COMANCHE HEART

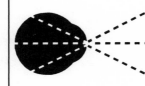

This Large Print Book carries the
Seal of Approval of N.A.V.H.

COMANCHE HEART

CATHERINE ANDERSON

WHEELER PUBLISHING
A part of Gale, Cengage Learning

GALE
CENGAGE Learning

Detroit • New York • San Francisco • New Haven, Conn • Waterville, Maine • London

GALE
CENGAGE Learning

LIBRARY OF CONGRESS CATALOGING-IN-PUBLICATION DATA

Anderson, Catherine (Adeline Catherine)
    Comanche heart / by Catherine Anderson.
        p. cm.
    ISBN-13: 978-1-4104-1893-7 (hardcover : alk. paper)
    ISBN-10: 1-4104-1893-6 (hardcover : alk. paper)
    1. Rape victims—Fiction. 2. Comanche Indians—Fiction. 3. Large type books. I. Title.
PS3551.N34557C65 2009
813'.54—dc22   2009019216

Published in 2009 by arrangement with NAL Signet, a member of Penguin Group (USA) Inc.

Printed in the United States of America
1 2 3 4 5 6 7 13 12 11 10 09

AUTHOR'S NOTE

As I wrote *Comanche Heart,* my mother informed me that I am part Shoshone, which explained my interest in and my affinity with the Comanche people, who were actually Shoshones who left their parent tribe to seek a warmer climate and better hunting on the plains. The Shoshones were sometimes called the Snake Indians because they lived in Idaho, a Shoshone word meaning "the land that is bitterly cold," and they often journeyed along the shores of the Snake River into central Oregon to hunt. I now live in Central Oregon and look out upon the terrain that my Native American ancestors often visited.

After leaving their parent tribe, the Comanche people called themselves the Snakes Who Came Back. They derived this name from the fact that they periodically traveled northward to revisit Idaho and the loved ones they had left behind. When they met strangers, they signed this name by holding their hands, palms down at the waist, and making a backward slithering motion.

This book is in memory of the Snakes Who Came Back — a great, noble people who still touch the hearts of everyone who reads about them and the trials they endured. Toward the end, just before the fall of the Comanche nation, the People often said, *"Suvate,"* which means, "It is finished." What a heartbreaking word, encapsulating a tragic story that still haunts so many of us today.

It is my hope that it will never be finished, not for any one of us, for if we can't learn from our past mistakes, we are doomed to repeat them.

PROLOGUE

Texas, 1876

Like a forlorn soul, the wind whistled and moaned as it funneled around Swift Antelope, whipping his hair across his face so that he saw the lonely grave through a shifting veil of black. He didn't blink. The sting in his eyes belonged to the living, and for this moment he lingered with the dead.

The rugged cross at the head of Amy Masters's grave, buffeted by the weather, had long since lost its battle to stand erect. He studied the crudely carved lettering in the wood, nearly obliterated by the hand of time, and wondered if the words sang Amy's life song. Somehow, he doubted *tivo tiv-ope,* white man's writing, could draw a glorious enough picture to do her justice.

Amy . . .

Memories flowed through Swift Antelope's mind, creating such clear pictures of her that he might have seen her only yesterday. Golden hair, sky blue eyes, a smile like sunshine . . . his beautiful, sweet, courageous Amy. With the memories came tears, which he shed with no shame yet much regret, for he should have mourned her long ago. He hunched his shoulders against the pain. If only he had come sooner. *Twelve years.* It broke his heart to imagine her waiting here, bound to him by a lifelong betrothal promise, only to die before he could fulfill his part and come for her.

Henry Masters's words, addressed to Swift Antelope only moments ago, rang inside his head. *She ain't here, you filthy Comanch. And it's a blessin', if ya ask me, with the likes of you comin' to court her. Cholera got her five years ago. She's buried out back, behind the barn.*

With an unsteady hand, Swift Antelope straightened the cross that marked Amy's grave, trying to visualize what her life must have been like, waiting for him on this dusty farm. When she lay dying, had she turned her gaze toward the horizon, hoping to see him there? Had she understood that it had been only the great fight for his people that had kept him from her side? He had sworn to come for her, and he had. Only he had been five years too late.

Swift Antelope knew he should climb back

on his horse and leave. His *compañeros* awaited him a few miles west, their saddle-bags filled with gold pieces, their gazes cast northward where they hoped to drive their ill-gotten cattle. But the will to place one moccasin in front of the other had deserted Swift Antelope. His plan to own a prosperous cattle ranch no longer filled him with purpose. Everything that he was lay here, with Amy, in a barren farmyard.

Lifting his head, Swift Antelope stared across the rolling grassland beyond the farm. Within him an awful emptiness took root, similar to that which he had felt a year ago upon entering the Tule Canyon. There, the September before, Mackenzie and his soldiers had slaughtered fourteen hundred Comanche horses and left the animals to rot. Though Swift Antelope had heard of the attack on his people in the Palo Duro Canyon, though he had known they were defeated, it had not seemed real to him until that moment when he saw the thousands of sun-bleached bones scattered across the canyon floor, all that was left of the Comanche remuda. It was then that Swift Antelope knew, deep within, that his people were finished; they were as nothing without their horses.

Just as he was nothing without Amy.

Pushing to his feet, he pulled his knife from its scabbard and slashed his cheek from eyebrow to chin, his final tribute to the spirited *tosi* girl who had touched his heart with so much love. His blood dripped onto the mound of her grave. He imagined it being absorbed into the earth, mingling with her bones. In this small way, a part of him would be here with her, no matter how far he might travel or how many winters passed.

Swift Antelope straightened his shoulders, sheathed his knife, and strode to his waiting horse. After mounting, he sat a moment, gazing into the distance. His friends waited to the west. Swift Antelope wheeled his horse and headed south. He had no idea where he was going. Nor did he care.

CHAPTER 1

March, 1879

Amy Masters touched the toes of her shoes to the floor to keep the rocker in motion. Despite the heat from her fireplace, cold seeped under her wool skirts, penetrating her petticoats and ribbed-cotton hose. Lighting the lantern might have helped, but for now she preferred the shadows. Somehow the firelight soothed her as it played upon the floral-patterned wallpaper in her sitting room, bringing to mind those long-ago summer nights in Texas when firelight turned the tepees of Hunter's village into inverted cones of glowing amber against a slate sky.

Faint voices and laughter drifted to Amy from outside. A door slammed. A moment later a dog barked, the sound distant and lonely. Everyone in Wolf's Landing was retiring for the night, as she should herself. Five o'clock would come early. Father

11

O'Grady from Jacksonville visited the settlement so seldom that she hated the thought of missing mass. He would leave the area tomorrow on a northward trek to his mission in Corvallis, then west to Empire on Coos Bay, then east to Lakeview. It would be weeks before he once again served mass at St. Joseph's in Jacksonville, let alone visited Wolf's Landing. With a husband, two children, and a visiting priest to feed, her cousin Loretta would need help preparing breakfast. Even so, Amy lingered.

Saying farewell to a cherished friend and precious memories took time.

Sighing, she lowered her gaze to the neatly folded page of Jacksonville's *Democratic Times* that she clutched in her hand. The horrible rumors about Swift Antelope had been filtering in to Wolf's Landing for a couple of years, but Amy had refused to believe them. Now that she had read this news story, she could no longer deny the truth. Her childhood sweetheart, the one and only man she had ever loved, had turned killer.

Leaning her head against the backrest of her rocker, Amy gazed at the charcoal sketch of Swift Antelope that hung above her mantel. She knew every line by heart, for she had drawn it herself. In the flicker-

12

ing light his profile looked so lifelike that she half expected him to turn and smile at her. Funny that, for she had little artistic talent. Such a beautiful face . . . Swift Antelope. His name whispered in her mind like a caress.

According to this news article, he went by Swift Lopez now; his Comanche name hadn't served him well once he'd escaped the reservation and started working as a cowhand. Even Amy had to admit it had been clever of him, Mexicanizing the last syllable of Antelope to Lopez. Despite the fact that he had been adopted by the People and raised as a Comanche, Swift Antelope's Spanish ancestry had always been apparent in his chiseled features. But, though she applauded his ingenuity and understood his need to escape the strictures of reservation life, she felt betrayed.

A comanchero and an infamous gunslinger. . . . The words from the news story replayed in her mind, conjuring images that turned her skin icy. For so many years she had held her memories of Swift Antelope dear, picturing him as he had been at sixteen, a noble, courageous, and gentle young man, a dreamer. Deep in her heart, she had believed he would keep his promise and come for her once the Comanches' battle for survival had ended. Now, she realized he never would. Even if he did, she would despise him for what he had become.

A sad smile touched her mouth. She was a little old at twenty-seven to be building castles out of dreams. Swift Antelope had made that heartfelt betrothal promise to a gangly twelve-year-old girl, and though the Comanches believed promises were forever, a lot had happened since, the destruction of his nation, the deaths of so many people he loved. Though the child in her hated to admit it, he would have changed as well, from a protective, gentle boy to a domineering and ruthless man. She should be thanking God that he had never come for her.

He probably didn't even remember her now. She was the strange one, living her life around other people, her heart bound to yesterday by promises that had drifted away on a Texas wind.

Bending forward, Amy tossed the newspaper page into the flames. The paper ignited in a *whoosh* of light. The acrid smell of smoldering ink filled her nostrils. She rose from the rocker and stepped to the mantel. With trembling hands, she grasped the sketch of Swift Antelope. Tears filled her eyes as she bent to toss the likeness into the flames.

When she looked at his face, she could almost smell the Texas plains in summer, hear the ring of youthful laughter, feel the touch of his hand on hers. *Keep your eyes always on the horizon, golden one. What lies behind you is for yesterday.* How many times had she found solace in those words, recalling every inflection of Swift Antelope's voice as he had spoken them to her?

She couldn't live the rest of her life trapped in the past. The Swift Antelope she had known would be the first to scold her for clinging to memories. And yet . . . She touched her fingertips to the paper, tracing the regal line of his nose, the perfect bow of his mouth, her own curving in a tearful smile.

With a ragged sigh, she returned the sketch to its place on her mantel, unable to surrender it to the flames, not quite ready to say a final farewell. Swift Antelope had been her friend, her innocent love, her healer. He had made her feel clean again, and whole. Was it so wrong to treasure those memories? Did it matter what he had become? It wasn't as if she would ever see him again.

Feeling inexplicably lonely, Amy turned her back on the portrait and circled the small, dimly lit sitting room, coming to a stop at the curio shelf. She ran her fingertips over a wooden figurine of a bear, carved by Jeremiah, one of her students. One shelf down from the bear sat a vase of dried flowers, gathered by the Hamstead girl. Seeing the gifts, simple though they were, brightened her mood. She loved teaching. How could she possibly feel lonely when her life brimmed over with people who loved her, not just her students, but Loretta and Loretta's family?

Though the deeper recesses of the house were dark, she turned and headed for the bedroom, once again forgoing use of the lantern. Afflicted since childhood with a severe case of night blindness, she had long ago familiarized herself with her home and could usually maneuver without mishap if she moved cautiously. Undressing quickly because of the damp chill that seeped through the walls, she tugged on her white nightgown and buttoned it to her chin. Shivering, she folded her underclothing and stacked it in a neat pile on her bureau, handy for morning. Then, drawing comfort from routine, she sat at her dresser, unplaited her hair, groped for her brush, and gave her long tresses their customary one hundred strokes.

She stared in the direction of her bed, unable to discern its outline. She should wrap some warm rocks in towels and slip them between the sheets, but she had no energy for it. It seemed to her that the impenetrable blackness drew closer, silent and oppressive. A peculiar tightness rose in her throat. She laid her hairbrush aside and, lured by the anemic glow of moonlight, went to the window, resting her fingers on the sash. Peering out through the steamy glass, she looked toward the main street of town, cheered by the glow of lights coming from the Lucky Nugget Saloon.

No stars peeked through the clouds. In March, southern Oregon got bursts of spring weather, but today had been drizzly. Fog hung in layers over the rooftops. In the muted moonbeams, she could see a mist of rain pelting the boardwalks. Tomorrow the streets would be a series of endless mudholes. Unlike the nearby town of Jacksonville, Wolf's Landing hadn't as yet undertaken the grading and graveling of its thoroughfares.

Another shiver ran up her spine. She hurried into bed, finding little warmth as the cold sheets settled around her. Pressing her cheek to the pillow, she watched a naked tree limb outside her window sway in the gusts of wind.

Amy dreaded closing her eyes, more so tonight than usual. Reading that newspaper article had resurrected the past, bringing to mind so many horrors best forgotten. In a few short hours dawn would break, but she derived small comfort from that when an eternity of darkness stretched before her. With that news story filling her thoughts, would dreams of the comancheros haunt her sleep? And if they did, would one of the brutal faces leering down at her be Swift Antelope's? Always before, when she had awoken from the dreams, her memories of Swift Antelope had soothed her. Now he rode with the men of her nightmares, killers, thieves — and rapists.

She imagined daybreak on the Texas plains, the eastern horizon layered with muted wisps of rose, the sky lead gray. Would Swift Antelope watch the sunrise? Would the north wind, sweet with the smell of spring grass and wildflowers, play upon his face? When he looked to the horizon, would he, for a fleeting instant, remember that long-ago summer?

As the sun lifted higher and higher in the sky, Swift Lopez sensed a building tension in the men who rode with him. Even his black stallion, Diablo, seemed to feel it, snorting and doing a nervous sidestep. Swift knew boredom worked on Chink Gabriel and his men like locoweed on horses; just a little made them crazy. For too many days now they had been traveling without incident. It didn't help that the warm morning air carried the scent of spring. This time of year made everyone restless. Only these fellows turned dangerous when they got to feeling edgy.

Tipping his black hat low over his eyes, Swift leaned back in the saddle and let the steady clop of his horse's hooves lull him. Birds twittered in the field grass, frantically flapping their wings when the horses drew too close. He spotted a rabbit hopping off to his right.

For an instant he found himself wishing the years could roll away, that he rode with good friends, his long hair drifting in the wind, that just beyond his line of vision lay a Comanche village. It was a frequent wish of Swift's and so sweet, so vivid, that he could almost smell fresh meat over open fires.

In the distance a church bell chimed, telling him what day it was and that a town rested over the rise. His mouth quirked, and he sniffed the air again. Judging from the scent, someone had a side of beef skewered over an open pit. He ran his hand along his whiskery jaw. Right now he could do with a bath and a jug of good whiskey.

Chink Gabriel, who rode beside Swift, reined his roan to a walk. "Be damned if that ain't a church bell. There's a town over yonder. Been so long since I sniffed a skirt, I'm as randy as a buck in rut."

Slightly behind them, José Rodriguez spat tobacco and said, "The last time I had me a gal, I was so damned drunk, the next mornin' I couldn't even remember givin' her a poke. I left town feelin' as randy as when I got there."

Bull Jesperson, whose name suited his massive frame, gave a disgusted snort. "One of these days, y're gonna pay dearly for drinkin' that heavy."

"Oh, yeah? How you figger?" Rodriguez challenged.

"Y're gonna tie up with somethin' diseased, that's how. You'll wake up some mornin' and yer pistol will be rottin' off."

"What'd'ya expect for two dollars?" another man grumbled. "Them last whores we run across was the durtiest bunch of females I ever saw."

Rodriguez chuckled. "The only clean spot on the one I had was her left tit, and that was because Bull went upstairs with her before me."

"Hey, Bull!" someone yelled. "Yer pistol been lookin' peculiar lately? José's is rottin' clean off!"

Laughter erupted, and the men began exchanging their favorite stories about whores. Swift listened with half an ear. He had paid a woman for her favors only once, not because she demanded money, but because her dress had been threadbare. Among the Comanches, a woman never had to sell her body to survive. To Swift's way of thinking, men who patronized sporting houses were encouraging a savagery far more heartless than any the Comanches had ever committed.

Charlie Stone, a stout redhead with a grizzled beard, pulled his gray to a stop. "My neck's swole, too. How's about you, Lopez?"

Acutely aware that the question carried a challenge and that his response was unlikely to sway the vote of twenty men, Swift removed his timepiece from his pocket and checked the hour. "It's early yet."

"Yep, all the little pleasure doves might still be abed," someone inserted.

"Mebbe business was slow last night," Chink countered. "If not, an extra ten dollars will wake 'em up right fast."

Swift didn't cotton to entering towns in broad daylight. He was especially leery today because Chink and the others were itching for trouble. Reining his horse around, he looked across the rolling open range. On the horizon he could see a ranch house. Returning his watch to his pocket, he withdrew a five-dollar gold piece and flipped it through the air to Chink. "I reckon I'll just take a snooze. Bring me back a bottle."

"Ya can't poke no goddamn bottle," Charlie retorted. "Y're not normal, Lopez. You figger y're too good for whores, or what?" When Swift made no reply, Charlie curled his lip. "Where we go, you go. That's the rule. Ain't that right, Chink?"

Swift swung off his black, his spurs ringing as the rowels caught in the grass.

"Y're jist runnin' short on guts, that's what," Charlie jabbed. "Afraid some green kid might recognize that purty face of yers and take it into his head to draw down on ya. That's it, ain't it, Lopez? Y're gettin' squeamish."

Keeping his face devoid of expression, Swift met Charlie Stone's gaze, all the while loosening his saddle cinch. After a few tension-packed moments, Charlie's larynx bobbed in a nervous swallow. He glanced away. Swift pulled the saddle off his horse and, skirting the other riders, carried it to a patch of sparse shade under a bush.

Chink sighed and wheeled his gelding toward town. Swift knew the comanchero leader resented it when one of his men didn't stay with the group, but Swift didn't count himself as one of Chink's men, never had, and would be damned if he'd start now. The only reason he had fallen in with Chink a year and a half ago was to stay on the move. Trouble had a way of dogging a man's heels, and he had to step smart if he wanted to avoid it.

"You sure you don't wanna come?" Chink called.

Swift ground-tied his stallion, then stretched out on his back in the shade, using his saddle as a pillow. Without answering, he closed his eyes. He knew Chink ran too short on guts to swap lead with him over something so trivial.

"Come on," Charlie said. "Leave the greasy son of a bitch to sleep."

When the sound of the horses' hooves grew distant, Swift pulled his nickel-plated .45 Colt revolvers from their holsters, habit compelling him to check the cylinders for cartridges. When he settled back against his saddle, he drifted off to sleep with the confidence of a man who had two loaded guns, sharp hearing, and fast reflexes.

Only a few minutes passed before Swift put both his hearing and reflexes to the test. Horses approached, coming fast. He shot to his feet and pulled his gun before he completely registered the sound. He relaxed a little when he recognized Chink Gabriel on the lead horse. The men were pushing their mounts, and that usually meant trouble nipped at their rumps. Swift holstered his Colt and quickly resaddled his black so he'd be ready to ride.

"Lookee what we found," Chink yelled as he barreled his horse up beside Swift's. "A girlee, and hot damn if she ain't the purtiest little thing you ever saw."

Swift squinted into the sun and saw that Charlie carried a girl draped over his saddle. Her blond hair had come loose and hung like a shimmering curtain down the horse's belly.

Swift's stomach lurched. Since learning of Amy's death three years ago, he seldom allowed himself to think of her, but every once in a while, like now, the memories came rushing back, bittersweet, filling him with a sense of loss. This girl's hair was yellow blond, while Amy's had been the rich gold of honey, but the similarity still struck him like a well-placed blow. Years ago Amy too had fallen victim to a band of comanchero.

Chink swung off his horse, his whiskery face split in a broad grin. Clamping a hand over his crotch, he gave himself a fondle. "She'll bring a mighty fine price across the border, but a little breakin' in won't hurt her value none."

Charlie rode up and dumped the girl off his gray. She screamed when she hit shoulder first on the grass, then staggered to her feet. She wore clothing like none Swift had ever seen, a pantlike skirt and a tailored blouse that skimmed her breasts like a second skin. Swift guessed that the outfit had been designed for horseback riding, but whatever its original purpose, the figure-revealing lines now served to whet male appetites — twenty of them.

The girl ran. Three men wheeled their horses to chase her, making sport of her attempts to escape. Swift set his jaw. He didn't cotton to rape, but he couldn't do one hell of a lot to stop it when twenty guns voted yea to his nay. The damned fool girl shouldn't have been out riding alone in the first place.

Chink left his horse's reins dangling and ran to catch the blonde, whooping with

25

laughter when she bucked and tried to kick as he carried her back to the spot of shade. The other men leaped off their horses and followed along like ducklings in a queue. Swift watched in passive silence as Chink tossed the girl down and grabbed hold of her blouse. The buttons flew. Cloth ripped. She gave a horrified screech and renewed her struggles to get free.

"Hot damn, Bull, ya won't hafta suck them tits clean," someone yelled.

"Somebody help me git her britches off," Chink ordered.

Swift turned and walked away. Only a fool would get himself killed over a female he didn't know. She'd been asking to get her legs spread, wearing clothes like that. He finished tightening the saddle cinch, doing a fair job of blocking out the girl's scream-ing. Did she think anyone could hear her way out here? No one who gave a damn, anyway.

Chink grunted as if he had been kicked. The next instant Swift heard the sickening thud of a fist against flesh. The girl screamed again. "Hold the little bitch still," Chink rasped. "Grab her ankles, you two. Not too tight. I like 'em with a little fight. You gonna fight me, sweet thing? You gonna buck and give me a ride to remember?"

Several men laughed and whooped encouragement. Swift knew without looking that Chink was getting into position. He turned his attention to his saddlebags, tightening the straps. The men's laughter nearly drowned out the girl's weakening cries. Even so, Swift's ears began to home in on the sobbing. Sweat popped out on his face. He gave one of the saddlebag straps a vicious jerk. Since there was little he could do, it seemed futile to stay and listen.

Grabbing his saddle horn, he stuck a boot in his stirrup. The girl screamed, "Oh, please, God!" Swift froze. Memories of Amy spun through his mind. This girl had no connection whatsoever with Amy, of course, except that she was blond and female. He closed his eyes, telling himself he would be ten times a fool if he interfered.

Then, before he could talk himself out of it, he removed his foot from the stirrup and took off his hat, looping the bonnet strings around the saddle horn. It *was* Sunday. Though Swift didn't hold with *tosi* religion, he didn't figure anybody who did ought to get raped on the Sabbath. He slapped his stallion on the rump so it would run off to safety, relieved when Chink's mount followed. There was no point in the horses getting hurt.

Swift slowly turned, heartened by the sight of Chink's bare butt shining in the sun. A man couldn't draw too fast with his britches down. "Chink!"

Sudden silence fell. Even the girl grew quiet. All eyes shifted to Swift, who stood with his long, black-clad legs spread, elbows bent and slightly behind him, his hands poised over his holsters. Chink's blue eyes narrowed. "You ain't plannin' to draw on twenty men," he said. "Not even a leather slapper like you would be that crazy."

Swift didn't need Chink to tell him what he was about to do was insane. He'd end up dead, and the girl would get raped anyway. It was mostly a question of how low a man wanted to sink, and he'd sunk as low as he could comfortably go and still live with himself.

"I'm taking you out first," Swift told Chink softly.

The girl sobbed and took advantage of the distraction to slither her hips away from the man who had nearly impaled her. Swift registered everything with sharpened senses, acutely aware of the breeze tossing his shortly cropped hair, the abrasiveness of his shirt collar against his neck, the weight of his guns where they rode his hips. For an instant he envisioned Amy's face, comforted by the knowledge that she waited for him in the Great Beyond, and that by doing this he could join her there with a clean heart.

Chink's eyes narrowed even more. "I'll see you in hell, then, you turncoat bastard." As the comanchero spoke, he went for his gun.

With the speed that had made his name legend, Swift drew, cocking the hammer of his gun with his thumb, bringing his left hand across his midriff to fan the hammer spur. Some of the others around Chink reacted, grabbing for their weapons. To Swift, they became faceless blurs of movement, targets that would kill him unless he killed them first. Six shots rang out from his gun in such rapid succession that they sounded like one explosion. Chink fell backward across the girl. Five other men sprawled, dead before they cleared leather. The girl began to scream, trying to pull her leg from under Chink's body. The horses, accustomed to gunfire, sidestepped and whinnied.

Swift threw himself to the grass and rolled. A slight rise to the ground provided him meager cover. Dirt geysered around him as the remaining fourteen men came to their senses and started firing. He drew his other single-action and, in a second blur of movement, fired three more shots. Three men went down.

In a lull between shots, Swift came up on one elbow, adrenaline numbing him to the fear, his palm poised over the hammer spur. "Which of you bastards wants it next?"

Between them, the remaining eleven men had at least a hundred cartridges, ready to fire. When no one ventured another shot, Swift said, "I'm as good as dead, and you all know it. But if I go, I'm taking three more of you with me." Well aware that José was the closest thing to a leader the men had left, Swift sighted in on him. "Rodriguez, you're going to be first."

A spasm of fear contorted the Mexican's swarthy face. Pupils dilating, he stared at the barrel of Swift's .45. After a moment he holstered his revolver and lifted his hands. "Ain't no woman alive worth gettin' plugged over."

Swift saw several of the other men cast bewildered glances at Chink. Without their leader spouting orders, Swift guessed they weren't quite sure what to do. Taking Rodriguez's lead, they all retreated a step, holstering their guns.

"You want her that bad, you can have her," one said.

"I don't want no trouble with you, Lopez."

Bull spat and shot Swift a murderous glare. "I knowed you was trouble the first time I set eyes on ya. You ain't seen the last of this. I promise you that."

"Shut up, Bull, and git on yer goddamn horse," Rodriguez ordered.

Swift remained prone on the grass until all eleven men had ridden off. Then he turned his gaze to the girl, who had gone strangely silent. She sat hunched over, buck naked and shivering, her blue eyes riveted to Chink's bare lower torso. Swift guessed she had never seen a nude man. There was no help for that. Seeing was far better than what had almost happened.

He rose and holstered his guns, his hands stricken with the uncontrollable quivering that always followed a gunfight. His gaze slid over the scattered bodies, and his guts twisted. He closed his eyes and flexed his fingers, the sweat on his body turning ice cold. *Killing.* He was so weary of it, so sick-to-death weary. Yet no matter what he did, it never seemed to end.

He whistled for his stallion and when the horse had trotted up he opened the saddlebag that held his store of extra cartridges. He wasn't taking any chances that Rodriguez and the others might come back. Only after he had reloaded his Colts did he clamp his wide-brimmed hat back on his head and walk over to where Chink lay. He dragged the comanchero off the girl's leg and then jerked up the dead man's pants.

"You all right?" he asked, more gruffly than he intended.

She slid a blank gaze from Chink's body to the other eight men sprawled around her. Swift sighed and raked a hand through his hair, uncertain what to do. If he took her to that ranch house on the horizon while she was in this shape, the only thanks he was likely to get would be at the business end of a rope.

He gathered up her clothes, which were torn and barely wearable. Kneeling beside her, he began the difficult task of dressing her, which he decided was pointless before he finished. He touched a fingertip to her cheekbone.

"He busted you a good one, didn't he?"

Her wide blue eyes flicked to his, blank with shock.

Striding to his horse, Swift pulled one of his shirts from his pack. The girl offered no resistance when he shoved her limp arms down the black sleeves. When his knuckles brushed her breasts as he fastened the buttons, she didn't so much as flinch. He guessed she was numb, nature's way of lessening the horror.

"I'm sorry I didn't shoot him quicker," he offered. "But I didn't think I stood a chance. I guess maybe that God of yours heard you hollering and decided to help me out."

She didn't seem to register the words. Swift sighed and fixed his gaze on the distant ranch, wondering if she lived there. Whether she did or not, it was the closest house, and time was playing out. He had to get out of here. Though he had never met them, he knew Chink had two brothers who wouldn't take his passing lightly. Once Rodriguez got to thinking things over, he'd be back. If he let Chink's death go un-avenged, the Gabriel brothers would kill him.

Swift carried the trembling girl to his horse. She seemed to come around a bit when he settled her onto the saddle. He mounted up behind her, taking care not to get his hand close to her breasts when he looped an arm around her.

"Thank you," she whispered in a quavery voice. "Th-thank you. . . ."

"No thanks needed. I was hankerin' for a little excitement."

They rode in silence for a couple of miles,

the girl finally relaxing against him. After several more minutes she took a long, ragged breath. "You saved me. You could've just rode off. Yet you didn't. Why?"

Swift swallowed and fixed his gaze on the house ahead of them. He wanted to say "Why not?" but he didn't. A girl her age would never understand how pointless life could become for a man who drifted from one town to the next, his people gone, his loved ones gone, his dreams gone.

"I've never seen anybody shoot that fast."

Swift nudged his black into a trot, making no reply.

"There's only one man who can handle a gun that way." She twisted her neck to look up at him, her eyes wide with a curious blend of awe and fear. "My daddy's talked about you. You're Swift Lopez. He has a scar on his cheek, and so do you! Now that I think on it, you even look like him!"

Swift struggled to keep his tone matter-of-fact. "I'm just a drifter who got lucky, that's all."

"But I heard one of those men call you Lopez."

Swift fought down a vehement denial. "Gomez, not Lopez."

"You *are* Swift Lopez." She turned slightly to study him. "I saw a photograph of you once. You're dressed all in black, and you're handsome, just like in that picture. Is it true you've killed over a hundred men?"

Feeling trapped, Swift dragged his gaze from hers. By this time tomorrow, everyone for fifty miles would have heard about this gunfight, and the number of dead would multiply in the retelling. And somewhere out there, a greenhorn kid who hankered for fame would hear the story and strap on his guns. Sooner or later Swift would find himself standing on some dusty street, facing that kid and having to decide whether he was going to draw or die. And, as always before, in that last split second, reflex would take over and his hand would slap leather.

The scenario never changed, and it never ended. Swift cursed the day he had first touched a revolver.

Turning his face westward, he contemplated the horizon. *Oregon.* These last few months he had been thinking of his lifelong friend Hunter more and more frequently. Swift was no longer sure if he really believed in the ancient Comanche prophecy that had led Hunter west. It didn't seem possible that Comanches and white people could live in harmony anywhere, at least not in this life. Hunter had probably settled in Oregon to find himself surrounded by nothing but more hatred. But that really didn't matter. To Swift, the thought of being among friends again, even if their number was few, had a powerful pull.

Hunter's *tosi* wife, Loretta, had sent a letter to the Indian reservation years back, welcoming any of the People who cared to join them in the west lands. Swift hadn't been present to hear the letter read aloud by the minister's wife, but he'd heard others talk about it, whispering the word *Oh-rhee-gon* and gazing with longing at the horizon. At that time Swift had given up on dreams of finer places, but now . . . A lump rose in his throat. With his life a living nightmare, a dream, even if it had no more substance than a wisp of smoke, had to be sought.

Swift had no idea what kind of a place Oregon might be, but three things recommended it highly: it was a far piece from Texas, the Gabriel brothers, and the legend of Swift Lopez. The minute he got this girl delivered to that ranch house, he was heading west.

CHAPTER 2

October 1879

Noon sunshine warmed Swift's shoulders as he guided his black stallion up the steep, rutted road to Wolf's Landing. After six months of traveling, some through desert, some through barren high plains, his senses felt bombarded by the sheer lushness of Oregon's vibrant display of autumn. He took a deep breath of the crisp mountain air and feasted his eyes on the colorful hillsides, which ranged from bright orange to dark rust and varying shades of green. Never had he seen so many species of trees in one place, oak, fir, pine, maple, and a beautiful evergreen he couldn't identify, with peeling trunks that twisted through the surrounding growth like gnarled fingers.

Children's voices drifted to him on the breeze as he crested the hill. He reined in his horse and sat a moment, taking in his first sight of Wolf's Landing, a bustling little mining town ten miles from Jacksonville, the county seat. The main street looked like any in a white community, with colorfully advertised shops lining the boardwalks. On the left, three two-story buildings loomed above the others, a saloon, a hotel, and a restaurant.

Up on the hillside, nestled behind a sprawling log house, Swift spotted two tepees. Judging from the smoke that trailed above the lodge poles, someone here clung to the Indian ways. He grinned as the words of the ancient Comanche prophecy ran through his mind: *A new place, where the Comanche and* tosi tivo *will live as one.*

The wonderful smell of baked bread floated on the air. Houses of varying size and structure, some impressive, some one-room shanties with bare dirt yards, peppered the thick woodland. In the distance Swift saw a woman hanging up clothes behind a squat log cabin. Farther up the hill from her, two cows ambled through the brush, one bawling, the other stopping to graze.

He relaxed in the saddle, a feeling of peace washing over him. It had been three years since he had escaped the Indian reservation — three long, restless years — and in all his wanderings he'd never come upon a place that spoke to him as this one did. Home. Maybe, just maybe, if he waited and lay low, he could escape his reputation here and hang up his guns.

A squeal of laughter caught Swift's attention, and he nudged his hat back to survey the schoolyard to his right. A small girl raced from the playground toward the schoolhouse, her gingham skirts flying as she tried to evade the boy who chased her. The next instant someone began beating a triangle with a steel bar, raising such a din that Swift's gaze shifted to the porch. He glimpsed a flash of golden hair, then heard a sweet, hauntingly familiar voice. "Time to come in, children. Recess is over."

Swift stared at the slender woman who stood on the schoolhouse steps, a vision in dark blue muslin. He couldn't move, couldn't think. *Amy!* Surely it couldn't be. Yet it sounded like her. The hair color was right, a rich honey gold. Could it be Loretta, Amy's older cousin? With her golden hair, fine features, and blue eyes, Loretta always had resembled Amy. If not for the difference in their ages, the two might have passed for twins.

The children raced for the schoolhouse. Their feet slapped the wood as they ran up the steps and went inside. Swift, drawn by the faint sound of the woman's voice, reined Diablo around and rode toward the school-yard. He pulled up by the stoop, swung out of the saddle, and draped the reins over the hitching post. For an instant he stood frozen and listened, afraid to hope.

"Attention, attention!" she called out.

The clamor of children's voices settled into silence.

"Jeremiah, you're first. If a gentleman meets a lady on the boardwalk, on which side should he pass?"

"His right," piped up a boy's voice. "And if the boardwalk's narrow, he will step off into the street and make sure the lady passes without mishap."

"Very good, Jeremiah," the woman said with a soft laugh. "You're answering my questions before I ask them. Peter, should the gentleman recognize the lady?"

"No, ma'am," replied another boy in a shy, unassertive tone.

"Never?" she prompted, her voice growing gentle.

"Well, maybe, if'n he knows the lady will favor a nod."

"Excellent, Peter."

Swift heard the pages of a book rustle. "Indigo Nicole? Is it proper for a lady to walk between two gentlemen, with a hand on the arm of each?"

A girl replied, "No, ma'am. A true lady gives her favor to only one gentleman at a time."

Swift didn't hear the next question. In a haze of disbelief he walked up the steps, his legs weak and trembling, a rivulet of sweat trailing like ice down his spine. He knew the woman's voice. Maturity had enriched its silken alto. The diction was more precise and proper. But the voice was definitely Amy's. He would know it anywhere, for it had haunted his dreams for fifteen years. *I'll wait for you, Swift. Just as soon as I'm old enough, I'll be your wife.* A promise that had become his greatest sorrow, now transformed into a miracle.

He stepped to the open doorway, peering out from under the brim of his hat into the shadowy room. So shaken he didn't trust his knees, Swift braced a shoulder against the door frame, his gaze riveted to the teacher, trying to come to grips with the reality of seeing her. Amy . . .

That grave behind Henry Masters's barn hadn't been Amy's. The cross Swift had so lovingly straightened hadn't borne her name and life song. His sweet, precious Amy was here, alive and well in Wolf's Landing. Three wasted years! For God only knew what reason, Henry Masters had lied to him. A wave of sheer rage hit Swift.

Then joy blotted out all else. Amy stood before him, breathing, smiling, talking, so beautiful the mere sight of her took his breath. Fifteen years ago she had been coltishly pretty, as thin as a bowstring, with an impertinent little nose dotted with freckles, a stubborn chin, and huge blue eyes outlined by thick dark lashes. Now, though still fragile of build, she had acquired the soft curves of womanhood. His gaze rested fleetingly on the white piping that edged her prim bodice, then dipped to her slender waist and the gentle flare of her hips, accented by two ruffled poufs that fell in a graceful sweep across her fanny. His throat closed off, and for a second he couldn't breathe. No dream this, but reality.

From the corner of her eye, Amy glimpsed a shadow looming in the doorway. Distracted from her place in *The Manual of Proper Manners,* she forgot what she was saying and looked up, taking in the tall man, clad all in black, with a wool poncho draped back comanchero style over one shoulder, a gun gleaming like silver death on his hip. With a shallow gasp she retreated a step, pressing her spine against the blackboard.

"M-may I help you, sir?" she asked in a

frail voice.

He didn't reply. With his shoulder against the door frame, he stood with one hip slung outward, his knee slightly bent, the stance careless and somehow insolent. The wide brim of his concha-banded hat cast his face into shadow, but light played on the twist of his sharply defined lips and the gleam of his white teeth. Touching the brim of his hat, he nodded to her and shifted his weight to the other foot as he drew to his full height, which seemed to fill the doorway.

"Hello, Amy."

His deep silken voice sent a wash of coldness over Amy's skin. She blinked and swallowed, trying to assimilate the reality of a comanchero standing in the doorway of her schoolroom, blocking the only means of escape. The fact that he knew her name terrified her even more. This wasn't Texas, yet the nightmare of her past had somehow found her.

Mouth as dry as dust, she stared at him, trying to think what to do. Were there others outside? She felt the uncertainty of her students, knew that they were frightened because they could see that she was, but courage, if she had any, eluded her. Fear consumed her, a cold, clawing fear that paralyzed her.

The man took a step closer, his spurs chinking on the wood floor. The sound swept Amy back through time, to that long-ago afternoon when the comancheros had kidnapped her. To this day she could remember the feel of their rough, hurting hands on her breasts, the cruel ring of their laughter, the endless haze of pain as man after man took his turn violating her child's body.

The floor dipped under her feet. In her ears, echoes from the past jostled with sounds of the present, a deafening cacophony that beat against her temples.

The comanchero moved closer, step by relentless step, the rowels of his spurs catching on the floor planks. She couldn't move. Then, coming to a halt a scant few feet away from her, he removed his hat. Amy stared up at his dark face, once so familiar, now chiseled by manhood, each line etched upon her heart yet changed so by the years that it had become the face of a stranger.

"Swift. . . ."

The whisper trailed from her lips, barely audible. Swirls of black encroached on her vision. She blinked and reached wildly for support, her groping hand finding only open air. As if from a great distance, she heard him repeat her name. Then she felt herself falling, falling . . . into the blackness.

"Amy!"

Swift lunged forward, snaking out an arm to catch her around her waist before she fell. She hung limp against his body, head lolling, arms dangling, eyes half-closed with the whites showing. No practiced swoon, this, but a genuine, out-cold faint.

Swift knelt on one knee to lower her to the floor. His heart slammed with unreasoning fear as he pressed his fingertips to her throat to find the uneven and weak thread of her pulse. Her pallor frightened him. Cursing beneath his breath, he grasped the high collar of her dress and struggled to unfasten the tiny buttons, frustrated by the ruffle of starched muslin sheer that formed an overlay at the neckline.

"Take your hands off her!"

The voice cracked on the last two words and squeaked. Swift threw up his head to find a knife blade gleaming inches from his nose, held in the steady brown hand of a boy he guessed to be about fifteen. Dressed in a buckskin shirt and blue jeans, the youth reminded Swift of someone, but with a knife nearly shoved up his right nostril, he couldn't concentrate on who. Swift studied the boy's sunburnished features and dark, wind-tossed hair.

"Don't try me, mister. I'll slit your throat quicker than you can blink."

Swift slowly lifted his hands from Amy's collar, eyeing the knife. Normally he wouldn't have been worried by a boy, no matter how vehement his threats, but the way this youth balanced the knife in his hand told Swift he could not only use the weapon, but with deadly accuracy.

"Just keep calm," Swift said softly. "There's no point in anyone getting hurt. Now is there?"

A little girl's frightened sob punctuated the question. Tension ran so thick in the air, Swift could almost taste it. He panned the room with a quick glance, discovering that every student, even those knee high to a jackrabbit, had stood up and looked ready to do battle. The thought crossed his mind that the infamous Swift Lopez could very easily meet his end in this schoolroom, mobbed by children.

A slow smile crossed his mouth. "The lady fainted, and I'm just trying to help her."

"The lady doesn't need help from the likes of you. Keep your filthy paws off her," the boy returned. "Indigo, run get our father. Hurry!"

A movement from slightly behind Swift's left shoulder drew his attention. He discovered that a tawny-haired girl stood two feet away, a classroom pointer gripped in her hands. She looked prepared to skewer him with it. He nearly smiled again at the murderous expression in her wide blue eyes.

"I'm not goin'! Send Peter!" she cried.

"Indigo Nicole, do as I say! Find our father!"

Swift guessed the girl to be about thirteen or fourteen years old, with a burnished tone to her skin that struck an almost breathtaking contrast to her hair and eyes. "Untamed" was the word she brought to mind, the impression underscored by her Comanche clothing, a loose-sleeved, beautifully beaded blouse, a flowing skirt, and fringed knee-high moccasins.

Swift inched his nose back from the weaving knife the boy held. Now that he had seen the girl, it suddenly occurred to him who this youth resembled. Little wonder he knew how to use a knife.

"Your father . . . Hunter of the Wolf?" Swift queried.

The boy's blue eyes darted from the girl back to Swift. "How'd you know his Comanche name?"

"I'm an old friend."

"That's a lie. My father wouldn't have any doings with the likes of you. Indigo, git! If you don't go right now, I'll thrash you good, you hear?"

The girl stood her ground. "And leave you alone? He's a gunslinger, Chase. Anyone can see that. You're no match for him!" She inched the pointer closer. "Peter, you go. And hurry! Tell our father Aunt Amy needs him!"

Peter, a carrot-haired ten-year-old, shot around his desk and hurtled toward the door. Swift, more concerned about Amy than he was about meeting his maker at the hands of children, lowered his gaze. "If you don't want me to touch her, Chase, you do something. Loosen her collar. Get her some water."

"You just mind your business," the boy ordered. He directed a concerned glance at Amy's chalky face and swallowed. "My father will be here shortly. Time enough then to tend Aunt Amy. You best be figuring what you'll say to him. He doesn't cotton to outlaws coming here."

Too late, Swift realized he did look like an outlaw, dressed as he was, which explained the hostile reception and Amy's fainting dead away at the sight of him. He sensed that the other children had pressed closer, frightened for their teacher. The little girl was still sobbing, swallowing the sounds now so they erupted through her nose.

Swift sighed. "Does the name Swift Antelope sound familiar to you?"

The boy's face tightened. For the first time he began to look uncertain. "What if it does?"

"Because *I* am Swift Antelope."

The girl holding the pointer inched sideways to study Swift's face, and after getting a good look, she gasped. "Oh lands, it is Swift Antelope, Chase. He's the man in the sketch."

"He isn't, either," Chase snapped, but even as he spoke he gave Swift a closer study. "Well, maybe he resembles him a little. That doesn't mean nothing. He's got a scar on his face. Swift don't."

"He could have acquired a scar, porridge brains." The girl lowered her pointer slowly. *"Hein ein mah-su-ite?"* she asked in rapid Comanche.

Hearing the language of his childhood made Swift's heart catch. "I *want* to take care of your aunt. After that, receiving the proper welcome of a trusted friend would be nice."

"You see! He understands Comanche!"

Sensing the boy's growing uncertainty, Swift bent back over to Amy to unfasten the collar of her dress. Peeling back the cloth, he glanced up at the girl. "Bring me some water."

Indigo tossed aside her weapon and ran over to a large jug that stood in the corner. The sobbing little girl made a wet, choked sound, and cried, "I want my ma."

Indigo flashed her a glance, her pretty face softening. "Don't cry, Lee Ann. Miss Amy just fainted. She's going to be fine."

Chase inched closer to Swift, his stance still threatening, his gaze darting from Swift's hands to his face. "If you're lying, my father will kill you for touching her."

Swift nodded. "I know your father's temper well. If I were you, I'd sheathe that knife before he gets here, or his anger may be directed at you."

Footsteps sounded on the porch just as Indigo returned to Swift's side with a cup of water. Lifting Amy in the bend of his arm, Swift loosened and removed the black kerchief he wore around his neck. Dipping one corner of the cloth into the cup, he gently bathed her lips. Her nose wrinkled with distaste, and her lashes fluttered against her pale cheeks.

"Amy," Swift whispered.

"What is happening here?" a deep voice boomed from the doorway.

All the children began to explain at once.

Chase drowned them out, crying, "This man came bustin' in! Scared Aunt Amy into a dead faint! Started undoin' her dress! He claims he's Swift Antelope."

Swift glanced over his shoulder at the tall, well-muscled man silhouetted in the doorway. Even without the long hair and Comanche leathers, Hunter would have been recognizable by the set of his shoulders. Lifting his gaze, Swift tried to see Hunter's face, but the sun blinded him. "*Hi, hites,* hello, my friend."

"Swift." Hunter stepped slowly across the room, his moccasins touching lightly on the floor, his blue-black gaze filled with disbelief. "Swift, it's really you."

Swift nodded and returned his attention to Amy, watching as her beautiful eyes fluttered open, confused and unfocused. "Can you take her, Hunter? Seeing me — that's what made her faint."

Hunter knelt on the other side of Amy and crooked an arm under her shoulders. "Amy," he whispered. "Ah, Amy."

Swift rocked back on his boot heels, a lump of tenderness rising in his throat as he watched Amy turn toward Hunter to grasp his leather shirt. "Hunter, a comanchero!"

"No, no, not a comanchero. It is only Swift, eh? Our old friend, come to visit us."

As if she sensed his presence behind her, Amy stiffened and threw a horrified look over her shoulder. The impact of her wide, frightened eyes hit Swift like a boulder in the chest. He searched those blue depths for any trace of fondness, of gladness, but found none. She was clearly shocked to see him and more than a little frightened.

Pain lashed Swift. That Amy, *his* Amy, should be afraid of him . . . The realization, coupled with the shock of finding her alive, left him feeling unbalanced.

Hunter turned toward the children, who stood frozen at their desks, attention riveted on the three adults before them. Swift noticed that the little redheaded boy named Peter was shaking. "School is finished, eh?" Hunter told them. "You go home to your mothers. Come back at the regular time in the morning."

"Is Miss Amy gonna be all right?" a boy of about twelve asked.

"Yes," Hunter assured him. "I am here now. Go on home, Jeremiah."

Like compressed springs, all released simultaneously, the students converged on the coatrack, grabbing lunch baskets and coats as they headed out the door. Swift watched them in bemused silence. Indigo paused at the threshold, and flashed him a shy smile, her blue eyes dancing.

"I'm glad you've come, Uncle Swift." With that, she bounced out the door after Chase.

Swift gazed after her, reassured because she had addressed him as "Uncle." Though not related by blood, Swift and Hunter had been brothers in spirit. It warmed Swift's heart to know that Hunter had spoken frequently of him to his children and raised them to think of him as a family member.

"The schoolchildren are wary." Hunter inclined his head at the gun on Swift's hip. "It's not often we see gunmen here."

"Men here don't wear guns?"

Hunter's firm mouth drew down at the corners. "Guns, yes, but not —" Amy stirred again, and he broke off to help her sit erect. When she passed a tremulous hand over her eyes, Hunter's chiseled face mirrored his concern. "You are all right?"

"Y-yes."

She slid a wary glance to Swift and twisted onto her knees. Swift rose immediately, offering her a hand up. She shoved to her feet unassisted, struggling against the cumbersome confines of her full skirts. Hunter caught her elbow to steady her.

"Amy . . ." Swift studied her face as he said her name, dismayed by its sudden whitening. She averted her gaze. "Amy, look at me."

She straightened her skirts, then buttoned her collar, her slender hands shaking so badly that Swift longed to help her. Drawing away from Hunter, she took an unsteady step toward her desk, then hesitated, looking disoriented. Swift reached to clasp her arm so she wouldn't fall, but when his fingertips grazed her sleeve, she flinched away, her blue eyes riveted to his black poncho.

Swift had never expected to find Amy here — Amy, with her accusing eyes. Removing his hat, he swept the wool poncho over his head and stepped to the coatrack to hang it on a hook. He put his hat back on his head and turned to look at her.

She had reached her desk while his back was turned. Now she stood gripping its edge, her knuckles white, her gaze riveted to his boots. Swift glanced at Hunter, nonplussed.

Hunter lifted one shoulder in a shrug. "Well! This calls for a celebration." His voice boomed with forced joviality, making Amy jump. "Let's go over to the house. Loretta will want to see you, Swift. She always claimed you would come for Amy one day, and, like most women, she likes nothing better than to be proved right."

Swift noted that Amy turned even whiter at Hunter's words, and suddenly he knew why she looked so appalled. As Hunter strode toward the door, Swift tried to imagine how she must be feeling and realized that if he didn't assure her now that he had no intention of rushing her fences, he might not find a private moment to do so later.

"Hunter?" Swift followed his friend toward the door, acutely aware that Amy had fallen in behind him, tensed to dart past him the second she saw an opening. "I'd like a moment alone with Amy."

"No!"

Amy's protest made both men turn to look at her. Swift had the distasteful feeling that if he yelled "Boo!" she'd faint dead away again. He glanced back at Hunter, requesting with his eyes that Hunter leave them. When Hunter complied and stepped across the threshold, Amy tried to bolt after him.

Swift foiled her attempt, grasping her arm and shutting the door. She tried to back away, hands clasped at her waist, her gaze riveted to the floor. Beneath his palm, she felt brittle with tension. He could see her pulse slamming in her throat. He released his hold on her, not wanting to unsettle her any more than he already had.

"Amy . . ."

Lifting her head, she fastened frightened blue eyes on him. Swift felt as if fifteen years had rolled away. He could recall her looking at him just this way that long-ago summer when he had dragged her from the village, day after day, to walk with him along the river. She had feared he meant to rape and brutalize her then.

"Amy, can't we talk — just for a moment?"

Her mouth quivered, then thinned. "I don't want to talk to you. How dare you even come here? How *dare* you?"

To Amy, the closing of the door had resounded like a rifle shot. Her head swam, racing with so many thoughts she couldn't begin to sort them. Swift was back. After fifteen years he had come for her. Swift, now a comanchero, a gunslinger, a killer. The words echoed inside her dazed mind like a witch's chant.

She knew firsthand how men like him treated women. She also knew that Comanches believed promises were binding until death. Swift would try to hold her to the betrothal vows she had made to him as a child. He would expect, perhaps even demand, that she marry him.

She stared up at him, unable to reconcile his features with those of the young Comanche warrior she had known. His burnished face, once so boyish and appealing, had become chiseled over the years, his muscular jaw set in a stubborn line and heightened by a squared, deeply clefted chin. Tiny lines etched the corners of his dark brown eyes. His arched, blue-black eyebrows had grown thicker. His once regal nose now sported a knot along the bridge. A thin scar ran from the outside tip of his right eyebrow to his chin. His mouth, once almost too perfect for a male, had grown firm, the dimples at each corner now furrowed into deep crevices that slashed his cheeks. Wind and scorching sun had weathered his skin to a leathery toughness.

Those weren't the only changes.

He had grown taller, much taller, and the years had hardened his body to a whipcord leanness, lending his shoulders a breadth they had lacked when he was younger. The boy she remembered was gone. Swift, her betrothed. A tall, dark, dangerous stranger who stood between her and the door.

"I thought you were dead," he told her softly. "You have to believe that, Amy. Do you think I'd have come riding in like this, out of the blue, without sending word to prepare you?"

"I have no idea what you might or might not do. And, as you can see, I'm far from dead."

"I went to the farm to get you, just as I swore I would. Henry told me you'd died of cholera five years before."

Hearing Henry's name made Amy stiffen.

"There was a grave out back. I couldn't read the writing on the cross." A wry smile slanted across his mouth. "It's a miracle, finding you here. I thought I had lost you."

Just in case he was entertaining the thought of embracing her, she took a step back. Gone was the stilted, charming English he had once spoken. Now he talked like a white man. Even the way he said her name had changed. In addition, he looked at her differently — the way a man looked at a woman.

"It — it was my mother's grave, but whose it was doesn't matter. It's been so many years, Swift."

"Too many years." His smile deepened. "We have a lot of catching up to do, don't we?"

Catching up? Amy tried to picture the two of them chatting over coffee. "Swift, it's been a lifetime. You've — changed."

"And so have you." His gaze swept over her and warmed with unmistakable appreciation. "You were a promise as a girl, and now that promise has been fulfilled."

His mention of promises unnerved her. As if he sensed that, his gaze sharpened, and a smile once again slanted across his mouth, tender with amusement this time. "Amy, would you relax?"

"Relax," she repeated. "Relax, Swift? I never expected to see you again."

He reached to touch a tendril of hair at her temple, his warm fingertips grazing her skin, sending jolts of alarm coursing through her. "Is seeing me again so bad? You're acting like my arrival somehow threatens you."

She inched her head back. "And you think it doesn't? I haven't forgotten Comanche customs. The past doesn't have a place in my life, now. I can't take up where I left off fifteen years ago. I'm a teacher now. I have a home here. I have friends and —"

"Whoa," he broke in. Glancing quickly around the cozy classroom, he withdrew his hand from her hair. "Why would you think my coming here is going to change any of that? Or that I would even want it to?"

"Because I prom—" She made fists in her skirt, staring up at him, uncertainty flooding through her. Perhaps she had been jumping to conclusions. "Are you saying that —" She licked her lips and took a deep, bracing breath. "I always thought — when you came here, I mean — well, I assumed that you'd come because we —" Heat stole up her neck. "Does this mean you no longer consider us — betrothed?"

His smile slowly faded. "Amy, does that have to be an issue right now? We've barely said hello."

"You walk back into my life when I haven't seen you for fifteen years, and you expect me to leave something that important hanging? To not feel threatened? I know how Comanche betrothals and marriages take place." She made a futile gesture with her hands. "Five minutes from now, you might decide to make a public announcement of our marriage and cart me off somewhere!"

A question crept into his eyes. "Do you really believe I'd do that to you?"

"I don't know what you might do," she cried. "You've turned killer. You've been riding with comancheros. I can tell you what I'd like you to do. I wish you'd climb back on your horse and go back where you came from. You're a chapter in my life that I thought was closed, that I want to stay closed."

"I've just ridden over two thousand miles

to get here." His teeth flashed as he spoke, straight and brilliant white against his dark skin. "And even if I had a notion to go, Amy, there's nothing for me to go back to."

"Well, there's certainly nothing for you here."

Swift had never intended for this conversation to turn ugly. But she was leaving him very little room to sidestep. What did she expect? That he should release her from their betrothal and ride out, pretending there had never been anything between them? "I'd say there's plenty for me here," he replied evenly.

She paled. "Meaning me, I take it?"

"Not just you. There's Hunter and Loretta and their children. Amy . . ." He heaved a tired sigh. "Don't back me into a corner on this right now."

"Don't back *you* into a corner?" Amy worked her mouth to speak, but for a second no sound would issue from her throat. She fastened her gaze on his silver-studded gun belt, shaking so badly she could scarcely stand. "Fifteen years is a long time. Too long a time. I won't marry you. If that's what you have in mind, now that you've found me here, then just forget it."

She stepped around him to the door. He planted a palm on the rough wood planks to bar her escape. She stood there with her hands knotted on the handle, her heart pounding, her senses electrified by his nearness.

"You're determined to have this out right now, aren't you?" His voice, pitched low and husky, flowed over her like ice water. "Why that surprises me, I don't know. You never did have much sense when it came to going up against bad odds."

"Is that a threat?" she asked shakily.

"It's just fact."

Her neck stiff with tension, she turned her head to look up at him. "Meaning?"

"You know damned well what I mean."

She tightened her hands on the door handle. "I knew it. The instant I saw you, I knew it. You're going to hold me to those promises I made, aren't you? It doesn't matter that I was only twelve years old. It doesn't matter that I haven't seen you in fifteen years or that you've betrayed everything that was ever between us. You're going to hold me to them."

The tensing of his jaw gave her all the answer she needed. She stared up at him, feeling trapped. As if he read her thoughts, he withdrew his hand from the door.

"Make no mistake, Swift. This is Wolf's Landing, not Texas. Hunter may honor many of the old ways, but he will never countenance your trying to force me into a marriage I would abhor."

With that, Amy ran out, slamming the door behind her. As she raced down the steps, she half expected to hear boots resounding on the weathered planks behind her. Relief flooded through her when she didn't. Scurrying past the black horse tethered at the hitching post, she pressed a hand to her throat, her one thought to reach Hunter and talk to him before Swift did.

CHAPTER 3

The smell of baked bread filled the large main room of the Wolf home. Amy paused just inside the door, trying to regain her composure. Hunter stood at the planked table. He held a slice of warm, honey-slathered bread halfway to his lips.

"Where is Swift?" he asked.

"H-he's coming," she replied, her voice shrill. The room rushed at her, familiar and comforting, yet strangely out of focus. To her left stood Loretta's prized Chickering piano, shipped from Boston around the Horn and hauled from Crescent City by Hunter in a wide-tread wagon. The well-polished rosewood glistened in a ray of sunlight. The braided rugs on the puncheon floors, bright and multicolored, seemed to swirl and undulate. The heat radiating from the wood cookstove seemed suffocating. "Hunter, where's Loretta? I have to talk to you both."

"She's down at the smokehouse getting a ham." His brows drew together. "You look like you just came across a skunk in the woodpile."

"I did." Amy concentrated on the family portrait hanging above the settee, taken shortly after her arrival from Texas, by a photographer named Britt, in Jacksonville. Typical of Britt's work, the picture was life-like, capturing Loretta's family and herself just as they had looked eight years ago. At that time, Amy had prayed Swift would come to Oregon. Now, ironically, those long-abandoned prayers had been answered. "I can't believe he's here," she croaked.

"I know seeing him made the ground turn to air under your feet, but now that you've talked, surely you're feeling better."

Amy swallowed and brushed her sleeve across her mouth. "I'm afraid he's going to make me honor the promises I made to him."

"Ah. And you don't want to? That isn't like you. Words we speak are for always."

"Surely you don't expect me to become that horrible man's wife."

Hunter took another bite of bread, chewing with maddening slowness, his indigo eyes resting thoughtfully on hers. "Swift, a horrible man? He's been my good friend for more years than I can count. When I rode with him in battle, I trusted him with my life many times. Have you forgotten all he did for you, Amy?"

"He's not the same person you knew. Not the same person I knew. He's a killer. And God only knows what else."

"And only God should judge him." He studied her. "It isn't like you to be unforgiving. Can you condemn Swift for what he's done? When I looked into his eyes, I didn't see a killer, just a lonely man who had ridden a long way to find his friends."

"I don't want to judge him. I just want to be free of him."

"The promises you made are between you and Swift. It is not my place to —"

"He was threatening to announce his marriage to me. To drag me off."

Hunter's gaze sharpened on hers. "Did he say that, or are those your words, Amy?"

She took another step into the room. "He didn't have to say it, Hunter. I could tell what he was thinking."

"It would be better if he found a priest so it would be a marriage for both the *tosi tivos* and the Comanches."

Amy stared at him, horror growing apace with disbelief. "You'd let him do that?"

Hunter glanced hopefully toward the

window, as if he wished Loretta would hurry and get back. He cleared his throat. "It isn't for me to say."

Amy advanced on him, fists knotted at her sides, shoulders rigid, so close to losing her temper that she shook. "I'm part of your family. Since the day you rescued me from the comancheros, you've always protected me and been my friend. How can you stand there now and — and eat!"

He studied the bread for a moment, then fastened confused eyes on hers. "I'm hungry?"

Amy found it difficult to breathe. She threw an arm toward the door, lungs convulsing, chest heaving. "That man is a killer. You've known it for months. Yet you'd let him take me? You'd just stand by and let him carry me off? I've just told you he threatened me, and you act as if you don't even care."

Hunter slid his gaze to the closed door. "He didn't pull his gun on you, did he?"

Amy gaped at him. She recognized that gleam in Hunter's eyes. He found this horrible turn of events amusing.

"If he draws on you, I will kill him," Hunter added, taking another bite of bread. "If he pulls his knife on you, I will kill him." He lifted one eyebrow. "But if all he threatens you with is marriage? That's between you and him, Amy. You shouldn't have made promises you didn't intend to keep."

"It's been fifteen years!"

"Ah, yes, a very long time. But, fifteen years or a lifetime, betrothal promises are unbreakable. I suppose you could ask Swift to set you free. . . ."

Amy clamped a hand over her heart in a futile attempt to stop its wild pounding. She couldn't believe this was happening. "He'd never agree to that. You know he wouldn't."

"Have you asked?"

"Not in so many words, but he must know how I feel."

Hunter smiled. "I think you're doing a lot of Swift's talking for him, instead of giving him a chance to speak for himself. How do you know he'd refuse you if you went to him and calmly asked to be released from your promises?"

"Beg him, you mean."

"Whatever it takes, eh?"

Amy swept past him toward the back door. "I can see where your sympathies lie. Well, we'll just see how you feel once I talk to Loretta. This is supposed to be a household where the Comanche and *tosi* beliefs are blended. It seems to me you're leaning mighty heavily one way."

Amy found Loretta just as she was stepping out of the smokehouse, golden curls escaping the braided coronet atop her head. Latching the door, Loretta noted the high color on Amy's cheeks and frowned. "Amy, love, surely it can't be as bad as that."

Amy clutched her collar, swallowing rising panic. She could count on Loretta. She only had to explain what was happening, and her cousin would march inside, give Hunter a tongue-lashing, and settle this matter with all speed. The problem was that Amy couldn't gather her thoughts to put them into words.

"Amy? Honey, don't upset yourself like this. I know it seems bad to you right now. But aren't you jumping the gun just a little? Give Swift a chance, hm? What can it hurt?"

"What can it hurt? He's going to hold me to the betrothal. You should have seen the look in his eye. You know that look they get when they're bent on something."

Loretta's blue eyes filled with concern. "Are you sure you read him right? Swift always loved you so much. I can't picture him riding roughshod over you. Maybe you took him off guard. Maybe he needs time to mull it over."

Amy swiped at a wisp of hair on her forehead, struggling for calm. "I know him,

I tell you. He means to marry me now that he's found me. I just know it. And Hunter said it's not his place to interfere. You have to do something."

"What do you suggest?"

Amy gestured at the house. "Go in there and tell Hunter that . . ." Her voice trailed off. A feeling of unreality swamped her, and she focused on her surroundings, wondering how such an ordinary day had gone so impossibly awry. To her right she heard the creek rushing. Delilah, the cow, came ambling up to the fence and mooed, sending the chickens that scratched nearby into a flutter. "Surely you can reason with him."

The tiny lines deepened at the corners of Loretta's eyes. "The first thing Hunter said to me when he walked into the house was that this was none of our business. He meant just that. Oh, Amy, do you realize what you're asking?" She stepped over to the fence and pulled a cloth sack of milk curd from the nail where she had hung it earlier to drain off the whey. "Hunter and I have spent our entire married life honoring both his ways and mine. How can I ask him to step into this and interfere when it's against his beliefs?"

"What about our beliefs, white beliefs?"

Loretta gave the sack of curds a little

shake to dislodge the remaining beads of whey clinging to its bottom. "I'm afraid you forfeited the right to those when you took part in a Comanche betrothal ceremony. It'd be different if you'd become affianced according to our ways. You could just say forget it. But, Amy, you made vows to Swift's gods, before his people. And you knew it was for forever when you did it."

"I was a child, an impulsive child."

"Yes. And if you'll remember, I wasn't exactly thrilled when I discovered what you'd done. But by the time I learned of it, you'd already betrothed yourself to him. There wasn't much I could do to rectify the situation then, and there isn't now."

"The man's a gunslinger, a comanchero. Have you and Hunter both lost your minds? Having him show up here is a nightmare!"

Loretta went pale. "I know how you're feeling, truly I do. I'm a little leery about having Swift here. More than you know. I have children in the house, and if he's as bad as the stories say, he can't be trusted."

"Then how can you —"

"How can I not?" Loretta pinioned Amy with a pleading look. "Hunter's my husband. Swift is his dear friend. Hunter thinks differently than we do, you know that. He looks forward, never back. No matter what

Swift has done, all that counts to Hunter is what he does from today forward. Am I to go inside and tell him his friend isn't welcome at my table? It's Hunter's table, too, Amy. And he puts the food there."

"What are you saying, Loretta? That you won't help me?"

"I'm saying I can't — not until Swift does something to warrant it."

A breeze picked up, whipping Amy's skirts around her legs. She shivered and hugged herself. "He's rumored to have killed over a hundred men, for God's sake."

"If he kills someone here in Wolf's Landing, we can start counting," Loretta replied gently. "Amy, love, have you tried just talking to Swift? Telling him how you feel? The Swift I remember would listen and weigh what you have to say. I'm sure he never intended to make your life a misery by coming here."

Amy tipped her head back, gazing up at a lofty pine, her eyes narrowed against the sun. "Do you really think he might listen to me?"

"I think you must try."

Swift ran the curry brush along his stallion's shoulder, his thoughts on Amy and the harsh words that had passed between them.

When the light in the barn dimmed, he knew someone stood in the doorway behind him. A sixth sense told him who. Pretending to be unaware, he spoke softly to his horse, continuing his chore, his body tensed as he waited for her to speak.

"Swift?"

She sounded like a frightened child. Memories swept over him, taking him back to that long-ago summer and those first weeks after the comancheros had stolen her from her family. He remembered how terrified she had been in his company. Back in the schoolhouse, he had seen that same panicked expression in her eyes, that of a trapped animal. He didn't want that.

Straightening, Swift turned to look at her. Sunshine slanted through the doorway behind her and ignited the coronet of braid at the crown of her head to a blinding gold. Because he looked against the light, he couldn't see her expression, but from the taut way she held herself, he knew what it had cost her to approach him alone, out here in the barn.

"I see y-you found everything — the feed and all."

"Chase showed me."

One of Hunter's horses neighed; Diablo nickered in answer, shifting sideways.

"That's a beautiful stallion. Have you had him long?"

He doubted she was sincerely interested in his horse. But if she needed to circle him for a bit before she got to her point, he had no objections.

"I raised him from a colt. He's not as ornery as he looks. If you'd like to pet him, he's pretty gentle with the ladies."

"Maybe later. Right now, I, um, need to talk to you."

He walked to the wall, spurs chinking, to rehang the brush on its nail. "I'm listening," he replied softly.

She surprised him by taking another step farther into the barn. Once out of the sun, her face became visible — a face so lovely and sweet it made his heart catch. Wiping her hands on her blue skirt, she glanced around uneasily, as if she expected ghosts to jump out at her. Swift indicated a bale of straw perched by the stall, but she shook her head, clearly too nervous to sit. Interlacing her fingers and bending her knuckles backward, she finally managed to drag her gaze up to his.

"I, um . . . first of all, I'd like to apologize. I didn't give you a very warm welcome. It's wonderful seeing you again."

Swift bit back a smile. Amy had never

been an accomplished liar. "Maybe we can start over, hm?" He held her gaze with his, wishing he knew a way to ease her fears. "Hello, Amy."

She licked her lips. "You used to call me *Aye-mee*."

He grinned. "Which sounded like a sick sheep. You have a beautiful name when it's said correctly."

"You've mastered English well," she said lamely.

"I didn't have a choice. I had enough counts against me without talking strange. If you practice hard enough, you can master anything."

Amy mourned the change. Swift's ineptness at expressing himself in English had often led him to say things that had seemed profound to her. *Wherever you put your face, Amy, your eyes see the horizon and your tomorrows, never yesterday. The sadness in your heart is a yesterday you can no longer see, so put it behind you and walk always forward.*

A lock of black hair curled across his forehead. She recalled touching his hair years ago, tugging his braids, repositioning the feathers he wore. Her gaze shifted from his dark face to the silver-studded gun belt that rode his narrow hips. Rawhide strings anchored the holsters to his muscular thighs. Though his stance seemed relaxed, she sensed a readiness about him, an alertness, as if even now he registered every sound around him. The black shirt and pants heightened the effect, making him seem all the more sinister. She wondered if he had chosen the color to intimidate his opponents.

"Swift . . . I have a request to make of you."

He glanced at her hands and saw that she had her fingers bent so far backward that they were in danger of breaking, her knuckles a painful white. "And what might that be?"

"Do you promise to consider carefully before answering?"

"If it's something I feel deserves consideration." Swift hooked his thumbs over his gun belt, waiting, knowing before she spoke what she meant to ask.

"I — would you —" She broke off and looked up at him with her heart in her eyes. "I want to be set free from the betrothal promises I made to you."

He turned back toward his horse and deftly unfastened the animal's bridle.

"You promised to consider."

"Do I take this to mean that Hunter still

honors the customs of the People?"

"You know he does!"

Swift smiled. "And he suggested you ask me to set you free? How quickly he forgets."

"What does that mean?"

"Don't you remember his marriage to Loretta?" He tossed the bridle onto the straw bale and turned back to face her. "He practically dragged her to the priest."

"It was different for them." In her agitation she came several steps closer, so close Swift could have touched her. "They loved each other, Swift."

"Do you think I don't love you, Amy?" He couldn't resist the urge. Lifting a hand, he brushed his fingertips along her pale cheek. She felt as soft as velvet. "Have you any idea how many times I dreamed of you these last fifteen years? How many times I wept because the great fight for my people kept me from being with you?"

Amy stared up at him, trying to imagine him with tears in his eyes. "You love a memory. I'm not the girl you knew."

His fingertips slid to cup her chin, the rasp of his callused skin warming her from the inside out like a gulp of medicinal whiskey. Amy shrank back, but his hand followed. He trailed his knuckles lightly along her throat, his gaze resting on her face, alert to every change in her expression.

"Aren't you the same girl?" he asked huskily.

"How could I be? You're not a foolish man. Why marry an unwilling woman when you could find someone else?"

"Are you unwilling, or only frightened?" His mouth twisted in a wry grin, and he closed the remaining distance between them. "You ever stumbled across a snake and thought it was a rattler? The first thing you think of is getting bit, and that scares you so bad you can't see past it. You don't look to see if it's really a rattler or if it's coiled. If you've got something in your hand to kill it with, you strike without thinking."

To her eyes, he seemed a yard wide at the shoulders. He smelled of leather and horse and gunpowder, distinctly masculine, a strangely heady combination in the close confines of the barn. Crooking a finger beneath her chin, he tipped her head back.

"I'm not a rattler, Amy, and I'm not fixin' to bite. Give me a chance to wash the trail dust off and have a cup of coffee."

"Then I have nothing to worry about?" Her voice shook. "I'm misreading you. Is that what you're saying? You have no intention of holding me to promises made fifteen years ago?"

"I'd like to discuss it later, that's what I'm saying. You need some time to walk a circle around me. And I need time to come to grips with the reality that you're alive. I have no intentions of making any announcements of marriage today, so you can relax on that score." He turned her face to regard her, his eyes smiling. "As for you not being the same girl I knew? You look like her, speak like her, smell like her . . ." He slowly bent his head toward hers. "Ask me to cut off my right arm for you, and I'll do it. Ask me to lay down my life for you, and I'll do it. But, please, don't ask me to give you up now that I've found you again. Don't ask that, Amy."

"But — I *am* asking it of you, Swift." She drew her head back as his advanced. "I'm begging it of you. If you truly love me, don't destroy my life like this."

Bent on kissing her, Swift tightened his hold on her chin. At the last possible second, she wrenched her face aside. With a broken sob, she whirled away from him and ran from the barn. Swift stared after her, his hand still uplifted.

After a moment, he stepped to the barn door and watched her fleeing down the center of the street. She bypassed Hunter and Loretta's house, heading for a small clapboard dwelling set among a cluster of tall pines at the other end of town.

Don't destroy my life like this. The words whispered in Swift's mind, a heartbreak he didn't want to face, but one he couldn't ignore.

After spending the afternoon and early evening catching up on old times with Loretta and getting to know the children, Swift accompanied Hunter to his lodge, where they sought privacy to talk. Hunter laid a log across the fire, then lowered himself cross-legged to the ground, eyeing Swift across the flames. Night wind slapped against the taut leather walls of the lodge, making a hollow, soft drumming sound that carried Swift back through the years. In the firelight, the age lines stamped upon Hunter's handsome face were invisible. Dressed in buckskin, with his mahogany hair still long, he looked just as Swift remembered him, a tall, lithe warrior with piercing indigo eyes.

"I can't believe you've kept your lodge all these years, Hunter. With a fine house like you've built, what's the point?"

Hunter glanced around them. "This is where I find myself. I live in one world, but my heart yearns for another sometimes."

His voice reed thin, Swift replied, "It's a world that no longer exists." As gently as he could, he told Hunter about the deaths of all his relatives. Tears filled Hunter's eyes, but Swift continued, knowing these things had to be said and that Hunter had brought him to the lodge to hear them. "At least they died free and proud, my friend," Swift finished carefully. "Their world no longer existed, so perhaps it was best they passed on to a better place."

Hunter swept his hand toward the lodge walls. "Ah, but it does exist, and as long as my children live, it will continue to exist, because I sing my people's songs and teach my children their ways." He thumped his chest with his fist. "The People are here, forever, until I am dust in the wind. It was my brother's last request of me, yes? And I have honored it. It was my mother's dream, and I have made it come true." He let out a ragged sigh. "I have known of their parting for a long time. My brother's spirit walks beside me. I feel the sunshine of my mother's love upon my shoulders. When I listen, I can hear them whispering gladness to me."

For years Swift had hardened himself against feeling anything, but now Hunter's tongue laid him open like a knife.

"For the Comanche in me, my life here

has sometimes been a lonely path, but within me there is a dream place where my people still ride free and kill the buffalo. When I come to this lodge, I listen, if only for a little while, to the whispering voices of lost souls, and a smile comes upon me."

An ache spread through Swift's chest. "I can't hear the whispers anymore," he admitted hollowly. "Sometimes, when the wind touches my face, my memories come so clear, I nearly weep. But the place inside me that was Comanche has died."

Hunter closed his eyes, his muscle-roped arms draped loosely across his knees, his body relaxed. He seemed to be absorbing the very air around him. "No, Swift. The Comanche in you has not died. You have only stopped listening. You feel the same to me as always, except that I sense great pain in you."

The firelight before Swift seemed to swim, and he realized he was looking at it through tears. "Not pain, Hunter, just a lost feeling. When the People fell, there was no longer a path for me to follow. No one to tell me where to walk, or how. And I began going my own way." He swallowed. "It hasn't been a good way. You've heard the stories." He looked up into his friend's eyes. "They're true. If you turn your face from me, I won't blame you. If your woman doesn't want me in your house tonight, I'll understand. My heart has little sunshine in it, only blackness. Blackness can spread to others."

Hunter smiled. "And sunlight chases away darkness. You've only to rise before dawn to see that. You've risked your life for me in battle, Swift. I trusted you enough to bless your betrothal to Amy. If your path has been a hard one, I'm sorry, but I see only where your feet rest now. You have been a brother to me. That will never change."

"Traveling here, I thought of you so often — of all the good times we shared. I hoped we could make new memories together."

A reminiscent silence fell over them. Then Hunter broke it by asking, "Yet you're planning to leave?"

Swift stiffened. "How did you know?"

"I see the good-byes aching in your eyes." Hunter leaned forward over his knees and prodded the fire with a stick of kindling. A spray of sparks shot upward. "Why, Swift? You've traveled so far to get here, and before one sleep, you're looking over your shoulder at the trail behind you. When a man finally finds his way, he is a fool to become lost again."

Swift closed his eyes, inhaling the wonderful smell of Hunter's lodge, weary in a way that went far deeper than his bones. "Sometimes a man has to do things he'd rather not."

"You leave because of Amy, don't you?"

Swift lifted his lashes. "My coming here has upset her. What she says is true. She *was* just a child when she betrothed herself to me." He hunched his shoulders. "As much as I love her, I'm not blind. She's changed, Hunter. The old fear is back in her eyes. I'm not sure I can get past it again. And if I couldn't, the only alternative would be force. I can't walk back into her life and do that to her. It wouldn't be fair."

"Wouldn't it?" Hunter grew pensive. "If you truly love Amy, I'm not so sure a little force would be a bad thing."

"Force, Hunter? That's never been your way."

"No." Hunter listened to the sounds outside for a moment, as if he wanted to assure himself none of his family had drawn close to his lodge. "Swift, what I'm going to tell you is for you alone. Loretta will burn my dinner for a month if she learns of it." A twinkle crept into his eyes. "She loves Amy very much, yes? And we don't always agree on what is best for her. Loretta sees with her woman's heart, and she shoos away shadows, trying to make Amy's world one of sunshine."

"It seems everyone here loves Amy. I thought her students were going to attack me today."

"Yes, very much love, but not the right kind." Hunter chewed one corner of his mouth, as if he weighed each word before he spoke. "Amy — she is like . . ." His eyes grew distant. "I once met a man in Jacksonville who caught beautiful butterflies. He kept them in cases, under glass. Amy's like that, living under glass, where nothing can touch her. You understand? She loves her schoolchildren. She loves me and Loretta and our children. Yet she claims no one for herself, so she can make babies of her own."

Swift ran his palms over the black denim that skimmed his thighs, then clenched his fingers over his bent knees. "Maybe she doesn't want babies, Hunter."

"Oh, but she does. I have seen the yearning in her eyes. But there is a great fear in her. She has . . ." His voice trailed off. "When she came to us from Texas, she had changed. She no longer has the courage she once had to fight for what she wants."

Swift circled that, remembering the dusty, barren farm and Henry Masters, swaying drunkenly in the doorway, a mescal jug dangling from his finger. "Did something more happen to her in Texas? Aside from the comancheros kidnapping her, I mean."

Hunter tossed the stick onto the fire. "I don't think so. Amy has no secrets from us." He shrugged. "What Santos and his men did to her — that has walked with her, always. Fear's a strange thing. When we face it, as she did that summer when you befriended her, fear becomes small. But when we run from it, it grows and grows. For a very long time, Amy has been running."

Swift considered that, trying to read Hunter's expressions.

Hunter met his gaze. "When she first came to Wolf's Landing, she made dreams about one day, when the Comanche fight for survival finally ended and you would come for her. They were very good dreams, and dreaming them was safe. You understand? You were her great love, but always for someday, never for today. She held herself away from others because she was promised to you. As the years went by and the dreams turned to dust, she filled her life with other things. My family. Her students." Affection warmed his voice. "She's a beautiful woman. There are many men who would marry with her and give her children, but she stays under the glass, where no one can touch her."

86

"More than twenty men raped her." The words came hard, catching behind Swift's larynx. "The hell they put her through would have destroyed most women. Amy was just a child. I guess if anyone has a right to live under glass, it's her."

"Yes, she has that right if you grant it to her and ride out tomorrow." Hunter arched a challenging eyebrow. "But is she happy? Being safe can also be very lonely."

Swift glanced away. "What are you saying, Hunter? I hate it when you talk around things. I remember when I was a kid, I always felt like I was on hot coals when you lectured me."

"The reason I talk around is so you will think through," Hunter replied with a grin. "I learned it from a very wise man."

"Your father." Swift laughed softly and then, on a sigh, whispered, "Many Horses . . . what I wouldn't give to see him again, just for an hour. To this day, I can remember sitting in his lodge, smoking with him and turning green, too young and proud to admit his pipe made my stomach roll."

"He was very good at talking around."

Still smiling, Swift pulled his Bull Durham pouch and La Croix papers from his pocket, then deftly rolled a smoke. Picking up the stick Hunter had tossed on the fire, he lit up and inhaled deeply. "Well, I like straight talk. What I hear you saying is —" He spat a fleck of tobacco. "You think I should stay. Even though she hates everything I've become."

"Does she? Or is it that she knows you will break through the glass and claim her, when no other man has dared? I think she is very frightened to have her dream turn out to be a flesh-and-blood man, a man who may not run if she lifts her nose high and scorns him." Hunter flashed an indulgent smile. "She is very good at lifting her nose. The men here try to impress her with their manners and end up tripping over their own feet."

"And you think I'll succeed where they've failed?"

"I don't think you'll approach her with a book of manners in one hand and your hat in the other."

"I couldn't read a book of manners if I had one. Jesus, Hunter . . ." Swift shoved the stick deep into the ashes, his thrust hard and angry. "She looks at me, and all she sees is the past coming back to haunt her. And she's right. I've seen things that haunt *me!* I've done things I couldn't forgive another man. She claims we no longer know one another, but the truth is, Amy knows me too well. If I stay here, I'll rip her life apart. She made promises to me long ago that give me the right to do that, but if I care anything about her, should I?"

"That is only for you to know." Pausing, Hunter stared for a moment into the fire, then looked up. "What will she have if you disappear over the horizon, Swift?"

"Her life here. Peace and quiet. Good friends. Teaching the children."

"Ah, yes. Like you, she walks her own way. But is it good?"

"It may be a whole lot better than what I can give her."

"No, because her life here is nothing." Hunter grew pensive again. "Chase found a wounded raccoon once, which he healed and raised to adulthood inside a cage."

Swift nearly groaned. "I hear one of your stories coming. How in hell can a raccoon possibly relate to this discussion?"

Hunter held up a hand. "Perhaps if you open your ears, you will find out." He smiled and settled back. "The raccoon — he always looked through the wire at the world, sniffing and yearning for freedom. Like Amy, he dreamed of yesterday and someday, but his todays were nothing. Chase decided it was cruel to keep him imprisoned, and he opened the cage door. The raccoon, who had been badly injured by another animal, was terrified and cowered in the back corner of his prison."

Swift set his jaw. "Amy isn't a coon, Hunter."

"But she cowers in the back corner, all the same." Hunter squinted against a trail of smoke. "The raccoon was a biter when he grew frightened, so instead of dragging him out of the cage, Chase prodded him with a stick, until the coon got so mad he forgot he was afraid and went out the door. Chase prodded him every day with that stick, and each time the coon left his cage, he stayed outside a little longer, until he finally lost his fear of the outdoors. It's a story with a happy ending. The coon's dreams of yesterday and someday became his today."

Swift snorted. "I can't go poking Amy with a prod. Talk sense, if you're gonna talk."

"I'm talking very good sense. I rescued Amy from Santos, yes? And I tended her wounds, just as Chase did the raccoon's. And like Chase, I have made a very safe world here for Amy, where she can hide and dream." Hunter swallowed, the muscles along his throat distended. When he resumed speaking, his voice rang taut. "My heart held only good things, but what I have done is very bad. The safety has become her cage, and she is trapped inside, afraid to leave."

With an index finger, Swift traced the Maltese cross imprinted on his folder of cigarette papers. "Do you realize that I have nothing? A horse, some gold pieces, and a pack of trouble riding my heels. That's it."

Hunter mused on that for a moment and, as always, offered no solution.

"It'd be a hell of a lot easier on both of us if I just rode out," Swift argued.

"Yes."

That single word held an unspoken challenge. "Doesn't it matter at all to you that I'm a gunslinger? That I rode with comancheros? If I met myself on the street, I'd say, 'Now there's a no-good bastard, if ever I saw one.' "

"I only know what I can see in your eyes."

"What if I turn her world upside down and my past catches up with me?" Swift tossed his smoke into the fire. "Tomorrow, next week, a year from now. It could happen, Hunter."

"Then you must turn and face your past. Just as Amy must turn and face hers." Hunter pushed to his feet, his shadow looming behind him on the leather wall. "Stay here in my lodge for a while, and listen to your heart. If, after you listen, you still ride out tomorrow, I will know it is the best thing and accept it. But find yourself first. Not the boy you were, not the man that boy became, but who you are tonight. Your path will then be marked for you. I leave you with one great truth. A man whose yesterdays rest on his horizon travels forward into his past. The result is that he goes a very long way to nowhere."

CHAPTER 4

Voices filled the Wolf home, bouncing cheerfully off the planked walls, drowning out the sound of silver chinking against china. Swift was full of questions about Hunter's mine, seemingly fascinated that his old friend had been so successful at unearthing gold. With his usual patience, Hunter explained the difference between placer and lode gold, describing the equipment and techniques used to mine each, and that his operation employed both. Loretta and the children inserted amusing anecdotes now and again, telling stories about the panned-out claims around Jacksonville and the more recent finds around Wolf's Landing.

"These hills are full of gold, no doubt about that," Indigo said excitedly. "Over in the Jacksonville jail, an inmate panned the dirt in the floor of his cell. It proved so profitable that he wasn't any too anxious to be turned loose. Then, right before his sentence was up, he hit bedrock and insisted he was staking a claim. The sheriff had to force him out of there at gunpoint."

Loretta winked at Swift. "The way this girl goes on, you'd think she teethed on a nugget. The Jacksonville jail has a double-layer log floor. Far as I know, it's the only jail there ever was."

In a warm voice Hunter said, "Indigo hopes to take over my mining operation when I grow old."

Chase snorted, clearly disgusted at the thought. Indigo's blue eyes flashed. "At least I know the difference between the real thing and fool's gold!" she cried.

"Bet you can't judge the height of a tree by the shadow it casts," Chase retorted.

"Who cares?"

Amy listened in silence, head bent over her plate, fingers clenched around the handle of her fork. With her assistance, Loretta had prepared a lovely dinner to celebrate Swift's arrival, but to Amy the food tasted like sawdust. Even the cottage cheese, more commonly known as "rag on the fence," had no taste. Amy rolled the curds across her tongue, feeling as if she were swallowing gravel.

When the children ran low on gibes, the conversation turned from mining to Swift's experiences since leaving the reservation. Bombarded with queries about Texas, Swift did most of the talking, and just the sound of his voice tied Amy's stomach into knots. When she actually looked at him, her nerves frayed like jaggedly cut burlap. A part of her still couldn't believe he was there or how much he had changed. He had a relentless look now, a hard, cynical, bitter look that made her heart catch. Yet somehow, despite that, he was as handsome as always, but in a more potent, powerful, and unnerving way.

Something else had changed about him, too, something far more recent and more subtle. Earlier today in the barn, when she'd pleaded with him to release her from her promises, he had looked uncertain. Now the uncertainty had vanished, replaced by a gleam of determination. Amy had the feeling that Swift and Hunter had talked about her out in Hunter's lodge and that whatever had been said had somehow strengthened Swift's resolve.

"So, Uncle Swift, tell us about your gunfights," Chase urged. "Is it true you've killed over a hundred men?"

A sudden silence fell, amplifying the soft *pling* of fork tines scraping china. Broad shoulders rigid, Swift cleared his throat. "I think the stories about my gunfights have been exaggerated, Chase." After a pause he added in a teasing tone, "I doubt I've killed more than ninety all together."

"Ninety? Boy!"

Loretta fastened disapproving blue eyes on her son. "Chase, your uncle Swift is teasing you."

Chase's face fell. "Then tell me true. How many?"

Indigo elbowed her brother. "Don't pester, Chase Kelly."

Swift's gaze collided with Amy's, and his smile tightened. "A man doesn't notch his belt every time he has to draw on someone, Chase. I've pulled my gun when I was forced to, and then I tried to forget."

"But you are the fastest in Texas. The paper said so. Ain't that right?"

"Isn't," Loretta corrected.

"There's always someone who's faster, Chase," Swift replied. "If you forget that, even for an instant, you're a dead man."

Chase nodded, clearly thrilled by the thought. "Now that you're here, will you teach me to handle a gun?"

Swift set his mug down with a decisive click. "No."

Indigo nudged her brother again, the seriousness of her expression making her seem far older than her thirteen years.

Chase glowered at his sister, then shot Swift an imploring glance. "But why? I'm good with weapons."

Taut with tension, Amy waited to hear Swift's reply.

"Because it's no way to live, that's why." A muscle twitched in Swift's cheek. He laid his fork on the side of his plate, a large piece of ham left uneaten. "Trust me on that. If I could go back in time and never touch a six-shooter, I would."

Amy glanced over and saw that Loretta had tears in her eyes. Swallowing down nausea, Amy followed Swift's example and set aside her fork, a part of her hating him for what he had become, another part as close to tears as Loretta. No one who looked could miss the haunted expression in Swift Lopez's eyes.

Hunter rose from the table and picked up his plate and mug. Carrying both to the dish counter, he said, "So tell me, Swift, what brought you out our way? And how long do you plan to stay?"

"I came here hoping to make a new start." Swift's gaze slid to Amy again. "Discovering my woman alive is like a dream come true. I'll be hanging my hat here, now that I've found her."

Another taut silence descended. Amy knew this was his way of letting everyone in the family know he hadn't forgotten her betrothal promise to him and that he expected her to honor it. The battle lines were drawn. Her gaze dropped to the intimidating expanse of his chest, to the play of muscle under the sleeves of his shirt. She had the horrible feeling that the outcome of this particular war might be a foregone conclusion.

Amy shoved back her chair. Keeping her face carefully blank, she began clearing the table, anxious to get the dishes washed. Chase hauled in water, which Loretta put on the stove to boil. Indigo, nearly as tall as her mother, drew an apron over her head and quickly tied the sash.

"Amy, Indigo and I'll do the dishes," Loretta offered. "You have to teach school in the morning. Why don't you go on home?"

Eager to jump at any excuse to leave, Amy pulled her shawl off the door hook and draped it around her shoulders. "It was a lovely dinner, Loretta Jane. Good night, Hunter." Her tongue turned cottony. "It's been nice seeing you again, Swift."

Indigo ran over to give Amy a farewell hug. Pressing a kiss to her cheek, she whispered, "No wonder you pined for him all these years, Aunt Amy. He's so hand-some."

Amy drew back, meeting Indigo's guile-less gaze, astounded that the child had said such a thing. It occurred to her that the little girl she had loved so well was approaching womanhood.

Swift rose from the table. With a lazy stride, spurs chinking, he approached the coatrack, pulled his gun belt from its hook, and strapped it around his hips. Next, he reached for his hat. Indigo dimpled one cheek in a mischievous grin and darted past Swift to help her mother clear the table. Amy was left standing there alone with him, horrified because he acted as if he intended to accompany her. A picture flashed in her mind of her and him, alone in the darkness.

"I'll see you home," he said softly.

"Th-that really isn't necessary. I walk home alone all the time. Don't I, Hunter?"

Hunter's only response was to smile.

"I'll walk with you anyway. It's bound to be a nice evening after all that sunshine we had today."

Amy clutched her shawl closer, searching wildly for some reason to forestall him. She settled for unembellished honesty. "I'd really rather you didn't."

His mouth quirked at one corner as he

settled his hat on his head. Tipping the brim down over his eyes, he replied in a dangerously silken voice, "And I'd really rather I did."

After casting Hunter a pleading look, which availed her naught, Amy jerked the door open and stepped out onto the wide porch. Determined to set a breakneck pace, she darted down the steps and across the yard, keeping a step ahead of the tapping boots and chinking spurs behind her. The crisp night air chilled her cheeks. She hugged her shawl more tightly.

"What's it say in that manners book of yours about ladies who run off and leave their escorts eating dust?"

She swung to a stop, peering at him through the moonlit gloom. "You're an uninvited escort, Mr. Lopez." His new name felt odd rolling off her tongue, yet she used it, a reminder to herself and him of who he was and what he had become. "A gentleman wouldn't force his company on a lady."

Farther down, a man staggered out of the Lucky Nugget. Swift came abreast of her, took her arm, and guided her to the far side of the street. As their feet touched the boardwalk, he said, "Even if I wanted to be a gentleman, I've never had proper manners taught to me. The closest thing I had to a teacher was a rancher I worked for named Rowlins, and all he knew was shootin' and spittin'. He was pretty good at both, and he taught me all he knew, but he wasn't and never claimed to be a gentleman."

"Obviously. Otherwise I wouldn't be walking on the street side of the boardwalk."

He laughed softly and, putting a hand at her waist, pulled her across his path so she walked next to the shop windows. He loomed beside her, a menacing shadow, the silver conchae on his hat and the studs on his gun belt gleaming in the moonlight. She flinched when she felt his palm touch the small of her back, then slip around to claim a resting place just above her left hip. The easy familiarity with which he touched her sent her heart into a skitter. The men in Wolf's Landing wouldn't dream of taking such a liberty.

"I haven't had much occasion to walk a lady down the street. Am I doing it right now?" He drawled the question, his tone amused. Then he tensed, as if to brace her. "Watch your step."

"I know this boardwalk like the back of my hand," she replied in a brittle voice, stepping over the unevenness in the boardwalk without difficulty.

"You must, as fast as you're walking. The

Amy I knew couldn't see the end of her nose when it got dark."

Amy bit back a retort, her one thought to get safely inside her house and bolt the door. To that end, she increased her pace. Swift's hand tightened on her waist.

"Whoa. The idea here is to stroll along and get reacquainted."

"I don't want to get reacquainted."

As if her wants were of absolutely no consequence to him, he ignored the rebuff. It seemed forever to her before they reached her porch. Amy hurried up the two steps and shoved open the door. "Thank you for walking me. Good night."

She stepped into the darkness and tried to push the door closed, only to find that Swift had braced a palm against the wood to prevent her.

"Won't you ask me in?"

"Most certainly not! I'm a teacher. I have a reputation to uphold. A lady doesn't allow a man —"

He shoved on the door, moving her back two steps. "Guess I'll just ask myself."

And with that, he sauntered inside. Whereas a moment ago she had been straining to shut the door, now Amy clutched the handle with frantic fingers to keep him from closing it. He won the tug-of-war by putting a shoulder into it. The door shut with a resounding finality, and he slid the top bolt into place.

"Two locks, Amy? I thought Wolf's Landing was a safe, friendly place to live. You locking yourself in, or the rest of the world out?"

Darkness had swooped over them. Amy stood rooted, her heart pounding. Dressed all in black, Swift blended so well with the shadows that she couldn't see him. But she could feel him, and with those horrible, nightmarish spurs chinking every time he moved, she could hear him as well. He had drawn far too close. The smell of leather and denim and tobacco filled her nostrils.

"Light the lamp," he said tersely. "We need to talk."

Making a beeline for the table, she groped for the lantern and the box of lucifers. Drawing the match through a pleat of glass paper, she ignited the head, showering sparks. She quickly turned up the lantern wick, set flame to it, and replaced the smoke-streaked mantle. The stench of the lucifer made her eyes tear, and she leaned back to escape its gaseous fumes while waving out the flame.

"You really shouldn't be using those things inside the house. You want bad lungs or a case of phossy jaw?"

"I — I don't usually. My tinderbox is low on cedar bark, and I haven't gone out to get more. It'd take a sight more than the number of matches I use to hurt my lungs or bones."

"You're shaking," he observed dryly. "Do I frighten you that badly?"

She made much of adjusting the light, ignoring the question.

"Can you at least try to talk to me about this?"

She carried the box of matches to the fireplace and crouched to lay a fire. When he stepped between her and the lantern, his shadow loomed across her, larger than life and threatening. The silent seconds stretched endlessly.

"Damn it, I'm speaking to you!"

Bending low to puff air at the feeble beginnings of the fire, Amy rearranged the wood so it would catch. "Don't curse in my house."

He let out an incredulous laugh. "As I recall, you taught me that word and several others. 'Hell and damnation' was your favorite phrase, remember? And when you were really bustin' mad, you'd say —"

"Do you mind?" She pushed to her feet, shoving the matchbox closed with so much force that she nearly crumpled it between her damp palms. "This is my home. I'd like to prepare for bed."

"Go ahead."

Amy blinked. In the leaping firelight he looked exactly like she imagined the Devil, tall, handsome, cloaked in black. Suddenly so weary she wanted to drop, she put the matches on the mantel, pressed the back of her wrist to her forehead, and closed her eyes. "Swift, please."

"Please what? Talk to me, Amy. Tell me what has you so upset that you can't even look at me. I know you remember how it was between —" He broke off suddenly. Then, in amazement, he whispered, "I'll be damned if that isn't —" His boots and spurs resounded on the planked floor, coming closer to the hearth. "Amy, did you draw that?"

Too late, she remembered the sketch. In a swirl of skirts she tried to edge past him and grab it off the mantel. Before her fingertips could grasp the frame, though, his deflected them.

"Don't," he said.

Defeated, Amy fell back, studying him as he studied his likeness. Seeing him standing there, his profile so similar to the boy's in the drawing, she was assailed by memories.

For an instant, an ache of longing washed through her. Swift, *her* Swift. Scenes from yesterday replayed in her mind. Two youngsters romping and giggling along a stream. Swift, leaping out at her from the woods, flowers clasped in his hand. Swift, teaching her to speak Comanche, shoot a rifle, use a bow, ride a horse, walk without making a sound. So many memories. At one time they had been such good friends. What had happened to them that they could stand together in the same room with such a great distance between them? There had been a time when she would have trusted him with her life.

And now?

Amy looked away. Now, she wouldn't trust him to walk her home — which he had done. Now, she wouldn't want him in her house when she was alone at night — which he was.

She heard his spurs chink, the one sound from out of her past that could reduce her to sniveling terror. Her stomach tightened. For a moment, long forgotten smells seemed to fill her nostrils — the smell of men and lust and blood, her blood. She swayed, trying to block out the pictures, but they sprang at her from all sides.

"Amy, look at me."

His voice had turned husky. He grasped her chin and lifted her face to his. She took one look into his eyes and knew what he intended. She wrenched away, backing up until she bumped into the wall. He followed. Once again she tried to twist away, but he braced a hand on each side of her, blocking her escape.

"Amy, for God's sake, what do you think I'm going to do to you?"

She tried to speak but couldn't. He stepped closer, so close she could feel his shirt grazing the bodice of her dress. The friction, whether intentional or not, titillated her nipples, and they strained against the cloth of her chemise, aching. Amy broke the contact by flattening her back against the wall. He removed his hat and sent it sailing in a wide arc toward the door. The conchae, the *hated* conchae, went *kerchink* on the wood. Santos, the comanchero leader who had kidnapped her, had worn conchae on his pants. Most of his men had worn them as well. She couldn't see the silver disks without breaking out in a sweat.

"Amy." Swift's lips grazed a loose curl at her temple. "Do you remember that day down by the river, when you taught me how to kiss?"

His grip relentless this time, he clasped

her chin and forced her head back. His dark eyes held hers.

"You closed your eyes, wrinkled your nose, and puckered up like a cactus button." His face drew closer. "It wasn't until years later I found out that wasn't the way to do things."

His chest met hers, sandwiching her between him and the wall. She strained her head back, trying to keep distance between their mouths. "Swift, don't . . . please, don't."

He bent closer until his breath mingled with hers, a warm mist, sweet from honeyed coffee.

"Do you remember, Amy?"

"Yes," she finally admitted on a soft sob. "I remember. It was a foolish child's kiss. That has nothing to do with now." She managed to get her hands between their bodies until she had both palms against his chest. With all her strength, she shoved.

Pushed off balance, he staggered back, and she took advantage, darting from under his arm. She put several feet between them, whirled, and hugged herself so he wouldn't see her shaking. Trying to keep her voice steady, she said, "It's over between us, Swift. Whatever we shared was between two children. We're grown now. Too much has happened. I'm sorry if you hoped differently. But that's the way it is."

He crossed the room and leaned a hip against her table, loosely folding his arms. The relaxed stance didn't console her. Every time he so much as flexed, she jumped, terrified of what he intended to do. Knowing Comanche custom as she did, Amy was all too aware that he might carry her to the bedroom and force himself on her. No one who believed as he did would frown on him for using strength of arm. God help her, she had granted him inalienable rights to her body and her life, and the possessive gleam in his eyes told her he just might exercise both.

Studying her with relentless intensity, he asked, "Is this all because I rode with the comanchero? If so, I can explain."

"Explain?" She ran a contemptuous gaze the length of him. "Do you think I don't know the evil things you must have done?"

"That's over and done."

She pressed a hand against her waist. Since his arrival her stomach had taken to doing cartwheels, fluttering crazily, sinking to her toes one minute, surging into her throat the next. "Over and done? Just like that, you think you can erase it?" She stared at him, waiting. "Did your comanchero friends kill people, Swift? Did they — rape women? Did they? Answer me!"

Swift swallowed, determined not to let his gaze falter. "I can't answer for what they did, Amy."

"Then answer for yourself. Did you steal and kill and rape? Did you?" Her voice rose to a shrill squeak.

"I'm guilty of some of that, but not all." A glitter crept into his eyes. "You don't really believe I'd rape a woman. Do you? Deep down . . ."

"You'd rape me," she countered. "Deny that, and I'll put on a pot of coffee. We'll have a nice little chat, catch up, just like you wanted. Swear to me that you'll never touch me."

Swift regarded her in silence, afraid for her in a way he never had been before. She looked as if an unexpected move from him might make her fly apart. Suddenly he understood what Hunter had tried to make him understand with the story about the raccoon. Amy was trapped here at Wolf's Landing, terrified of anything or anyone that threatened to change her world.

"You can't swear that to me, can you, Swift?" Her voice quavered as she spoke. "If I don't honor my promise to you, you have every intention of making me honor it.

Don't you?" She stared at him, her pupils so dilated that her huge eyes shone nearly black. "Answer me. You've betrayed all else between us. Please don't add lying to the list."

Swift felt as if he stood on a precipice with someone nudging him to leap. He didn't want to lie to her. But he could see the truth would terrify her, driving the wedge ever deeper between them. "I'll never hurt you, Amy. You have my word on that."

The skin across her cheekbones drew taut, the delicate muscle beneath twitching, until her face became a caricature of its beauty, skeletal and harsh. "Painless rape? Where did you learn that trick?"

Swift's guts knotted. "Amy, for God's sake. Why are you prodding me like this? You started in on me the minute I got here, and you haven't let up since."

Amy had no answer. The last thing she should do was infuriate him, yet she couldn't let the matter drop. She had to know what he intended. She couldn't bear the thought of spending an entire night wondering.

"Do you want a confrontation?" he asked softly. "For me to make threats? Is that it? So you'll have a reason to hate me?"

"I've plenty to hate you for as it is. I'm

asking for honesty, if you're capable of it anymore. I want to know what your intentions are. I think I've every right to that. It is my life we're discussing. Are you too big a coward to answer me?"

"All right, goddamn it, yes," he said, pushing away from the table. His sudden movement made her jerk. "You want it on the line, Amy? You're mine! You have been for fifteen years. No one forced you to betroth yourself to me. You knew exactly what you were doing. And you wanted to do it as much as I did. If you try to welsh on our agreement, I'll force you to honor it. That's the way it is, and that's the way it's going to be."

She braced herself, as if she expected him to hit her. Swift froze, his body taut, his skin clammy.

"Do you feel better now?" he asked hoarsely. "It's out in the open. You know where you stand. I'm here, I'm staying, and you'd damned well better figure out a way to deal with it."

She looked as if her legs might buckle. Swift yearned to reach for her but didn't dare.

"Amy." His voice shook with emotion, foremost regret because the last thing he had ever dreamed he might do was deliberately frighten her. "Do you know the safest place you could be right now? Come here and I'll show you. Just three steps, and I swear to your God and all mine that nothing and no one will ever harm you as long as I've got life left in my body."

She looked at his outstretched hand in horrified disbelief.

"You trusted me once. You can trust me now. Come here and let me prove it to you. Please. . . ."

"I trusted Swift Antelope. Swift Antelope is dead."

Swift felt as if she had slapped him. He slowly dropped his arm and curled his hand into a fist. "If I were dead, honey, you wouldn't have a betrothal promise hanging over you. You're making this a lot harder than it needs to be, and you're going to be the one who suffers for it."

"Maybe, but I'll go down fighting." Even as she spoke she retreated a step, her voice thin and quavery. "Make no mistake in that, for I will fight you. With my last breath. I'd rather die than let a man like you put his hands on me again."

Brave words, but they had no force behind them. Swift studied her, and he grieved over what he saw. What had happened to the Amy he had known — the courageous girl who had once stood alone, challenging sixty Comanche warriors with a rifle she wasn't big enough to shoot? Even if it meant losing her, he longed to see that fire back in her eyes again, if only for an instant. As Amy was now, she was only a shell — a beautiful, untouchable shell — of the woman she should have been.

"A man like me? You know nothing about me."

"I know you're not the boy I loved! That's all I need to know."

"You can't get rid of me quite that easy." He strode toward the door and bent to pick up his hat. After he dusted it clean on his pants, he turned to regard her. "A betrothal promise is forever, Amy. I realize fifteen years is a hell of a long time, but it's nowhere close to forever. You promised yourself to me by the central fire. Nothing and no one can change that. I'll give you some time to get used to the idea, but not too long. The way I figure, too much time has been wasted already."

He opened the door.

"Swift, wait!"

He paused and glanced back.

"Y-you can't really expect me to honor a promise I made as a twelve-year-old."

"Yes, Amy, I really can."

He could see how badly she trembled, even from across the room.

"Even though you know I'd rather die?"

Swift ran his gaze over her. "I'm not too worried about you dying on me. You might wish you could, but wishing and doing are two different things. You can give it a try. We'll see if you're more successful than I was. But my advice is to spend more time getting used to the idea of marriage — just in case wishing yourself dead doesn't work. It'd be a hell of a note to kid yourself right up until the last minute and find yourself being touched, despite all your wishing, by a man like me."

He waited, hoping she'd throw the challenge back in his face, but instead she only grew pale. With a sinking heart he walked out and softly closed the door.

After a poor night's rest, Amy awoke just after dawn to the ring of an ax. Slipping from bed, she approached the window, wondering who would be in her yard chopping wood. Pressing her face to the glass, she peered out into the grayish gloom.

"Swift!"

Her fingers tightened on the window sash when she spotted him. His black, collar-length hair was wind-tossed and damp with sweat, but those who didn't know better might think it was mussed from sleep and damp from washing his face. Naked to the waist, he afforded her a view of his sunburnished upper torso. With every movement, muscle bunched across his broad back. Except for the gun belt strapped around his waist, he looked like a man who had just crawled out of bed to chop wood for the breakfast fire. A fire that people would assume was to be built in her stove.

"What do you think you're doing?" she called, glancing anxiously toward town to see if anyone had seen him.

He didn't seem to hear her. Infuriated, Amy grabbed her wrapper, shoving her arms down the sleeves as she dashed from the bedroom. When she threw the door wide and yelled the question again, he ceased swinging the ax and turned the full impact of his gaze on her, beginning at her toes and working his way up to her face, his interest lingering at several points in between.

"I'm chopping my woman's firewood," he explained with a lazy grin. "That is how you white folks do things, isn't it?"

"I'm not your woman! And I don't appreciate your parading about my yard half-dressed. I'm a schoolteacher, Swift. Do you want me to lose my job?"

He balanced a partially split chunk of wood on the block, stepped back, and rendered it in two with one mighty swing.

Sputtering, Amy ran onto the porch. "You get out of here. People will see you and think you've been here all night."

"Now why didn't I think of that?"

She watched him split another log, her temper rising with each report of the ax. When he continued to ignore her, she braved the yard barefoot, uncertain what to do once she reached him but convinced she had to do something.

"I said get off my place."

"Our place."

"What?"

"Our place. What's yours is mine, what's mine is yours. You know how it goes."

"You don't have anything but a horse."

"He's one hell of a good horse, though." His eyes met hers, dancing with mischief. "My, my, Amy, you are a fetching sight in that nightdress. From a distance, I bet we look like we're making eyes at each other."

Amy felt heat rising up her neck. "Get out!"

He gave her a measuring glance. "You giving me the boot?"

She wanted to wrest the ax from him but

didn't quite dare. "Teaching is my life. Do you understand that?"

"Yeah, and it's a hell of a waste."

"It isn't a waste. I like it. I love it!"

"Fine with me. Teach to your little heart's content. They don't have anything against married women teaching, do they?"

Amy stared up at him, legs quivering with rage. She knotted her hands. He noted the gesture and grinned, his laughing eyes daring her to strike him. Amy came close to accommodating him. Only the thought of what he might do in retaliation stopped her.

"The men on the school committee will terminate me on the spot if they think I'm engaging in — in improper behavior. Unlike you, I can't steal for a living."

He cocked an eyebrow at her, his grin widening. "Would you listen to yourself? Are you the same girl who helped me tug all the ropes coming from Old Man's lodge one night and then hid with me in the brush to watch all his wives run to join him in his buffalo robes? Improper, Amy?"

Lips parted, she gazed up at him, unable to speak. It had been years since she had thought of that night. She and Swift had rolled in the grass, bent double with laughter, fighting to make no sound while Old Man tried to placate his wives. The memory hit her so suddenly and with such clarity that for a moment she nearly forgot why she was standing there. Looking into Swift's eyes, she felt for a timeless instant as if she were floating, that there was no present, only yesterday, she a child, he a carefree young man.

"Do you think he ever figured out it was us who tugged the ropes?" Swift asked.

Amy blinked. Old Man had been slain in a massacre shortly after that night, murdered by border ruffians. Reality and all its harshness came sweeping back to her. With it came self-awareness. She was no longer a child, and Swift didn't look at her as if she were. They both knew what Old Man's wives had been hoping for when they ran so eagerly to his lodge.

She couldn't drag her gaze from his. To know that he, of all men, had seen her behave with such a total lack of propriety made her feel dangerously vulnerable. And here she stood, attired in nothing but a nightdress and wrapper, in what was fast approaching broad daylight. "I —" She searched desperately for something, anything, to say. "I'm going to be late."

With that, she turned and scurried for the house. The rhythmic sound of the ax continued the entire time she dressed for school.

She grabbed a chunk of bread and an apple for lunch, then left the house, slamming the door with such force the windows shook. Swift upended the ax on the chopping block and propped an arm on the handle's end. His gaze followed her as she swept past him in a blaze of anger. There was only one word to describe that look in his eye, *predatory*. And, God help her, she was his prey.

CHAPTER 5

The first thing Amy clapped eyes on when she stepped inside her classroom was Swift's black poncho hanging on the coatrack. As soon as she'd set down her books, she walked over to dispose of the disgusting thing, but when she reached for the coarse black wool, her arm began to shake. Try though she might, she couldn't force her fingers to clasp the garment.

Slowly the children began to filter in. Aside from the concern for her welfare because she had fainted the prior afternoon, it seemed like any other day, yet not, for she knew Swift lurked somewhere in town and that he might, at any time, appear in the doorway. Just in case, she closed the door but soon reopened it when the children began to look flushed. It was an uncommonly warm morning for October, and the classroom was a misery without some fresh air.

Before Amy called class to order, she heard a distant popping sound. *Gunfire.*

Swift always had been one to practice with his weaponry, so hearing the shots shouldn't have surprised her. Memories assailed her, of Swift teaching her to throw a knife, his strong hands enfolding hers, his chest against her back, his deep voice whispering next to her ear. If only they could go back. If only the years hadn't changed each of them so.

Amy licked her lips and dragged her mind back to the present, to the gunfire. Swift was no longer a gentle boy. He had killed more men than he could count and had joked about the number last night. *Not more than ninety.* One was too many.

Another volley of shots rang out. Distracted by the sound, nerves leaping, Amy relied on ingrained habit and opened the day's lesson with arithmetic, then proceeded to spelling. When the distant sound of gunfire ceased, her senses, alert for the slightest sound, became riveted to the doorway. During recess, she refused the girls' invitations to join them outside for a game of jacks. Instead she sat at her desk, back to the wall, nibbling her apple and trying without success to read.

By the end of the day, Amy's nerves had

frazzled. As relieved as she felt that Swift hadn't visited the school, she still had the remainder of the afternoon and the evening to get through. In no hurry to go home, where he was sure to find her, she sat at her desk to check her notes on the next day's lessons.

When a shadow suddenly fell across the room, she stiffened and glanced up to find Swift standing in the doorway. Because she hadn't heard him approach, she dropped her gaze to his boots. His silver spurs had been removed. As much as she detested the chinking noise the spurs made, a perverse anger swept over her. Why had he taken them off? The better to sneak up on her?

Brown-red dust coated the toes and heels of his boots. She swallowed and trailed her gaze upward. More dust clung to his pants. Dressed all in black, with his hat over his eyes and the gun belt low on his hips, he looked every bit the heartless gunslinger, the kind of man who was lightning quick to anger and deadly on the draw. The kind of man who would rule a woman's every thought, word, and action.

The sleeves of his shirt were rolled back over his corded forearms, as if he'd been working. The collar hung open, the top three buttons unfastened to reveal a V of bronzed chest.

"M-may I help you?"

"Something that belongs to me is here," he replied silkily. "I thought I'd walk over and collect it."

Amy gripped the edge of the book so hard her knuckles ached. "I thought I made myself clear last night and this morning. I'm not yours. Nothing on God's earth could convince me to marry a man who hasn't even the common decency to remove his weapons in a schoolhouse. Hunter may not step in on my behalf, but there is law here in Wolf's Landing. If you bother me again, I'm going directly to the jail to tell Marshal Hilton."

He tipped his head so the sunshine slanted under the brim of his hat, revealing his slow, taunting grin. His hatband of silver conchae flashed into her eyes like a mirror.

With a flick of his fingers, he unbuckled his gun belt and slung it over his shoulder as he stepped inside. "I was talking about my poncho, Amy. I worked all day with Hunter up at the mine, and it gets damned chilly if I go underground. The poncho's the closest thing to a jacket that I've got."

"Oh." She swallowed, feeling ridiculous. How could she have forgotten the poncho? Swift rattled her so badly that she was fortunate to recall her own name when he was around.

So he'd been working at the mine all day, had he? No doubt catching up on old times with Hunter. That was just like a man, making threats and leaving a woman to stew, never giving it another thought, while she thought of nothing else.

He stepped to the coatrack. "I'm sorry if I startled you. It was so late, I figured you'd be gone."

To her dismay, instead of collecting his poncho, he hung his gun belt on a hook and strolled around the classroom, hands clasped behind him. Her attention centered on the knife and scabbard attached to his pants belt. She recognized the hand-carved handle; he still carried the same knife he had years ago. She could almost feel the smooth wood against her palm, still warm from his hand, the thrill of hitting her mark.

He paused before a display of drawings. "Not a bad likeness of a horse. Who drew it?"

"Peter Crenton. His father owns the Lucky Nugget Saloon. He's a little red-headed boy. You may have noticed him."

He nodded. "That carrot red hair was hard to miss."

"His name is in the bottom right corner."

"I can't read, Amy. You know that."

A pang of sadness hit her at the life he had led, but she pushed it away. "What can you do, Swift? Besides ride a horse, steal from the God-fearing, and sling a gun, I mean?"

He nudged his hat back, the movement slow and lazy, then turned to survey her, his mouth still curved in a grin. "I make love real good."

Fiery heat flooded up her neck to her face, pooling in her cheeks. She stared at him, her eyes dry, her eyelids stuck open.

"What can you do?" he countered. "Besides teaching children and scaring off men by spouting rules of etiquette, I mean."

Amy ran the tip of her tongue across her lip.

"Do you make love good, Amy?" he asked softly. "I'll bet you don't know. I reckon there are lots of rules for courting, and I'd wager every piece of gold I own that you know them all by heart. I'll bet any man who's ever come close to you got so sidetracked trying to start off right, he never got past saying, 'How do, Miss Amy.' " He turned to regard her. Because his hat shaded his eyes, she could only guess where his gaze might be lingering. "It's too bad you were so young fifteen years ago. I'd have made love to you, and you wouldn't be in this fix."

"Are you quite finished?"

"I haven't even started yet," he came back with a low chuckle. He strode toward her, his feet touching the floor planks so lightly that she felt as if she were being stalked. "Lucky for you, no rule book about manners is going to muddy my waters." He braced his hands on the far side of her desk, leaning toward her. "It'd be a shame, wouldn't it, if you lived the rest of your days a starched virgin with her nose in the air?"

"I'm no virgin, and you know it."

"Aren't you? I'd say you're about as untouched as a woman can get. You've never made love, Amy. You were used, and there's a hell of a difference."

The blood drained from her face. The Swift she had known never would have taunted her about the comancheros. "Get out," she whispered. "So help me, if you don't leave, I'm going for Marshal Hilton."

He smiled and straightened. "So he can fight your battles for you? What's happened to your backbone? The girl I knew would have spit in my eye. Or socked me. She gave as good as she got, to hell with the consequences. You called *me* a coward? Honey, you haven't got enough guts left in you to make a smear if someone smashed you."

"I'm not the girl you knew. I told you that. Now please leave before you embroil us in a nasty and completely unnecessary confrontation with Marshal Hilton."

Moving toward the coatrack, he began to whistle. The tune came clear after a moment. Scarcely able to believe he still remembered it, she threw a glance at his broad back. After taking his gun belt and poncho off the hooks, he turned and looked at her again. His voice pitched low, he said, "How did that song go? 'Up in the hayloft with a girl named Sue . . .' " His eyes met hers, alight with laughter. "You taught me the words, remember? Did you even know what they meant? You didn't, did you?"

"It — it was a song I'd heard my — my stepfather sing. At that age, it never occurred to me it might be —" She broke off and averted her gaze. "What's the point in all this, Swift? To embarrass and humiliate me? If so, you're doing a good job."

He hesitated at the door, looking back at her over his shoulder. "I'm just reminding you that there was a time when you laughed and sang and ran wild with me on the Texas plains. That chapter in your life isn't closed. The last half hasn't even been written yet. Like I said, I'll give you some time to get used to the idea of marrying me. Make good use of it."

With that, he walked out the door.

For the next several days, Amy expected Swift to sneak up on her at every turn. During school, the slightest sound outside made her whirl, heart slamming. En route home, she jumped every time a bush moved. At night, certain he would come and force a confrontation, she paced, ears pricked for footsteps on her porch. When he didn't, instead of feeling relieved, she grew angry. He had turned her life into a living hell, and now he was off doing whatever it was men did, forgetting all about her.

Was this what he meant about giving her time to get used to the idea of marrying him? This torturous waiting? Not knowing, from moment to moment, when she'd turn and find him there?

She avoided Hunter and Loretta's house as though the occupants were in quarantine, going directly from home to school, then back again, double-bolting her door against the night, only to pace until the wee hours, unable to sleep. She didn't dare bring her tub inside and bathe, for fear he'd choose that moment to shoulder her door open. When she dressed, she did so with the speed of a harried actress changing costume backstage between scenes.

The first afternoon, she saw Swift at a distance when he came into town after working at the mine. A few minutes later, she saw him out riding his black stallion bareback, impressing Chase with his Comanche riding skills. On the second day, she spied him walking with Indigo along the boardwalk. He behaved like a man without a care, his hat low, his gait loose-hipped and lazy. He never spared a glance for the women who passed him on the street, apparently unaware that they made a cautious circle around him. Late the third evening, she saw him and Hunter in the woods at her end of town, throwing axes and knives at a stump. Having fun, damn him!

By the fourth afternoon, necessity drove Amy up the street to the shops along the boardwalk. She was out of bread, low on eggs, and she needed kerosene, flour, sugar, and molasses. She hurried to get her shopping done, hoping to pick up a loaf of bread and eggs from Loretta's before the men came in from work.

Samuel Jones, at the general store, grinned broadly when he saw her. "Well, hello, Miss Amy. How are you this afternoon?"

"Fine, and you?" she asked, moving toward him, her green muslin skirts swirling with each step.

"Now that your smile is brightening the place, I couldn't be finer," he teased. "I just got a shipment of new threads. Care to look them over? Lots of tempting colors."

"I haven't had much time for crocheting of late."

"Haven't seen you out and about much. You been spending all your time visiting with Hunter and Loretta's houseguest? I hear he's been a friend of the family for years."

Amy stiffened. "Yes, he has. However, that isn't what's kept me at home. I've been occupied with lesson planning and such. The beginning of the school year is my busiest time."

She glanced at her shopping list and read off the items she needed. Sam quickly stacked her supplies on the counter, casting her curious glances while he worked. "Is it true he's *the* Swift Lopez, the gunslinger we've been reading about?"

Amy crumpled the list in her palm. "Yes."

Sam gave the sack of flour a pat. His face was pockmarked thanks to Jacksonville's smallpox epidemic of 1869, but the scars enhanced his looks, lending him a rugged appeal.

"People are fidgety about him being here. Even makes me nervous. If it wasn't for Hunter being the founding father of our community, I think there'd be a petition circulating by now to have Mr. Lopez escorted out of town by the marshal."

Family loyalty prompted Amy to say, "You know Hunter would never countenance a troublemaker in our midst. As I understand it, Mr. Lopez has come here to make a new start. I'm sure he has no intention of using his guns again."

"He'd be wise not to. You know what they gave John Wesley Hardin, don't you? Twenty-five years in the Texas State Prison. He'll be an old man by the time he sees freedom." He went to fetch her kerosene. As he sat the container of fuel on the counter, he shook his head. "Hard to believe we may see the day when lanterns will be outdated."

Amy forced a smile. It never ceased to amaze her how many topics of conversation Sam could dream up to keep her in his store. He was a nice man and more than passably handsome, but Amy wasn't interested.

"Lanterns, outdated? How so?"

"The electric light." Leaning forward at the waist, Samuel folded his muscular arms

132

on the counter and flashed her a grin. His blondish brown hair gleamed as he bent his head. "They say Edison is inches away from developing a bulb that'll burn for prolonged periods of time. Don't you keep abreast of the news?"

"I haven't much time for reading the newspapers. As I said, my students keep me fairly busy."

His blue eyes warmed on hers. "You should make time. The way things are changing, you ladies need to be on top of things. Why, just this February, President Hayes signed a bill allowing female lawyers to argue cases before the Supreme Court."

"It's high time, if you ask me." Amy put the kerosene on top of her packages, gathered the lot into her arms, and turned to go. "Just put this on my account, would you, Mr. Jones?"

"Sam," he corrected. "As long as we've known each other, Miss Amy, I'd think you'd call me by my first name."

"That would be unseemly, Mr. Jones. I am the schoolteacher."

"The committee won't terminate you for calling me Sam."

Still smiling, Amy wove her way between the floor displays toward the doorway. As she left the general store, she saw Swift standing outside, his back to her, a shoulder braced against the building. Amy froze. A woman stood on the other side of him.

Leaning out to see around him, Amy identified Elmira Johnson, one of the unmarried girls in town. She stood with her head back, batting her eyelashes and giggling. The silly twit. Naturally a mysterious man like Swift Lopez would fascinate her. At eighteen Elmira was foolhardy and naive enough to be tantalized by danger. If her father, a burly miner, caught her flirting with trouble, he'd have her hide.

Amy gathered her packages close and stepped off the boardwalk, hoping to cross the street and reach Loretta's while Swift was preoccupied. Unfortunately he didn't seem too interested in what Elmira was saying and glanced around when Amy moved away from the building. Amy increased her pace. From the corner of her eye, she saw him straighten. She felt clumsy and awkward. Trying to walk gracefully while loaded down with packages was no easy feat.

"Amy! Wait!"

His deep voice had the same effect as a leash around her neck. He strode into the street and, without another word, took the packages from her.

"I've been doing for myself for five years,

Swift — ever since I moved into my own place."

Somehow he managed the load with one arm so he could take her elbow. The grip of his fingers burned through the sleeve of her dress. "You don't have to do for yourself anymore," he replied, steering her up the street toward Loretta's. "I'm glad you finally came out of hiding, by the way. I was starting to worry, and so was the rest of the family."

"The children see me every day, and I wasn't hiding."

"Keeping to yourself, then."

"I always keep to myself."

"Not according to Loretta. She says you usually come by every day after school. I don't bite, Amy." His eyes twinkling with mischief, he slid his gaze to her neck. "Not hard, anyway."

She jerked her arm from his grasp and hurried ahead, taking the steps of Loretta's porch at such a speed that she nearly tripped on her skirts. Swift followed her inside, set her packages on the table, and lowered himself onto a straight-backed chair. Stretching out his long legs, he crossed his boots at the ankle and clasped his hands behind his neck, his mouth sporting a half grin.

"Amy!" Loretta cried with delight. Abandoning the dumplings she was making, she came across the room, flour-covered hands held out to her sides, cheek turned for a kiss. "I've missed you so. Why haven't you been coming by to see me after school?"

Amy felt Swift's amused gaze on her. While giving Loretta a hug, she said, "I've just been busy."

"I've extra bread made up for you. And I'll wager you're low on eggs."

"Yes, as a matter of fact, I am." Amy fetched the egg basket off the drain. "I'll go gather my own. Don't fuss, Loretta. Finish the dumplings. I can get everything myself."

Loretta gave her a concerned look. "Can't you take a moment for coffee? It seems like forever since we chatted."

Amy couldn't see herself chatting with Loretta while Swift looked on. She toyed with the rust-colored grosgrain ribbon on her bodice. "I, um, actually, Loretta Jane, I've a busy evening planned." She searched wildly for an excuse and seized upon the one she had just given Samuel Jones. "Lessons, you know."

"I thought you had those done already, from prior years."

Amy licked her lips. "Yes, well, I still have to go over them."

Loretta didn't look as if she believed that. With Swift sitting there, it would be unforgivably rude to admit the real reason for her prolonged absence. Perhaps Loretta would figure it out on her own, if she hadn't already.

"Well." Amy turned toward the back door. "I'm off to rob the hens. Be right back."

After leaving the house, she tucked the ends of her shawl under her sash. When she reached the henhouse, she gathered her green muslin skirts into a loose knot just below the knees to prevent her hem from trailing in the filth. Collecting some eggs took only a few minutes. When she emerged from the pen, she wiped her shoes clean on a clump of grass. As she straightened, she spied a pair of black boots a few feet away.

"Swift! You startled me."

He stood with his back against a nearby madrona. "It doesn't take much to startle you. Sometimes I think breathing wrong might do it."

His gaze fell to her exposed petticoat and he stepped forward, extending a hand for the egg basket. Flustered and horribly embarrassed because she had forgotten she had her skirts hiked up, she relinquished her hold on the basket handle and bent to untie the knot in her skirts.

"How long is this going to continue, Amy?" he asked softly.

She glanced up. "How long is what going to continue?"

"You holing up over there and peering out your window at me. I meant to give you some time to circle me, but you're cutting a mighty wide berth. If I hadn't knocked off work early today, you'd have come and gone without seeing me."

"There's always Elmira."

"Jealous?"

She gave a little snort of derision.

When she headed for the house, he stood his ground. "You're forgetting the eggs."

She turned back, clenching her teeth and avoiding his gaze as she extended her hand. He didn't offer to relinquish the basket. Left with no choice, she finally looked up at him. The creases that bracketed his mouth deepened, his lips pursing slightly as he regarded her.

"It's up to you how we go about this."

"Go about what?"

He ignored the question. "The hard way or the easy way, it's up to you. If you go on hiding out over there, I'll take matters in hand. And you may not like my methods."

It took all her strength of will to keep her voice steady. "Don't threaten me, Swift."

He handed her the basket. "I'm not threatening. I'm promising. You can't run from this, Amy. You can't pretend I don't exist. I won't let you."

"What, exactly, are you saying?"

"I wanted to give you a chance to get to know me again — here, with your family around. You haven't made any attempt."

"Because I don't want to know you again."

A glint crept into his eyes. He took a deep breath, exhaling with exaggerated slowness. "Fair warning. Make hay while the sun's shining. If you don't, the first thing you know, I'll cloud up and rain all over you."

Amy's legs felt suddenly weak. She licked her lips, glancing off into the trees.

"I'm going to be bagging gold dust this afternoon, getting it ready for Hunter to take to Jacksonville." His voice turned low and husky. "Why don't you help me? Chase and Indigo will be there. We'll get a big fire going, and Loretta says she'll make hot chocolate. You can stay for supper. It'll be fun. Who knows, you might find out I'm not so terrifying after all."

All Amy wanted to do was run. "I'm busy tonight."

He sighed. "Fine. Have it your way."

She tightened her grip on the wire handle of the basket. He stood there a moment, studying her, then inclined his head at the house. She spun on her heel and hurried ahead of him. When she burst inside, she grabbed some towels off a shelf to wrap her eggs and bread, acutely conscious of Swift's entrance behind her.

"Did you get plenty?" Loretta asked.

"Enough for a few days." Amy gathered her packages together, placing her eggs and bread on top.

"I could help you carry that," Swift inserted.

"Thank you for offering, but I can manage fine."

Their gazes locked. With a forefinger he touched the brim of his hat, inching it back so he could capture her gaze with his. His eyes had a mischievous glint in them that made her spine tingle. "Don't be such a stranger from now on."

Amy's throat tightened. Though he had said it teasingly, they both knew he meant it as a warning.

"Thank you for the bread and eggs, Loretta."

Loretta rolled her eyes. "It's part of your teaching contract. If you need more, there's always plenty. I'll have Hunter bring you a fryer. How's your ham and bacon holding up?"

"Fine."

Amy said her good-byes. Because her arms were full, Swift opened the front door for her, then followed her onto the porch. As she descended the steps, he called, "If you don't show up here tomorrow, it'll be a hard row to hoe from here on out."

Amy glanced back. Four levels above her, he seemed to loom, broad of shoulder, lean of hip, long legs stretching forever. His gaze held hers for an instant, relentless and piercing.

"It's your choice," he added. "One more day, Amy. Then we do things my way."

She struck off up the street. Damn him. She felt as if he had a noose around her throat and was slowly tightening it.

Furious that he had that kind of power over her, Amy rebelled by dragging her bathtub into the kitchen the moment she got home. She wouldn't let him rule her every waking moment. After hauling in water and setting it on the stove to heat, she made certain all the windows were securely fastened and barricaded the front door with sitting room furniture. Only then could she find the courage to undress. It was the most miserable bath she had ever taken in her life.

■ ■ ■ ■

The following afternoon, Amy went by the dry goods store to select some cloth for a dress. After haggling with Mr. Hamstead on the price, she purchased the yardage in a delightfully lightweight blue serge and splurged on a quarter yard of ecru lace to accent the collar, bodice, and cuffs. She had a gorgeous cut-to-size pattern that she had found in *Harper's Bazaar,* with a fitted bodice, gently flared skirt, and a three-ruffle pouf in back. While admiring a sewing machine in one of Mr. Hamstead's catalogs, she gave him a wistful smile.

"Still saving?" he asked with a chuckle. He bound her packages with twine and gave them a pat. "They get more expensive in every issue, you know."

Amy gnawed her lip, tempted to order one straight away. If she did, though, her savings would be sorely depleted, and she felt more secure with some money set aside. "Never fear, I'll be in to order one soon. Why, if I had a machine, I could have this dress on its way to being finished after a couple of evenings' work. I could sew for Loretta and Indigo. Make shirts for Hunter and Chase." She snapped her fingers. "And be done just like that."

His blue eyes twinkled. "The wife sure loves hers. And Tess Bronson ordered one last week."

"She didn't!" Amy leaned back over the catalog, filled with yearning. "As hard as she works in the restaurant, she deserves it."

"Being a teacher isn't exactly light duty," he reminded her.

"It doesn't make one wealthy, either," she came back. "On a single income, I have to watch my pennies."

"Make Sam Jones a happy man, and he'll buy you a sewing machine for every room."

"He's a very nice man, but I'm not in the market for a husband. I'll just save up, thank you."

"Anytime you're ready to order, I'll still give you the discount I promised."

Amy winked at him. "As if I'd let you worm your way out."

Happily contemplating the day when she could place an order for a sewing machine, Amy gathered her packages, bade Mr. Hamstead good-bye, and headed for the door, promising herself that tonight she would stay busy and never spare a thought for Swift Lopez.

After leaving the shop, she gathered her

courage and went to Loretta's for a visit, as had always been her habit each day after school. As she had hoped, Swift and Hunter hadn't come home from the mines yet. She nearly grinned with delight. Swift couldn't very well cloud up and do much raining, at least not for another day. She had shown up. He couldn't argue with that.

"Is Swift going to work for Hunter?" Amy asked shortly after her arrival. She dreaded the answer but felt a need to know.

"I think so," Loretta replied, stooped low over the oven to check her bread. "Lord knows there's enough gold in that mountain to share, and Hunter could use a partner to carry part of the load. Who knows, maybe having Swift here will free him up so he can enjoy life a little more. Those other men who work for him can't wipe their own noses without him telling them how."

Amy knew Hunter worked too hard and that she should be pleased there might be an end to that in sight, but she couldn't rejoice when salvation came in the form of Swift Lopez.

Loretta, cheeks flushed from bending over the oven, closed the stove door and swiped at a stray tendril of golden hair, her blue eyes shadowed with anxiety.

"What's wrong?" Amy set her packages

on the table.

Loretta threw up her hands. "Oh, Amy, I'm worried sick about Indigo."

"Why?" Amy stepped across the room. Loretta wasn't one to stew over nothing. "She hasn't come home yet, or what? She left school at the regular time."

"No, she came home." Loretta's mouth twisted. "Then immediately left again. I swear, Hunter's too lenient. The Comanche way of child rearing isn't enough in our society. He forgets that our people, men in particular, don't always do the noble thing with a pretty, starry-eyed girl Indigo's age."

"This sounds serious."

"It is serious. She's carrying a torch for that Marshall fellow, the one from Jacksonville who's so high-falutin that his name has a number stuck on the end."

Amy couldn't hide a smile. "Perfectly ordinary people can be the third person in their family to bear the same name, Loretta." She gave her cousin a comforting pat. "However, I agree. Mr. Marshall seems to have far too high an opinion of himself. I've seen how he acts when he comes to town. He never misses an opportunity to let us know he's from Boston."

"Wherever *that* is. He walks like old Mrs. Hamstead just dosed him with sheep dung tea," Loretta said with a sniff.

Amy wrinkled her nose. "Sheep dung tea?"

"Her latest remedy. Runs a body to death making trips to the necessary. It's supposed to get the impurities out of you."

Momentarily forgetting her worries about Swift, Amy giggled. "I reckon if it has that effect, then maybe she's right and it does. Now what's this about Indigo and Mr. Marshall?"

"She thinks the sun rises and sets in him, that's what. Mark my words, that young man'll do her wrong if he gets half a chance. I've seen that look in his eye. As far as he's concerned, the rules don't apply with a girl like her."

"Because she's part Indian?" Amy's scalp prickled. She had seen enough prejudice in this region against the few remaining rogue Indians and the Chinese to understand Loretta's concerns without her voicing them. "Have you told Hunter?"

"Yes, and he's confident Indigo will send the man packing if he tries to touch her." Loretta shrugged. "Hunter's right. I'm sure she will. It's her heart I'm worrying over, not her chastity. I've tried to talk to her, but she turns a deaf ear. She doesn't understand how cruel some people can be to those of mixed blood. Hunter's never allowed me to talk about it, for fear his children will feel ashamed of their heritage. I don't want to make her feel inferior, God knows. But I don't want her hurt, either."

Amy gnawed her lip. "Would you like me to talk to her?"

"Oh, would you, Amy? She listens to you. For some reason she discounts half of what I say."

"What can her mother possibly know about falling in love?"

"Enough to turn my hair gray. Was I ever that stubborn?"

"You weren't raised by Hunter. And our lives were — harder." Amy picked up her packages. "I'll take a turn through town and see if I can find her. If not, don't let on I've looked for her. I'll just wait and get her off alone tomorrow after school. If she realizes you talked to me, she'll get her back up."

"There, you see? That's what I try to tell Hunter. About her getting her back up. A girl her age should kowtow. She needs a firm hand, and he refuses to discipline her."

"That isn't his way. Indigo will be all right, Loretta." Amy clutched her packages more tightly. "Better for her to have a father like Hunter than one like Henry Masters was to you and me. At least Indigo's not afraid to speak her mind."

"Amen." Loretta's eyes darkened with distaste as she recalled their childhood on Henry Masters's farm in Texas. "God forbid that any child should have a father like Henry." She shivered slightly, then seemed to shake off the memories. "At least Hunter has taught Indigo to stand up for herself. God pity the man who marries her, though. She'll be okay on the love and honor part, but obey isn't in her vocabulary."

She laughed. "I guess I shouldn't speak ill of Henry. He did take care of you for three years after Aunt Rachel passed on. I'll be forever grateful to him for that. Many a man would have sent a stepdaughter packing and let her fend for herself."

Not quite able to meet Loretta's gaze, Amy pretended to be preoccupied with straightening her shawl. "Well, I'll get on my way. No telling where Indigo may be off to." She paused before opening the door. "Um, Loretta, give my best to Swift, won't you? Tell him I'm sorry to have missed him?"

Loretta's blue eyes sharpened with suspicion. "Sorry to have missed him? Does this mean you've had a change of heart?"

Amy nibbled her lip. "It's more like a change in tactics. Just tell him, please?"

Clearly perplexed, Loretta nodded. "All

right."

Amy walked the length of town twice and then circled behind the buildings into the woods, hoping to find Indigo sitting beneath a tree daydreaming, as the girl often did, but she was nowhere to be found. Before Amy knew it, the sun had dipped behind a hill. Assuming that Indigo had gone home, she decided to do likewise before she found herself in the woods without light to see by. Darkness fell swiftly in the mountains, and she knew her own shortcomings.

Arms aching from carrying her packages, she hurried toward her house. As she approached, she gave the yard a quick once-over, frustrated by the black shadows. After hurrying up the steps, she shoved open the door, stepped inside, and shifted her packages so she had a free hand to manage the bolts.

"Feel safe now?" a silken voice asked the moment she had shoved the locks home.

CHAPTER 6

Amy's heart leaped, and she whirled, dropping all her packages. *Swift.* Dear God, he had come in her house. She peered through the darkness. Faint traces of leather and tobacco smoke teased her nostrils. Pressing a hand to her throat, she croaked, "Wh-where are you, Swift?"

"Right here."

The whisper by her ear made Amy squeak with startled annoyance. "Hell and damnation! Are you trying to make my heart fail?" She turned, straining to see. "Why are you in my house?"

"Our house. We're betrothed. What's yours is mine," he reminded her, his voice coming from a slightly different direction this time. "*You* are mine, as far as that goes."

She made a sound of protest but couldn't articulate her thoughts.

"Amy, love, you've forgotten everything I taught you. As blind as you are when the sun goes down, you should be more careful. It's foolish to come in and bolt the door before you're sure you're alone. You didn't even listen first. Someone could be hiding in here some night, waiting for you to lock up. You'd never undo the bolts quick enough to get away from him."

The veiled threat wasn't lost on her. "I'm within hollering distance of Hunter and Loretta's."

"*If* you could holler. When a man's up to no good, the first thing he does is clamp a hand over a woman's mouth."

Amy homed in on his voice and turned. "Until you came, I never had to worry about being accosted in my sitting room."

"And that's your problem, isn't it, Amy? You live in a safe little world, in a safe little town, in a safe little house, and life's the same, day in and day out." A strong arm caught her around the waist and drew her against a hard, lean body. Amy's breath gushed from her lungs. "Now I'm here, and you can't be sure from one minute to the next what might happen."

"I went to Loretta's to visit today," she cried.

"While I wasn't there. Sorry, Amy. I gave you your chance. Now we'll try it my way."

With that, his lips claimed hers. For a

crazy moment the kiss so bedazzled her that she couldn't think, let alone feel afraid. She clutched his shoulders to arch away. Velvet over steel. That's how his arms felt around her. She fought to keep her lips closed and lost the battle. He slanted his mouth and drove his tongue deep. Too late, she realized her teeth were parted.

She tried to say his name, to wrench away, but his hold gave her no quarter. And his mouth. He bent her head back and kissed her until her senses spun. When he drew back for breath, she hung limp against him, legs atremble, her breath coming in ragged little spurts against the curve of his neck.

Then fright coursed through her. The door. Both bolts were driven home. She was locked in here with him and hanging in his arms like a mindless lump, a sure invitation for him to kiss her again. And possibly more. More . . .

Moving her hands to his chest, she gave a shove, surprised when he fell back. She knew he had more than enough strength to hold her — if he chose. She staggered away from him. At least, she hoped it was away. She still couldn't see him.

"Please, Swift, I w-want you to leave." From out of the darkness his knuckles feathered along her cheek, startling her so that she leaped. His touch was light, so incredibly light that her breath caught. "Please, Swift."

Her voice shook. His hand withdrew. She swallowed and closed her eyes, expecting him to reach through the blackness and grab her again. Instead she heard him draw the bolts. The door swung open, throwing his tall frame into silhouette against the backdrop of moonlight that bathed her porch.

"No more hedging, Amy. I'll be back." His voice slid over her like chill air, though in reality it held no menace, just a warm, vibrant promise. "Again and again. Until you forget to pull away, until you forget to be afraid, until you forget everything but the fact that you love me."

Moving as if he had no more substance than a shadow, he stepped out and closed the door, plunging her back into darkness. Amy stumbled forward over her packages and groped for the bolts. When she had driven them home, she pressed her forehead to the wood, weak with relief, her pulse erratic and racing.

Through the cracks between the planks, his voice drifted to her. "Feel safe now?" She thought she heard him chuckle. Fury brought her head up. "A locked door won't stop me, Amy. You know damned well it won't. So why bother?"

Amy listened. Had he left? Temples resounding with her own heartbeat, she turned, ears pricked for any noise at the windows, knowing even as she did that Swift could enter a house as stealthily as a cat.

The seconds dragged by, mounting into minutes. Amy pressed her back against the door. Damn him! This was her home. It meant everything to her. He had no right to come in here.

Shaking and disoriented, she groped her way to the table, lit the lantern, and crept to the bedroom. The coverlet on her bed was mussed, as if he had lain there, which to Amy was the ultimate invasion of privacy. A saucer from her kitchen sat on the nightstand, a snuffed cigarette in its well.

She turned a slow circle. The things on top of her bureau had been moved, her brush, her mirror, her perfume. Her attention shifted to the underwear she had washed last night and draped on the bedstead to dry. She thought she remembered hanging the pantalets with the waist toward the bed, the ankles toward the room. Now they hung the opposite way. Rage filled her, a tremulous, blinding, impotent rage.

Setting the lantern on her nightstand, she

sank onto the bed to stare at the floor. She imagined his hands touching her underthings. What could she expect from a man who could kill in the blink of an eye, who had ridden with comancheros? Men like Swift made their own rules, as the mood struck.

Amy hugged herself and tried to stop shivering. She knew Swift too well. He had declared war. How long would he remain satisfied with taunting her? Not long, if she guessed right. If nothing else worked, he would bend her to his will, one way or another. The thought terrified her as nothing else could. To be his wife, his property, forced to submit to him, to spend her life scurrying about, trying to please him so he wouldn't get in a temper, to have no lawful recourse . . .

The tree limb outside her window scraped against the glass, making her start. Trembling, she cupped a hand over her eyes. How much longer could she bear this constant tension? What in God's name should she do? Swift had been raised by the Comanche. All his life he had seen men possessing reluctant women, Hunter included. Spiriting her away in the dead of night would be a game to him. And after? Memories of the comancheros slid through her mind. Those, and other memories. . . .

Not again. Please, God, not again.

Beads of sweat rose on Amy's face. A year ago she never would have believed Swift capable of hurting her, but he wasn't the same person she had known. Life had hardened him, turned him bitter and harsh. She feared him now, with bone-deep foreboding, and detested him for making her feel so horribly helpless.

Gray morning light slanted through Amy's window. She yawned and snuggled deeper into the down mattress, enjoying the drowsy contentment of awakening slowly to the smell of pork slab and coffee. Loretta was already up and fixing breakfast.

Opening her eyes, Amy stared at her window, registering reality in measures. The white lace curtains, the floral paper, the post of her bedstead. She stiffened. This was *her* house.

Coming wide awake, Amy shot from the bed, grabbed her wrapper, and crept to the doorway. Silence. She ventured through the sitting area to the rear of the house, noiselessly touching her bare feet to the floor, wincing when the boards creaked. Leaning around the door frame, she peered into the tiny kitchen. Feeble light from the small, high window cast the room into shadow.

"Who's here?" she called. "Indigo, is that you?"

No one. Frowning, Amy stepped across the threshold, her gaze settling on the table. Three red roses stood in one of her vases. From Loretta's flower bed? The bushes behind the Wolf house still had a few bedraggled blooms. Skin prickling, she turned and saw that her cast-iron skillet sat on the stove, brimming with fried potatoes, strips of pork slab, and eggs. She touched her palm to the coffeepot. Boiling hot.

Amy crept back to the sitting room and stared at the door. The bolts were still driven home. "Hello?" Her throat tightened. "Swift, it has to be you." No answer.

Hurrying through the small house, Amy checked every hiding place, ending the search in her bedroom. Perplexed, she dug her toes into the rag rug and planted her hands on her hips. How had he gotten in, fixed a meal, and left with the door still locked?

A splash of red on her pillow caught her attention. A rose lay across her pillowcase. She inched forward, staring at it. She hadn't noticed it earlier when she got out of bed.

Swift. He had come in, somehow, and then left. Despite the pure perfection of the rose, Amy was certain it hadn't been left as a romantic gesture. He meant it to carry a message. *Lock your door and windows. That won't stop me. Nothing will. I stood over you while you slept, and you never knew I was here.*

She clamped a hand over her diaphragm, struggling to breathe. She had to do something to make him back off, and she had to do it soon.

Swift swung the ax, driving the blade through the log until it hit home on the block. Sweat trickled down his temples, yet he continued to work, so frustrated he had begun to doubt whether Hunter's supply of unsplit logs would last through his temper.

The little coward! She had gone off to school as if nothing had happened, never even glancing toward Hunter's house. How far did he have to push her before she struck back? Swift clenched his teeth, swinging the ax again with a grunt of disgust. He had expected more from her. Some sort of confrontation, at the very least. Even if she quivered and shook while she faced him.

Arms aching, lungs spent, Swift upended the ax and leaned on it, gazing toward the schoolhouse. *What's happened to you, Amy?* She had hidden in her house for four days!

It was as if something vital inside her had been snuffed out. He could understand her being intimidated by him, but not to this degree. Where was her fierce pride? And the glorious temper she had once had? Now her answer to everything was to turn pale and shake.

A sad smile twisted his mouth. *Admit it, Lopez. Deep down, you were hoping she might like the roses, that instead of a confrontation she might even say "thank you" and call a truce.*

"Mr. Lopez?"

Swift whirled at the voice, unsettled because he had let someone sneak up on him. He'd be a dead man if he let that happen too often. He focused on the tall, hefty man who walked toward him, skirting Loretta's chickens, which pecked the ground looking for seed. Sunlight glinted off the badge on the man's shirt. Swift cursed under his breath.

"You must be Marshal Hilton."

The lawman nodded and drew to a stop a few feet short of Swift, glancing uneasily at his guns. "I'm sorry to introduce myself this way. But there's been a complaint lodged."

Swift swiped at the sweat on his jaw, glancing toward the school. "I figured that when I saw your badge. She threatened to go see you. I didn't think she meant it."

"You thought wrong." Marshal Hilton frowned. "I understand you entered Miss Amy's house last night without her permission . . . twice. Do you deny that?"

Swift tightened his grip on the ax handle. "No."

"Seems to me a man could find better things to do than torment a helpless woman."

Breakfast and roses were considered a torment? Swift shifted his weight. "Helpless? You don't know Amy very well, Marshal. She's hell in a tailspin when she gets riled."

The marshal scratched his chin. "I'm going to have to insist that you leave her be. Do I have your word on that?"

Swift straightened his shoulders. "No, sir, you don't."

The marshal slid another anxious glance at Swift's guns. "I either get your word, or I lock you up. I know she's a pretty little thing, but there are appropriate ways to court a lady. Entering her house isn't one of them." Pursing his lips, the man met Swift's gaze. "I know your reputation." His voice shook a little as he spoke. "I reckon you can kill me where I stand, 'cause I'm no fast draw. But I have to uphold the law. You can't pester a helpless woman in my town and get away with it."

Swift respected that. "I've never shot a man yet who didn't draw on me first," he replied through clenched teeth.

The marshal relaxed somewhat. "I'm no fool."

Furious, Swift buried the ax blade into the chopping block and reached for his shirt. "When Miss Amy lodged her complaint, did she happen to mention that she and I are betrothed?"

The marshal's eyes registered his surprise. "Betrothed?"

Swift sauntered toward him, shoving his arms down the sleeves of his shirt and fastening the buttons. "Have been for fifteen years. According to Comanche law, she's my woman."

"I don't recall her mentioning that. Of course, Comanche law isn't my concern, so it wouldn't make much difference. White law forbids a man to terrorize a woman."

"Terrorize? I fixed her breakfast and left her red roses!"

Looking confused, the marshal digested that bit of information and sighed. "There's no figurin' women sometimes."

Swift drew abreast of him. Pretending an indifference he was far from feeling, he said, "You can lock me up, I guess. But for how long? A day, maybe two?"

"I reckon a day will cool your heels a bit. But it'd be a sight easier if you'd just agree to leave her alone."

"I can't do that." Just the thought of being locked up made Swift's belly lurch. "As for cooling my heels, you reckon wrong. The minute I get out, I'm going right to her house and shake her until her teeth rattle. She's carried things too far by bringing you into this. Over roses! I can't believe it."

The marshal cleared his throat. "Mr. Lopez, don't threaten her in front of me. I'll lock you up and throw away the key."

Swift struck off toward the jail, stabbing his fingers under his belt to tuck in his shirttails. "I'm not threatening, I'm promising." He swung around, arching an imperious eyebrow at the lawman. "Well, are you coming or not?"

Amy had never seen Hunter so angry. She scurried along beside him, trying to reason with him. "I can't just leave my classroom. It won't hurt Swift to wait until school is out."

"He's waiting in a cell," Hunter retorted. "You know how the People feel about bars, Amy! Indigo and Chase can handle the schoolchildren until you return."

162

Amy nearly tripped on her petticoats. "I never meant for him to get tossed in jail, Hunter. You have to believe that."

"You went to the marshal."

"Yes, but only to ask that he intervene. I figured once he talked to Swift that Swift would leave me be." Amy lifted her gray-striped satin skirts to step up onto the boardwalk. "Dumb gunslinging comanchero, anyway," she muttered under her breath. "Why wouldn't he just promise to stay clear of my place? The marshal never would've done this if Swift would be reasonable."

"Reasonable?" Hunter shot her a glare. "It's his house, too. The marshal doesn't understand that, but you do."

"According to your beliefs," she reminded him.

Hunter came to a stop. His mouth white with rage, he pinioned her with glittering eyes. "Until now, you have honored my ways. When the day comes that you no longer do, then you are no longer part of our family. You understand?"

Amy couldn't believe she had heard him correctly. "Hunter," she whispered, "you don't mean that."

"I say what I mean," he replied. "Swift is my friend. He's living in my house. Because of you, he is in jail."

"What else could I do? I'm no match against him, and you know it. You've turned a blind eye and refuse to protect me."

Hunter's jaw tightened. "Has he harmed you? Has he even so much as grabbed your arm and tightened his fingers until his grip caused you pain?" He paused, waiting. "Answer me. Yes or no?"

Tears burned behind Amy's eyelids. Her mouth dry, she managed a weak, "No."

"Louder!"

"No!"

Hunter nodded. "And he is in jail. Settle your differences between you. Never bring Marshal Hilton into it. Understand?"

With that, he struck off up the boardwalk, his destination the jail. Amy followed, feeling more alone than she ever had. Hunter threw open the jailhouse door with such force it cracked into the wall. He stepped inside and boomed, "Marshal Hilton!"

Stepping across the threshold, Amy peered through the gloom. At the rear of the small jail, she saw the marshal standing by the only cell, his shoulder pressed to the bars. Hunter didn't speak, which led her to believe he was waiting for her to. Amy glanced past him at the dark man who reclined on the cot inside the cell. Every line of his body radiated how trapped he felt.

Licking her lips, she said, "Marshal, it seems you misunderstood my intentions when I came to see you this morning. I, um, never meant for Mr. Lopez to be incarcerated. I only wanted you to discourage him from pestering me."

"He didn't discourage too good," the marshal replied in an amused voice. "Fact is, he still hasn't agreed to stay clear of you. To the contrary, he's threatening worse."

Amy's nape prickled. She glanced at Hunter to find him glaring at her expectantly. Her throat froze up. Eyes drawn to Swift, she clasped her hands. Swift's eyes glittered at her, promising reprisal she couldn't even contemplate.

"Amy . . ." Hunter's voice came out in a low growl.

"I, um . . ." Amy looked into Swift's eyes. There was no mistaking the message in them. Her legs quivered. "The way I see it, Mr. Lopez has no one but himself to blame. If h-he would just . . ." She hesitated, aware of Hunter beside her. "If he'd just promise to leave me alone, we could let him loose."

"Ai-ee!" Hunter exclaimed under his breath.

Amy waited, imploring Swift with her

gaze. His answer was to settle his head more comfortably on his arms and close his eyes, as if he were prepared to stay there until hell froze over.

"I guess that —" Amy broke off, her mind racing frantically ahead to the inevitable moment when she would have to face him — alone. Yet she had no choice. Hunter had made his position clear, and he and Loretta were her only family. Taking a deep breath, she tried again. "I g-guess you'd better just turn him loose, Marshal Hilton." She turned an accusing glance on Hunter, then spun and left the jail.

Swift opened his eyes and watched her leave, his jaw set. Keys jangled. The next instant the door swung open. Making an effort not to reveal how anxious he was to escape the enclosure, he rose, lifted his hat from the hook, and stepped out of the cell. The marshal handed over his knife and guns.

Strapping on his gun belt, Swift said, "Nice meeting you, Hilton. Hope I don't see you again any time soon."

With that, Swift clamped his hat on his head and followed Amy out the door, Hunter behind him.

CHAPTER 7

Nerves frazzled beyond repair, Amy dismissed school early and went home, bolting the door and making certain the windows were locked the moment she went inside. Swift would come; it was only a matter of time. She paced the floor, her body clammy with nervous sweat. He'd be angry — probably so angry he'd be livid. There was no telling what he might do.

Time passed. Amy kept glancing at the clock, but from one time to the next she couldn't recall where the hands had been a moment before and was therefore unable to guess how many minutes elapsed. Hunter had turned against her. She couldn't believe it. Hunter and Loretta were her only family, the only support she had. Swift's arrival had threatened that. She hated him.

A soft knock on the door made Amy leap. She whirled, staring at the bolts. "Wh-who is it?"

"One guess," a deep voice replied.

She pressed her palms against her middle, feeling as if she might vomit. "G-go away, Swift."

"I'm not going anywhere, Amy. Open the door so we can talk. That's all. Just talk."

His smooth, deceptively calm tone didn't fool her. "You're angry. I won't talk to you when you're angry."

"I'm going to stay angry until we talk," he called back, his voice a little louder. "Unbolt the goddamn door!"

She retreated a step, glancing around her wildly. "No. You go away and calm down. Then we'll talk."

She heard him curse. After a long silence he yelled, "I'm not going to calm down. Not until we talk. You had me locked up. Do you know how bad I hate that? I can see you doing a lot of things, but going to the marshal, Amy?"

"It was your own fault. Why couldn't you be reasonable!"

"Reasonable? You call going to the marshal reasonable?"

"I — I didn't mean to get you put in jail," she called, her voice quavery. "I truly didn't, Swift."

"Open the door and tell me that," he replied not quite so loudly.

She stood frozen.

"Amy . . ." She heard him heave a sigh. "Listen real close, okay? I'm not going to hurt you. I just want to talk."

"You're furious. I know it," she squeaked.

"Yeah, I'm that all right."

"And you expect me to open the door?"

"Let's put it this way. If you don't, I'm going to kick it down. And when I get in there, I'll be a shade madder than I am right now. It's what you call a bad hand, Amy, no matter how you call it. So throw it in now."

She closed her eyes, trying to stop shaking. "D-do you promise not to touch me?"

"I promise not to hurt you. Isn't that good enough?"

She wrung her hands. "I want you to promise not to touch me."

"I'll go to hell in a handbasket first."

"I knew it. How stupid do you think I am?"

"Bright isn't exactly your middle name. Come on, Amy. If I kick in this door, I'll be all day tomorrow fixin' the damn thing. What's the point in that?"

Amy retreated another step, listening. She heard his boots thudding and knew he was deliberately making the noise so she'd know he was backing up to get at a good kicking distance.

"W-wait! I, um . . ." She clamped a hand over the coil of braid atop her head. She had to get out of there. Where could she go? Hunter wouldn't help her. She'd have to hide. In the barn, maybe, or perhaps the woods. In the mood Swift was in now, there was no telling what he might do. "I'm not dressed!"

"Why are you undressed at this time of evening?"

"I, um . . ." She backed up another step. "A bath, I was taking a bath."

"Amy, if you're lying, I'll skin you alive."

"No. No, I'm not. Give me two minutes. Just two, and I'll open the door. Please?"

"All right. Two minutes, but not a second more."

Whirling, Amy ran toward the kitchen. Approaching the window, she rose up on her toes to unfasten its latch and swing it wide. Staring upward, she wondered if the hole was large enough. Not that she had much choice. All the other windows faced the front of the house. Heart in throat, trying her best to be silent, she dragged a kitchen chair over to the opening and climbed up on it.

With her full skirts to hinder her, she nearly lost her balance trying to get one leg high enough to push it over the sill. Getting a grip on the frame, she hauled herself upward. Finally she sat astraddle the sill. She curled into a ball and tucked her head, trying to fit her shoulders through the tiny opening. Wincing, she drew up her other knee. After straining and twisting, she managed to get her bent leg wedged. Now, all she need do was get turned around enough so she could jump.

"Just one more minute, Swift."

"You'd better count on five," a voice said from outside in the yard behind her. "I think you're stuck."

Amy started and nearly fell through the window backward. A large hand, planted firmly on her left buttock, righted her again. "Swift?" she squeaked, straining her neck to see over her arm, which was looped around her knee.

"Who the hell do you think?"

"Oh, God . . ."

Hands grasped her waist to pull her on through the window. Pain shot from her knee to her hip and across her shoulders. If she hadn't been wedged into the opening before, she was now. She cried out.

"Goddamn, you *are* stuck," he said from below her. "Amy, why in hell did you choose this window? It isn't big enough to spit through."

"It was the only one you couldn't see."

"I didn't need to see. With all the racket, I knew what you were doing. And now look at the fix you're in. It's a wonder you didn't fall out and break your fool neck." He tugged on her again. "Well, if this isn't a hell of a mess, I don't know what is. Can you stick that leg back inside?"

With her head bent to her chest, she could scarcely breathe. "It's stuck."

His hands fell from her waist. "You know, I oughta just leave you there."

"Go, then. I don't need or want your help."

"You're a fine-looking sight, waving your drawers at the world. What would little Peter Crenton think if he could see you now? I bet a *proper* lady doesn't climb through windows."

Amy squeezed her eyes closed. "Oh, God, are my drawers truly showing? Pull my skirt down."

"Not on your life." He laughed softly. "Prettiest damn drawers I ever saw."

Amy clenched her teeth. "I hate your guts. I detest you. You're turning my life into a nightmare! How can you stand there when a woman's underwear is showing and — and just look!"

"You're right. That's plain disgusting. I'll

172

have me a smoke while I'm at it."

Seething, Amy strained and shoved to dislodge her foot so she could get her leg inside. A sob of frustration crawled up her throat. "You slimy bastard! Just stand there, why don't you?"

Swift made no reply. She tried to twist her neck to see him, couldn't. "Swift?"

Nothing. She grew still a moment to listen. He had left her! She jerked furiously on her foot. The window frame dug painfully into her shoulders, bringing tears to her eyes.

"Be still. You're gonna keep on till you pop through like a grape out of its skin, and I'm not out there to catch you."

She started at the sound of his voice coming from inside the house, to her right. "Scare me to death! I thought you left."

"I'm not quite as slimy as that," he said with a chuckle. She heard the chair scrape the floor. "It was tempting, though. If I wasn't scared you'd break that spindly little neck of yours, I'd do it." He grasped her ankle and tugged. "Relax, Amy. You're stiff as a board. If I'm going to get you out, you'll have to loosen up."

"It's easy for you to say. It's my hind portion planted up here."

"Hind portion? Sounds like a slab of beef.

How about behind? Or fanny? Or —"

"So help me, Swift!"

He laughed again and gave another jerk on her foot. Her leg came loose. As it did, her upper body pitched in the opposite direction. Swift snaked an arm around her waist to catch her, plucked her off the sill into his arms, and stepped off the chair.

"Butt," he finished with a grunt, making a half turn with her still cradled in his arms before setting her on her feet.

Amy staggered away, straightening her bodice and smoothing her skirts, cheeks aflame. "I didn't hear you kick in my door."

"Didn't. I came in your sitting room window."

"It was locked."

"I *un*locked it."

"But if you could —" She broke off, staring up at him. "Why'd you make all that fuss about the door, then?"

His mouth slanted into a grin, flashing white teeth. "Because I was mad. Unlocking a window wouldn't be very satisfying. Busting it, maybe. But then you'd have been without glass until we could get a new piece ordered and delivered."

Her eyes widened. "This is all nothing but a game to you!"

"And you're losing."

There was no denying that. Amy averted her face. "Well, you're in. N-now what?"

"I've a mind to give you a kick on that cute little *hind portion* of yours."

Amy glared at him. "Do it. And leave a bruise, damn you. One mark on me, and Hunter'll kill you."

Swift met her fiery gaze and grinned again. "You'd bare your fanny to show him? I bet I could paddle you black and blue, and you'd never do it. That'd be a sight I wouldn't want to miss, Miss Amy with her skirts hiked up and her bare ass shining."

"You're disgusting."

"And you're infuriating. Jail, Amy? When Marshal Hilton showed up, I couldn't believe my eyes."

She leaned toward him, body shaking. "If it hadn't been for Hunter, I'd have let you rot in there."

"Now we get to the truth. I thought you said you never meant for me to be locked up?"

She advanced a step, hands knotted into fists. "I lied. Anyone dumb enough not to back down when the marshal comes calling deserves to be in jail."

Swift stood his ground, watching her. She looked furious enough to hit him, and he was willing to let her, if only she had the courage to dare. She stopped a pace away from him, her blue eyes blazing, each cheek dotted with crimson, her lips drawn back over her teeth.

"I didn't realize breakfast and roses would make you so mad." He jutted his chin at her. Tapping a finger on his jaw, he taunted, "You want to hit me? Come on, Amy. Now's your chance. Or are you too yellow? I'll give you one free shot!"

"It wasn't the breakfast and roses. You broke into my house. I'm tired of being stalked and tormented and threatened."

"*Our* house."

"*My* house, you arrogant, addle-brained Mexican."

With that, she swung. Swift saw her fist coming at him one second and went blind the next, pain exploding up the bridge of his nose. He grabbed for his face. "Jesus Christ!"

"And don't curse in my house."

Her shoe glanced off his knee. He lost his balance and staggered backward against the stove. Something warm dripped through his fingers where they were cupped over his nose. He blinked, trying to see. He half expected her to strike again, now that she was getting into the swing of it, so he kept his shoulders hunched. Silence fell around him.

"Swift?" She said his name in a shaky little voice.

He blinked again. The room spun into focus.

"Swift, are you all right?"

"Hell, no, I'm not all right. You broke my goddamn nose."

He heard her quick intake of breath. Her skirts swished closer. "Oh, my God! Oh, my God, you're bleeding all over my floor."

Swift cupped his other hand over his nose. "I can't help bleeding, Amy," he told her in a muffled voice. "Get me a rag."

He heard water slosh. A moment later a cold cloth touched the back of his hands. He pressed it over his nostrils.

"Oh, Swift, I'm sorry. Come sit down and let me look."

"I'll be fine," he protested, allowing her to pull him by the arm toward a chair.

She pressed him down and leaned over him, her small face taut with concern as she gently drew the cloth back. Looking up at her, Swift decided then and there that a broken nose was worth having seen her lose her temper. Though tears streamed from his eyes, a smile tugged at his mouth. She touched the knot along his bridge, wincing as if it were she in pain.

"Oh, Swift, I think it *is* broken."

"A horse kicked me once. It never set right, so it doesn't take a lot." He mopped at the blood on his lip, jerking when her fingers touched the broken spot. "Easy! It hurts like hell."

She drew her hand back, her expression agonized. "I never meant to hurt you."

Swift couldn't bite back a grin. "You little liar. You damn near shoved my nose through my brain."

Her wide eyes met his, filled with incredulity. "You're not mad?"

"I dared you to do it. Why be mad?" Gingerly he clasped the bridge of his nose between thumb and forefinger, trying to straighten it. "I have to say, though, that I was expecting to get it on the jaw. I should've known you'd go for blood if I once got your dander up." Giving a sniff, he tested the airflow, then angled a look at her. "It'll mend, Amy. It's not the first time I've rebroke it, and it won't be the last."

Dragging out another chair from the table, she sank onto it, as if her knees had given way. She heaved a weary sigh and cupped her hand over her eyes. "Oh, Swift."

He took another swipe at his lip with the rag, studying the top of her golden head.

"I can't take any more of this," she admitted in a quavery voice. "I truly can't. You have to stop."

"Marry me, and I will stop."

She lifted her head, fastening miserable eyes on him. "Don't you see that I can't?"

"Amy, I could just settle the matter and ride off with you slung over my horse."

The color washed from her face.

"Why do you think I haven't? I'll tell you why. I want to make you happy. Won't you give me a chance? I'll do everything I can to make sure you never regret marrying me, I swear it."

"I would abhor marriage to you."

"You won't, I swear it."

"How could you make me happy, Swift?" she asked in a thin voice. "You planning on stealing and killing to make a living?"

"You know better than that."

"Do I? It isn't just your past that bothers me. But your refusal to change. Look at yourself. Still wearing those guns, still dressed all in black like walking death, still intimidating people. You're not in Texas, living with the comancheros. You're in Oregon in the *tosi* world now, and if you plan to stay, you can't behave like a heathen."

Swift's eyes held hers. "I went with Marshal Hilton today. Is that how a heathen

179

behaves?"

"And five seconds ago, you threatened to sling me over your horse and ride off with me." Her eyes brightened with tears. "You were mad because he locked you up, because you hate being confined! How do you think you're making me feel? Trapped!" She waved her hand at the house. "You've invaded my home, snuck up on me out of the darkness. You've turned my family against me, getting them on your side, so I can't even ask the marshal for protection. There's no place I'm safe from you."

"Amy, you're safe from me right now. That's what I've been trying to make you see." He gripped the rag in his hand and leaned toward her. "What did you think I meant to do when I got in here?"

She caught her lower lip between her teeth, the tears in her eyes welling over her lashes onto her cheeks. "You wouldn't promise not to touch me."

"Because it's my right. I love you. Do you think I'm going to promise away the one edge I've got? Just because I won't relinquish that right doesn't mean I'm going to exercise it."

"You were angry. I thought you might."

"And you were wrong. But say you hadn't been. What if I decided, right here and now, to toss you over my shoulder and carry you to bed? Do you really believe I'd hurt you?" He pressed closer. "Look at me and tell me you think I'd harm you."

One corner of her right eyelid began to twitch. "Harm, Swift? People can bleed inside, where you can't see."

His voice went low and husky. "I know you're frightened. If you'll only trust me, I can make that feeling go away."

"No. Nothing will ever take it away."

"You believed differently once."

"I was a child then. I'm older and wiser now."

After taking another swipe at his lip, Swift trailed a finger up a stripe on her gray satin skirt. "I know you don't think much of me and the things I've done. But you do still trust my word, don't you? For old times' sake?"

She looked wary. "I suppose if you swore to something, knowing as I do that you were once a Comanche and never lied, I'd lean heavily toward believing you."

He curled his fingers over her knee. "Then take this promise and hold it forever. No matter what happens, no matter how angry I might be, even if I take you, I'll never hurt you or use you roughly. I won't ask you to believe it'll be good between us, because I don't think you're able to believe that. But I swear on my life that it won't be bad."

For an instant she thought of Hunter and Loretta and all that they had, wishing with all her heart that she and Swift could weave the same magic, that a home and children of her own were a possibility. But that was the child in her, spinning dreams. Reality seldom turned out so magical. "Swift, why won't you just let it go? Even if there wasn't all the other standing between us, we're worlds apart. We could never make a marriage work."

"And if I change? If I try, will you try, too?"

Her small features tightened, and she averted her face, staring at the roses on her table. "I don't know if I can."

"What have you got to lose? I think I've made my stand pretty clear. If we can't work things out between us, I'll settle it the only way that's left. Why not try it the easy way? Will you at least try? I'm not asking for surrender, just for a declaration of peace. I'll meet you more than halfway."

Her mind raced with all the possibilities that trying might pose, but foremost in her thoughts was the consequence that would undoubtedly occur if she refused. "I — I guess I can make an effort, though I don't see how that will —"

"You promise?"

She sighed, feeling as if she had lost important ground. "I promise to try, nothing more."

"That's good enough," he whispered.

A sense of purpose filled Swift as he left Amy's house and strode down the main street of Wolf's Landing toward Hunter's home. Change. It had sounded simple enough when he had agreed to do it, but now that he had time to consider, he had no idea how to begin. Only one thing seemed certain: Amy wanted nothing to do with a gunslinger who dressed like a comanchero. If he wanted her, and he did, he had to acquire a new look.

When Swift stepped into the Wolf home, he found Hunter sitting at the kitchen table, head bent over a large book, the pages lined with green columns and chicken-scratched with writing. Glancing up, Hunter riveted his gaze to Swift's face.

"What happened to you?"

"The coon came out," Swift muttered, stepping to the stove to pour a cup of coffee. "Where is everybody?"

"Mrs. Hamstead's sick, and Loretta went to check on her. She took Chase and Indigo to help chop wood and tidy the house."

"What's she ailing with?"

"Her mother-in-law's sheep dung tea." Hunter smiled when Swift turned from the stove. "What did your coon hit you with? That nose looks broke."

"It is. More fool me for sticking my chin out and telling her to slug me."

Hunter's grin widened. He leaned back in the chair and laid down his pencil. "I haven't seen Amy lose her temper in years. Congratulations."

Giving his nose a tentative probing, Swift tried to sniff, only to discover his nasal passages were already swollen closed. "Don't get carried away celebrating. Just because she gave me a poke doesn't mean I've accomplished anything." Heaving a sigh, he pulled out a chair and sat down. Taking a sip of coffee, he said, "I don't know what to do, Hunter. Is this game I've been playing helping, or am I just making things worse?"

"Things must get worse for her to see she has to change." Hunter reclaimed his pencil, toying with it idly. "I think you've done well. Unless she leaves Wolf's Landing, she has no sanctuary. That leaves her no choice but to adjust."

"I'm tempted to do just what she expects and take her. It'd be easier and a sight quicker."

"Yes, but quick isn't always good, especially considering what Amy has been through." Hunter's gaze softened with memories. "Gaining Loretta's trust took time, but in the end it was worth the wait."

Swift fished in his shirt pocket for his tobacco pouch, then forgot what he was doing and dropped his hand. "I'm just talking, anyway. As if I could take her, even if I wanted to. I'd hate myself afterward worse than she would."

"Perhaps."

Swift narrowed his eyes. "Have you ever forced a woman?"

"A little bit."

"How do you do it a little bit?"

Hunter's eyes filled with amusement. " 'For a little while' is probably more accurate. Until my woman forgot to struggle. That was Loretta, though. Amy's story is much harsher." He studied the tip of his pencil, as if the mysteries of the world might be answered there. "Loretta saw her mother brutalized, and that made her very much afraid. Amy didn't just see, she was the victim of twenty-three cruel men. It has been many years, and living with fear every day is an unpleasant thing. She has journeyed beyond it, I think, into a place where she doesn't feel. Until you came, that is."

Swift raked his hand through his hair. "She asked me to change." Bluish oil ribboned the surface of his coffee. Tipping the cup, he gazed into the murky depths. "She doesn't like my appearance or the fact that I wear my guns. I don't think she believes I can provide for her without resorting to my old ways."

"Can you?"

Swift felt heat rising up his neck. "I can work with you or get a farm. I'm not lazy, Hunter."

"I could use a partner in my mine. Chase has his eye on the timber, and one day I expect him to try logging. But is Amy's concern truly your ability to earn money? Or is it that you are an acorn in a bowl of walnuts?"

"Meaning that I don't fit in? I can buy some new shirts. Take the conchae off my hat. I'm not so different from the people here."

Hunter shook his head. "You misunderstand. Your clothes are a small thing. The man who wears them is not." He gestured at the book before him. "To be my partner, you must know your letters and numbers, and you don't."

"You expect me to learn how to read?"

Swift stared at him, scarcely able to believe Hunter, of all people, placed importance on book learning. "I can't read, Hunter. I can't even spell my name."

"I was one dumb Comanche, and I learned." Hunter tapped his finger on the writing. "My books. They say how rich I am. And I put all the numbers here. If I can do this, you can. You talk of a new shirt? Anyone can buy a shirt, Swift. What will that prove to Amy?"

"That I'm willing to try."

"But only a little bit. This is a white man's world. Our world, as you say, no longer exists, except within our hearts. You claim a white woman as yours, and you plan to marry with her and live in her world. To do that, you must make yourself a little bit like a white man, so you can care for her."

Swift swallowed, his gaze dropping to the writing on the paper. Anger filled him. "I don't need to know my letters to care for her. Damn it, Hunter, that's asking too much. It's enough to consider taking off my guns now and again. I never know when someone may discover I'm here and come looking for me."

Hunter lifted one shoulder in an eloquent shrug. Swift clenched his teeth. "It'd take me years to learn letters and numbers," he argued.

"A little time if you study hard. I learned quick."

"Yeah, well, maybe you're smarter than me."

Hunter shrugged again. "You are right. It is too high a price to pay for a woman."

"That isn't it, and you know it."

"What is it, then? Are you afraid to try?"

Swift bristled. "I'm not scared of anything, let alone a bunch of letters on a page."

"We will see."

"Are you daring me?"

Hunter looked bewildered. "Me, Swift? You came to me, and I have said my thoughts. That is all. You don't like my thoughts, and that is fine, but they are still my thoughts. Amy is a schoolteacher, and she makes much of letters and numbers. I think she would be pleased if you showed interest in what is important to her. You ask Amy to do all the compromising. This way, she will see you making a big effort."

"All right," Swift said through clenched teeth. "I said I'd try, and I will. You teach me."

Hunter grinned. "I can't teach you, Swift. I must work in my mine to feed my family. And Loretta is very busy with her work. You could study with Chase and Indigo at night, but that would take a very long time."

"Well, how in hell can I learn, then?"

"Maybe you should go to school."

Swift stared at him, incredulity striking him speechless for a moment. "With the children, you mean?"

CHAPTER 8

Morning sunlight slanted over the roof of the schoolhouse into Swift's eyes. He shuffled his boots, not quite able to force himself up the steps. The feelings sweeping through him reminded him of the first time he'd bedded a woman. He had been uncertain of himself then, afraid of failing. Making love had turned out to be something he had aptitude for, but he wasn't sure he could master academics with the same flair.

What if he *was* stupid? What if, no matter how he tried, his mind couldn't make sense of the scribbles? Amy would see and know. He'd never again be able to stand proud before her. Years ago he had impressed her with his many skills, but those skills meant nothing here. Wouldn't it be wiser not even to try than to risk revealing his inadequacies? She might never guess if he tried real hard to do good at everything else.

Children's laughter floated from the building. Swift imagined that laughter was being directed at him. Sweat filmed his palms. He could face a man on the street in a gunfight, but this was different. For the first time, he wanted to run. Pride wouldn't allow him to. What would Hunter think if he found out? Swift could admit to many things, but never to cowardice.

He walked slowly up the steps.

Amy stood at the front of the classroom, her slender back straight, head held high, her voice ringing like a bell as she gave instruction on some arithmetic problems. When she glimpsed Swift, she turned in surprise, her eyes widening in question. Swift felt like a fly in the honey.

"Good morning, Mr. Lopez." She glanced at the children, and they chimed in, saying, "Good morning, Mr. Lopez."

It was small consolation that the kids didn't seem wary of him anymore. Swift shifted his weight from one foot to the other. Tipping his hat, he said, "Mornin'."

"Did you have a specific reason for coming?" Amy asked, her gaze dropping to his gun belt, then drifting upward to his hat.

Swift yanked the hat off his head and swallowed, shooting a glance at the youngsters. "I —" He cleared his throat. "I've come to —" He met her gaze. "Do you have room for a new pupil?"

"Of course. For whom?"

"Me," Swift mumbled.

"Who?"

He swallowed again. In a louder voice he repeated, "Me."

"You?" She stared at him as if she didn't believe she had heard correctly.

"I want to learn my letters and numbers," Swift said with more conviction. One of the children snickered.

Amy didn't look elated over his request. He shared her sentiments. But he had come. And he'd be damned if he'd back out now.

"You're a little old to be attending school, Mr. Lopez."

"I'm a late bloomer." Swift strode to the coatrack. After hanging up his hat, he unfastened his gun belt, acutely conscious that everyone in the room was staring at him. He draped his guns over a hook and turned to face them. Flashing a grin, he said, "Maybe I'll learn quicker since I'm older."

There were no empty seats near Chase or Indigo. Peter, the little redhead, returned Swift's smile. Since there was an unoccupied desk behind the youngster, Swift headed in that direction. The desk was a problem. Once he folded himself into it, he wasn't sure he'd ever get out. Thinking of Amy stuck in the window, he glanced up at her and grinned again. She narrowed her eyes on his swollen nose. Since he felt fairly certain she couldn't read his mind, he decided grinning might be against the rules. He mashed his lips together and tried to look humorless.

The silence began to feel uncomfortable. Swift wondered if Amy would ever regather her composure or if she was going to stand there staring at him all day. He stared back at her and slowly relaxed. He might not learn anything, but the view was breathtaking. He could think of several less pleasurable ways to spend his days. His gaze trailed from her face downward.

After a moment Amy clamped a hand over the line of buttons on her bodice, as if she guessed where his attention had centered. She turned a very pretty pink, a nice contrast to her somber gray dress. "Well . . ." She looked nonplussed, as if she might have forgotten what she had been saying. Her eyes turned a stormy blue. He knew what that meant. When she got angry, her eyes never failed to look dark and turbulent. "Far be it from me to turn anyone away. If you really want to learn, Mr. Lopez, this is the place to do it."

She clearly had her doubts about his sincerity. Swift forgot that it might be against the rules to grin. He was enjoying himself more by the moment. To spend hour after hour flirting with Amy Masters and making her cheeks turn pink was about as close to the Great Beyond as a Comanche could get.

Straightening her shoulders, Amy returned to her desk and searched frantically for her notes, which had been buried beneath the homework the children had just handed in. Arithmetic. But she couldn't recall today's lesson. Swift Lopez, in her classroom? Her throat tightened with unreasoning panic. He'd sit there staring at her all day, she just knew it. He no more wanted to learn numbers and letters than pigs yearned to fly.

Amy at last found her notes. Clutching them in one hand, she turned to face her class. Swift's gaze slid slowly from her breasts to her waist, then lower. Fury welled within her. He had come to torment her. And if not for that, to further his cause with her. Well, she'd nip this nonsense in the bud. She would give him so much homework that he'd be up half the night finishing it. He'd very quickly decide this was her territory and, unlike her home, inviolate, unless he was willing to go through a great deal of self-sacrifice.

Somehow Amy waded her way through the arithmetic lesson, seeing to it that each age group understood the instructions and were busily doing the problems. Then she advanced on Mr. Lopez with her arithmetic book. Her determination to bowl him over flagged a bit when she realized he couldn't recognize any number, except those he had come across in a poker deck. Determined not to soften, she dragged over a desk and sat down.

"I guess we'd better start at the very beginning," she said sternly, determined not to let the wary expression in his eyes get to her.

He leaned her direction to look at the pages of the book. When he saw the enormity of what he was undertaking, he whispered, "Shit!"

She sent him a reproving look. He glanced around at the other students and apologized.

"This is a schoolroom," she reminded him. "Remember that always."

"Yes, ma'am." Swift met her accusing gaze and grinned. "So start teaching me, Miss Amy."

Amy didn't know how, but he managed to make those harmless words carry a sensual undertone. She embarked on a quick lesson, showing no mercy as she gave him in-class and after-school assignments, one of which was to write the numbers one through twenty 100 times. Given the fact that Swift had never held a pencil, she figured that alone would take him until sometime next week. Feeling for the first time that she had the upper hand, she allowed a slight grin to settle on her mouth.

"What's she trying to do? Have you reading the New Testament within a week?" Loretta asked that evening as she bent over Swift's shoulder while he painstakingly drew his letters. "A hundred times the first day? You'll be up all night."

Swift flexed his cramped fingers, staring at the ugly-looking *J* he had just finished. "I've gone without sleep before. This much work is good. I'll learn fast."

Loretta made a disapproving noise. "I think she's trying to discourage you, that's what I think. That isn't at all like Amy. She's usually such a dedicated teacher." She patted his shoulder. "Not to worry. I'll talk to her, Swift."

"No. This is between her and me, Loretta."

"But —"

"No," he repeated more gently. "Would that be fair? Who can she go to for help? You, Hunter, the marshal? It's our war. Let us fight it."

"But this is different. You have as much right to learn as anyone else, and she's deliberately making it impossible."

"I'll survive," Swift assured her. "And I won't quit. Let me handle this in my own way. Once Amy realizes I really want to learn, she'll teach me. But she has to realize it by herself."

Amy crawled out of bed and went to the window. Rubbing a dry place on the steamy glass, she peered through the night at the Wolf home at the other end of town. A dim glow of light still shone through the parlor window. She grinned and marched happily back to bed. He would never get all that homework done, not in a night. And he would never admit to failure in front of the whole class. Mentally brushing her hands clean of Swift Lopez in her classroom, Amy snuggled deep in the down and closed her eyes. Sleep claimed her almost immediately.

Drifting in black mists, Amy's mind plummeted her into the past. Only not into the past. Wrists tied to the spokes of a wagon wheel, she found herself gazing across her classroom instead of flat grassland. Frantic, because she knew the comancheros would soon start coming, she fought to free her wrists from the rawhide.

"Help me, Jeremiah," she called. "Chase, Indigo, someone!"

Cruel hands settled on her thighs, the fingers biting. She threw her head back. Swift smiled down at her, eyes gleaming.

"Swift, no. Not you!"

"You're mine," he said, laughing at her frenzied attempts to escape his hands. "I warned you, didn't I? You promised to try. You won't give me too much homework again, will you, Amy!"

Pain slashed through her. She threw her head and screamed, her only defense against the agony. . . .

Amy jerked awake, her breath coming in uneven little gasps, her hands knotted in the quilt. For a moment, reality and dream melded. As her surroundings broke the dream's spell, she jackknifed to a sitting position, burying her face in her cupped hands. Oh, God.

Amy hunched her shoulders, knowing the nightmare stemmed from guilt. It had been wrong to give Swift all that homework. She had a duty to teach anyone who came to her, and she was trying to drive Swift away.

When she began letting her personal feelings influence her, she would no longer be a good teacher. And teaching was her entire life.

Swift tipped his head, listening for the sound to repeat itself. Glancing from the table over at Hunter, who sat whittling by the fire, he asked, "Do you have big cats in this country?"

"Cougars," Hunter replied, not looking up from his work.

"I think I just heard one." Swift studied his friend's profile, wondering how it was that he had detected a sound when Hunter hadn't. "Did you hear it? Sounded just like a woman screaming. Enough to curl my whiskers, if I didn't know what it was."

"It wasn't a cougar."

"What in hell was it, then?"

Hunter's knife paused in its downward course along the wood. "It's a sound we sometimes hear. Nothing to worry about, Swift."

"What kind of an animal is it?"

Loretta stopped pushing her rocker to and fro, her blue eyes shifting from her darning ball to her husband.

"It isn't an animal," Hunter said solemnly.

Swift laid down his pencil, a tingle creeping up his spine. He glanced from Loretta's worried expression to Hunter's deadpan one, and then he shot up from his chair.

"Don't," Hunter said, never looking up from his knife. "She is awake now, and the bad time will soon pass. It's easier for her if we pretend the nightmares don't come. She can't help the screams, and it shames her to know everyone hears."

"Easier?" Swift curled his hands into fists. "I've never heard anyone scream like that. Shouldn't someone be with her?"

Hunter at last looked up, not at Swift but into the leaping flames. "You've never seen what it is she screams about, either. If you could be with her inside the dream, perhaps then you could help, but you cannot. And now the dream is over."

The next morning, Amy knew the moment Swift entered the schoolhouse. A different feeling touched the air, an electrical feeling, like that right before a storm, when the air seemed too thick to breathe, when all living things grew silent, waiting. Even the children quieted, which was phenomenal. She didn't look up from her desk until his dark hand passed under her nose.

"My homework," he said softly.

With tense fingers, Amy accepted the

papers. Very quickly she leafed through, checking the assignments. All had been completed. Almost afraid to look up, but unable not to, she lifted her gaze to Swift's weary countenance.

His nose looked better today, but that was the only improvement. Even if his sleepless night hadn't shown on his face, she would have known he had been up all night working simply because he had delivered the assignments. Even a sloppy effort, inexperienced as he was, would have taken hours. She was also quick to note he had come to school minus his hat and guns.

"I think I did it good," he said.

Dry-mouthed, Amy nodded, her voice failing her. Swift waited a moment, as if he expected comment. Then he turned and went to the desk he had occupied yesterday. Amy took a moment to go through the work. Two-thousand six-hundred perfect letters. Tears stung beneath her eyelids. She leafed to the numbers. She knew without counting that he'd formed all two thousand. Swift, the Comanche warrior, the hunter, the gunslinger? He had humbled himself coming here yesterday, putting himself on the same level as children, but she had never expected him to go this far.

Seeing no alternative, Amy met his gaze

across the room and said, "You did every-thing perfectly, Mr. Lopez. I'd say you deserve an A-plus on each assignment."

"Is that good?"

A few of the children giggled. Amy shot them reproving looks. "It's the very best grade a student can get. It means better than excellent."

Swift straightened in his seat. There was no mistaking the prideful gleam in his eyes. Amy smothered a smile. Forming letters and numbers might seem like child's play to her, but to Swift it clearly had been an almost impossible feat.

Her emotions in a confused tangle, she pushed up from her desk. All else aside, she was first, last, and always a teacher. Swift wanted to learn. No man would slave all night on a whim. She could spurn him with no regret when he approached her as a suitor, but she couldn't rebuff him when he came to her, minus his hat and guns, asking her to do the one thing God had put her on earth to do. It looked as if she had another student.

Amy assigned Swift a much lighter home-work load that day. When school was dis-missed, he waited for the children to leave and then approached her desk. She grew still, not quite able to look at him, wishing he had left with the others and spared her the necessity of doing what she knew she must.

"Swift, I, um . . ." She dragged her gaze up from her desk. "I owe you an apology. Yesterday I gave you way too much work, hoping you wouldn't come back to school." She waited a moment for him to speak, but he didn't offer her an out. "I'm sorry, truly sorry. You can expect fair treatment from now on."

"I appreciate that." His eyes warmed, not with laughter, but with another indefinable emotion. "It's real important to me to learn my letters and numbers."

"I — I never realized. . . ."

"Well, now you do." He studied her a moment. "What you said about me not being in Texas anymore — it made sense. If I'm going to take care of you, I have to fit in here."

"It's a great deal of work to embark upon when you have no guarantee of the reward."

He flashed her a slow smile. "But I do have a guarantee. Two, as a matter of fact."

"Two?"

"You promised to marry me, and the other night, you promised to try if I'd meet you halfway. When I walked up those schoolhouse steps, I came my fair share of the distance."

"What is it you're expecting from me?"

"That's for you to decide. And when is up to you, too. I won't push you anymore, not like I did. I didn't mean to make you feel like you were inside a jail." He paused and cleared his throat. "You gave me your word to try, and I trust you to live up to it."

Over the next few days, Amy found herself heartily regretting her decision to allow Swift in her classroom, and she began despising her job with an intensity that she never would have dreamed possible before his enrollment. Swift applied himself to learning with the same tenacity he had once applied to Comanche warfare. Though she couldn't for a moment doubt his sincerity, he was not a man with a one-track mind. His initial reason for acquiring knowledge had been to win her favor, and he persevered in that quest with the same fervor as before.

Because they were surrounded by children, Swift's tactics became more subtle, but his effect on Amy was just as devastating. While she taught, his piercing gaze followed her. He never missed an opportunity to touch her. Once, when she leaned over his shoulder to assist him with his work, he turned his face so that his cheek grazed her breast. The contact took her breath. Sometimes she wondered if he truly needed her hand to guide his when he was forming letters or if he merely liked having her fingers pressed to his.

Though the teacher in Amy had to admire Swift for his determination to learn, and though she felt a sense of pride in seeing him gain ground, she also resented his disruption of her life. Jeremiah, who sported a schoolboy crush on his teacher, had begun disturbing class, clearly jealous of Swift. Little Peter Crenton, who had an abusive father, came to school with bruises one morning and didn't come to her for comfort, as he had always done in the past. Even the smaller girls began acting silly about things they never had before, trying to get their handsome schoolmate's attention.

On top of that, a delegation of mothers visited Amy one day after school, concerned about Swift's questionable character and his influence upon their children. In addition to assuring the mothers that Swift's behavior at school was exemplary, Amy found herself defending his right to an education, which left her emotions in a confused tangle by the time the mothers left, appeased. Was she risking her position as schoolteacher by keeping Swift in the classroom?

Amy spent a great deal of time wondering why she had bucked the delegation of mothers. Was it that she was beginning to feel drawn to Swift? The thought terrified her. She didn't begrudge him an education, but she couldn't help wishing that he would attend school in Jacksonville, far away from her.

On Wednesday, exactly one week after Swift enrolled in school, the monthly spelling bee fell due. Because Swift had no background whatsoever to arm him for such competition, Amy meant to excuse him from participating before the children chose captains and began dividing up into teams. The moment she announced that intention, however, a general grumble of "That's not fair!" reverberated through the room. It had always been the rule that everyone in class had to participate in the spelling bees, and the children took exception to anyone getting off.

"That's all right, Miss Amy," Swift cut in when she started to explain. "Rules are rules."

Amy knew Swift had no idea what a spelling bee entailed, and it was on the tip of her tongue to insist he sit this one out. But then it occurred to her that this might be the answer she had been praying for. It wasn't as if she hadn't tried to spare Swift. But, if he insisted . . .

"All right, class," she conceded. "Let's pick captains."

It immediately became apparent how the wind was going to blow. Swift was the last person to be chosen as a team member and only then because he was the last choice Jeremiah had. Swift went to stand on Jeremiah's side of the room, his tall frame looming over the little girl in pigtails beside him. He looked ready for anything, his body slightly tensed. He truly didn't have an inkling of what the competition was going to entail. In his experience contests were won by strength of arm, agility, speed and wit. Unfortunately Swift's wit hadn't been honed for this particular type of jousting.

"The questions should be easy for Mr. Lopez," Jeremiah suggested. "Or it won't be fair."

Swift's face tightened. Amy knew he had never had anyone make concessions for him and that having a child do so stung his pride. She already hated herself for having allowed things to go this far. Swift would be overwhelmed by even the simplest word, and she had let him go up there, like a lamb to slaughter.

The spelling bee began. Swift's expression altered when Amy presented the first word. Indigo's team went first, Indigo the lead speller. She zipped through the word *dangerous.* Amy turned toward Jeremiah's side of the room, her gaze drawn to Swift. He looked back at her, his dark face solemn, his mouth drawn. The expression in his eyes could only be described as wounded. And perhaps accusing. Understanding had dawned.

To his credit Swift remained standing and faced the humiliation that was sure to come — like the warrior he was. When his turn finally came and Amy had to ask him to spell a word, she felt like the enemy about to destroy him. He raised his head, pride shining in his eyes, and met her gaze. Searching her mind for a word, any word, that he had the remotest chance of spelling, Amy seized upon his name, which he had been printing each evening on his homework papers.

"Swift," she said shakily.

One of the children laughed. Amy's cheeks felt as though they were on fire. She shot a glare in the direction of the sound. "That's a perfectly fair word, Beth. It means fast and fleet of foot."

Swift swallowed and stood a little taller. His eyes clung to Amy's. "S-u-i-f-t," he recited quickly.

Amy's heart felt as though it dropped to her knees when a few of the children began whooping with laughter. "He can't even spell his own name," one of the boys cried.

"Soo-ift!" another inserted, dragging out the syllables.

A little girl leaped to Swift's defense, saying, "He came close. He just got his *u* and *w* mixed up."

"This isn't fair," Jeremiah grumbled. "Our team's gonna lose just because we have one stupid player. What's he doin' in school, anyways! If he was gonna learn to read, my pa says he should've done it years ago."

Before Amy could react, Swift shoved away from the wall. For a frozen instant, their gazes locked. And in that instant she knew Swift was hurt far more by her betrayal than he was by the ridicule. He stood there a moment; then, without a word, he left the schoolroom, closing the door very softly as he went out. Amy held herself rigid, hands clenched around the edges of her lesson book, one thought passing repeatedly through her mind. She had won, but at what cost?

The children's laughter amplified in her

ears. On the one hand, Amy understood how funny Swift must seem to them, a tall, dangerous-looking man hunched over in an undersize desk, his big hands struggling to wield a pencil. But, just the same, their laughter was inexcusable.

"Enough!" she cried.

Silence blanketed the room. Indigo pushed away from the wall, her large blue eyes blazing. Stepping to her desk, she picked up her lesson books. Turning back to Amy, she said, "That's the meanest thing I've ever seen anyone do. The very meanest." And with that she fled the schoolhouse, slamming the door so hard the walls reverberated.

Numb, Amy called a halt to the spelling bee and dismissed school early, which once again earned her a word from Jeremiah. "My pa says we've been let out early so much since Mr. Lopez came we might as well not bother coming. He says the school committee's going to hire a new teacher if it keeps up."

Amy stood rooted, watching all the children leave. Maybe Wolf's Landing should hire a new teacher, someone who wouldn't let personal feelings interfere with her dedication.

"Aunt Amy?"

Chase's husky voice jerked Amy back to the moment. She turned, feeling strangely unattached to reality, and focused on Chase's handsome features. His blue eyes searched hers.

"Indigo didn't mean it," he offered.

Amy took an uncertain step toward her desk. "I'm afraid she did, and I can't really blame her. It was cruel of me to let him go up there."

"He's been just as cruel to you."

Taken aback, Amy glanced over her shoulder. Until that moment, she had seen Chase as a child. Now, looking into his eyes, she realized the little boy she had entertained with stories so long ago had become a young man.

A flush crept up Chase's neck, and he shrugged. "I know he doesn't mean to be cruel, that to him it's just —" He averted his gaze. "Indigo's too young to know about stuff like that, so she hasn't paid any mind to what's been going on. I know Uncle Swift's been making things pretty miserable for you."

Tears nearly blinded Amy. "Thank you for that, Chase," she said tightly.

He shrugged again, clearly uncomfortable wearing the cloak of manhood, even for these few moments. "Ma hasn't ever said what happened to you exactly, but I've heard whispers when she and my father think I'm asleep." He licked his lips. "I know that you've been feeling like we all stopped caring. I just —" He blinked and stepped toward her. "I love you, Aunt Amy."

The next instant Amy found herself vised in Chase's strong arms, her feet skimming the floor as he hugged her. Curling an arm around his neck, she returned the embrace, wavering between a smile and tears. It was tempting to cling to him, to weep and pour out all her troubles, but Amy couldn't allow herself to do that. Hunter had made it clear that his loyalties lay with Swift. She couldn't drive a wedge between Hunter and his son.

"I love you, too, Chase," she whispered. "I appreciate your understanding. But warranted or no, I did a great wrong to your uncle Swift just now. And somehow I have to undo it."

"I know." He tightened his arms around her for one final hug. "Sometimes my father's ways make things hard. I'm glad you're my aunt, even though you aren't truly, by blood. But it doesn't seem fair that Uncle Swift is my uncle when he isn't. Not when it makes us choose between you. I just wanted you to know I'm not mad at you. And that Indigo's just too young to understand. I'll go find her and talk to her. And I think once Uncle Swift thinks it over, he'll stop being mad, too."

Amy squeezed her eyes closed. She knew Swift wasn't angry; he was hurt. "I'll speak with him."

"Would you like me to go with you?"

Amy pulled away, scrubbing tears from her cheeks and sniffing. "No, thank you. This is something I have to do alone."

"You sure? I know you're a little scared of him."

Looking up into Chase's worried blue eyes, it was all Amy could do not to grin. He truly believed she'd draw comfort from his presence while facing a man of Swift's ilk? It would be like siccing a puppy on a wolf.

"Actually, Chase, your uncle Swift and I are old friends."

It wasn't a lie; she and Swift had been friends, once upon a time. The best of friends, as only children could be. Now he had grown into a man, she into a woman, and life's realities formed a wall between them. Wall or no, though, the memories still existed between them. Amy knew Swift had trusted her when he joined the spelling bee competition. She had betrayed him, not in what she had done or said, but by what she hadn't.

CHAPTER 9

Amy found Swift at the far end of town, sitting beneath a madrona tree, back pressed to the red trunk, one leg extended, his muscular arms draped over an upraised knee. Seeing him surrounded by the woods, with the wind tossing his black hair, his gaze fastened on some distant place she couldn't see, she was transported back in time. For an instant, brief though it was, she glimpsed the boy she had once loved so dearly, in the regal lift of his head, the wisdom in his eyes, the solemn pensiveness of his expression. Swift Antelope, painfully proud, sometimes insufferably arrogant, as he had been raised to be, a blooded warrior, a hunter, a horseman without equal. And she had allowed him to be ridiculed by children.

For him to have lowered himself to the status of a student, to have sat hour after hour letting a squaw teach him anything, had been a great concession. In retrospect, she could hardly believe he had done it. She could have saved him this. There was plenty of time after school to tutor him privately. Instead she had forced him to publicly admit to his own ignorance, a thing most white men wouldn't have done. The fact that Swift had, and that he had done it mainly for her, made her feel ashamed — deeply, horribly ashamed.

She approached him slowly, seeing a vulnerability in him that she hadn't looked for until now. He couldn't go live in Jacksonville with strange whites and attend school any more easily than she could take up quarters in the saloon and support herself the way May Belle, the local pleasure dove, did.

Her shoes crunched on small twigs and dried autumn leaves as she drew near him. She knew he was aware of her presence, but he didn't betray that by so much as a flicker of his eyelid. "Swift?"

He kept his gaze locked straight ahead. Swallowing her own pride and a great deal of uneasiness, Amy sat down beside him. The wind funneled leaves around them, a dizzying cone of burnished orange and yellow, beautiful yet somehow depressing, significant to her because autumn was the death of spring's bounty, and she felt that she was fast approaching the autumn of her life, childhood and its beauty far behind her.

For a long while, they sat in silence. Amy wasn't certain what to say, and when she at last found the courage to speak, her words seemed pitifully inadequate. "I'm so sorry, Swift."

He finally stirred but didn't look at her. "I know."

Pain cut through Amy. He could have said anything but that. She started to reply that she hadn't meant to hurt him, but that wasn't entirely true, and if there was one thing she and Swift had always shared, it had been honesty. "It was so uncomfortable having you in the classroom. I wanted to get rid of you."

"You have. I won't come back."

She bit her lip until tears filled her eyes, but the new pain in no way took the edge off the other inside her. "Swift, I could tutor you privately, after school."

"It's no use, Amy." He sighed, the sound so weary and defeated that she ached. "Jeremiah's right. I'm too stupid to learn. You've no idea how hard I worked just to make the right lines on paper. I'll never get them memorized, so I can spell any word I want. I realized that today. I'm lucky I've learned to speak English as well as I have.

Even that didn't come easy. I had to practice constantly while I was out riding fence lines."

"You aren't stupid!" she cried. "And you wouldn't think you were if I'd given you a halfway fair chance."

He still refused to look at her. Studying his profile, Amy realized she wasn't the only one who felt ashamed. What had she done to him? Since his arrival in Wolf's Landing, she had been so preoccupied with her own concerns and feelings that she had forgotten Swift had feelings as well, that she might have as much power to hurt him as he had to hurt her.

"*Suvate,* it is finished," he said softly. His dark eyes trailed over the leaf-swept clearing. After a moment he swallowed and added, "Many great men before me have had the wisdom to say those words. Even Quanah finally said them."

"Quanah?"

"He fought the great fight for the People. Defeat came for him when Mackenzie slaughtered our horses. I rode with him on Adobe Walls. I know he would have died, rather than surrender, but sometimes dying won't come. Winter always does. The babies began to cry with hunger. Quanah surrendered so they might eat." A bitter smile twisted his mouth. "They didn't defeat him with war, but by leaving him no way to feed his people. One of the greatest warriors of all time, and it was the wails of children that made him lay down his weapons. It's funny, isn't it?" He tipped his head, as if he were listening for something, tasting the air. "And I'm defeated by lines on paper. I don't know why I came here, Amy. The world I belonged in is gone."

"No." Her voice came out in a raw whisper.

He smiled, but his eyes didn't warm with the gesture. In fact, Amy had never seen anyone's eyes look so empty. He studied her for a moment, as if he were looking at a memory, then glanced away.

Amy's heart wrenched. "Swift, you have to at least give it another try. You can't just give up."

His nostrils flared. "I tried, and I failed."

With a sinking sensation, she realized he would be just as stubborn about quitting as he had always been about everything else. Once he got something in his head, swaying him from his course was nigh unto impossible. She knew what she had to do . . . if she wanted him to stay. The question was, did she?

For a moment, fear held Amy paralyzed.

Until today she had wanted him to leave, prayed for him to. Her reasons for that hadn't changed. This man had the power to rip her safe world apart, then to rebuild it under his iron rule, to suit his fancy. If he remained here, he would do just that. It was as inevitable as rain during a cloudburst. What no one knew was that eight years ago she had fled a living nightmare, and she had sworn never again to allow anyone dominion over her. Was she going to let the emptiness in Swift's eyes make her forget that?

Hopelessness filled Amy, for she knew that question had already been answered long ago, a lifetime ago, when a gentle young man had rocked a sobbing twelve-year-old girl in his arms.

Clenching her hands into fists, she leaned toward him. "Don't be an ass, Swift. You started something, and you should finish it. You're the last man on earth I ever thought I'd see feeling sorry for himself."

His gaze flew to hers, and she knew she had chosen the right tactic — the only tactic. She didn't allow herself to think about the trouble she might be inviting. The important thing now was that she had done him a terrible injustice, and she desperately wanted a second chance to put it right.

"I never realized you had it in you to be

such a quitter."

A glint crept into his eyes.

She gave a little laugh. "I can't believe you've had me quaking in my shoes, terrified of you. Don't flatter yourself, comparing your situation to Quanah's. He had babies crying. The only crier you've got to worry about is yourself. Look at you, beaten after one measly week, giving up because you've failed to learn in five days what it takes other people years to conquer."

The glint in his eyes had turned to fire. "I'm no quitter. And you know it."

"Really? Look at you, moping because a few children laughed at you. You don't belong in this world? Hog spittle! What're you going to do, Swift? Go back to Texas and starve on a reservation, daydreaming about the good old days? Or maybe go back to the comancheros? You supposedly came here for a new start. Today went badly, and I apologized for that. I even offered to tutor you privately, and you turned that down. That's a quitter in my books."

"Be careful what you say, Amy."

She sprang to her feet. "Oh, yes, intimidate me and prove what a big, brave man you are. A physical battle with me would be easy. Learning to read isn't. It takes courage to face a book day after day. Your problem isn't between your ears, it's in that backbone of yours."

He rose slowly to his feet. "Amy, I'm warning you, I'm not in the right frame of mind for this. You can accuse me of a lot of things, and I'll take it, but don't call me a coward."

"Coward, quitter, it's all the same." She met his gaze. "I'll be at my house tomorrow at three o'clock, lesson book ready. If you're not a quitter, be there."

The next afternoon Amy paced the floor of her sitting room, glancing repeatedly at the clock. Five minutes after three. Swift wasn't going to show up. She sighed and sank onto her dark blue velvet settee. *The world I belonged in is gone.* If she couldn't convince Swift to give book learning one more try, those words were going to follow her to the grave.

She would have felt bad about discouraging anyone who had come to her for instruction, but she felt doubly bad about failing Swift. Whether she liked to admit it or not, he had been her salvation once, the only person who had cared enough to spend endless hours forcing his company upon her, giving her hope where she had none, pride that had been stripped from her, and renewed self-confidence. And he had given her all those things with unfailing gentleness and an understanding far beyond his years.

In return, when he had fled his destroyed world in Texas and come to Wolf's Landing seeking old friends, she had scorned him, spurned him, and then crowned everything by humiliating him beyond repair. No matter what he had become these past fifteen years, no matter what he had done, he deserved better than that, especially from her.

Rising from the settee, Amy grabbed her shawl and draped it around her shoulders. Maybe if she spoke to him one more time, he would reconsider. She stepped to the door and stared at the bolts, heart in throat, well aware of what she was about to do and the possible consequences. If she left things as they were, there was every possibility Swift might leave Wolf's Landing and return to Texas. She would be a hundred times a fool if she did anything to stop him. And yet, how could she not?

Decision made, she slid the bolts back and, gathering her shawl against the crisp autumn breeze, stepped out onto the porch. As she did, she caught movement from the corner of her eye. Turning, she came face-to-face with Swift, who had just planted a black boot on the bottom step of her porch. Their eyes locked, sending messages neither of them seemed able to voice, his angry, hers relieved.

"You came," she said at last.

Making no reply, he stomped up the steps, swept by her, and went inside the house. Amy stared after him, her mouth suddenly dry. He made her nervous enough when he was acting nice. She followed him inside, closing the door behind her, but not bolting it, just in case.

He went into the kitchen. Jerking out a chair, he turned it, straddled the seat and folded his arms across its back. Amy moseyed toward him, pretending with little success to be unaffected by his stormy behavior. He angled her a sharp glance and inclined his head at another chair. Heart pounding like a kettledrum, she sat down, settled her navy blue skirts around her, and opened her lesson book. Having him here was what she wanted, wasn't it? She was getting her second chance to teach him something, and she wasn't about to let it be spoiled. He couldn't stay angry forever, after all.

Determined, Amy began the lesson with some two-sided letter cards she had made with this exercise especially in mind. She held up the *A,* explained what he was to do, and then waited while he regarded her in sullen silence.

"Swift, I know you recognize this letter," she admonished him. "Are you going to apply yourself to this challenge or not?"

"Which of us is the biggest coward, Amy?" He leaned forward slightly. "You called me a coward for giving up on book learning, so here I am, willing to let you teach me. Now I'm calling you a coward, for giving up on life. Do you have the guts to let me teach you a few things?"

Amy stared at him, the card still held aloft.

He reached over and snatched it from her taut fingers. "That's an *A,* as in *ass.*"

Clinging to her composure, she watched him lay the card on the table. "It also has a long sound, as in plate."

"Or as in waist." His gaze dropped to her middle. "I could span yours with my hands, if you'd ever let me get close to you."

Amy set her jaw and held up the next card. He gave it a lazy perusal and said, "That's a *B,* as in *bottom* or *breast.*" He trailed his gaze to her bodice and arched an eyebrow. "Nice, very nice."

"It's also a *B* as in *bastard!*" Amy shot up from the chair, disappointment, embarrassment, and anger warring for supremacy. "I can see you didn't come here to learn anything. If you think I'm going to sit here, suffering your verbal abuse for an hour, you've got another think."

"Have I made a mistake? *B,* the buh sound, breast. I think I got it right."

She slapped the cards down on the table, so furious that she dropped several on the floor. He bent over to sweep them up. "That's an *H,* as in *honey,* and I'll bet that's how you taste." He flashed her an infuriating grin. "Honey, from one sweet end to the other."

"That is quite enough."

"No, sweetheart, that's life."

"Maybe in your books. But I can do without that particular facet of living, thank you."

"Because you're shaking-in-your-boots scared, that's why. The Amy I knew was a fighter. You ran out and faced a war party of Comanches when you were twelve, toting a rifle bigger than you were. Do you remember that?"

"Loretta's life was on the line. I had no choice."

"And now it's your life on the line, and mine. And you still don't have a choice. Because I'm not going to give you one, damn it! The Amy I knew didn't jump at her own shadow and run from what she knew she wanted. Are you willing to let what Santos did to you ruin your whole life? It's been fifteen years. And he's still torturing you every day and every night. Fight back, Amy. Bury him."

Chest heaving, she retreated a step. "How can you claim to know what I want? I have what I want, Swift." She gestured at the house, her hand trembling. "A home, a job I love, friends. And you want me to give it all up? For what? So you can tell me what to say and when to say it? What to do and how to do it? Maybe my life isn't what you think it should be, but I'm happy."

"Are you? Do you even know what you're missing? Let me give you a taste of what you could have. Haven't you ever looked at Hunter and Loretta and *wanted?* A home, with a fire in the hearth at night, and kids, and laughter?" He laid the cards that he had gathered on the table. Nodding toward the top one, he said, "That's an *L,* as in *love,* and I love you more than I'll ever be able to tell you with words. I want to tell you in other ways. In the way I kiss you. In the way I touch you. In the way I hold you. Won't you let me say it my way, just once?"

She glared at the upturned card. "That's

not an *L.* It's a *T.*"

He gave a soft laugh. "I don't believe you sometimes."

"The feeling's mutual. You need your mouth scrubbed with lye soap."

"Look at me, Amy."

She knew she shouldn't, that he was in a dangerous mood and that she was feeling particularly vulnerable, but the gentle plea in his voice compelled her. She immediately regretted complying. The moment her gaze met his, a rush of dangerous emotions swept through her.

"I promised you I'd try to change, because I'm in the white world now and I want —" He broke off, looking deep into her eyes. "I want to live. Really live. And you're my last chance. Wolf's Landing is my last chance. Can you understand that? If I can't make it here, among friends, where in hell can I make it?"

"Oh, Swift, don't . . ."

"Don't what? Tell you the truth? Don't make you feel sorry for me? By God, I'll play on your sympathy if I have to."

She squeezed her eyes closed. "Don't."

"Do you think I rode two thousand miles on a whim? I was running, damn it, running for my life!" He half rose from the chair, hands braced on its back. The sound of movement brought her eyes open. "And when I got here, I found you — alive and so beautiful it was like finding a dream. I can't turn my back on that. I *can't!* Not because I'm a stubborn bastard, but because there's nothing else. Nothing. Do you understand?"

The heartbreak was that she did.

He gestured at himself. "No conchae, no guns, no spurs, no poncho. I'm clean-shaven. Loretta trimmed my hair last night. And I'm here to try, one more time, to learn my letters and numbers. What have you done to fulfill your part of the bargain? You said you'd try to meet me halfway. What have you done?"

"Nothing," she admitted. And then in a rush she added, "I don't know how to fulfill my part. Every time I think about it, I feel —"

"You feel what?"

"Trapped," she whispered.

"You promised to try," he reminded her. "And I've waited patiently, which isn't in my nature. I want equal time, Amy."

"What?"

"Equal time. I'll learn my letters and numbers, but in return, you have to make an effort to learn to trust me again."

Amy's first inclination was to say no. But then uncertainty hit her. These last two weeks Swift truly had made an effort to change, trying every way he knew to please her. But more important was what he hadn't done, which was to throw her across his horse and run off with her, as she had at first feared he might. Because he hadn't, her attitude toward him was changing already, which tantalized her and made her wonder. Was the Swift she once knew lurking under the hard, dangerous facade of Swift Lopez? If he was, Amy yearned to find him. For, hesitant though she was to admit it, she had never stopped loving him.

"Equal time," she ventured hesitantly. "What exactly do you mean by that?"

"Just how it sounds. For every hour I spend on book learning, I want you to spend an hour with me."

She nibbled her lip, watching him, trying to read him. His expression gave nothing away. "Would you promise not to . . ."

"Not to what?" he asked softly.

She gathered her courage and plunged ahead. "Not to touch me while we're together."

His eyes warmed on hers. "No promises, Amy. The whole idea is for you to trust me."

"I thought the idea was to get reacquainted."

He smiled. "Exactly. And I don't want a

bunch of rules muddying the water."

She made the mistake of looking directly into his eyes again, and an electrical feeling charged the air between them, making her skin tingle.

"Say yes," he urged. "Trust me, Amy — one more time. You did once, a long time ago. Remember? And I never broke faith. Can't you take another gamble on me?"

Her heart began to slam.

"I've already promised you I'll never hurt you," he reminded her. "If you stop and think about it, doesn't that pretty much cover most of the things you're afraid might happen?"

In Amy's experience, it covered them all. Her fear was that she and Swift had different definitions of hurting. "Yes."

"Well then?"

She licked her lips, feeling reckless, as if something wonderful just beyond her line of vision awaited her and she had only to step forward to see it. "If I say yes, will you give me the option of calling the whole thing off if I'm not comfortable with it?"

He hesitated a moment, as if thinking that over, then grinned. "That sounds fair, as long as you don't call it off when you still owe me time. Agreed?"

"Agreed."

For a long moment, he looked up at her. Then, so softly she almost couldn't hear him, he said, "You won't regret this. I promise you that."

Legs atremble, Amy perched stiffly on the chair and gathered up the cards again. Swift watched her, looking smugly pleased with himself. She hoped that didn't bode ill.

Amy had planned an hour's lesson, but Swift somehow managed to stretch one hour to two. She suspected that he did so with an ulterior motive, which became apparent the moment they finished working. He demanded his two hours of equal time, right away.

"Now?" She glanced up at the small window above them. "But it's dark. Loretta will be waiting dinner on you. Besides, what could we possibly do to pass two hours?"

"We can take a walk — and talk. I told Loretta I'd be late."

Amy liked the hesitation in his voice before he said "talk" even less than she did the mischievous twinkle in his eye.

"I can't go walking after dark. It's out of the question. If people saw us, you know what they'd think. I have my teaching position to think of."

"Who'll see us? Do you think people peer

out their windows at your front porch all night?"

"But they're bound to see us walking. People do come and go around town after dark."

"I have no intention of walking around town."

Her eyes widened. "Where do you plan to go walking, then?"

"In the woods."

"What?"

"Trust me, Amy." He draped her shawl around her shoulders and steered her toward the door. "That's what all this is about, remember? Trust. Do you really believe I have anything other than your best interests at heart?"

"I'm just afraid you might have an entirely different idea of what's good for me than I do," she admitted.

He laughed and pulled the door closed behind them. Amy peered into the gloom, liking this idea less by the moment.

"Swift, it's going to be pitch dark any minute, and you know how blind I am at night."

"I can see fine." His hand closed around her elbow. "I won't let you fall, Amy. Relax. Remember when we were kids, running wild along the river after dark? You'd grab my belt and trail along behind me when you couldn't see."

"I remember you tripping once, too, and both of us falling down a bank."

He led her across her yard toward the trees. About two hundred yards away, the schoolhouse loomed like a ghostly specter.

"I tripped on purpose."

"You didn't."

"I did." He angled her a warm look. "I stole a hug at the bottom of that bank, if you'll recall."

Amy squinted to see ahead of them. "Swift, the woods are so dark. Let's walk along the boardwalk."

"Nope. I want you alone with me, out of shouting distance of everybody."

Her heart leaped. "Why?"

He drew her closer as they circled a tree in their path. Taking advantage of the moment, he released her elbow and slipped his arm around her. His hand, large and warm, stole under her shawl to settle on her side, his fingertips staking claim just below her right breast. Amy stiffened and grabbed instinctively for his wrist.

"Trust, Amy," he reproved. "That hand's not going anywhere."

She shot a glance over her shoulder toward town, her heart sinking when she saw that they were already beyond shouting distance. Her throat tightened. Against her better judgement, she relinquished her hold on his wrist.

The two hours loomed ahead of her, promising to be the most nerve-racking of her life. She began to wish she never had sought Swift out yesterday, that she had used her head and encouraged him to leave for Texas instead of challenging his pride. More fool she, for here she was, traipsing toward the woods with him, half his size, blind as a bat, and undeniably stupid for ever letting him talk her into this insanity in the first place.

Swift led her toward Shallows Creek, *led* being the operative word, because it soon grew so dark inside the timber that she couldn't see. An owl hooted and swooshed down at them, nearly scaring her out of her skin. She instinctively pressed closer to Swift, and once he had tightened his hold on her, he seemed loath to loosen it. Her hip bumped his thigh as they walked.

Soon she could hear the rushing of the water. They came upon a clearing, bathed in bright moonlight, the trees gilded silver, the shadows cast into frightening blackness. Swift led her to a huge fallen log and, seizing her by the waist, swung her up to sit on it. She braced her palms on either side of her, gazing down at him nervously, unsettled to have her feet dangling so far above the ground when she couldn't see what lay below her.

A looming shadow dressed in black, he hopped up beside her, looping his arms around one knee. The moonbeams shone upon his face and glistened in his ebony hair where it curled across his forehead. Looking over at him, she could only wonder what in God's name she was doing out here alone with him.

After gazing at the water for a long while, he turned his head to study her, his eyes black splashes against the dark planes of his face. "Well, Miss Amy, this is the moment you've been dreading, isn't it? You're completely alone with me. There's no one to come if you scream. What's supposed to happen next? I'd sure hate to disappoint a lady."

She swallowed and toyed nervously with the fringe on her shawl. "I, um . . ." She glanced over at him. "I guess that's up to you. That was the whole idea, wasn't it?"

His teeth shimmered in the moonlight as he grinned — a slow, smug grin that sent her heart into a skitter. "I was thinking about doing something you never expected, something that would take you totally by surprise, now that I've got you out here, completely at my mercy."

"L-like what?" she asked in a small voice.

"Like talking." His grin widened. "That is the last thing you expected, isn't it?"

Relief made her feel giddy. "Yes," she admitted with an airy little laugh. "What shall we talk about?"

"I don't know. Anything about me you're dying to know?"

Her smile faded. "Yes. What made you start carrying a gun? You never were one to kill merely for the sake of killing or for fighting without a cause. How did it happen that killing became a part of your daily life?"

"It wasn't exactly daily, Amy. Sometimes I went weeks, even months, without using my gun." He sighed and shifted his position slightly. "As for picking up a gun in the first place, it was fate, mostly. You know me and weapons. Rowlins, my boss, taught me to shoot a revolver." He shrugged. "It's a necessary skill when you're a cowhand. And once he taught me the basics, I practiced every day, until I felt I could handle it well."

She remembered how accomplished Swift had been with other weapons, how important that had been to him as a warrior. "So, of course you became excellent."

"Fair."

"Swift, I read the news story. They say you're the fastest gun in Texas, maybe the fastest anywhere."

He scowled into the darkness. "After the first gunfight, I had to be fast. Once you kill a gunslinger, there's no end to it. Your reputation follows you everywhere you go, and there's always someone who wants to test his skill against you. You either draw or die. In my first fight, I had the misfortune of killing a man who had a name. I went to town with the fellows one Saturday night, he saw me, didn't like my looks, and challenged me. From that night on, my life became a nightmare."

"What if — what if someone follows you here?"

He sighed. "I hope no one does."

"But if someone does?"

He turned to regard her, all trace of a grin gone. "The coward in me will draw on him. Remember what I said to you about wishing you could die, and it not being that easy? I know firsthand. I've tried not to go for my gun at least a dozen times — promised myself I wouldn't — but when the smoke cleared, I was still standing." He studied her for a long while. "You're not the only one to ever feel afraid, you know. We all do sometimes. Unfortunately for the other fellow, the more afraid I am, the faster I can draw."

"Surely you don't wish —" She tried to read his expression and couldn't because of the shadows. "Those men would have killed you. Why would you want to let them?"

"They weren't always men." He gazed into the trees, his body immobile, not even appearing to breathe for a moment. "You saw Chase's eyes that first night when he was asking about my gunfights. Some were kids, Amy, just a few years older than Chase. Legally, I guess you could call them men . . . nineteen, twenty, some a little older. But that isn't much consolation when you look into their faces." He waved a hand as if he couldn't find the words to express how that had felt. "Boys who practiced slapping leather until they thought they could take me. They were dead wrong." He swallowed. When he continued, his voice sounded hollow. "Me or them, that's what it boiled down to, and sometimes — sometimes I wished it was me."

Amy dug her nails into the bark of the log. Averting her face, she said, "I'm sorry, Swift. I shouldn't have asked about something so painful." She yearned to ask him about why he had become a comanchero, how he could have betrayed her that way, but now, after hearing the pain in his voice, she couldn't.

His voice went gravelly. "Don't be sorry. I think it's something you need to know. I never set out to be a gunslinger. It just happened." He grew quiet a moment. "What else do you want to know?"

Her heart aching for him, she sighed and glanced at his face. "Who took a knife to you?"

His mouth twisted. "I did."

She turned to stare at him. "You? But why?"

"It's a mourning scar," he said huskily.

Amy knew enough about the Comanches to realize that men only scarred their faces when close relatives or their women died. "You lost someone very dear to you, then?"

"I lost everyone who was dear to me," he replied. "This scar was for the woman I loved. Because of the war, we were separated. When I learned of her death, I marked my face."

Amy closed her eyes. She had always known, deep down, that Swift was bound to have found someone else. Fifteen years was a very long time. She took a deep, cleansing breath and opened her eyes again. "I'm so sorry, Swift. I didn't know. . . . Did you have children?"

He tipped his head, studying her. "We haven't yet."

She nearly nodded, then realized what he had said. "But I thought you said she —" Amy's eyes widened and shifted to the scar. A horrible trembling seized her. "Oh, God, Swift, no."

"Yes," he said solemnly. "You're crazy if you think I ever loved anyone else. There have been women — I won't lie to you about that. Lots of them, over the years. But I never felt anything but a passing fondness for any of them. Everyone has one great love in his or her life, and you were it for me."

Tears blinded Amy. "I never dreamed . . . Why didn't you tell me that first night? Why did you wait?"

"I didn't want you to feel like I was using it against you. You would have felt bad. Hell, you feel bad now. I just didn't think telling you was fair."

"I don't feel bad," she said tightly. "I feel devastated. You're face was so — so beautiful."

He narrowed one eye at her. "Beautiful? Amy, you're beautiful."

"So were you." She caught her lip between her teeth. "You still are, in a different way.

The scar gives you a certain look — *character,* I guess would be the word."

"That's because it has your name on it."

The tears in her eyes spilled over onto her cheeks. "Oh, Swift . . . you truly did love me, didn't you? Every bit as much as I loved you."

"I still love you. Die on me, and I'll slash my other cheek. I'll be so ugly no other woman will have me. And I won't care. You're the only woman I ever wanted, the only one I'll ever want." He fished in his pocket and pulled out his Bull Durham pouch. "And you know what?" he asked as he rolled a cigarette. "You still love me just as much as you ever did. You're just too damned scared to admit it."

She wiped at her cheeks. "I love the memories of you," she whispered. "I never stopped loving the memories. Even when I learned you were a comanchero, I couldn't burn my sketch of you, because I still loved the boy you were."

Swift struck a lucifer and lit his cigarette. Waving out the match, he flicked it into the creek with his finger, then took a deep drag, slowly exhaling smoke. "I wish we could go back." He turned his head toward her, his shadowed eyes looking haunted. "I wish I could undo everything I've done, Amy. But

I can't. I'm not the boy you knew. I never can be again. I can only be who I am now."

"We've both changed."

Swift nodded. "I know I refused to accept that when I first came here, but it's the truth, and only a fool denies what smacks him right between the eyes. I've changed. And so have you — so much that sometimes I'm not sure the girl you were ever existed. At first I tried to force you to be the way I remembered you. But it isn't in you anymore. You finally popped me in the nose, but only because I pushed until you didn't have much choice."

Amy shivered and hugged her shawl close. "I was a very foolish girl back then, with more temper than brains sometimes."

He chuckled. "You were glorious! If ever anyone had Comanche heart, it was you, blond hair, blue eyes, and all. Even at the very worst times, when you were the most terrified of me, I could see the courage in your eyes. What happened to you, Amy? Have you ever asked yourself that?"

She tipped her head back, smiling at the memories with a trace of sadness she couldn't quite conceal. "Life happened," she said softly. "The little girl grew up, and she found out the hard way that all the courage in the world didn't put any thrust behind her fist when she pitted herself against a man."

Swift studied her intently, watching the bitter twist to her mouth, knowing that she smiled only because the alternative was to weep — which she would never do. "Santos? Tell me, Amy. I thought — well, after Santos, I thought you came through it, that you were all right."

She shivered again and spoke slowly. "A person never gets all right after something like that. I lived through it and kept my sanity. Wasn't that enough?" She turned tear-bright eyes on him again, eyes that reached clear down inside him and wrenched his heart. "I'm sorry I'm a disappointment to you. But like you, I can't go back. I am the way I am."

"Honey, you're not a disappointment to me. Don't ever think that."

"Yes," she said in a taut voice. "I'm even a disappointment to myself sometimes. But there we are, hm? The cloth's been cut. I am who I am."

"I just want to know you as you are," he said softly. "The other night, after you hit me, when you described how I was making you feel, I realized I was going about things wrong. I'm sorry for that. But, mistakes or no, I love you, Amy, the girl you were, and the woman you are."

She shook her head. "No. You don't know who I am, Swift, not really. You loved a girl who was glorious. You said it yourself. There's no glory left. I'm just a humdrum teacher, in a safe little town, in a safe little house, with a safe little life." She peered through the gloom at him. "You should find someone glorious. You should! A woman you can admire, someone feisty, like Indigo will be. A woman like me has to have her battles fought *for* her."

"Then let me be the one who fights them," he said huskily.

Her luminous eyes caught the moonlight, shimmering at him like prisms. "Until you came along, there weren't any battles to fight. I liked it that way."

He conceded the point by inclining his head. Studying the orange tip of his cigarette, he said, "I let you ask me questions. Now it's my turn for one. Agreed?"

She hesitated, then with reluctance said, "I lead a pretty boring life, but I guess that's fair."

He lifted his head, snubbed out his cigarette, and slid off the log. Stepping over to her, he leaned his chest against her knees and encircled her waist with his arms. After looking up into her face for a long while, he said, "What is it that you dream about?"

She smiled. "What does everyone dream about? Lots of things."

Swift watched her, feeling the sudden tension in her body. "That isn't fair, Amy. I answered your questions. I've only asked this one, and I'd like a truthful, complete answer."

Even in the moonlight, he saw her grow pale. "I dream of Santos and his men. And sometimes about —" The corners of her mouth quivered. "Sometimes about my stepfather, Henry Masters."

Swift knew by the pain in her expression that she had told him the unveiled truth. "And what happens in your nightmares?"

"How do you know I have them? Did Hunter tell you?"

"Yes." It wasn't actually a lie. Swift didn't want to embarrass her by admitting he had heard her screams. "What happens in them, Amy?"

She fidgeted in his embrace, her gaze chasing off from his. "You know what I dream of. Over and over, the same thing."

"And the dreams about your stepfather?"

She hesitated, looking more and more uncomfortable with his questions. "You know how silly dreams are. Half the time they don't make much sense."

Swift's stomach tightened. He struggled to pose his next question matter-of-factly, not wishing to press her for information she didn't want to reveal, but feeling a need to know more. "How old were you when your mother died, Amy?"

"Sixteen." She brushed at her forehead, her trembling hands a telltale sign that she was hiding something. "Cholera took her. It hit fast, and within two days, I was digging her grave."

Swift remembered the writing on the cross, how he had touched his fingers to the letters, never dreaming that Amy's hand had carved them. "How old were you when you came here?"

She looked uneasy and took a deep, shaky breath. "I was, um, about nineteen." She flashed him an unconvincing smile. "My, how the years do fly. It hardly seems possible I've been here eight years."

Swift's throat closed off so that he had difficulty asking the next question. "Why didn't you wait for me in Texas, Amy, like we agreed?"

She couldn't seem to meet his gaze. "I . . ." She wrinkled her nose. "I never did like Texas very much. Not where we lived. And Henry cottoned to the mescal jug a little more than I liked. So one night, when he was in his cups, I got a bee in my bonnet and left."

Swift saw the haunted look in her guileless eyes, the fragile pride in the determined lift of her chin, and the guilt he felt nearly bent him double. He still wasn't certain what had happened to her. He only knew that he had promised her he would come for her, and the war had kept him from doing so. While he had fought so valiantly for his people, there had been no one to fight the battles for Amy.

Chapter 10

Holding Amy's face between his hands, Swift moved his thumbs along her fragile cheekbones, his fingertips electrified where wisps of her silken hair touched. Bathed in moonlight, she shimmered, her coronet of hair a halo, her skin gleaming like polished silver, her beautiful eyes aglisten and so deep that he got lost looking into them. He couldn't imagine anyone hurting her. But apparently someone had. Henry Masters? And if so, what had he done? After so long a time, Swift supposed it no longer really mattered. The here and now was what he had to deal with. And yet . . .

"Did you say you decided to leave Texas at night?"

She shrugged. "Well, not exactly at night. One evening. It was still light out."

"What'd you do? Take one of Henry's horses?"

Her mouth trembled. "I, um, we didn't

have a horse. Henry sold it. He wasn't much for working. And the drink cost him. He ran low on funds there at the last and sold it to a peddler."

"Oh." He considered that for a moment, wishing he could just let it drop. "One of the mules, then?"

He felt the resistance drain out of her. "I walked."

"What?"

"I walked," she repeated. "One night, after he got drunk, I got my extra shoes out of the loft and I set out walking."

Swift swallowed a rush of fear, which came eight years too late. "What happened to the mules?"

"One got sick."

"There were two. What happened to the other one?"

"He, um —" She licked her lips, avoiding his gaze. "He shot it."

Swift's heart started to slam. "Why in hell did he shoot the mule?"

She twisted her face from his grasp and looked around her, as if seeking a way to escape. "I — You know, it's getting awfully chilly out here." Gathering her shawl around her, she shivered, still avoiding his gaze. "Winter's coming. I can feel it in the air — can't you?"

Swift eased back, giving her some space, which he sensed she needed — perhaps desperately. "Yes, it's getting nippy all right." He waited a moment, picturing her walking across the endless Texas plains. Suddenly he realized he didn't know the meaning of the word *courage.* "Amy, why did Henry shoot the mule? Was it ailing? Or was he just having a temper fit?"

With a panicked look in her eyes, she jerked away from him and pushed off the log. Swift managed to catch her from falling. When he set her on her feet, she twisted away from him. He dogged her heels, afraid she might trip over something she couldn't see. "I want to go home now," she said in a thin voice. "I'm getting awfully chilly. Really I am. And I —" She broke off and took a jagged breath. "Don't ask me any more questions, Swift. Please?"

He stepped around her so he could see her face. "Amy, can you look at me?"

She made a strangled sound and averted her face. "I want to go home now."

"Amy . . ."

"I want to go home."

"All right. But look at me for just one minute."

"No. You'll just ask more questions. I don't want to talk about it, not now, not ever. I never meant for you to know, and now I want you to pretend you don't."

Swift still wasn't exactly sure what he supposedly knew. He could only guess. The suspicions roiling through him made him feel sick. "I can't pretend we never talked like this."

"Then stay away from me."

"I can't do that, either. Amy, don't look at the ground."

"Don't start."

"Don't start what?"

"Preaching."

Swift made a futile gesture with his hands. "I'm the last person to preach. I just say things that are true."

"I know all about your truths . . . tomorrows on the horizon and stars in the heavens, and keeping your eyes ahead of you."

"You've got a good memory."

"I also know what happens if you walk around without watching your feet. Don't waste your breath saying pretty things to me, Swift."

He reached out and touched her bowed head. "Amy, without pretty things, what do any of us have?"

"Reality." She sniffed and finally looked up at him. "Will you take me home now?"

Swift knew the mere fact that she believed

he would take her home was a small victory. For tonight he'd have to settle for that. "Can I say just one more thing first?"

Resignation crossed her face. "I suppose you'll say it anyway, so do it and get it done."

"I'm sorry I wasn't there."

Her mouth tightened, and an ache crept into her eyes. "I'm sorry you weren't, too."

Swift slid his hand to her nape and drew her forward into a walk, guiding her through the darkness as he would have liked to guide her through the rest of her life. Amy had become a whole lot more than just night blind.

When her house came into view, Amy felt relieved. Swift hadn't even tried to kiss her while they were in the woods. She wondered if it was because of what he had learned about her. She shoved the thought away, determined not to let it hurt. Very little got past her defenses nowadays.

She didn't want to be kissed, anyway. Not by him, not by anyone. Especially not by him. The thought terrified her. Once he got into a habit of that, he'd press for more. If he ran scared after tonight, so much the better. Her life could return to normal. After him, she'd never have to worry that another man might gain power over her. She'd be able to stop feeling threatened, stop feeling off balance, stop feeling, period.

Swift was dangerous for her in more ways than one. He always had been a dreamer, reaching for pretty things over the horizon that didn't exist. As a child, she had let him spin his dreams around her, and she had believed . . . for a while. Dreams had a way of shattering, though, and when they did it was sometimes impossible to pick up the pieces.

As she stepped onto her porch, he pulled his timepiece from his pocket and tipped it in the moonlight.

"I timed that perfectly," he said. "We made it with ten minutes to spare."

Amy hugged her shawl close. "How can you tell time when you can't count?"

He closed the watch and returned it to his pocket. "I can't tell it real good. But what I do know, Rowlins taught me. The straight numbers make more sense to me than your curly ones."

The breeze picked up, cool and brisk, slipping icy fingers down the collar of her dress. She shivered and hunched her shoulders. "Curly ones?" She considered that a moment. "I guess my numbers are kind of curly, aren't they?"

He didn't seem interested in pursuing the topic. He put a boot on the bottom step and brought his face level with hers. She liked being eye to eye; it made him seem less intimidating.

"Well . . ." She shivered again. "Thank you for the nice walk. It was a pleasant two hours."

"Less ten minutes," he reminded her. "We're still on my time. I figure that's plenty of time to say good night."

"I've never taken ten minutes to say good night in my life."

"There's a first time for everything."

He placed a hand on her waist and drew her against his chest. His other hand cupped the back of her head. Looking into his eyes, Amy knew he meant to kiss her. So much for his running scared. She started to move away, but his fingers fisted in her hair to hold her still, and his hand slid from her waist to the small of her back. She felt the leashed strength in him and knew struggling would be futile. As it had always been.

"Swift, please don't."

"It's my equal time, Amy. Ten more minutes. You're welshing on our bargain."

Her gaze fell to his mouth. Suddenly she couldn't breathe.

"What can happen on your doorstep?" he

asked huskily, his mouth coming closer and closer to hers. "Relax, and see for yourself how my kisses feel. Now, while you feel safe, while you have the security of other people nearby."

She couldn't deny that his reasoning made sense. As long as no one saw them, it was better that he kiss her here, if he was bent on doing it, than down along the creek somewhere. She tipped her head slightly, bracing herself, quite certain his mouth would be as hungry and demanding as the glow in his eyes.

His warm breath mingled with hers. Amy swallowed and closed her eyes, keeping her teeth tightly clenched. And then his lips touched hers, so lightly, with such incredible gentleness, that the contact seemed whisper soft. Carefully . . . so very carefully that it took her breath and made her want to weep. There was no demand here, no bruising hunger, only a promise of incredible sweetness that made her lips part, wanting and expectant. She clutched his shirt, leaning closer, but he maintained the featherlight pressure, refusing her what she sought. Which was just as well, because she wasn't sure what it was she wanted, only that . . .

"Amy . . ." Her name came off his lips

256

like a caress. He trailed his mouth across her cheek to her ear, then explored the curve of her neck. "Amy, my sweet, precious Amy. I love you."

And suddenly she knew what he had meant about giving him the chance to say it his way. His hand trembled on her back. His lips worshiped. No harsh taking, no grasping, no force. Just tender, whisper-soft kisses that set her skin afire and her senses reeling. She couldn't feel her legs and feared she might fall, but his strong body was there to hold her erect, warm and solid, his heart thudding robustly, a steady cadence in contrast to the wild fluttering of hers.

When he at last lifted his head, she couldn't move away from him. He ran his hands up her arms, touched her cheek, the tip of her nose, a curl at her temple, soothing her, as if he knew how painfully her heart lurched and how weak her legs felt. The expression on his face when he looked at her made her feel cherished and, at the same time, vulnerable.

"Promise me something," he murmured.

"Every time I turn around, you're asking for another concession," she whispered.

"I know, but this one is important." He cupped his hand to her chin and looked deep into her eyes. "When you lie down tonight and close your eyes to fall asleep, take me with you. If the nightmares come, dream that I'm there." He pressed his cheek to hers. She felt wetness touch her skin. "Don't face them alone anymore."

She couldn't have spoken if she tried, so she only nodded. He turned and strode away into the darkness. Amy stood there staring after him for a very long time and then, with trembling fingertips, touched the tear on her cheek.

Swift saw that a light was still burning in the parlor when he walked up the steps to Hunter's house. Uncertain whether Loretta had left it on for him or if someone was still awake, he opened the front door as quietly as he could. Loretta glanced up from her rocker, her darning needle poised in midair.

"Hello there," she whispered, flashing him a smile.

"I'm surprised you're still up," he whispered back.

She inclined her head at the sock she was mending. "I wanted to finish this first. Are you hungry?"

"Not really." Swift crossed to the hearth and pulled Hunter's stool around so he could sit and warm his hands at the fire. The lantern on the small table at Loretta's elbow made a steady hissing sound that was oddly soothing. "It's a chilly one out there tonight. Winter won't be long in coming."

She lowered her work to her lap, studying him for a moment. "What are you so low in the lip about?"

He forced a smile. "Do I look low in the lip?"

"Is Amy all right?"

"Right as rain. We just got back from a nice long walk."

Loretta arched a brow, her expression incredulous. "Amy went for a walk? Alone with you? After dark?"

"Just down to the creek. But it's a start."

Her mouth turned up at the corners, and a twinkle crept into her eyes. "I'd say you're making fine progress."

"Better than a kick in the fanny, anyway." He braced the heels of his hands on the stool and shifted his weight. "We just talked, catching up on the years a bit." He hesitated. "I never realized until tonight that Amy stayed in Texas with her stepfather for quite a while after her mother died."

Loretta nodded. "For about three years." She darted her needle in and out through several threads on the sock heel, then tugged the weave tight. "The moment we heard about Aunt Rachel's death, Hunter and I sent Amy money to come to Oregon. She sent it straight back, along with a nice letter telling us she was perfectly happy in Texas and that Henry needed her on the farm. She didn't feel right deserting him so soon after Aunt Rachel died, and I can't say as I can fault her for that. Families should stick together in times of loss."

"Did she write often?"

"Fairly often. Which relieved our minds."

"Why's that?"

Taking more bites with her needle, Loretta touched her toes to the floor to set the rocker in motion. "There was a time when Henry wasn't exactly what you'd call easy to get along with. Hunter and I were concerned at first about Amy living clear out there alone with him." She glanced up. "Aunt Rachel always did claim he had some good in him, and if we looked hard enough and long enough, we'd finally see it." She chuckled. "I reckon she was right. After she died, he was good to our Amy, and that wipes the slate clean as far as I'm concerned."

The hair on Swift's nape prickled. "You two didn't get along well, then?"

Loretta's hands froze over her darning. After a moment she resumed her stitching. "I guess you might say that once I matured out, Henry tried to get along too well with me." She wrinkled her nose. "I suppose, me just being his niece by marriage and him being Aunt Rachel's second husband, he didn't think of me as being blood kin. He always did have a wandering eye that took him off to the fancy house in Jacksboro about once a month." Her mouth tightened. "When I got up in years, his eye didn't have to wander quite so far."

"That must have been hell for you, living in the same house with him."

"Luckily, Hunter was there and intervened the one time Henry tried to press the issue, and before it ever happened again, Hunter took me away from the farm."

Swift gripped the edge of the stool. "What was Henry like otherwise?"

She squinted down at the sock and took another stitch. "After his being so good to Amy, I hate to speak ill of him. He mended his ways. A body should forgive and forget."

"It'll never go beyond me."

She sighed. "Well, to be honest, there was a time when he had a mean streak a mile wide."

"How was he mean?"

She stopped the rocker, her eyes growing distant. "Oh, nothing that awful, I guess. Although, when I was on the wrong end of

261

a razor strop, it seemed pretty awful, especially when I didn't feel I'd done any wrong to deserve it." She met his gaze, her face softening with memories. "Mostly, though, it was Amy who took the brunt. Her growing-up years weren't easy. For a long while, Aunt Rachel seemed afraid to stand up to Henry. And I was mute after my parents were massacred. Amy was the only one to give him lip. He never quite measured up to her real father in her eyes. And he tended to settle arguments with Aunt Rachel by using his fists. You remember what a little spitfire Amy was. She'd jump right into the fray. Henry wasn't one to take sass, and sass was her middle name."

Swift smiled. "More temper than brains, is how she puts it."

"Yes, well, that pretty much hits the nail on the head. No matter how many times Henry took after her with the strop, she never quite learned the art of keeping her mouth shut if she thought he was doing wrong. Given the fact that he tended to get a little too enthusiastic in the woodshed, it wasn't a good mix. He never did her any real harm, I guess. But there were times when I'd have made him stop if I'd been big enough."

She tied off her thread and bent her head

to bite the strands in two. Lowering the mended sock to her lap, she looked up at him.

"It's hard to explain what he was like back then." A frown pleated her brow. "I always had the feeling —" She broke off and smiled. "Lands, talk about water under the bridge."

"What kind of feeling?"

"Oh, I don't know. The feeling he was holding back, that he would've been even ornerier if he could have gotten away with it. I think he knew he could only push Aunt Rachel so far."

"So he kept himself in check?"

"To a degree. All heck broke loose when he found out I was pregnant with Chase Kelly, though. He threatened to kill the baby when it was born — because Hunter was Comanche. Aunt Rachel finally stood up to him then and taught him some manners at the business end of a Sharps carbine. Up against three feisty females who'd had enough of his foul temper, his disposition improved remarkably." She smiled again. "I guess he got into the habit of being nice and got to liking it, hm?"

Swift's face felt stiff. "I guess he must have." After gazing into the fire for a moment, he ventured, "Amy never mentioned

Henry being ornery to her after her mother died, did she? In any of her letters or after she came out here?"

"No. Why? Are you aware of something I'm not?"

"No reason. Just curious, that's all." Swift rolled his shoulders and rubbed the back of his neck, recalling the frantic look on Amy's face when she'd stressed that she had never wanted anyone to know about what he had learned. The problem was that he still wasn't sure what it was he supposedly knew. "I —" He drew his hand from his neck. "I guess if she never said anything, he must have treated her good."

"I'm sure she would have written and come to Oregon if he hadn't."

Swift couldn't argue with that. "And in her letters everything sounded fine?"

"Better than fine! Real cheery — telling us about all the improvements Henry was making on the house, about her garden and the things she put up for winter, about her sewing projects. She sounded happy as a bug."

"If she was so happy, why'd she leave?"

"Mostly just loneliness, I think. The nearest neighbors were miles away. She sent us word that she was working up in Jacksboro for her board and room until she received the money from us for her trip out here. She said the isolation on the farm had been driving her crazy. And Henry was pretty much over losing Aunt Rachel. I reckon she must have felt a long enough time had passed for her to leave."

"How did she get from the farm to Jacksboro?"

"I don't recollect that she ever said. I just assumed Henry took her. Why?"

"No reason. Just curious. Jacksboro's quite a way from the farm, if I recall."

"Is there something you're not telling me?" she asked softly, her large eyes filled with concern.

Swift forced another grin. "No. I'm just piecing the years together, that's all. Amy's changed a lot. Sometimes I get to wondering if something might have happened — something she never told."

Loretta's face relaxed. "Amy has no secrets from me." She studied him a moment. "Don't expect too much, Swift. Amy went through a terrible ordeal with the comancheros, you know. You can't expect her to have come through the years unaffected."

Swift swallowed and looked away. "No, I don't suppose so."

"Give her time. Good things come to he who waits. Deep down, Amy never stopped loving you. That makes her vulnerable. I imagine it's mighty scary to her when she thinks on it."

He took a deep breath and exhaled slowly. "I'm trying to be patient, believe me."

Smiling, she stowed her darning in her work bag and pushed up from her rocker. "It's been a spell, you know. Amy has to get to know you all over again." She placed a hand on his shoulder. "Let her do it in her own time."

He nodded, keeping his gaze averted. He heard her stifle a yawn.

"Well, it's time this old woman got some rest for her weary bones. Good night, Swift."

"G'night, Loretta."

"I'm pleased to hear you convinced Amy to take a stroll."

"No more pleased than I am."

She gave him a pat as she walked past him. Swift returned his gaze to the fire. He heard the soft click of the bedroom door as Loretta closed it behind her. On the heel of that sound, he heard the echo of Amy's voice. *I walked. Got a bee in my bonnet one night and set out walking.* He curled his hands into fists, remembering the haunted look in her eyes.

Over the next week, Amy's routine was

altered to accommodate her tutoring sessions with Swift. For every hour they spent at lessons, Swift demanded that she give him an hour of her company, during which she had to venture away from the settlement with him. Since she taught school during the day and he worked in the mine, their walks occurred at night, after study hour. Amy soon lost her fear that anyone would see them and draw the wrong conclusion. She found herself worrying instead that no one would see them, that some night, after luring her away from town, Swift might take advantage of their aloneness.

That she trusted Swift so little seemed to amuse him, and he made a point at least once every evening of tormenting her about it, making it clear he could take advantage if he chose, but that he didn't choose to that particular night. He was very careful in the way he phrased it so that she didn't misconstrue things and think he meant that he never would. Amy remained uncertain from one moment to the next of what he might do.

That didn't seem to bother Swift in the least. It was as if he were saying, "Think the worst. I don't care. Watch every move I make. Sooner or later, you'll let down your guard." Amy wasn't certain why he toyed with her. Sometimes she longed for him to promise he would never touch her, even if it was a lie, so she could relax and enjoy being with him.

But Swift came with no guarantees.

Her experiences with him were many and varied. One moment he would be serious, the next teasing. Memories of yesterday became steady companions for her. She glimpsed the old Swift sometimes, the carefree boy she had loved so dearly. But usually she was escorted by Swift Lopez, a man with a harsh face and somber, shadow-filled eyes that ached with sorrows she couldn't begin to name. She could only guess at the pain he had suffered, the loved ones he had lost, the hopelessness he had felt.

The following Saturday, a dance social was to be held at Wolf's Landing. Swift asked her to make an appearance there.

"I never go to the socials, Swift," she replied nervously.

"I've only met half the people here in passing. Please, go, Amy. Just for a while. Who am I going to stand with?"

"Don't go."

"I want to go. I'd like to get to know everyone better. I see people on the street, but it isn't the same. And with my reputation on their minds, they're leery. The social will give me a chance to show them I'm just ordinary, like them. That I want to be part of the community."

Swift, ordinary? "I'll think about it," she conceded.

"Think real hard. It's just one silly social. If you hate it, you don't ever have to attend one again."

Amy agonized for three days over whether or not she should go, her heart slamming every time she imagined dancing with Swift. In all her adult life she had never attended a real dance, and the thought gave her butterflies. What if she went, and Swift didn't come? What if she didn't, and he did? He might be left standing alone, shunned by the townspeople. Or he might meet someone else. . . .

That thought panicked Amy, though she wasn't willing to analyze why. If he found someone else, it would be so much the better, wouldn't it? She sought Loretta's advice. Loretta immediately searched her wardrobe for a dress Amy might wear.

"This one is perfect!" Loretta cried, swirling around her bedroom with a blue silk gown held before her. "It's just the color of your eyes, Amelia Rose. Swift will take one look at you and think he's died and gone straight to heaven."

"But, Loretta . . ." Amy fingered the low-cut bodice. "I can't wear this. It's beautiful, but it just isn't me."

"Lands, Amy, do you think Swift doesn't know you've got bosoms? This dress is modest compared to most. Be a little daring for once in your life. I'll help you with your hair. You'll be so lovely. Why, I'll bet he pays a fortune to buy your dinner basket so he can eat with you."

"I'm not taking any dinner basket."

"But all the unmarried women take dinner baskets to the auction. Either you'll fix one or I will. Do you want him buying someone else's?"

"I've never even attended a social before, and I've sure enough never taken a dinner basket to the auction. And I'm not going to start now. It's undignified, women letting strange men bid for their company." Amy wrinkled her nose.

"You're just afraid someone besides Swift might buy it."

"Maybe I wouldn't even want him to. If I spend an evening with a gentleman, I want it to be because I choose to, not because he's paid five dollars of his hard-earned money. I'd feel obligated to spend the entire evening there."

"Oh, Amy, what will Swift do if you leave early? I'd like this evening to go well for him. Why not go all out? Take a basket to auction. Swift will be hungry after working all day."

"I can pack a basket and not put it up for auction," Amy reminded her, swatting wrinkles out of the dress's skirt.

"What fun would that be? You're not an old married woman like me. It's supposed to be exciting, having a man pay through his nose to spend a night with you."

"Ask May Belle over at the saloon how exciting it is."

"Lawzy, Amy, you are odd turned. How can you compare a dinner basket auction with May Belle's profession?"

"Because a dinner basket auction is sort of the same. Do you think those men buy a basket so they can just sit down and eat? They can eat what their mothers bring."

Loretta giggled. "I reckon maybe you've got a point. Thinking back on it, I can remember Hunter polishing off more than a few meals and then looking at me like I was dessert."

Amy grinned. "Wear this dress Saturday night and I bet he has dessert before dinner."

Loretta blushed. "With two kids in the

loft, we have dessert a long while after dinner, and that's a certainty." She heaved a wistful sigh, running her fingers over the silk. "Oh, Amy, I do wish you'd take a basket and let Swift bid on it. You've missed out on all the fun things, you know it?"

"Pardon me, Loretta, but having a man nibble a chicken leg while he's got his eye on me isn't my idea of fun. I don't want any money changing hands, and that's that."

"Well, will you at least wear the dress?"

Amy gnawed her lip, running a loving hand along one sleeve. "It is glorious, isn't it?"

"And perfect for you."

"What're you going to wear, if I wear this?"

"My rose silk. It's Hunter's favorite." Loretta shoved the dress into Amy's arms. "Take it."

"I'm not even sure I'm going to go yet."

"If you don't go, I'm gonna skin you alive."

"What if the widower, Mr. Black, asks me to dance?"

Loretta shuddered. "Tell him you don't dance. It isn't a lie. Except for here at the house, I've never seen you so much as toe tap."

■ ■ ■ ■

On Saturday morning, Amy ventured into Loretta's backyard and tried to catch a chicken. Since Hunter and Chase usually took care of that for her, she hadn't kept in practice. Her long skirts complicated matters, slowing her down and scaring the hens. Before she knew it, she was out of breath and wet with perspiration. Her braid had come unwound. She had a rock in one shoe. And she was overall disgruntled.

She hated to think about the neck wringing and head chopping that had to follow. Since her experience with the comancheros years ago, she had an aversion to violence, even when it was a domestic necessity. Poor, helpless chickens. She ate more than her fair share of them, but when she did, she didn't allow herself to think about where the poultry came from.

"Come here, chick-chick-chick," she called softly, her sights set on a nice plump hen that was showing no enthusiasm whatsoever for gracing a skillet. "Come here, chicken. Come to Amy."

"I don't think she likes you," a deep voice said.

Amy straightened and whirled, her hands

flying to her hair. "Swift! I thought you were at the mine."

"I was. I need to go to the general store for a new shirt, so I took off from work."

Amy could only wonder why he wanted to waste good money on another shirt. With the black one he was wearing unbuttoned halfway down his chest and the sleeves rolled back over his corded forearms, he looked more handsome than any man she had ever clapped eyes on.

"If you aren't a sight, Amy. What're you trying to do?" Swift ran a twinkling gaze from her tumbling braid to her soiled hem.

"I need a hen for my dinner basket." Heat flooded to her cheeks, for she hadn't intended to say anything about that. "Not for the auction, mind you. Just to take along, in case I get hungry."

His gaze once again shifted to her hair, making her fidget and try to tidy it. The more she poked and repositioned the heavy braid, the looser it got. She finally gave up, acutely aware that he watched her with unveiled curiosity. Probably because she looked so silly.

"So, you're going to the social after all, are you?"

"I thought I'd go and watch for a while."

"I'm proud of you, Amy. I know it's not

high on your list." He scanned the yard. "I can catch the hen for you."

"No." Since she hoped that he would join her for dinner, it didn't seem right that he should help get the makings for it. "I mean, that's okay. I'm enjoying myself."

"You look ready to drop." He took off his hat and set it on the woodpile. Rolling his sleeves farther back, he sighted in on a fat hen. "There's a trick to chicken chasing, you know."

"There is?"

He walked slowly across the yard, wiggling his fingers like he was dropping seed. Hens converged on him. "Females are all the same. If you chase them, they run. So instead, you let them" — he leaned slightly to one side, his hand opening — "chase you, until you catch them."

With that, he lunged, missed the chicken, and fell full length in the dirt.

"That's the slickest trick I've ever seen," Amy said with a giggle. "My, my, I'll bet a smooth operator like you has women hanging all over him."

He narrowed an eye at her. "Here lately, my luck's been running sour."

Amy grinned and bent her mind to chicken catching again. Swift joined her. Before she knew it, they were running around the yard, laughing like fools, the hens flapping and squawking and leading them a merry chase. When they ran themselves out of breath, Swift collapsed on the chopping block, bracing one arm on his knee. He grinned up at her.

"Would you settle on a cow?"

Amy pressed a hand to her aching diaphragm and laughed again. "A cow? It'd be a mighty big dinner basket. And I doubt a cow would be any easier to catch."

"I could shoot a cow. If I shoot one of those chickens, there won't be much left to eat."

The back door slammed, and Amy turned to see Loretta on the back stoop, hands on her hips, eyes narrowed against the October sunshine that slanted through the trees. "Those chickens aren't going to lay me any eggs for a week with you two chasing them like that."

Swift swung a hand at the hens. "Well, you just come out here and catch us one, Loretta Jane."

"You're supposed to get them into the pen first, Mr. Lopez. I can see you don't know squat about farming. And Amy's nose is never out of a book long enough to mind anything that's going on. How're you two going to get by on your own?" She gathered her apron into a bowl and came down the steps. "You see? They'll follow me right in."

Swift raised an eyebrow. "I don't have an apron."

"You don't have good sense, that's what you don't have, chasing chickens till the feathers fly."

Two minutes later, Loretta emerged from the henhouse holding a frenzied, squawking chicken by its neck. She marched to Swift and handed the hen over.

Rising from the stump, he held the chicken out in front of him. "Now what?"

"Wring its neck."

Swift glanced over at Amy, and there was no mistaking the pity in her eyes as she regarded the flapping, squawking chicken. He'd seen enough chickens swung to know how to do it, quick and with a snap. The chicken's neck felt warm and fragile within the circle of his fingers. He knew he could wring it, slicker than grease. Yet how dare he with Amy looking on? He could just hear her the next time she got in a dither at him, calling him a good-for-nothing, gunslinging, chicken-killing comanchero.

"You gonna do it or not?" Loretta asked.

Swift felt Amy's eyes on him. Big, worried blue eyes. He sneaked another look at her. She was biting her lip. He started to feel pretty silly, standing there holding a frantic chicken, his arm jerking up and down, while two women watched him, one with dread, the other with impatience. In his lifetime he had taken scalps, slapped leather, gutted buffalo, and slain deer, bears, wolves, and just about every other kind of creature. Killing one brainless chicken should have been easy.

"Let's just go shoot a cow."

Amy rolled her eyes and took the chicken. "Lands, Swift, I'd think with all you've done, chicken killing would be a snap."

And wasn't that the problem? He didn't need another count against him. "I've never wrung a poor bird's neck."

Amy bent slightly at the waist, getting ready to swing her arm. Then she looked down at the frantic hen and lost her impetus.

"Oh, for Pete's sake!" Loretta reclaimed the chicken, her cheeks flushed with indignation. "As much chicken as you eat, Amelia Rose, you'd think you'd be a little less squeamish."

Amy stepped back, wrinkling her nose, bracing herself. Loretta tensed to swing her arm, then hesitated and fastened wide blue eyes first on Amy, then on the flapping hen. "Lawzy! We can't kill this hen! This is Henrietta. She's gonna be one of my best layers, mark my words. Hunter'd have my hide."

Swift grinned. "I think we're back to a cow."

Loretta turned the chicken loose and shooed it away with her apron. "How about ham. Do you like ham, Swift?"

"It's not for me. It's for Amy's dinner basket." Swift gave Loretta a slow wink. "What do you think, Amy? Will ham do?"

Remembering Swift's first night in Wolf's Landing and the large piece of ham left on his plate, Amy turned questioning eyes on him. "I — do you — if you were a fellow, what would you like? Chicken or ham?"

Swift arched an eyebrow. "If I were a fellow?"

She blushed. "Well, of course, you're a fellow, Swift. I meant a fellow eating dinner at a social. Would you want chicken or ham?"

"Either one, I guess. Unless, of course, I had to kill the chicken. Then I'd lean real heavy toward ham."

CHAPTER 11

Amy felt like a trussed-up sausage in the blue silk dress. Loretta had insisted that she wear a corset, which made her bulge in places she'd never bulged in her life. The sounds of fiddles dug at her temples, and stomping feet sent vibrations through the floor of the community hall. Amy longed for home, for the quiet there and the certainty that she knew what would happen next.

"He'll come," Loretta assured her, leaning sideways so Amy would be sure to hear. "He and Hunter just worked late. I'll bet they're over at the house right now, washing up."

Amy gnawed on her bottom lip. "I think I'll just go home. This isn't fun like I thought it'd be."

Loretta caught her wrist. "You'll do no such thing."

Indigo swirled past them, caught a trifle too closely in her partner's arms, her black high-top shoes flashing beneath the hem of her pink dress. Loretta's gaze followed her daughter.

With a sigh, she released Amy's arm and said, "What a waste, her wearing that dress for the likes of him."

Amy studied Brandon Marshall, Indigo's partner. A tall blond with dancing blue eyes, he was every young girl's dream. Handsome, smartly dressed, suave. She could see why Indigo was starry-eyed and why Loretta was so worried. Brandon Marshall looked to be about twenty, far too old to be courting Indigo.

"I never found her that evening, when I offered to talk to her," Amy admitted. "Then I got so wrapped up in my own —"

Loretta lost her daughter in the jostle of dancers. "It's just as well." She flashed a smile. "Sometimes I forget my loved ones must experience life for themselves. I can't spare her everything. It's a mistake, that." Loretta's gaze shifted from the dancers to Amy. "I've done it with you, too, you know."

The sadness in Loretta's expression made Amy's heart catch. "Don't be a ninny, Loretta Jane. You've been wonderful to me."

"Have I? Look at you, panicked by a silly social."

Amy narrowed her eyes. "I think the term

panic is a bit exaggerated. Not everyone enjoys this sort of nonsense."

"Let's see how you feel once Swift arrives."

"Maybe he decided everyone would stare at him."

"Amy, he bought a new shirt for tonight. Of course he'll come. Just relax, would you?"

"Is that why he got a new shirt? For tonight?"

Loretta smiled. "Why else would he buy a new shirt?"

The widower, Mr. Black, approached. Amy felt like a bug on a pin, the way he looked at her. She longed for her shawl and glanced toward the coat hooks by the door, tempted to go get it.

"Miss Amy, you don't often grace us with your presence at functions like this. May I have this dance?"

"I don't dance," Amy replied softly, not wishing to offend him. In addition to being the coroner, Mr. Black did carpentry and served on the school committee. "I enjoy watching."

His gaunt face twisted into a grin. "I noticed you brought a basket. I'll surely bid on it." His gaze moved to her chest.

"You misread the tag. I didn't bring an

auction basket."

Loretta eased away to a nearby group of women. Amy glanced after her. Loretta knew how she disliked Mr. Black. He had beady frog eyes that made her feel like a fly about to be eaten.

"I hear you have a new pupil — Mr. Lopez, the gunslinger, according to the concerned mothers at our last meeting. I was pleased when you began working with him after hours. Odd, that, a gunslinger attending school. Of course, with a pretty teacher like you, I might go back to brush up on my alphabet myself."

Amy swallowed, her poise deserting her.

Loretta returned and broke into the conversation. "Mr. Lopez is a friend of our family, more like a brother, actually. He's working at the mine now, so Amy's tutoring him each day."

"Privately, I understand." Mr. Black raised an eyebrow, as if that somehow smacked of impropriety.

Amy fidgeted. Had someone seen her going off into the woods with Swift at night? Her stomach jumped. Her job was her independence. "Tutoring him is my only recourse, Mr. Black. Surely you don't begrudge the man an education."

"Of course he doesn't." Loretta smiled as

if Black had just announced the Second Coming was imminent. "Mr. Black's on the school committee. Education, for one and all, is his mission. Isn't that right, sir? I bet he's pleased you're so dedicated."

Black puffed up with pride. "I certainly am." He placed a cold hand on Amy's bare shoulder. "I'm quite an admirer of this little lady. She's a fine teacher."

Amy yearned to move away. He slid his fingertips across her skin — cold, clammy fingertips. Angling a peek at him, she wondered what he'd do if she swatted him a good one.

The fiddlers ceased playing, and all attention turned toward the front of the hall. Mr. Black got a little more bold with his finger gliding. Was she encouraging him by standing there? His hand on her shoulder was innocent enough, in itself.

Randall Hamstead, who owned the dry goods store, stepped up onto a box with a dinner basket held high.

Loretta leaned close. "I'll bet next week's egg money that *he* hasn't been dosed with his mother's sheep dung tea."

Amy started to giggle, then froze, her gaze fixed on the blue wicker basket in Hamstead's hand. She threw a horrified look at Loretta, then glanced toward the coatrack.

Her basket wasn't sitting where she had left it.

Noting where Amy's attention had flown, Loretta made an exasperated little noise. "They should be here by now."

"Loretta Jane . . ." Amy forgot all about Mr. Black's fingers and jerked from under his grasp. "What in blazes have you gone and done?"

When Loretta got caught pulling a fast one, her eyes rivaled dinner plates. "I didn't mean any harm, Amy. It's all in fun. Swift said he'd be here."

Amy had a good notion to give her cousin a kick. "Loretta Jane, how could you? Of all the sneaky, low-down, mean tricks!"

Loretta threw a look at the door. "Where is that man?"

"Attention, gentlemen," Hamstead yelled. "We're startin' with a prize. Ham, potato salad, raised bread, and apple pie."

"Get to the important part," one man shouted. Several men near him laughed and slapped him on the back.

Mr. Hamstead chuckled. "This basket belongs to . . ." He checked the tag and winked. "Miss Amy, our schoolteacher."

Since Amy had never attended a social, let alone participated in a basket auction, several of the bachelors hooted with enthusiasm and pushed closer to the table.

"Seven dollars," someone yelled.

Amy's stomach dropped. Seven dollars? That was outrageous.

"Eight," another deep voice chimed in.

"Ten. A man can't skimp on a lady who can teach him his p's and q's."

Amy threw another horrified look at Loretta. Her cousin's eyes grew even rounder. "It isn't my fault. They should've been here by now."

"Not your fault?" Amy cried. "You stole my basket and entered it in the auction, and it isn't your fault?"

"Eleven dollars," someone yelled.

Mr. Black roared, "Fifteen dollars. Let's see ya top that."

Amy slid her gaze to Mr. Black, resigned to her fate. Mr. Hamstead yelled, "Fifteen dollars. Fifteen. Going! Go—"

"One hundred dollars," a deep voice called.

A gasp rose from the crowd. Amy felt as if she might faint. One hundred dollars? She turned toward the door to see Swift at the threshold, Hunter and Chase behind him. A light blue shirt hugged his broad shoulders and muscular arms, the color striking a marked contrast to his dark skin. Amy's pulse accelerated just from looking at him.

He stepped into the building, tall and confident, sweeping his black hat from his head with a flourish only Swift could manage. Hanging the hat beside her shawl on the coatrack, he paused to scan the room, settling his dark gaze on her. A mussed lock of damp black hair fell across his forehead.

"Pardon me, sir? Did you say a hundred dollars?"

"That's right, a hundred." Swift shouldered his way through the crowd and set a stack of gold pieces on the table. Then he turned and looked at Amy, as did everyone else in the hall. A hundred dollars wasn't just an unheard of amount for a man to spend on a basket, it was crazy, insane, outrageous. Tongues would buzz for a year. If May Belle from the saloon had set up business in the street, she couldn't have stirred more buzzing.

Mr. Hamstead seemed so taken aback that he didn't bother saying, "Going, going, gone." A man could attend every single social and buy baskets for five years with a hundred dollars. Hamstead handed the basket to Swift, the bid uncontested.

Loretta nudged Amy forward. "Go, you ninny. How long do you expect him to stand up there waiting for you?"

Amy couldn't feel her feet. She walked

toward Swift, the silk dress swishing with every step, her cheeks warm beneath his penetrating gaze. Unlike Mr. Black, Swift didn't look at her chest. He never stopped looking into her eyes.

When Amy finally reached him, he crooked his arm, the possessive gleam in his gaze unmistakable. She knew everyone in the building was staring. Miss Amy and that man. She could almost hear them.

She curled her hand around Swift's arm. They'd think she was cavorting. She'd lose her income, her independence. Where would that leave her? Looking for a man to take care of her, like every other dumb female in town, that's where.

Swift's arm felt rock hard, the cloth of his sleeve slightly damp and warm. She knew he had scrubbed up and thrown on his shirt while still dripping wet to get there. As he shouldered a path through the crowd, Amy bent her head, cheeks burning. "A hundred dollars, Swift? Why'd you do something so outlandish? My reputation will be ruined."

"Ruined?" She felt him stiffen. "Ruined? I honored you, paying a hundred dollars. Hunter says no one's ever paid that."

It hit Amy then. Comanches showed regard for their brides by the bride price they paid. The more horses they left before a future father-in-law's lodge, the greater the honor. Swift had seen the auction as a way to express his high regard for her. And he had. Irrevocably.

"Oh, Swift, you don't understand. People will think something's going on between us. They're going to wonder what you're going to get for your hundred dollars, don't you see?"

He stopped at the rack for her shawl, draping it over her shoulders. His dark eyes twinkled at her. "What am I gonna get? A chewing? You're the prettiest woman in town. If you don't smile, I'm going to go put another hundred dollars on the table."

"Where'd you get so much money?" she squeaked. "You didn't steal it, did you?"

"I don't steal money from people." He clamped on his hat, took her arm, and drew her out the door. "I came by it honest."

"How?"

"Selling horses and cows. When I left the reservation, I planned to start a spread. I worked and saved." He glanced down. "The plan fell through. I never spent the money."

As they stepped into the night, the chill air curled around Amy. She took a deep breath, glad to escape all the suspicious eyes. "Thank goodness for that much. I'd hate to think you bought my basket with ill-gotten gains." She angled a glance at his dark profile, squinting to see as the light from the building fell behind them. "Where'd you get so many horses and cows?"

"Watch your step."

Amy saw nothing in her path, but then in the dark she usually didn't until she tripped. "Are you going to answer me?"

"Careful, Amy." He drew her closer to his side.

"Hell and damnation! You stole them, didn't you?"

"Don't cuss. You want your mouth washed with lye soap?" He tipped his head, his face shadowed by his hat brim. "Where do you want to eat?"

Amy narrowed her eyes. "How much money do you have, Swift?"

"Amy, if you're gonna hang me for stock stealing, you'd better hang every man in Texas. Those cows I sold had been across the Rio so many times, they didn't need droving."

"How's that relate?"

"The Texans steal from the Mexicans, and vice versa. The cows learn the way real quick." He led her to a sprawling oak. "Don't be mad. They were stolen cows and horses before I stole them. This is a special evening. I even bought a new shirt."

"How much ill-gotten money have you got, Swift?"

He set the basket down. In the moonlight, she saw a leaf flutter down and settle on his broad shoulder. He flicked it off. "Enough to keep you in lace drawers for a good long spell."

Amy's neck tingled. "I don't wear lace drawers."

"You ought to. That day when you fanned your underwear out the window, all I could think was that they should've been lace." He nudged his hat back and grinned at her, moonlight gleaming on his teeth. "Would you stop glaring at me?"

"What am I going to do if I lose my job?"

"You can marry me and have babies."

"I don't want to. I want my teaching position, and my own life, with no man telling me what to do and when to do it."

Swift folded his arms across his chest. "I won't tell you what to do and when to do it. Sit down, Amy, so we can eat." When she didn't oblige him, he leaned toward her. "I won't steal any more horses or cows. I promise."

"Swift, I don't care if you steal. It's not my concern."

"Then why are you mad?"

"Because you spent the money on my basket. Not to mention spending so much. If I don't lose my job, it'll be a miracle."

"You worry about that job too much."

"That job buys my bread and butter."

"If you get the boot, I'll bring you more bread and butter than you can eat. You'll get fat eating it all. And I won't tell you what to do and when to do it, I promise. Now, sit down. I didn't buy your basket to fight. Do you like my shirt?"

She studied him for a moment, unhappily aware that he vowed not to order her around, then commanded her to sit, all in the same breath. "Yes, I like it. You look very nice."

He grinned again. "You look so beautiful in that dress, I almost forgot to bid when I heard your name called. Who was that man standing with you?"

"Thank you for the compliment, and his name is Mr. Black. He's on the school committee."

"Well, I can forget you winding up without a job and needing me to take care of you then. I'd say he's stuck on you."

Some other couples came from the hall, finding spots beneath the trees to eat. Following their example, Amy sat on the grass, taking care not to soil Loretta's dress. Swift sat beside her. She gnawed her lip. "Oh, Swift, I'm sorry for being sharp. I know you didn't mean any harm, paying so much for my basket."

"Of course I didn't. Is it my fault white people think crazy?" He braced an arm behind him and lifted the towel from the basket. "Mm, Amy, this looks good."

She leaned over, eyes narrowed to see. Laughter floated through the moon-touched darkness, a woman's laughter. Amy's throat tightened. It was a sure bet no man had spent a hundred dollars on her basket. Poor Swift had spent a fortune and got scowls. "I made apple pie. Do you like apple pie?"

"I love apple pie." He glanced up. "Especially yours."

"You've never tasted mine."

"I don't need to."

Feeling dull and horribly inadequate, Amy began setting out the food, acutely conscious that Swift watched her every movement. They ate in silence. To Amy it seemed an uncomfortable one, especially when she heard other ladies all around her giggling and talking. The potato salad grew to gigantic proportions in her mouth.

She heard Elmira Johnson say, "Oh, Samuel!" *Teehee.* "Get away with you!" Swift glanced up from his plate. "Amy, would you relax?"

She gulped the salad down, wondering if he thought it tasted dry, too. "I've never come to a dance social before. You should have bought Elmira's basket so you could be with someone fun."

"She sounds like a duck."

Before she caught herself, Amy giggled.

"What's worse, she looks kind of like a duck. You ever noticed how her skirts poke out behind her when she walks?"

"That's a bustle, Swift, the absolute latest in fashion. I've heard tell that everyone will wear them in a year or so. Elmira has an aunt who travels abroad."

He arched an eyebrow. "You're not wearing one. When she walks down the boardwalk, her bottom sticks out so far behind her, you could set a plate on it." He angled her a rakish grin, "And who says you're not fun? I kind of like being chewed out if it's the right lady doing the chewing."

He served himself a huge piece of apple pie and made an appreciative noise. "Amy, you've got to marry me and make me apple pie every week. Where'd you learn to make this crust?"

"My ma." Sadness cut through Amy. She shoved the memories away. "She was quite a hand at cooking and baking."

He cleaned his plate in record time, then stretched out on the grass. One by one, the other couples began drifting back to the hall and the music. Amy finished her meal and put away the food, placing the soiled dishes on top so she could wash them later. She wished some of the other couples had remained outdoors. Any moment now Swift might suggest they go inside, too. Then he might expect her to dance with him.

Swift watched Amy from the corner of his eye. Moonbeams touched her small face, turning her eyes to shimmering spheres, making her mouth glisten. The coronet atop her head shone like silver, the curls above her ears and at her nape tempting him to touch them. Her hand rested on her skirt, her slender fingers keeping time to the fiddler's beat. She looked so beautiful in the shifting moonlight that he yearned to move closer, to feel her warmth, to have the sweet scent of her in his nostrils.

"Shall we go in and dance?" he asked, gesturing toward the brightly lit hall. A line of dancers swept past the door, boots stomping, skirts aswirl. "Sure looks like they're having fun."

"Oh, no, I couldn't." Even in the dim light, he saw the flush on her cheeks. "I enjoy just listening." She settled her gaze on a nearby wagon and team of horses. "Look at that old fellow. I swear he's got that front hoof tapping to the rhythm."

Swift shifted onto his side, propping his head on his hand. He had a feeling Amy had spent all her life just listening. From the way she fidgeted, he suspected she would love to do a whole lot more. He supposed, at her age, it would be awfully embarrassing to dance her first dance in front of half the town.

"You know, I always wished a lady would teach me to dance." It wasn't a lie. The only women Swift had ever danced with hadn't been ladies. "Do you know how, Amy?"

"I know some, but not nearly enough to teach you."

"Can you teach me the some you do know?"

She glanced at the hall. "Everyone would stare at us."

"Not here." He pushed to his feet. "Come on. It's fun."

Looking more than a little hesitant, she took his hand and let him pull her up, away from the tree's shadows and into the direct moonlight. He swept the shawl from her shoulders and tossed it next to the basket.

With a frown puckering the skin between

her fair eyebrows, she peered down at his feet. "I hope I don't show you backward. Or, worse yet, step in a hole and fall flat." She moved sideways, gnawing her lip. "Can you even see me?"

"I can see you fine. Can you see me?"

"Not good enough to read your large print if you were a newspaper, let's put it that way."

Swift swallowed a chuckle. He'd danced in practically every saloon in Texas, and whatever step Amy was trying to execute, he'd never seen its like. She heaved a sigh.

"I'm not very good to be teaching anyone, I'm afraid." She dipped in a graceful slide to her left. Swift followed suit, and she giggled. "I think that's the lady's part."

The music stopped. She stood before him, arms out from her sides, waiting. Then the lilting strains of a waltz began. Swift stepped forward and settled a palm on her waist, reaching for her hand. She went rigid at the close way he held her.

"Relax, Amy. Just move with me."

When he swept her in a circle, she glanced worriedly over her shoulder at the dark ground.

"I can see fine. Put your hand on my shoulder."

She did, tipping her head back to look at

his face. "Swift, you dance beautifully! Where did you learn?"

"You're like air in my arms," he whispered, pulling her closer. "Close your eyes, Amy. Let the music take you with it."

Her lashes fluttered closed, and a rapturous expression crept across her small features. Swift imagined her lying beneath him with a look like that on her face, and he missed a step. Amy, in her inexperience, didn't note his error. His throat tightened. In so many ways she was still a child. He wanted to keep her there in his arms forever.

The waltz ended, but Swift kept dancing. Amy was all the music he needed. Another waltz began.

"It feels like flying," she whispered, her eyes still closed. "Oh, Swift, it's wonderful!"

He wanted to kiss her. So badly that he ached. He wanted to carry her off into the shadows and slide the silk dress down her arms, to feel the warmth of her skin, to hear her say how wonderful *he* made her feel. He wanted to change her nightmares into dreams, to make her yesterdays dim memories, to build her a life full of love and laughter. He wanted to feel her belly swollen with his child, to see that child's dark head pressed to her breast, to see the love he knew she'd feel shining in her eyes. He wanted that, more than anything. So far, no one had followed him to Oregon. It didn't look as if anyone would. He had done the impossible and escaped his past. Now he had to help Amy escape hers, so they could build a future together.

But for this little while, the night was Amy's. To dance, because she never had. To giggle, because she did so seldom. His gift to her, in lieu of all else, because she wasn't ready for more. And if she was never ready for more, Swift knew he'd take what she could give, even if it was only a smile, because a morsel of Amy was worth a thousand other women giving their all.

He loved her. He had loved the skinny little girl of fifteen years ago, he loved the beautiful woman she was today, and he would love the wrinkled old woman she would become, simply because the essence of Amy went far beyond the physical. Amy, his sunshine. The one perfect joy that had ever touched his life, lost to him for so long. Now that he had found her again, he couldn't imagine life without her.

CHAPTER 12

Amy didn't think anything could spoil the evening. Dancing. Really and truly dancing. It didn't matter that they swirled beneath an oak tree, alone. She didn't need onlookers to make it official. A man held her in his arms, and she was wearing a beautiful silk dress, gliding to a waltz. It surpassed her wildest dreams. She wanted to dance and dance and dance, until the moon drifted from sight and dawn streaked the sky.

Looking up at Swift's dark face, she decided he was the handsomest man in the whole world. To think that he had bought *her* basket. And for the unheard-of price of a hundred dollars. Delicious, that was how she felt. Beautiful. The night was magic, Swift was magic, everything was magic.

It didn't even matter anymore that he'd come by the hundred dollars stealing. Raised as a Comanche, Swift had grown up learning to be a horse thief. The fact that he'd learned the craft so well shouldn't have surprised her. His promise that he would never steal again enabled Amy to forget that he had.

When a stitch started in her side, she tried to ignore it. This was the one night of her life, and she wanted to make it count. When Swift slowed his steps and swung her up against his chest, she tried to protest but didn't have the breath.

"You're tired."

"Oh, Swift, must we stop? It feels so glorious."

"We'll have other nights, Amy."

He bent his head. Too late, Amy realized that she had melted against him like a dollop of butter on a hot biscuit. The magic feeling fragmented. For several wonderful minutes she had fallen under his spell, as she had so many years ago, forgetting her yesterdays, that she was a woman in a world where men had absolute power. But a person couldn't stay in a pretend world.

She drew her face back, frightened by the gleam in his eyes and the firmness of his arm around her, arching her toward him so that his arousal was apparent, even through the layers of denim, silk, and muslin. As blind as she was in the dark, moonlight gilded his face, revealing the hardened set to his features, the grim determination of his mouth, the flare of his nostrils. Amy had seen that look on men's faces before, but never on Swift's.

His passions had become aroused while dancing with her. And when that happened to a man, the animal in him took over. She could smell the change in him, see the sheen of sweat filming his face, hear the quick, urgent way he breathed. It struck her suddenly that he stood between her and the community hall.

He drew her arm around his neck and released his hold on her hand to settle his own on her waist. Only, of course, with the need coming over him, he didn't keep his hand on her waist. As his mouth claimed hers, his palm slid up her ribs, his fingers probing, frustrated by the network of whalebone in Loretta's corset. He homed in on the only softness, her breasts, which swelled above the stays, cupped to midnipple with the wispy cloth of her chemise and covered with only the silk.

Amy jerked. The heat of his hand scorched her. When she gasped, his hot, silken tongue dove into her mouth, striking a rhythm she knew too well, plundering deep, allowing her no quarter. He found the peak of her breast, his thumb and fingers capturing it through the silk. A shock of sensation zigzagged through her. And in its wake came mindless panic.

She tried to jerk her face from his, to twist from his arms. He was rawhide lean and roped with muscle. He held her as easily as he might have a struggling child. His body hunched around her, hardening to steel, his kiss turning more demanding and determined, as if by forcing her he could convince her to like what he was doing. She tried to say his name, to plead with him to stop, but the words went into his mouth, a jumble of whimpers.

The world became a swirl of moonlight and madness. Swift wasn't Swift anymore; he was just another hurtful man, taking what he wanted. She was no longer Miss Amy, safe in Wolf's Landing, under a sprawling oak outside the community hall, with music floating on the air. Animal instinct drove her just as it drove Swift, and she fought for survival.

During that heartbeat of time when Amy metamorphosed from woman to trapped animal, Swift whispered her name, gentled his arm around her, and withdrew his hand from her breast. But Amy didn't register the change. She wrenched her mouth from his and struck out, blind with panic, her one purpose to get away from him. How she accomplished that, she didn't notice. Swift's unexpected attack had set her on a stimulus-and-reaction course.

He released her, and she ran.

"Amy!"

His voice, thick with desire, sounded like a stranger's, and it spurred Amy forward. She didn't know where she was going, didn't care, just as long as it was away.

"Amy, honey, come back. Not into the trees. Amy, don't!"

Amy's scope shrank to a tunnellike path. There was only the rasp of her breathing, the slamming of her heart, the ragged little cries tearing up her throat. She barely felt her feet slapping the ground. A branch hit her in the face. She staggered. Brush loomed before her, specters blacker than the blackness, to tear at her clothing, grab at her legs.

And then she heard boots thudding behind her, coming hard and fast. Her skin shriveled. She threw herself forward into a faster pace, frantic, beyond thought. *Oh, God — Oh, God — Oh, God.* There was no safe place, no safe person. Swift was like all the others, racing after her, six feet of unleashed power. She wouldn't be able to fight him or stop him, until he finished tearing into her, shuddered with his own satisfaction, and fell on her, an immovable anchor of sweaty flesh that pinioned her under the terror. *Not again — not again.*

"Amy! Watch out! There's a log — Honey, watch out!"

Something hit her from behind. Amy screamed as she fell, manacled in a horrifying tangle of rock-hard arms and legs. Swift spun with her in midair, so he hit the ground first and cushioned the impact. But Amy scarcely registered that. She grunted and twisted, trying to escape him, and when that availed her nothing, she pressed a frontal attack, going for his face.

He swore and grabbed her wrists. Whipping his body, he came up off the ground, catching her in the backlash to pin her beneath him. She kicked, but her skirts tangled around her. He angled a muscle-roped thigh across hers and dragged her jerking arms above her head.

Breathing fast, his face a dark shimmer of menace above hers, he cried, "It's all right, Amy. It's all right."

But it wasn't all right. He had her. Black treetops, silhouetted against the sky, loomed and shifted, sentinels to witness her shame. She couldn't move, couldn't breathe. He anchored her wrists above her head with one hand, which left his other free. She knew what was coming. A scream welled within her, tearing up her throat to be born as a pitiful mewling.

"Forgive me, Amy. I didn't mean it. Sweetheart, I didn't mean it." His hand, which she expected to tear at her clothing, settled with trembling lightness on her hair. "It's all right. I swear it, Amy. I'm not going to hurt you."

The words came from a great distance, the same words, over and over, but the hard, heavy body on top of hers spoke much more clearly. She strained until she was drenched in sweat, until her muscles no longer twitched in response to the messages from her brain, until the fear moved back a little, hovering, waiting to reclaim her. She quivered and jerked, sobbing, unable to utter the pleas for mercy that crowded into her head.

"It's all right," Swift said again. "I'm sorry, Amy. I lost my head for a minute. I shouldn't have. I'm sorry. I won't hurt you. I swear it. Not now, not ever."

He moved his hand from her hair to her neck, his warm fingertips curving over her nape, caressing the wispy, damp curls that lay against her clammy skin.

"D-don't t-touch me. Don't . . ."

His hand tightened on her nape. "Honey,

I won't hurt you. I swear it. Relax. There's my girl. Take a deep breath."

Amy did and burst into tears. Wild, hysterical tears. Swift swore and rolled off of her, carrying her with him in the circle of his arms until she lay atop him. It seemed to Amy his trembling hands were everywhere, on her hair, her back, her arms, caressing, soothing, forcing the brittle tautness from her.

"I'm so sorry," he said again and again. "Please don't cry. I'd rather be horsewhipped than hear you cry. I mean it. I'll go to Hunter's barn with you. You can lay me open with the strap. I deserve it. But please don't cry."

Lying on top of him as she was, Amy could feel his heart slamming. Her cheek was pressed to his shirt. She shuddered and went limp, soothed by the raw sincerity in his voice and the quivering regret she felt in his lean body.

Time passed, measured in her ear by the erratic thumping of his heart. The wind whispered, bending the trees, rustling boughs and parched leaves. Amy closed her eyes, her throat too raw to speak, the energy to weep drained from her. Insanity had surely struck, for it made no sense to flee a man in terror, then lie upon him, relaxed and motionless, once he caught her. But lie here she did, at peace in a way she couldn't understand and didn't have the presence of mind to contemplate.

Her feelings for Swift had never made sense, anyway.

After a very long while he threaded his fingers through her loosened braid, toying with it, running the strands over his knuckles. "I meant tonight to be perfect for you."

His voice vibrated through his chest and into hers, hoarse with emotion. Amy nuzzled her cheek closer to him, soothed somehow by the smell of clean skin and soap and leather.

"I never meant to go after you like that," he whispered. "Please believe me. It just came over me, and it happened so quick — you didn't give me a chance to stop before you ran."

She squeezed her eyelids closed against another rush of tears, "Oh, Swift, I wish with all my heart men weren't subject to being overcome, especially you." She gulped and shivered. "It turned you into someone I don't know. And it frightens me to think that stranger lurks within you now, ready to pounce on me when I least expect it."

"I deserve that, I guess. But, Amy, it's not a stranger inside me. I want you like that all the time, and the wanting just got bigger than I was for a second. You felt so sweet, leaning up against me."

Uneasiness niggled up her spine. She was lying against him now. Sighing, he cupped his hand to her cheek.

"Don't be afraid." His voice went husky. "I think I'd rather hear you cry, and hearing you cry about kills me."

Digging her elbows into his chest, she levered herself up to peer at him, still alarmed by his admission. "I th-think we'd best get back to the social."

"We can't. You're a sight. Your reputation *would* be ruined if anyone saw you like this." He brushed a stray tendril back from her face. "Not that you aren't beautiful, with that hair falling around your shoulders like spun silver and gold." He trailed his knuckles along her cheek, then traced the tip of one finger over her lips. "Kiss me, Amy. Would you do that for me?"

Amy decided then and there that she wasn't the only one suffering a bout of insanity. "What?"

"Kiss me," he repeated gently. "I won't force myself on you. Just kiss me. One time. A real kiss, with your lips parted and your tongue touching mine. A nice, long kiss. I'd like you to meet the stranger in me when he's got his head on straight. If you don't, you'll be leery of that side of me forever, and I don't want that."

The way Amy figured, it would be far smarter to stay leery. It was a trick, she just knew it. She started to roll off him, but he caught her at the waist, holding her fast.

"Please. I won't ever make you do it again if it's awful. How's that for a bargain? One kiss. If you hate it —" He broke off and seemed to ponder what he was about to say. "If you hate it, I'll set you free from the betrothal promise."

That got her attention. He might trick her, but she'd never known him to outright lie. She could scarcely credit her ears.

"If you hate kissing me, we'll just be friends from now on," he added in a strained whisper. "I'll never pester you for more."

Friends. That would be a dream come true — to be able to be with Swift and never have to worry. Her pulse went wild just at the thought of kissing him, but if he truly would release her from the betrothal promise if she hated it, which she would, she'd be crazy not to consider doing it. "D-do you m-mean it?"

"Have I ever lied to you? Name me one time, Amy."

Swift watched her, heart in throat, afraid

she might refuse, more terrified that she might not. If she kissed him and detested it, he would lose her. It was a hell of a lot to gamble on — the rest of his life. Her inexperience was bound to make even her best effort a fumbling pressure of mouths, not the stuff dreams were made of. But it was a risk he had to take. If he let her leave these woods with his pawing, panting attack on her foremost in her mind, he'd never get within ten feet of her again, unless he took her down in a flying tackle and forced her.

Her expression revealed her every emotion and thought, most of them unflattering. But there was also a shimmer of determination in her eyes. A release from their betrothal was clearly a powerful temptation. He had no choice but to accept that. Lying perfectly still beneath her, he waited.

After regarding him suspiciously for several moments, she let out a shaky breath and dropped her gaze to his mouth. Then, as if she had reached a decision that she feared she might heartily regret, she scooted upward, so her face hovered above his. Swift didn't know which torture was worse, the scooting or the taste of her sweet breath on his lips. Her huge, luminous eyes settled once again on his mouth. She looked about as enthusiastic as a woman who had just been asked to jump off a cliff. He struggled not to smile. All he had asked for was a kiss, not a consummation of the sexual act. This was clearly a very daring feat for her to consider undertaking.

"Do — do you promise not to get overcome?" she asked in a dubious little voice.

Swift had been overcome by the mere sight of Amy ever since he had first seen her, a furious little hellion, with glorious blond hair and flashing blue eyes. It was strange, that. He'd fallen in love with her because she had such fiery courage, and now he loved her even more because she lacked it. This Amy, who had suffered so much and, because of that, fled from him in mindless terror, brought all his protective instincts to the surface, and he wanted nothing more than to shield her for the rest of her life. Except, of course, from himself.

"I promise not to lose my head," he amended. "If I get your meaning correctly, I think I'm already what you'd call overcome."

She stiffened and looked as if she were about to leap off him. Swift tightened his arm around her.

"Amy, it's natural. Sometimes I just look at you and it happens. Or I smell your hair and it happens. I'm overcome most of the time I'm around you."

A thoroughly horrified expression filled her eyes. "Oh, dear. Swift, let's go." She planted her palms on his chest and shoved to get up. "Now. Please."

He kept his hold tight to keep her where she was. "Not until you kiss me. Don't you want to? Think of it, Amy. If you don't like it, we'll just be friends, like you are with Hunter. That's what you want, isn't it?"

"It wouldn't be like that, though. My hair doesn't bother Hunter. I — I want to go. Right now."

"Amy, listen to me. There's nothing to be frightened of. A man aches with wanting a woman sometimes, and I ache for you. I was aching tonight when we were dancing. And when you leaned against me, I forgot everything but that, just for a second. People kiss each other all the time, and nothing happens. Try it. Come on. It can't be so hard as all that. Think of what you stand to gain." And what he stood to lose.

She went back to staring at his mouth again. And then, curling her hands into taut fists in his shirt, she bent her head and touched her lips to his. He parted his mouth a finger's width, enough to allow her access but not enough to startle her.

She deepened the kiss ever so slightly, the

contact so moist and sweet and shy that his heart started to slam and every muscle in his body screamed to hold her. Swift splayed his hand on her back, thoroughly and irrevocably *overcome* as the tip of her small tongue darted out and flicked the sensitive underside of his upper lip. He allowed her the touch-and-flee experimentation, careful to do nothing that might unnerve her.

Finally, as if she'd assured herself it was safe, she pressed her lips to his, shyly running her tongue across the edge of his teeth. He struggled to remain passive, but so much rode on this kiss that he forwent caution and put his other hand on the back of her head to get some control. Pressing downward, he settled her mouth more firmly against his, angled his head, and very carefully touched his tongue to hers. She flinched, but Swift firmed his hold on her until she relaxed.

As he felt the tension drain from her, his own lessened somewhat, and instinct took over. He knew he had won by the way her body molded to his. Amy, his Amy. Almost reverently, Swift explored her mouth, drawing upon all his experience with women and the love he felt for her to make this kiss beautiful.

For Amy, the world went into a spin.

Swift's mouth pulled on hers, hot and warm, his tongue teasing, retreating, the touch so tantalizing that she grew braver and thrust her own forward, wanting more. Which he gave her, groaning deep in his chest.

Someplace in the back of her mind, Amy tried to remind herself that it was crucial she not like this. Freedom rode on her not liking it. Independence and survival rode on her not liking it. If she responded, she could say good-bye to any hope at all of controlling her own life.

When it came, she felt the change in him, just as she had earlier. The passion sweat filming his body, the urgency of his breathing, the whipcord tension in the way he held her. But this time he held her tenderly. His hands floated over her like air, so lightly that her skin came alive and tingled with expectancy. She didn't feel threatened, just treasured.

And feeling treasured was her undoing. Swift groaned again and rolled with her, coming out on top. Everything was already in such a spin that it didn't matter. This time he didn't touch her breasts. But he did touch her elsewhere. The electrical graze of his hands through the silk felt so wonderful that she didn't want him to stop.

"Amy . . ."

He said her name as though he were uttering a prayer. Dizzy and flushed with heat, she fluttered her eyelashes, vaguely aware that his mouth had left hers and ventured to her throat, but she was so caught up in sensation, she couldn't surface to protest. Featherlight lips traced the line of her collarbone, then trailed to the swell of her breasts. Amy blinked, but blinking didn't slow Swift, and before she could think of some way to more actively relate her dislike of the liberties he was taking, he persuaded her into liking what he was doing after all.

He dove his tongue under the edge of her gown, tugging up on the lace, slipping under, grazing the peak of her breast. She gasped and made fists in his hair to pull him away. Before she could, her breast, shoved so high by the bones of the corset and tugged upward by his tongue, popped free of the flimsy lace and into his mouth. Shocked by the sensation that shot into her belly, she arched her back to buck, and Swift took full advantage, drawing hard on her nipple.

All thought fled. Amy forgot where she was, what she was doing, everything. Swift and his hot, relentless, demanding mouth was the only reality. She whimpered, then moaned as he nipped the swollen nub of her nipple until it throbbed, until her areola sprang taut and tingled with longing.

Sweet torture. Grazing and pinching lightly with his teeth, he soon had her trembling with frustration, pressing his head to her breast, begging with her arching body for the full heat of his mouth. Which he refused her. Amy felt as if she were melting, her bones turning to liquid fire that pooled low in her belly.

"Swift . . . Swift, please . . ."

The instant she voiced the plea, he drew all of her back into his mouth, not carefully this time, but hungrily, sucking hard and long, his mouth so hot that she trembled and jerked with every drag of his tongue. An ache started deep within her, a sharp, tingling, insatiable ache.

A spiral to heaven, the fires of hell, Amy felt a bit of both, the strange need building, hurting, tightening inside of her. She wanted. There was no definition in her mind of what she wanted, just a primal recognition of a need as old as womankind, and she fell prey to it with quivering helplessness, too mindless to analyze what was happening.

Above her, Swift struggled for self-control, knowing he could push now for more, take her as he had been longing to do. But the risks. He had promised not to take her, damn it. And here he was, about to toss up her dress and do it on the hard, half-frozen ground. She was his. He was so close.

In all his life, Swift had never broken a promise. In the last few years everything he valued had been stripped from him, except his honor, which no one could steal, unless he abandoned it himself. To do so now, by breaking a promise to Amy, when the very fabric of her trust depended on his word, would be an irrevocable mistake. If one thing went wrong — one lousy thing — like her becoming frightened at the moment their joining began, what seemed so perfect could turn nightmarish.

He swallowed, trying to slow his heartbeat, to pace his breaths. Lifting his head, he gazed down at her sweet face, twisted with yearning he had built within her and only he could slake. "Amy, love . . ." His voice shook. "Amy . . ."

She quivered, clutching his shirt. Swift lowered his head back to her breast, gentling the kisses, slowly bringing her down. He scooped her small, perfect breast back into its cup of lace and smoothed the silk back over it — the hardest thing he had ever done in his life.

"Amy . . ."

He trailed light kisses up her throat to her mouth, whispering her name until sanity slowly returned to her eyes. With the sanity came disbelief. Swift reared back as she jerked to a sitting position. Placing his hands on his knees, he regarded her in watchful silence, not sure how she might react.

She touched her wildly mussed mane of golden hair, glanced dazedly around them, and said, "I — you — oh, my . . ."

It wasn't exactly what Swift had expected, but at least it wasn't accusatory. "Are you okay?"

She looked at him as if she didn't believe anything would ever be okay again and pressed a hand over her bodice. Even in moonlight, he could see the painful flush creeping up her neck.

"Amy . . ." He looped an arm around her and, shifting his position, drew her across his lap. Pressing her head to his shoulder, he brushed a light kiss across her forehead. "It's all right, honey. Trust me, it'll be all right."

"No," she whispered. "Don't you see that it can't?"

He closed his eyes, inhaling the scent of her hair, flyaway tendrils of which tickled his nostrils. "Did you hate it?"

He felt her start to shake, a horrible, palsied shaking. Fear lanced through him. "Y-yes! Of course I hated it."

He hunched his shoulders around her, touching his lips to her ear. "Do you remember when I used to hold you like this?"

Amy did, and the memories brought tears to her eyes. "Yes." She bit her lip, struggling to stop the horrible shaking that had taken hold of her body. Oh, God, he had won. She had melted under his mouth, quivering and begging. She had betrayed herself, condemned herself. He'd insist she marry him now. How could she have been so stupid as to accept his challenge and kiss him? She should have known he felt confident of winning the wager, or he never would have made the offer. And she, like a brainless ninny, had put herself into a position where he could push past her defenses.

"I'd really like to go home now, Swift."

Swift ran a hand up her slender arm, wishing he knew what to say to her. "If you want to go, I'll take you."

She fastened wide blue eyes on him — eyes that reflected an entirely new kind of fear, not just of him any longer, but of herself as well. Swift couldn't understand or comprehend, but it was there all the same.

Amy had just come face-to-face with her own passion, and for some reason completely beyond him, that seemed to make her feel even more vulnerable than she had before.

Chapter 13

En route back to town, Swift had one thought. Amy had lied to him about hating their kiss, flat-out lied. He circled that realization, trying to come to grips with it and understand it. She had never been one to lie, not about something important. Little things, maybe, in the heat of anger or when she felt threatened. But never about something like this.

He didn't know how to confront her or if he even wanted to. She looked so damned scared, a trembling, heart-slamming scared. He wasn't certain why. All along he'd been convinced it was the thought of sex that terrified her. Now he realized though her fears might center around that, they went far deeper, encompassing other issues as well, issues he hadn't considered and that he might not even be capable of comprehending.

As they neared her house, she turned on

him. "I suppose you're going to be the typical, arrogant male and insist I liked what you did back there."

Off balance, he stared down at her, not sure what to say. "You've never lied to me about anything important, Amy. If I had to choose the one thing in this world I knew I could count on, it'd be your word."

She stiffened and averted her face as if he'd struck her. Swift knew by her reaction that he'd pricked her conscience. Closing her eyes, she breathed raggedly through her nose, her small nostrils flaring. He glanced down and saw that her hands were clenched into fists. After a moment she cried, "You think you're so smart. You'll appeal to my honor and make me admit I liked it, right? Think again. I'll never admit it, never."

"Amy, I'm not trying to —"

"Don't lie." She riveted anguished eyes on him. "You think you've won with one little kiss. We're back to the betrothal. You'll insist I marry you. I know you — don't think I don't."

Swift clenched his teeth.

"You see? You can't deny it, can you? You men are all the same. You want control, and one way or another, you get it. You knew what would happen. And you tricked me, saying you'd release me from the promise, knowing I'd go for the bait. You knew you'd win before you ever posed the challenge."

Swift didn't point out that she had just as much as admitted that she had enjoyed the kiss. "Amy, that's insane. Why would I trick you?"

"Why?" She leaned toward him and jabbed a finger at his chest. "Understand something. This is one woman who will never kiss your boots. Never!"

Swift swallowed. "My boots? Amy, when have I ever —"

"I've done all the groveling I'm going to do. No one's ever going to have that kind of power over me again. No one!"

With that, she whirled and ran across the yard, tripped on an exposed tree root, stumbled up the steps, and wrestled with the door, as if she thought he rode her heels. He watched her, afraid to press her when she was so upset. "Good night, Mr. Lopez, and good riddance," she snapped over her shoulder.

She escaped inside and slammed the door. An instant later he heard glass breaking, then a broken, sobbing "Damnation!" that made his heart catch. He moved closer, cocking an ear to listen.

"Amy, are you okay?"

"I'll be okay just as soon as you get off my place."

He heard a thud and an "Ouch!" that made him cringe. An instant later, light flared. Swift leaned against the tree in her yard, trying to decide whether he should have this out with her now. She was more likely to confess what was bothering her while upset. But a confrontation now would be unavoidably nasty.

While he mulled over his options, Amy came to the sitting room window and cupped her hands to the glass, peering out into the darkness. She looked straight at him, then sagged with relief, which told him she hadn't seen him and thought he had gone. His mouth tipped in a tender smile.

The lantern light moved from the sitting room to her bedroom. Through lace curtains, Swift could see her too well and knew a white man would probably leave. A gentleman would, at any rate. He had been in her bedroom at night, and her curtains looked far more concealing from the inside.

She twisted to unfasten the blue silk dress. His throat tightened as she slid the sleeves down her slender arms — as he had imagined doing. She bent to untie the laces on the back of the corset and tossed the garment aside. As she walked to her bureau, she kicked off her pantalets and petticoat en route.

Laying a nightdress on the bureau, she tugged her chemise off over her head. Swift braced himself as she flung the garment away from her. His mouth went as dry as dust.

She was so beautiful, so damned beautiful.

Her body seemed to undulate behind the film of lace, a shimmer of delicious white, her narrow back dipping to a tiny waist, then flaring out into the nicest behind he'd ever seen. His woman. White society might frown upon him for standing out here gaping, but the way Swift saw it, he was making a big concession. If looking was a sin, he'd go to hell smiling.

And then he saw them. Scars. Faded to white, but there, a network of white ridges crisscrossing her back and bottom. He felt as though a horse had kicked him in the guts. The ground disappeared from under his feet. If it hadn't been for the tree, he would have fallen. Someone had whipped her. Not Santos. Once, years ago, Swift had seen Amy's back while she was swimming, and she had borne no whip marks after her ordeal with the comancheros. Nausea surged up his throat.

The little girl grew up, and she found out the hard way. You know how dreams are. Sometimes they don't make any sense. Her voice echoed in his mind, deceptively gay to hide the pain. And then his own words came back to haunt him as well, nearly breaking his heart because he had said them. *You haven't got enough guts left in you to make a smear if someone smashed you. What happened to you, Amy? Have you ever wondered that?* She had looked at him with those huge, luminous eyes, without rancor, without accusation. *I'm sorry if I'm a disappointment to you. I survived and kept my sanity, Swift. Isn't that enough?*

Tears ran down his cheeks, tears of helpless, impotent rage. *I've done all the groveling I'm going to do. No one's ever going to have that kind of power over me again. No one!* Swift clamped an arm to his middle and slid down the tree until he sat on the ground. *Why didn't you wait for me in Texas, Amy, like we agreed?*

There, alone in the darkness, he wept — with shame because she had waited for him there on that dusty farm, believing he would come, as he had promised — with regret because he had been too blind to see that the courageous, glorious girl he had known was still just as courageous and glorious, only in a different way. *You want to hit me, Amy? Or are you too yellow? I'll give you one free shot.* And bless her heart, she had taken up the challenge and done it, even though she must have been terrified.

Every memory cut through him. He had been so cruel to her without realizing it. *I could just throw you over my horse.* He cupped a hand over his eyes. *No, that's life, sweetheart. You don't have a choice! You're mine! I'm here, I'm staying, and you'd better damned well figure out a way to deal with it.*

Time became meaningless to Swift. The lantern went out, casting a fading glow through the bedroom. The wind shifted, blowing his hair, cutting through his shirt. And still he just sat there, staring, punishing himself over every thoughtless word he had uttered to her since his arrival in Wolf's Landing.

Amy saw him the moment she got out of bed the next morning. Just sitting out there beneath her pine tree, not wearing a coat, his blue shirt dirt-streaked, her dinner basket and shawl beside him. She inched closer to the window, peering through the lace at him. He looked stricken, as he might if someone had died.

Fear clutched her. She raced to the door. The chill morning air cut through her gown, making her shiver.

"Swift? Oh, God, what's happened?"

Her first thought was Loretta's family, that one of them had been hurt, and he had been sent to tell her. He certainly looked haunted enough for that to be the case. She scurried down the steps and out into the yard.

"Swift? Wh-what's happened?"

"Nothing, Amy. I've just been sitting here, thinking."

"Thinking?" she repeated. "Have you been here all night?"

"Yes. I have to talk to you."

"Oh." She straightened, suddenly uneasy. "Aren't you cold?"

"I could use a cup of hot coffee."

"I'm sure Loretta has the pot on."

"I want a cup of your coffee. Can I come inside?"

"Well . . ." Amy glanced uneasily toward town. "What do you want to talk about?"

"Us. A lot of things."

"Let me get dressed."

He glanced at her nightdress. "You're fine like you are."

"Nonsense."

Gathering her things, he pushed up from the tree, stiff and slow. "No nonsense to it.

Let's get some coffee on the stove."

With that, he strode unsteadily past her to the house. Glancing down at herself, she followed him inside warily. She could already hear him clanging around in her kitchen.

"I'll be right with you."

He poked his head around the door frame. "Amy, you're covered from chin to toe. Come in here by the stove, honey. You're shivering. There are hot coals, and I already put in some wood. Here in a couple of minutes, we'll have a fire."

She stood rooted, uncertain whether she wanted to get near him or not. After last night, what was he thinking?

"Amy . . ."

She moved toward the doorway, every step a decision. He glanced up from the coffeepot when she appeared in the doorway. Motioning her toward a chair, he said, "Have a seat. It's time we had a long talk."

She didn't like the sound of that. "Will I ever have peace and quiet in my own home again?"

"Maybe sooner than you think."

Amy slid onto a chair, tucking her nightgown around her knees and plucking nervously at the bodice, afraid he might be able to see through the cotton.

"Relax. I saw more than that last night, and I didn't kick the door down. I think I can stay civilized now."

He turned a chair and straddled it, sitting down with a tired sigh. Amy turned over his words, examining them.

As if he knew what she was wondering, he said, "I stood under the tree last night and watched you undress."

Indignation washed over her in a scalding wave. "You what?"

"I —" He broke off. "You heard what I said."

"How dare you!"

"I'm a low-down skunk."

"You most certainly are."

He folded his arms on the chair back and rested his forehead on his wrists. "I'm sorry. I know it's not worth much, but I'm sorry. In a way, at any rate. In another, I'm glad I did it."

"I'm to accept an apology when you're not really sorry?"

"It doesn't matter." He lifted his head, planting a hand over his face. "Hell, nothing matters anymore."

Amy had never seen him like this. "Swift?"

"I'm leaving," he said softly.

"Leaving?"

"Yes."

"Wh-when?"

"Today." He heaved another sigh. "You've finally won, Amy. I'm not going to hold you to the betrothal. You're free."

Amy couldn't credit her ears. "Because of last night?"

He moved his hand up his face and over his wind-tossed hair. His weary eyes settled on her. "Yes, but not for the reason you're thinking." His mouth twisted in a tender smile. "I didn't lose that wager, and you know it. You didn't hate what happened, you hated the position it put you in. The betrothal promise is gone on the wind — over. You can be honest now."

Her cheeks felt hot. "Is this a trick?"

He laughed softly. "I don't need tricks. If I wanted to be an ass, I'd just be an ass. Carry you to the bedroom, rip off your clothes, and lay my claim." He cocked an eyebrow, as if he waited for her reaction. "And don't take that as a threat. I'm just stating fact. Why would I bother with tricks?"

Amy didn't know. "Then why — why are you leaving?"

"Because I'm making your life miserable, and I know why, and I don't blame you a damn bit." He stared into her eyes, tears filling his own. His throat worked. "I saw the scars, Amy."

Amy froze on the chair. Her senses sharpened. She could hear the fire snapping, the clock ticking, the wind whispering outside. She couldn't speak, couldn't drag her gaze from his.

"I'm not asking you to talk about it," he said in a low voice. "I'm not now, and I never will. I don't think you've ever told anyone, have you?" Met with her telling silence, he continued. "How did you keep Loretta from seeing your back?"

Amy's mouth felt powdery. "I bathed in my room."

He nodded. "So it's been your secret. That's a powerful lot to pack around, isn't it? Especially when you're only nineteen years old and scared to death."

"I've never feared Hunter. And it wasn't a lot to pack around. It was a lot to explain. So I didn't."

Swift considered that. "Because you were ashamed."

"It's nothing to be proud of."

His eyes delved into hers. She had the horrible feeling he could see too much, read her too well, that she had no secrets left. He knew Henry had done far more than just beat her.

"Last night, when you said you'd never

kiss my boots, I thought it was just a figure of speech, but it wasn't, was it? The bastard really made you do it, didn't he?"

Amy's stomach knotted. A hundred lies sprang to mind, but she knew before she uttered a word that lying to Swift was as impossible as lying to herself. So she said nothing.

Swift tightened his grip on the chair back, watching her as she lifted her head a notch higher, her eyes brilliant with shattered pride. "Amy, sometimes life gets bigger than we are, and we do things we never dreamed we could just to survive. There's no shame in that. If you think you're the only person who's ever been brought to his knees, you're dead wrong."

Amy felt naked and so ashamed she wanted to die. *You were glorious.* He would never think her glorious again. More tears rushed to her eyes, and she blinked, trying to hold them back.

"Amy . . ."

The tears overflowed onto her cheeks, hot and ticklish. "I don't want Hunter and Loretta to know," she said shakily.

"I won't tell them. You have my word on that." He muttered something under his breath, gazed at the ceiling a moment, then riveted those all-seeing brown eyes on her again. "One question. Loretta said you wrote her letters, saying everything was fine. Why, for God's sake? Did you doubt for a second that Hunter would come? He'd have walked the whole way if he'd had to."

Amy gulped, then found her voice. "I, um, Henry stood over me and told me what to write. Until the last mule died, he took the letters to a neighbor's and had him post them. I couldn't write myself without him knowing." She forced herself to meet his gaze, then stared at him, words deserting her for a moment. "Wh-when did you say you were leaving?"

"Today. You anxious to see my dust settle?"

Amy saw the hurt in his expression. She folded her hands in her lap, swallowing back a denial.

"I wish you had leveled with me," he whispered. "When I think back on everything I've said and done, I —" He broke off and moved the coffeepot off the direct heat so it wouldn't boil over. "I might have understood you a lot better."

She bent her head, gazing at the cracks in her bleached floor. The bloodstain by the stove still discolored the wood. "I don't need to be understood. I just need to be left alone."

"I realize that now." He heaved another sigh. "About last night —"

"I lied." She looked up, and their gazes locked. Silence stretched taut between them. "I lied because I was afraid."

"I know."

"No, you can't know." She closed her eyes, unable to bear looking at him. "You're a man. Things are different for you."

"I think I can come close." Swift yearned to brush the wetness from her cheeks, to gather her into his arms, to hold her while she wept. But she was fighting the tears, battling the memories, afraid, for reasons beyond him, to share either with him. And until she did, he didn't dare touch her. "You were afraid if you admitted you liked the kiss that I'd demand more, that I'd marry you. And then your life would never be your own."

She made a strange sound, half sob, half laugh. "What life?" She lifted her lashes and brushed at the tears on her cheeks with tremulous fingers. "Do you realize this house and everything I've saved would become yours if I married you? Even my clothing! If you decided to sell everything and give away the money, I'd have absolutely no say in it."

"Of course you would."

"Not by law."

"Is that what this is about? About the things you own?"

Bright crimson dotted her pale cheeks. "No, it's about being owned. By you! By anyone!"

The words shot from her mouth, stark and ugly, crackling between them. By her expression, Swift guessed that she hadn't meant to say them, that she wished she could call them back.

"Owned, Amy?"

"Yes, owned! Have you any idea how it feels to be — someone's property?"

Swift knew he had finally drawn the truth from her, but he was left feeling as confused as ever. Naturally he would consider her his property if he married her, just as she would him. "I'm not sure I understand what you mean."

"It's simple. If I married you, you would own me. If I bore children, you'd own them. Do you know what the neighbors said when I ran away from Henry and asked them for sanctuary?"

Swift stared at her. "No. Tell me."

"They said he was my father. And I had to go home. That I should try not to rile him. As if *I* were to blame!" A haunted look crept into her eyes. "I was in no shape to take off walking to get out of there that night, let me assure you. It was all I could do to reach them. The man saddled up his horse and took me home, as if that were the noble thing to do."

Swift didn't want to hear the rest. "What happened?"

"What do you think? Henry was furious. And drunk, as usual. Do you think he patted me on the head and said it was very bad of me for going to the neighbors?"

"Amy, Henry was the world's worst bastard. One man in a thousand."

"No!" She shook her head and pushed up from the chair. Pacing, she ran her hands over things, the coffee grinder, the butter churn, a decorative plate on the wall, her eyes not seeming to focus on what she touched. "Right here in Wolf's Landing, it happens. The man has all the power. Men make the laws, and there are precious few to protect wives and children. God forbid they should lose control of their families."

"That's an exaggeration."

"Think what you like."

"After what you've been through, I guess it'd be mighty scary to put yourself in a vulnerable position again."

"Scary? No, Swift. Scared is when something jumps out at you and your heart leaps." She ran a hand over her hair. "Did you notice the bruises on Peter when you were attending school?"

Swift thought back. "I — yes, one on his cheek."

"His father, Abe Crenton, gets in his cups over at his saloon and goes home for the big finale."

"Have you gone to the marshal?"

"I talked Alice Crenton into going."

There was a world of heartbreak in her eyes. Swift stared at her. "And what did Marshal Hilton do?"

"He threw Abe in jail for five days."

"And?"

"When Crenton got out, he went home to *his* house and beat *his* wife for having him locked up." She dampened a rag and wiped off the table, which looked spotlessly clean to Swift. After finishing, she clenched her hand around the cloth. "Really beat her, so she'd never dare file a complaint against him again."

"She could leave, Amy. No one has to put up with that."

She stared down at the cloth a moment, then lifted her gaze to his. "Really? And where would she go, Swift? She has no way to earn a living and five children to feed. She can't throw him out. It's his house. She looks on the bright side. Her kids aren't starving. A few bruises aren't so bad."

"Are you telling me that Hunter stands by and lets some man in this town beat his wife and kids, and he does nothing?"

"I've never laid the problem at Hunter's doorstep. What could he do? Beat Crenton? There are laws against that." She laughed softly, bitterly. "Hunter would end up in jail, and for a whole lot longer than five days." She held up her hands. "That's the way it is. Peter comes to me for comfort after the bad times." Her voice turned thin. "And I hug him and put medicine on his cuts. And I say the unforgivable. 'He's your father, Peter. You've got to go back home. Try real hard not to rile him.' And he does his best, until the next time."

Swift closed his eyes.

"I hate myself for saying that to him, but that's life, right? You said that to me, remember? That's life. . . ."

"Amy, I'm sorry. You can't doubt I love you."

"No. But —" She made a frustrated sound and tossed the rag onto the table. Curling her hands into fists at her sides, she said, "I just can't take the leap of faith other women take. I can't, Swift. After Ma, I was Henry's whipping post for three miserable, endless years, with no way out. Do you know what finally drove me to leave on foot? He had sent for a preacher! He was going to marry me! There wouldn't have been an escape for me, not ever. I preferred to die of thirst on the plains. So I left and swore I'd never give anyone dominion over me again."

"I understand." And the heartbreak was that he truly did.

"There's a dark side to you, Swift, a side you've never let me see, but I know it's there."

"Yes, there's a dark side. Don't we all have one, though?"

"Yes, and that's the problem. We can't escape the fact that we're all just human beings, with faults and weaknesses." Tears welled behind her lashes again, brilliant, turning her eyes into shimmering pools. "I'm not condemning you, truly I'm not."

"Aren't you?"

Her small face twisted. "No! I understand the situation you were in was impossible, that you survived the only way you could. It's just —" Her breath caught and came out of her in a jagged rush. "If I married you, it might be wonderful. Then again, after the new wore off, maybe it wouldn't be. There are no guarantees in life. Marriage, especially for a woman, is a big gamble. And the stakes are just too high for me."

"I'd never lift my hand against you. Surely you know that."

"I know you don't believe you would. But the magic wears off, Swift. Daily life gets dull and frustrating, and there are hardships. People quarrel and lose their tempers. Men drink. They come home in nasty moods. It happens. Can you swear to me it wouldn't? You've led a violent life. You've killed so many men you've lost count. Can you truly put that behind you?"

A muscle began to tic along his jaw. "Amy, I can't promise you a life with no rough spots, if that's what you're wanting. I can't promise I'll never lose my temper. All I can promise is that I'll never hurt you. No matter how mad I get. If I really blew up, I might take the house apart, or scream and yell and threaten. But I'd never lay a hand on you."

She dug her teeth into her bottom lip, her gaze clinging to his. Swift knew she waged a battle. He also knew the fear within her overwhelmed all else. After a while she whispered, "I wish I had the courage to give you the chance to prove that. But I don't. I'm sorry. I know you don't understand. . . ."

"But I do understand. I did a lot of thinking last night." He took a deep breath and glanced up at the window, letting his eyes fall closed for an instant. "That's why I'm leaving." He returned his gaze to her. "I don't want you to feel threatened. We never made it to being lovers, but no one's ever had a more beautiful friendship. You don't make a friend's life hell, not if you can help it."

He rose and took two mugs from her cupboard. She turned to watch him, her eyes shadowed. Filling each cup with coffee, he handed one to her, making a valiant effort to smile as if his heart weren't breaking. "Have a swig with an old friend?"

Amy took the mug, stared at it a moment. "Wh-where will you go?" she asked in a faint voice.

"I don't know. Wherever I light, I guess."

"Will you — ever come back?"

Swift avoided her gaze. "To do what? Spar with you? Make you unhappy again? I love you, honey. I wish we could be just friends, but that isn't possible, and you know it. I want more. I can't help wanting more." He shrugged. "I'd like to come back now and again to see you, but I probably won't."

"We were such good friends, though." She clutched the coffee mug, trembling so that

343

the dark liquid sloshed over the porcelain edge. "We had such fun together."

"We were kids. I'm no kid anymore, Amy. I need more than you're able to give. Last night, when we were dancing, I told myself I could settle for just seeing you smile." He raked a hand through his hair. "And if it was just me I had to think of, maybe I could. But what if I'm not that noble? I'm not the only one who'd suffer. You would, too. I couldn't take that."

With a shaking hand she set her mug on the table, memories washing over her, so sweet she yearned to recapture them. She stood there, rigid and shaking. "Why can't you just love me? Why does it have to be dirty?"

Swift's guts contracted into a knot and he nearly choked on his coffee. He swallowed hard. "Amy, it isn't dirty. It's beautiful with the right person."

A closed expression came over her face. "H-how far away do you think you'll go?"

He sighed and reclaimed his chair. "I don't know. Until the urge comes over me to stop and hang my hat, I guess." He gazed up at her. "Won't you sit down with me, honey? This one last time, as friends."

She sank onto a chair, the closed expression still on her face. Swift ached at that look, for he had secretly hoped she might beg him to stay, that the love he knew she felt for him might give her the fragile courage to take a chance on him.

They drank their coffee in frigid silence, a far cry from the camaraderie of old friends. When Swift finished off the last sip, he stared into the dregs and abandoned all hope that she'd say the words he longed to hear. An image of her back flashed in his mind, the network of scars that were testimony to all she had suffered, and he understood her letting him leave. He understood, but that didn't stop it from hurting.

"Well . . ."

She didn't lift her eyes from her coffee mug. Her hands were clenched around the porcelain, her knuckles white and rimmed with red. Swift had the horrible feeling he was deserting her, yet how could he not?

"I guess I'd better see to my horse and get my gear together," he said softly.

She still didn't look up. He rose from the chair, set his mug on the dish board, lingered, praying to her God and all his that she'd fly up from the chair and into his arms. But she didn't. And she never would.

"Good-bye, Amy," he said in a husky voice.

"Good-bye, Swift."

She kept her head bent, never moving. He went toward the door, each step tearing a chunk out of his heart. When he reached the threshold, he looked back. She remained where he had left her, clinging to the coffee mug as if it were her lifeline.

Hunter sat on the straw bale, watching Swift saddle his horse. The time had come for saying last words, something neither man wanted to face. They were the only two of a kind, in a strange and sometimes hostile world.

"I hope the sun shines upon you," Hunter said.

Swift smiled through the sadness. "My sunshine's up the street, Hunter. Take care of her for me, will you?"

"I always have."

Swift tightened the saddle cinch. His good-byes to Hunter's family had been said. The time had come to leave.

"Hunter . . ." Swift rested his hand on Diablo's neck. "There are things about Amy you don't know."

Hunter's blue eyes lifted and sharpened. "Yes?"

"I gave her my promise that I'd never tell you."

"Amy has no secrets from us."

"Yes . . . she does, Hunter. Terrible secrets." Swift's throat constricted. He had never willingly broken a promise in his life. "You said you'd built her a safe world, and that you'd done a bad thing. I'm asking you to let her hide here and dream her dreams, for as long as you can. Don't let anything threaten that. For Amy, the world you've given her is her survival."

Hunter's face tightened. "What are these secrets?"

"I can't tell you that. And don't press her to tell you." Swift led Diablo in a circle to turn the stallion toward the door. "Some things are best left buried."

"Henry . . ." Hunter whispered the name, his eyes taking on a gleam of anger.

"Don't press, Hunter." Swift hesitated, gazing over his saddle at his friend. "I won't betray her trust. She's been betrayed enough to last her a lifetime. Just be there for her."

Hunter looked sick. He closed his eyes, his throat working. "But the letters — everything was fine."

Swift offered no explanation for that. Because of his promise to Amy, he couldn't.

"I think I must go to Texas," Hunter whispered.

Swift's hands started to shake. "Jesus! You can't do that. Don't talk crazy, Hunter."

Hunter met his gaze. "Where are *you* going?"

Swift averted his face. "I told you, wherever I light."

"Maybe in Texas."

"Who's to say?"

"If you go there, you'll never come back. You know that, and I know that. Does Amy know? That is the question."

"What I do is no concern of hers."

Hunter pushed up from the straw bale. "I will pack."

Swift swore. "You'll do no such thing. Loretta and your children need you here, and, damn it to hell, so does Amy."

Hunter clenched his hands. "What did he do to her?"

"You don't want to know, my friend."

In a blur of movement Hunter came across the barn, grabbed Swift by the shirt, and threw him against the wall. For an instant Swift was so taken by surprise that he drew back his fist. Then he focused on Hunter's rage-contorted face and forced his body to relax.

"What did he do to her?"

"I won't fight you, Hunter."

"You will tell me! She is part of my heart!"

"No. I promised her, and I won't betray

her. If you're my friend, you won't ask me to."

"Why did she never tell me herself? Why?"

"Because she's —" Swift pushed Hunter away, straightening his shirt with a shrug. Raking his hand through his hair, he paced, then turned. "Some things are mighty hard to talk about. She never told me, if that's what's eating you. I found out by digging and —" Swift threw up his hands. "She doesn't want anyone to know. She's hidden it from you and Loretta all these years. It's not my place to say anything."

"Yet you go to Texas?"

"I never said that."

"Your eyes say it. You're going to reclaim her honor. He raped her, didn't he?"

Swift picked up his hat where it had fallen during their scuffle. Clamping it on his head, he led his horse from the barn. Hunter followed, rigid with anger. His gaze shifted from Swift to Amy's little house at the other end of town.

"Don't say anything to her," Swift said. "Promise you won't. It'd just about kill her if she found out you knew."

"Why?"

Swift sighed, hesitating with one foot in the stirrup. "Shame, maybe."

"Shame!" Hunter's face drained of color.

"Shame? It's Henry's shame, not hers! Never hers!"

"To our way of thinking. But Amy wasn't raised like we were. Just let it go, Hunter. The wound's healed over."

"Healed? The man she loves is riding out of her life!"

Swift felt as though someone had plunged a knife into his stomach. "Whether or not she loves me is another thing entirely. She doesn't trust anymore, and who can blame her? Bringing it all out — shaming her — won't change how she's come to feel."

Swift swung into the saddle. Hunter grabbed the stallion's bridle. "Swift, if you're going, take her with you. Ride down there, throw her on the horse, tie her on, if you have to, and take her with you. Don't leave her here to live the rest of her life with nightmares."

"Hunter, I'm her nightmare."

With that, Swift spurred his horse into a gallop. The horse's hooves threw up dirt as it careened onto the street and leveled out in a run.

CHAPTER 14

Amy clutched the windowsill, staring through the steamed glass as Swift rode his black up the street. Tears filled her eyes, and she began to shake. He drew his horse to a walk as he passed her house. Her gaze shifted from the gun belt that rode his hips to the conchae on his black hat, then fell to the roll of black wool across the back of his saddle, the hated poncho.

A comanchero, a gunslinger, a killer. She forced herself to repeat the words in her mind, to remember who and what he was. But she could no longer find the fear she had once felt. He was just Swift, a curious blend of past and present, a hard, bitter man with a capacity for violence she couldn't fathom. Yet he touched her with such gentleness.

He rode to the top of the hill and wheeled his horse to look back. She had the feeling he could see her at the window, but she didn't drop the curtain or pull away. She couldn't. She wanted to drink in the sight of him, memorize every detail, because she knew, deep in her heart, that once he disappeared she would never see him again.

A sob swelled in her throat. She willed him to ride off so the hurting would stop. But he just sat there on his horse, buffeted by the late October wind, staring at her house, as if he were waiting, giving her this one last chance. *Trust me,* he seemed to be saying. *Come out of the house, Amy. Run into my arms. Take a chance on me.*

"I can't, Swift," she whispered to no one. "I can't."

Whirling from the window, Amy clamped a hand over her mouth and squeezed her eyes closed. She wouldn't watch. She'd pretend he had never come. She'd get on with her life. She wouldn't wish for things she couldn't have.

The world I belonged in is gone. You're my last chance. Rigid, she stood there, the seconds measured by her slamming pulse, each one an agony because she knew he might have left by now, that if she turned and looked, the hilltop would be empty.

As empty as her life.

Swift nudged Diablo into a trot, tightening

his hands on the reins. The wind whipped against his jaw, cut through his shirt. He reached behind him for the poncho, hesitated, then jerked it free from the ties. It didn't matter now if he wore it. It never would again. Giving the stallion free lead, he took off his hat to shove his head through the slit in the wool. The protective layer of clothing didn't warm him. But then, the chill he felt went deeper than the flesh.

Taking up the reins again, he settled his gaze on the skyline, an endless expanse of trees and mountains. *A man with yesterdays on his horizon travels a great distance to nowhere.*

Diablo snorted and pricked his ears. Swift listened, heard nothing. The stallion snorted again. Reining him to a walk, Swift twisted in the saddle to look back. *Wishful thinking,* he chided himself. *Just keep riding. Don't torture yourself.* But he listened all the same. And then he heard it. A cry, carried on the wind, so faint he nearly missed it.

Then she appeared on the hilltop, gray skirts blowing, wisps of golden hair flying from her braid around her face. He focused, blinked, afraid he was imagining her. *Amy.* Gathering up her skirts, she came tearing down the rutted road at such a breakneck speed he feared she might lose her footing and fall.

About twenty feet away, she staggered to a stop. Tears streaked her face. Her eyes looked tortured, so blue against her pale skin they reached out and grabbed him. She clasped her hands over her waist, short of breath, sobbing.

"Swift . . ." She gasped and swallowed, struggling to speak. "Wait . . . until tomorrow. Please? Just one more day."

His heart felt like a rag she was wringing out. "What difference will one more day make, Amy?"

Her face contorted, twisted. She cupped a shaking hand over her eyes. "Don't go. Please don't go."

Swift swung off the horse. The poncho caught in the wind, the fringe whipping up and lashing his cheek. He should take it off; he knew how she hated it. But, as she said, a man couldn't outrun his yesterdays, no matter how he tried.

"Amy, look at me."

She dropped her hand, focused on him through shimmering tears, her mouth atremble. "Won't you stay with me one more day?"

Swift let his gaze trail off to the trees, steeling himself against the plea in her voice. "Why, Amy? So we can go through this again tomorrow? It's better this way, quick and clean."

"You'll never come back." She took several steps toward him. "I don't want you to leave."

"For one more day?"

"I don't want you to leave at all."

He leveled a gaze on her. "Why? Say it, Amy."

She closed her eyes and braced herself. "You know why, damn you! You know why!"

"That's not good enough. I want the words."

"Because . . . I love you!"

Swift's stomach twisted. "Look at me when you say it. I'm no sketch on the mantel. I can't go back and become the boy you knew. You have to take me the way I am now. *Look* at me."

She slowly opened her eyes. Her gaze traveled from his concha-banded hat to the poncho, touching on his guns, settling on his silver spurs. Then, her face draining of all color, she looked directly into his eyes. She swayed slightly, as if the wind might carry her with it.

"I love you."

The words carried no conviction. He regarded her, acutely aware that their future, if they even had one, depended totally upon her and what pitiful measure of courage she had left.

"If you really love me, Amy, then take those three steps I asked you to take that first night. But understand that if you do, your freedom's gone. You call it owning, but I call it loving. And I want it all, your love, your life, your body. I won't settle for less."

She wrung her hands, staring at him. "T-today, you mean?"

It was painfully obvious that her attention had centered on only a part of what he had said. Swift clenched his teeth. As frightened of lovemaking as she was, he couldn't allow her to hold part of herself away from him. They'd end up right back where they started. He knew now that the thought of anyone having power over her terrified her. She might never move beyond that unless he forced her to surrender to him. Only then could he prove her fears were groundless.

With supreme effort, he finally managed to speak. "Maybe today. Maybe right now, right here. That isn't the question. You know it isn't. What difference does when make, Amy, if you trust me, if you truly believe I love you? When you love someone, you care about their feelings. If you don't believe, with all your heart, that I care about yours, then do us both a favor and go home."

"I believe it."

"Then you know what you have to do." He held her gaze, hating himself but convinced he had no options. "It's your choice. I gave you your freedom. If that's what you want, take it and run. If it's not, you've got three steps to take, and I can't help you take them."

She just stood there, as if her feet were pinned to the dirt. Swift waited. It was the longest wait of his life. And she still didn't move.

Turning toward his horse, he said, "Goodbye, Amy."

"No!" she cried.

Swift glanced back to see her running toward him. He barely had time to turn before she catapulted. He caught her, staggering under the impact of her weight. Then he tightened his arms around her. She trembled, clinging to him. Tears burned behind his eyelids. He bent his head, pressing his face into the sweet curve of her neck, reveling in the feel of her against him, all reservations gone. He had yearned for this, dreamed of it, but nothing compared to the reality of Amy in his arms.

"D-don't leave me," she cried. "Please, don't, Swift. I'll take the risks. I'll change. I will, I truly will. If you'll only give me a chance. Just one more?"

Freeing a hand, he pulled the folds of his poncho around her to protect her from the wind, then hugged her close again. She pressed nearer, if that was possible. Swift ached for her, wishing he could undo all that had been done. But he couldn't.

"Oh, Amy, love, I don't want you to change. I don't care if you come to me afraid," he whispered gruffly. "I don't care if it takes us years to make things right between us when we make love. The only thing I care about is that you come to me freely." He swallowed back a rush of fear, afraid to press her, yet knowing he must. "Say you're mine, Amy. I want your betrothal promise. Not one from fifteen years ago, but now, from the bottom of your heart. Can you do that?"

The tension in her body told him what it cost her to say the words. "I'm yours. I'll marry you. I — I promise."

"And if I choose to make love to you right now, under one of those trees over there? Does the promise still hold?"

A shudder shook her. "Y-yes."

Swift's arms convulsed, tightening around her. In the back of his mind, a warning went off. She was delicately built. He might be hurting her. But, damn, he loved her so. To hear her say yes, even with trepidation, was such a joy he wanted to hug the breath right out of her, to meld their bodies into one, so he'd never have to fear losing her again. He struggled for control, forcing his arms to relax. Placing one hand on her hair, one on her back, he swayed with her in the wind, soothing her with his touch, receiving solace himself when the tension eased out of her and she relaxed against him.

"You'll never regret this, Amy. Never."

He swept her up into his arms and carried her to his horse. Swinging her into the saddle, he arranged her skirts around her, then mounted behind her, encircling her waist with his arm. She threw a dread-filled glance toward the trees but didn't ask his intentions. He knew the silence didn't come easily for her.

He drew her snugly against him and bent his head to hers. The brim of his hat cut the wind. "Do you remember my saying that you used to have Comanche heart?"

She nodded, saying nothing. Swift brushed his lips along her temple. "You still have Comanche heart, Amy. More so, I think, than anyone I've ever known."

"No," she said in a hollow voice. "Not anymore."

Tears turned to ice on his cheeks. "Oh, yes. Do you think courage means being fearless? Or daring? Courage, real courage, is taking three steps when it terrifies you."

Firelight played upon their faces. Stretched out on the rug before the hearth, Swift held Amy in the crook of his body, one arm at her waist, a hand splayed over her midriff, his fingertips inches below her breasts. The silence between them made room for inconsequential sound, the wind whistling along the eaves of her little house, the tree limb outside her bedroom window squeaking forlornly on the glass, their hearts beating, their lungs drawing breath, the clock ticking away the minutes of their future, which yawned before them now, an unfulfilled promise.

Swift ran his fingers over the cloth of her dress, touching the tiny buttons that ran so primly to her high collar. She didn't flinch away, and that pleased him. It also forestalled him from touching anything other than the buttons.

"I'm going to have to go see Hunter, tell him I'm not leaving," he whispered.

She stirred slightly. Swift guessed she was probably drained after last night and this morning, that numbness had set in. He had stayed; evidently that had become her one reality, the only thing she could deal with, for now. This time together, with the firelight and the silence, was their lull before the storm. She had to realize he wanted more, that he would eventually demand more, but for now he allowed her the moment.

Memories drifted through Swift's mind. He sensed that she remembered, too. With the firelight and the wind outside, it was easy to believe the walls around them were leather, that the whistling wind came from the north, sweeping across grassy plains. Children, huddled by an evening fire, bellies full, limbs tired and relaxed from running all day under an endless summer sky, laughing and playing. It was that long-ago bond of friendship, of trust, that held them together now. Such a precious gift, that friendship, and they had nearly lost it.

Swift realized that he had to reach back through the years and recapture more than just memories, that somehow he had to bring laughter and magic back into their relationship. For Amy's sake. And maybe for his own.

He sat up slowly, careful in his every movement, so as not to startle her. Drawing her up before him, he studied her blue eyes. Mostly she looked bewildered and wary, as if she weren't quite sure how she had come to this pass and was dreading what came next. Reading those emotions, Swift knew how dearly she must love him. She had thrown caution aside to keep him here, and Amy had far more reason than most people to be cautious.

Sitting on her heels, her skirts fanned around them, she looked very like the child she had once been. He ran a finger along the shadowy contour of her cheek, uncertain what to say.

"Do you know how beautiful you are?"

Her gaze fell to his mouth. She clearly expected him to make a move, and she was braced. He sighed and trailed his hand to her braid, slowly pulling the combs, unwinding the heavy length of gold, loosening it into a shimmering curtain with his fingertips. His gut contracted as the strands slid across his arm, warm and silken, as he imagined her skin. To finally have inalienable rights and not exercise them was sheer torture.

"Someday you're going to come to me wearing nothing but your beautiful hair," he whispered huskily.

A tiny muscle at the corner of her mouth twitched as he lifted a palm of the gold ripples and touched them to his cheek.

"I promised to be yours, Swift. That's all I promised. Don't expect more than I can give."

"That's just it, Amy. I don't want what you can't give."

Her eyes darkened. "Wh-what are you saying?"

Swift sighed. He wasn't sure what the hell he was saying. "I just don't want you to be frightened."

"I can't help that."

"But I can. Do you really believe I would rape you?" He caught her chin so she couldn't look away. "Do you?"

She regarded him like a trembling rabbit might a hungry hawk. He realized that a loving physical relationship was beyond her scope and totally at odds with her memories. She saw sex as one-sided, a dirty thing that men demanded and women were forced to render.

Her voice rang thin and thready, like an off-key note on a reed flute. "But I — there's no question of that now."

That fact clearly terrified her. Swift nearly smiled, not because he found her fear amusing, but because he knew how unnecessary it was. If Texas hadn't been so far away, he would have paid a call on Henry Masters.

Forcing away his anger, Swift studied her

small face. "Do you know what I want more than anything? I want to laugh with you — like we used to."

Her eyes clouded with memories. "We did laugh a lot, didn't we? I think —" She broke off and studied him, her expression melancholy. "Do you know that you were my one and only best friend? I never had another, growing up so far away from neighbors as I did. Sometimes, while I was still on the farm in Texas, when I grew lonely, I'd sit under the pecan tree and pretend you were there with me."

An ache crawled up his throat. "I wish I had been."

"I'd remember things that we did together." She smiled slightly, her eyes shimmering up at him. "It was almost as good as actually doing them again. Or I'd tell you my troubles and imagine what you'd say. You gave me some very good advice."

"What did I tell you?"

"To look at the horizon." Tears filled her eyes. "You'd say, 'Look into tomorrow, Amy. Yesterday is over.' And I'd find the courage to go on, just one more day, because tomorrow might be the day you'd come for me." She sighed and lifted her hands in a little shrug. "I couldn't give up, you see, because tomorrow was only one night away."

It pained Swift to think what troubles she might have had and that he hadn't been there to do anything about them. Perhaps someday she would share those experiences with him and purge herself. He knew how it felt to hang on for just one more day. He also knew how bad things had to be for a person to live beyond the present, his only hope an elusive tomorrow that never came.

"We have a second chance, you and I," he whispered. "A chance to be best friends again."

"We're no longer children," she reminded him. "We can't go back."

"Can't we? That's what I want — what we used to have. Making love together will just happen, when it feels right."

She drew herself up, lifting her chin a notch. "Swift, I have to tell you that I don't believe it'll ever feel right to me. You have to understand that."

Appreciating her honesty, knowing how difficult it must be for her to dispense with subterfuge, especially when she risked so much, he said, "I'll know when the time is right. It isn't now. So relax and just enjoy being with me."

"But —" She caught her lower lip between her teeth, worrying it for a moment. "Don't you see? I can't relax when I know that —

that it might happen."

"Then I'll warn you first. How's that sound?"

"You'll warn me?"

"Yes. And until I do, there's nothing to worry about. So there's no need to feel frightened if I touch you or kiss you."

A glimmer of hope shone in her eyes, along with a great deal of doubt. "You promise?"

Swift had a feeling this was a vow he might have to repeat again and again until she began to believe him. "I swear it, Amy."

CHAPTER 15

That evening, the Wolfs had a huge Sunday dinner in celebration of Swift's decision to stay. Amy attended, as she always had their Sunday meal before Swift's arrival in Wolf's Landing. And for the first time since his coming she could be herself, embraced by those she loved, laughing and talking and teasing. Acutely aware of how his presence there had stripped her already lonely life, robbing her of her family and their support, Swift felt his throat tightening more than once.

Toward the end of the meal, Amy surprised even Swift when she suddenly stood and said she had an announcement to make. Everyone looked up at her. As she met Swift's gaze across the table, her cheeks turned a shy pink, her eyes a brilliant blue. She clearly had reservations about whatever it was she planned to say. His body drew taut. Before she spoke, he guessed her intent, and he could scarcely believe she had worked up the courage to take such an irrevocable step so quickly.

"I know Swift may not tell you this, out of regard for me," she said in a shaky little voice. She swallowed, looking nervous. "After all the fuss I've made since his arrival here, I think it's only fair I tell you that I renewed my betrothal promises to him today."

Silence descended, a rigid, breathless silence, as if everyone at the table had frozen in place. The muscles in Amy's thighs knotted. She pressed a hand to her skirt. There, she had said it. No turning back now. Calling on all her courage, she looked into Swift's eyes. He looked like a man who had just drawn four aces in a high-stakes poker game.

After a long while Hunter said, "I hope the sun shines upon you both."

With a little cry, Loretta leaped from her chair and gave Amy a heartfelt hug. "I knew it would work out. I knew it."

Another wave of uncertainty rushed Amy as she returned Loretta's embrace. Nothing had been worked out as yet. She could feel Swift's gaze on her. She wondered what he was thinking, why he didn't speak, why he was smiling that way.

"So you're going to be married?" Indigo piped up with childish enthusiasm. "Oh, that's grand! I think we should have a big party to celebrate. Maybe Brandon Marshall will come." She fastened blue eyes on Loretta. "May I invite him, Ma?"

Pulling away from Amy, Loretta threw her daughter a flustered look. "Let's get the party planned first, Indigo. Then we'll discuss invitations."

Swift held up a hand. "There'll be no party." His voice rang with determination. "Not for a while, anyway."

"Whyever not?" Loretta asked.

Swift's left eyebrow rose a fraction. "Because I don't want anyone beyond these walls knowing until we decide we're ready."

Hunter broke in. "That isn't our way, Swift. Betrothals are always announced publicly."

"It's my way." Swift leaned back in his chair and curled one hand around his coffee mug. His gaze, dark and unreadable, caught Amy's. "We have a lot of catching up to do. Getting married soon is out of the question."

"There's nothing wrong with a long engagement," Loretta assured him. "What can it hurt if you make an official announcement?"

Swift turned his gaze on Amy again, his mouth tipping in another mysterious smile. "Amy's job is very important to her. I'd like for her to be able to keep it."

Amy blinked, trying to make sense of what he had said, but before she could assimilate it, Loretta cried, "Why would an announcement about your engagement jeopardize her job?"

Once again, Swift seemed to have eyes only for Amy. "I'm not exactly the most popular person in Wolf's Landing. If tongues started wagging . . . well, it doesn't take a genius to figure out what might happen. I don't want to take that chance. Holding off on telling everyone will give people an opportunity to know me better. Maybe then it won't matter if their schoolteacher marries an ex-gunslinger."

"But tongues are bound to wag even worse if people don't know you're engaged," Loretta argued.

"Not if we're careful about being seen together too much. We've been fairly successful at that so far."

Swift rocked back in his chair, his shoulders relaxed, one arm crooked over the chair back, a hand resting on his thigh. Amy could almost feel the warmth of those strong fingers splayed beneath her breasts, the

370

strength of his arm around her.

"If you're going to be married, Aunt Amy won't need a job," Chase inserted. "She'll stay home and cook and take care of kids."

"Who says?" Still balancing the chair on its back legs, Swift turned his head toward the boy. "Why does she have to give up everything to be married?"

"Yeah, Chase, how come?" Indigo demanded. "Women can do other things besides keep house and wash clothes."

Chase rolled his eyes.

Laughing, Swift held up a hand. "I didn't mean to start a war here. It's just that the white way of doing things doesn't sound fair to me. In fact, now that I can write my name, I'm going to sign a paper that says Amy's house is her house, and that her money is hers, too."

Amy's heart soared. So touched it was all she could do not to cry, she clamped a hand to her bodice. "What did you say?"

"You heard me."

"You're going to sign away rights to my house and wages?"

"That's outlandish!" Loretta cried. "What wife would want a division of property?"

"A wife who needs to feel independent." Swift slanted Hunter an amused glance. "Do you have a problem with that?"

Hunter shrugged. "It is a good way, the way of the People. We signed no paper, but a woman's property was her own."

"Then it's settled. Right, Amy?" Swift watched his bride to be, waiting patiently for her to speak. When she simply stood there, staring at him, he said, "Well, do you agree or not?"

Amy tried to speak and couldn't. Finally she simply nodded. Swift's mouth tipped in a slow grin. For an endless moment, Amy forgot everyone else in the room. There was only Swift and the tenderness she saw in his dark eyes.

When the meal was concluded and the dishes had been washed, Swift invited Amy for an evening walk. She accepted without hesitation. Once they gained the trees behind the house where no one might see them, they slowed their pace to a lazy stroll.

When he took hold of her hand, Amy took a cleansing breath, exhaling on a sigh. "You haven't changed. In so many ways, you haven't changed."

"How's that?"

She smiled and met his gaze. "One minute you're demanding promises, the next you're changing your mind. I didn't expect —" She broke off and arched an eyebrow. "You didn't have to make any of those concessions during dinner. Yet you did. Why?"

The lines deepened along his brows and under his eyes. "I don't think your people's way is fair."

Amy circled that. "Most men like having the laws in their favor. Their house, their money. They have control that way."

"I'm not most men." He made a loose fist and lightly touched his knuckles to her chin. "As long as I don't beat you once a week to keep my arm in shape, you'll never need that paper. Signing it's a small thing to me, if it makes you happy."

Matching her pace to his, she leaned her head against his arm, gazing at the trees ahead of them. Swift studied the top of her golden head. Taking yet another deep breath, she let it out slowly, as if a huge weight had been lifted from her.

"You used to do the same thing, demanding the most frightening things possible of me and then taking very little once I surrendered them to you." She tipped her face up. "I still remember the first few times you dragged me off for a walk after Hunter rescued me from the comancheros. You took me to hell and gone out there along the river, as far away from the village as you could. You knew what I was thinking."

"It wasn't hard to guess," he replied with

a grin. "You needed to learn that you didn't need the security of others to be safe with me. That was the only way to prove it to you."

"You're doing it again. Trying to prove something to me. You lead me to expect the very worst of you. And then you do none of the things I expect. You made me agree to make love alongside the road today. Yet you never intended to do any such thing, did you? Just when I think I know where I stand, you turn everything inside out."

With a sigh, he drew up and pulled her into the circle of his arm.

He bent his head and brushed his lips across her cheek. A shiver of reaction raced down her spine, and her breath caught when his mouth brushed the corner of hers.

"It's so simple, Amy. All I want, all I've ever wanted, is your trust. If I have that, I have everything. Don't you see? The rest will just happen."

With tears in her eyes she touched the scar on his cheek, then pressed her forehead against his chest. "It's not easy for me."

He smiled and hunched his shoulders around her, content to hold her close. "I know. But it'll come if we give it time."

When Swift lifted his head, he saw tears shimmering in her eyes.

"I love you, Swift," she whispered raggedly. "I never stopped."

"I know."

Looking down at her, seeing the fragile trust in her eyes, Swift could scarcely believe his good fortune and felt a sudden rush of anxiety. For over half of his life, happiness of any kind had eluded him. He hadn't dared allow himself to dream. Now he held the world in his arms. Amy. He loved her so much. What if something went wrong? What if he lost her again?

"Swift? What's wrong?" she whispered.

"Nothing. Everything's right."

Shoving the fears aside, he forced a smile and lowered his head, brushing his lips over hers. In the magic of the night, recapturing their love from childhood was enough. He'd deal with the future one day at a time.

CHAPTER 16

Exactly one week later, at about the same time of evening, Swift stood with a shoulder against Amy's porch post, his lips still tingling from her innocent good-night kisses, his guts knotted with yearning for more. After seven days of handling her with kid gloves, his patience was about as fragile as a wet bowstring. Leaving her was the hardest thing he had ever done. His every instinct demanded he go back inside and sweep her into his arms. She'd give herself to him. He had no doubt of that. And it would be the sweetest joining in his life. All he had to do was go back to her. . . .

Swift closed his eyes, the painful ache low in his guts making his stomach churn. All Amy's life, men had taken her with force. Tonight she had trusted him enough to let him hold her. She needed to go through this to see the contrast between being used and wanting to make love. Their union would be all the sweeter for it, and that was worth another night of frustration.

Clamping his hat on his head, he forced his feet down the steps, each stride a decision and a sacrifice. But in the end, he kept walking because he loved Amy far more than he desired physical release with her.

As had become his habit this week, Swift went to the saloon, hoping to find solace in a stiff whiskey and a friendly game of cards. Mainly in the whiskey. With his body screaming with longing for Amy every night, sleep took a long time coming, and he had to be at work early each morning in Hunter's mine. A drink relaxed him.

Randall Hamstead sat alone at a corner table inside the saloon. Swift went to the bar and ordered a drink, smiling politely at May Belle, a brassy blonde, who sat on a nearby barstool. She gave him a once-over while he waited to be served. In the bright lantern light the lines in her face stood out, making her heavily powdered skin look like crinkled paper. Above her black bodice, her breasts swelled like overripe melons.

Swift couldn't help but wonder how someone as attractive and kindhearted as she had wound up here, an aging whore, shining up to men she probably despised. Sometimes he wasn't sure who the savages were, Comanches or whites.

Swift paid for his drink and slid his change down the bar to her. She regarded the money with one artfully drawn eyebrow raised high. Picking up his drink, he sauntered between the tables to join Randall Hamstead. Pulling out a chair across from him, he said, "Well, Randall, how did the dry goods business do you today? You got enough spare change to play some poker with those cards, or are you just planning on looking at them all night?"

Randall grinned. "Just waiting for a sucker to come along. I was beginning to think you weren't coming in tonight."

"Ah, so I'm the sucker you were waiting for, am I?" Swift tossed a dollar onto the scarred surface of the table. "Ante and deal, my friend. We'll see which of us is the bigger fool."

Several hands of five-card stud later, Swift turned up two of a kind, ace high. "Doesn't beat a flush," Hamstead said, fanning his cards across the table. "You lose, Lopez. Again."

Swift grinned. "The way I figure, you haven't won back everything you lost to me two nights ago."

A group of miners at another table overheard Swift's gibe and laughed. Randall threw them a warning glance. "I'm only two dollars shy."

"Three." Swift took a drag off his cigarette, making a sweep with one hand to gather the cards. "I'm learning how to count, remember? Save your pride some other way."

From a nearby table, Abe Crenton brandished his empty whiskey bottle. "Pete!" he yelled. "Bring me another jug."

Randall cast the intoxicated saloon owner a look of disgust. "At least he doesn't like to play cards when he's like that."

"Is he good?"

Randall grinned and whispered, "He cheats. Don't ever bet your life savings when he's sitting in."

Swift hoped Crenton wouldn't go home drunk and make life hell for little Peter and his family. "Seven-card stud, four down and dirty," he said, slapping the deck on the table. "Care to slit your own throat?"

Hamstead cut the cards. "Here comes my three bucks home to me. I can feel it in my bones."

Swift dealt the first two cards face up and chuckled. "My lady beats the hell out of your ten. I'll see your dollar and raise you one."

Crenton leaned toward their table, so

drunk he nearly lost his seat. "What's that you say about your lady, Lopez?"

Swift lifted his gaze from the cards, his smile fading. "Pardon me?"

Crenton focused bleary blue eyes and flashed a nasty grin, his grizzled red beard so saturated with whiskey that he reeked from several feet away. "She as good in the sack as she looks?"

"Who?"

"Miss Amy — who in hell you think? You don't really think anyone b'lieves that you're doin' book learnin' o'er there at her house, do ya?"

Swift laid his cards on the table. He yearned to jump up and rearrange Crenton's face for him. Only regard for Amy forestalled him. If he didn't handle this right, he could do irreparable harm to her reputation. He forced himself to smile. "I wish I was having as much fun as everyone thinks I am. That woman's got so much starch in her drawers, they could walk off without her."

Crenton threw back his head and barked with laughter. Hamstead blushed and looked uncomfortable. "Miss Amy is a fine lady. You two shouldn't speak of her disrespectfully."

"I respect her," Swift countered, swallowing the last swig of whiskey in his glass and whistling as the liquor burned its way to his belly. "It's the only thing you can do with a lady like her. Not that I haven't tried. She's a beautiful woman."

"Amen to that," Crenton said, waving his empty whiskey glass. "So tell me, Lopez, if ya haven't been compromisin' her, why in hell'd you pay a hundred dollars for her dinner basket?"

Swift set down his glass and leaned back in his chair. "It was the only way I could think of to pay for my schooling. The committee wouldn't accept payment or even a donation from a man with my reputation. And Miss Amy, she won't accept money on the side. I figure the town ought to benefit in some way."

It was a lame explanation, but the only one Swift could come up with on such short notice. Crenton, however, seemed to think it made sense. He nodded and belched. "I reckon I'd feel the same. It's not as if you're one of the children. And" — he belched again — "the good folk in Wolf's Lan'ing prob'ly didn't want ya in their goddam uppity school anyhow."

Just then, the saloon doors banged open. Two men sauntered between the tables toward the bar. Because of their concha-banded hats slanted over their eyes, Swift couldn't make out their featutes. His attention centered on their clothing, and wariness washed over him. Silver conchae decorated one man's pants. The other wore a beaded, fringed leather vest. Both wore silver-studded gun belts. Their holsters rode low on their hips. They walked with cocky swaggers, shoulders high, arms slightly bent, carrying with them an air of tension, as if they disliked having their backs to strangers. Swift knew the feeling well.

"Two whiskeys," the man with the concha-studded pants called to the barkeep. "And line us up with a full bottle."

Swift slowly sat erect, uncomfortably aware that he wasn't wearing his guns. He glanced at the other customers in the saloon. No one but him appeared to think the two newcomers seemed out of place.

"You gonna finish the deal or sit there?" Randall asked.

Forcing himself to relax, Swift picked up the cards and, drawing on long practice, continued the game, his attention centered on the men at the bar.

"Pete! You comin' with that bottle?" Crenton yelled.

"On my way, boss."

The bartender served the two strangers.

As he hurried between the tables, bearing the second bottle for his boss, the stranger wearing the fringed vest turned and hooked a boot heel over the foot rail, one elbow braced on the bar, glass to his lips. He panned the room, his blue-eyed gaze touching on Swift, then sliding past him without hesitation.

Pete plunked the bottle down on the table in front of Crenton. Turning back to the bar, he struck up a conversation with the newcomers. Swift cocked an ear, hoping to glean information, scarcely noticing when Abe Crenton grabbed his bottle and staggered drunkenly toward the door.

"What brings you fellows to our fair city?" Pete asked.

"Been over in Jacksonville," said the man wearing the vest. "Heard there was strikes bein' made over this way."

Pete jerked a towel from off his shoulder to polish a glass. "Lot of gold in these hills, if a man's patient enough to look for it." He flashed a grin, making a swipe at the countertop. "You thinkin' to placer mine, or what?"

The man seemed to mull over his answer. "Well, to be honest, we're not certain sure. Never done much minin' before. We thought we'd do some brain pickin' before we did much of the same with dirt."

"Hunter Wolf's the fellow to see. He doesn't mind helping newcomers out like most do. Of course, his claim doesn't appear to be anywhere close to played out, so he can be generous." Pete flashed a friendly smile. "There's a nice hotel next door. Next door down's the restaurant. No finer cook than Tess Bronson."

"We'll probably be steady customers, then."

"Where you two from?"

"Around," the other man replied.

"You gonna ante?" Hamstead asked, forcing Swift's attention back to the game.

Swift tossed another dollar into the pot. "Sorry, Randall. Couldn't help but notice those two fellows who just came in. They look like trouble to me."

Randall glanced toward the bar. "Yeah? Well, we get all kinds drifting through. All you gotta do is holler 'Strike!' and gold seekers come from everywhere."

"They don't look like the type to be in these parts."

"After you, nothing surprises me." He smiled. "We're not cut off from the world nowadays. The stage from Sacramento goes through Jacksonville en route to Portland every day." Randall studied the cards Swift dealt. "I'll be damned if my three of a kind doesn't beat your pair of ladies, my man. I made my three dollars back and got five to boot."

Swift shoved over the money and the cards. "That's my cue to mosey on home. Good night, Randall. Enjoyed the game."

Pushing up from his chair, he nodded good evening to May Belle and left the saloon, relieved when the fresh night air bathed his face. Stepping off the boardwalk, he paused, regarding the two horses tied to the hitching post. After glancing back at the saloon doors, he closed the distance, making a circle around them, his gaze riveted to the garishly tooled saddles, pommels gleaming in the moonlight. Bending low, he lifted one horse's leg to run his hand over its shod hoof. Well-worn. He probed the tendons in the animal's foreleg and knee to check for telltale swelling, a sure sign of a long journey.

"What you doin', Lopez? Thinkin' on horse stealin'?"

Recognizing the voice, Swift turned and peered into the shadows between the saloon and the general store. "Good evening, Marshal. Been a spell since I saw you."

Hilton eased out from the darkness. "I make it a habit not to be seen. A lawman learns more that way."

"I had you pegged as a smart man. Seems I was right."

Hilton paused beside the horse. "Well?"

"Well what?"

Hilton snorted. "Have they come a far piece or not?"

"Far enough," Swift replied.

Hilton sighed and tipped his hat back to gaze at the saloon. "My wife used to say I shouldn't take an instant disliking to people. But it's been my experience that my first hunch is usually correct." He slid his gaze toward Swift. "Take you, for instance. The minute I clapped eyes on you, I didn't figure you to be near as mean as your reputation paints you."

"I hope that's a compliment."

"If it weren't, your ass would still be behind bars. Can't have a no-good gunslinger threatening our schoolteacher. A respectable one, though, that's different."

Swift started to hook his thumbs over his gun belt, noted its absence, and moved his thumbs a notch higher to his pants belt. "Is there such a thing as a respectable killer, Marshal?"

Hilton chuckled. "That's what I like about you, Lopez. Straight talk." He grew quiet a moment, squinting at Swift through the gloom. "You an eye man?"

"Come again?"

Hilton smiled. "I read a man by his eyes. You don't have the look of a killer."

"Then your eye reading doesn't work. I'm a killer, Hilton. Not that I'm proud of it."

As if Swift hadn't spoken, the marshal smiled and scratched his chin. "Nope, you got the look of a man with his back to the wall. You'll draw if you're pressed, but you don't go looking for it. Never have, if I read you right. And I'm seldom wrong."

"What're you getting at?"

Hilton ran his hand over the horse's saddle, his brow pleated in a frown. "That I don't like the looks of those two in there any more than you do."

"You think they're trouble?"

Hilton pulled his hat back down to shade his eyes. "Could be." He started to walk off, then hesitated. "I guess what I'm really trying to say is, if Wolf's Landing is where you plan to put your back to the wall and trouble does come calling, you've made a friend."

Swift swallowed. "I'll remember that."

Hilton nodded and sauntered away to disappear again into the shadows. Swift stood there a moment, mulling over the conversation. Then he gazed thoughtfully at the saloon doors, his jaw set.

Chapter 17

The following day the two strangers visited the mine, asking Hunter questions. Swift continued to work, but he kept one ear pricked. The men seemed genuinely interested in finding gold. Hunter supplied them with what information he could and listed several items they would need from the general store to rig themselves out for prospecting. After the men walked off, Swift abandoned the rocker box he had been manning, circled a pile of gravel, and strode over to Hunter.

"Well?"

Hunter frowned, his gaze still fixed on the men, who descended the slope toward town. "They claim they're brothers. Lowdry, they say their name is, Hank and Steve Lowdry."

"Do you believe them?"

"I'm not sure. We will see, eh? If they gear up for prospecting, then you can relax. If not . . ."

Swift braced himself against the wind, then slapped at the leg of his greased overalls. "Did they seem to be watching me?"

"No." Turning, Hunter placed a hand on Swift's shoulder. "Maybe you're chasing shadows, my friend. I admit they're a rough-looking pair, and their clothing puts me in mind of a comanchero's. But Wolf's Landing is a very long way from Texas."

"I don't suppose Texas has a corner on rough men."

"You and I are in Oregon, yes?"

With a laugh, Swift returned to his work.

Amy sat on the schoolhouse steps to eat her lunch during noon recess. Surrounded by chattering children, she couldn't help drawing a comparison between the simplicity of their lives and the tangles in her own. With the exception of Peter, her students led sheltered lives. She hoped they could remain innocent. How wonderful it would be to trust and see only goodness in others.

As her gaze trailed over the playground, Amy sighed with a touch of wistfulness, for she knew she was wishing on rainbows. Pain and heartache were part of living. Take Indigo, for instance. Her fascination with Brandon Marshall was destined for disaster, but unless the girl met her share of skunks, she'd be slow to recognize a truly good man when he finally came along.

Amy searched the clusters of children for her niece and experienced a chill of unease when she didn't see her. Indigo didn't usually leave the schoolyard during breaks.

Brushing crumbs from her palms, Amy went down the steps and cut across the schoolyard to gaze toward town. Nothing. Frowning, she interrupted some children who were playing tag to ask if any of them had seen Indigo leave.

"Yup," the littlest Hamstead girl said. "She went walking."

"Alone?"

"No."

Amy waited, and when she saw the child didn't intend to volunteer more information, her mouth curved in a smile. "Anna, if she wasn't alone, who was with her?"

"A fellow."

Amy folded her arms. "Are you a woman of few words, Miss Hamstead?"

Anna looked perplexed.

"Who was the fellow?" Amy prompted.

Anna wrinkled her freckled nose and shrugged. "I dunno."

Amy bent forward. "Can you tell me what he looked like?"

"Fancy."

Amy straightened, growing more uneasy by the moment. "Which direction did they go?"

Anna jabbed a finger toward the woods. "Thataway."

"Thank you, Anna. You've been very helpful."

Striking off toward the trees, Amy lifted her skirts to circle a puddle. She didn't dare walk far and leave the children unattended. A little way into the woods, she paused to listen. Laughter came from the right. She headed that way, pulling her skirts tight around her legs so they wouldn't become soiled on the maze of bushes. "Indigo!"

A moment later the tawny-haired girl came bounding into sight, her eyes sparkling, her cheeks flushed. "Hello, Aunt Amy. What are you doing out here?"

Amy leaned to one side, craning her neck. "The question is, what are you doing out here? And who have you been with?"

Indigo smiled and leaned forward, as if to share a secret. "I have a beau, Aunt Amy. Brandon Marshall! He's so handsome, my heart nearly stops when I look at him."

Amy's nearly stopped at the look she saw in Indigo's eyes. "And you sneaked off from school to tryst with him in the woods?

Indigo, that isn't the behavior of a proper young lady."

"I didn't do anything wrong. We just talked."

Hesitating, Amy regarded Indigo's lovely face, not wishing to say anything that might hurt her. "I'm sure you didn't do anything wrong, love. The thought never occurred to me, in fact. But the sad truth is, people's tongues wag very easily."

Indigo's eyes grew round with indignation. "You sound just like Ma. It's Brandon, isn't it? You don't like him because he's rich and comes from Boston. You didn't think he'd give a girl like me a second look. And now you're mad because he has."

Amy touched her niece's shoulder. "That isn't true. I think you're a beautiful young girl, Indigo. Any boy would be honored to court you, even a rich one from Boston."

"Then why are you so against my talking to him?"

"I'm not." Amy paused. "But Brandon's a lot older than you. I don't want you to get hurt."

"That's exactly what Ma says."

Amy sighed. "You must admit, Boston's wealthy neighborhoods are far different from Wolf's Landing. And Brandon is different, too. Not just older, but more sophisticated."

"Meaning?"

"Just that Brandon will probably return to Boston one day. He might never intend to hurt you by befriending you and then leaving, but it would hurt nonetheless. And there's also a possibility he may feel it's okay to sow a few wild oats here. You've caught his fancy, but is it because he genuinely cares about you or because you provide him with a diversion?"

"What you're really saying is that he thinks less of me because I'm a breed. He'll toy with my affections, get what he can, and leave without a twinge of conscience."

"No . . ."

"Yes, it is! I'm not as good as everyone else, that's what you're saying. He won't care if he hurts me because girls like me don't count the same as white girls."

Amy swallowed. "Indigo, you can't possibly think —" The lie turned to dust. Indigo had seen too much prejudice, against her father, the few remaining rogue Indians in the area, and the Chinese laborers, to believe a lie. "There are ignorant people in the world," she tempered. "You're a beautiful young lady. There are unscrupulous men in this world, men who'd take advantage of you without a qualm. Because you're part

Indian."

"Brandon isn't unscrupulous!"

"I pray not," Amy whispered.

Indigo's eyes filled with angry tears. "I'm proud of my blood. Proud, do you hear? And Brandon likes me for who I am. You'll see. You and Ma both. You'll see!"

With that, Indigo raced past Amy toward the schoolhouse. Shaken, Amy gazed after her. Then she scanned the surrounding woods, wondering how Brandon had disappeared so quickly. What did a young man have in mind when he secretly met with a girl Indigo's age in the woods?

Amy toyed with the edge of lace on her collar, afraid for Indigo and uncertain what she should do to steer the girl away from trouble. Amy could only hope Indigo's upbringing would stand her in good stead.

As she hurried back to the schoolyard, Amy sent up a silent prayer that Indigo would be there. Relief filled her when she spied the girl sitting on the front steps. Sulking, but there. Amy vowed to give the situation serious thought and talk to Indigo once more. Perhaps if she changed tactics, the girl would be less defensive and take some well-intended advice.

Amy's relief to see Indigo was short-lived. As she crossed the playground, she heard a yelp of pain and turned to see Peter skidding in the dirt on his belly. Breaking into a run, Amy reached the child just as he rose to his knees, sobbing and holding his shirt out from his chest.

"I didn't mean to push him," Jeremiah cried. "I didn't, Miss Amy, I swear."

"I wasn't accusing you, Jeremiah," Amy replied. "You're always very careful of the younger boys."

Shooing children from her path, she helped Peter to his feet, then led him across the yard and up the steps into the schoolhouse. She aimed for her desk, where she kept clean squares of cloth, a roll of bandages, and medicinal salve.

"Here, love, sit down," Amy crooned, wiping at Peter's cheeks with her handkerchief as she pressed him onto her chair. "You must have taken an awful fall. You're always tougher than a pine knot."

Peter glanced up, his face so pale his freckles looked like splatters of mud, his blue eyes huge. He placed a protective arm across his middle. "I want to g-go home for tending. My ma knows all about tending."

A great admirer of Alice Crenton, Amy smiled, wondering if Peter was suffering an attack of boyish modesty. "I'm sure she's far better at it than I. However, I can't in good conscience send you running along home without knowing how badly you're hurt. Now, can I?"

"No, Miss Amy," Peter squeaked, looking miserable.

Amy patted his head, then reached to untuck his homemade pullover shirt. "It's not as if I haven't seen a young man's chest before."

"No, ma'am."

"I'll tell you a secret, if you won't spread it around," Amy added conspiratorially. "I'm so bashful, I'd rather take a dose of Widow Hamstead's sheep dung tea than go see the doctor." Peter studied her, clearly at a loss as to how that related. Amy felt her cheeks grow warm. "Just in case you're feeling shy, I thought it might help you to know other people feel shy, too."

As carefully as she could, Amy lifted the flannel, intending to pull the garment over Peter's head. As the cloth cleared his belly, her gaze riveted on his bruised and swollen ribs. She gave an involuntary gasp.

"Oh, Peter . . ."

"I fell real hard."

Amy knew by the reddish purple color of Peter's bruises that his ribs hadn't been injured in the last few minutes. More than likely it had happened yesterday or last night. She swallowed, uncertain what to say. His fright was all too apparent; she didn't want to make matters worse. An almost irresistible urge came over her to cuddle him close and rock him. But Peter would resent being babied.

"Peter, what happened?" she asked softly, assailed by sudden guilt. There must have been signs that Peter was hurt, yet she'd had him in the classroom all morning and never noticed.

"You saw. I fell."

Amy pulled the shirt off over his head, feeling sick. Rising, she looked at his back. As she feared, he was bruised there as well. "Peter, I know your father did this to you."

"Don't tell my ma. You gotta promise, Miss Amy."

Amy strove to keep her voice level. "She doesn't know?"

"Not how bad it is. I told her it was nothing."

"Then why did you want her to tend you?"

"I didn't. I don't want anyone to. It'll just cause a fuss. I don't want tending."

Amy felt a sheen of perspiration pop out on her forehead. She wanted to scream and curse, to find Abe Crenton and pulverize him. Instead she took a steadying breath and said, "But, Peter, I'm afraid a couple of

398

those ribs might be broken. They need to be wrapped. And you should be in bed until you mend some."

Tears filled Peter's eyes again. "No! If I tell my ma, she'll get upset and sass my pa, and —" He closed his eyes, gulping air. "He'll hit on her again. My ribs'll still be broke either way. So why make a fuss?"

Amy pressed trembling fingers to her throat. Peter was seriously hurt. If he fell again, one of those ribs might puncture a lung. She had no choice but to do something.

"What set your father off this time?" she asked.

"Nothing. He just came home in his cups last night, like he does sometimes. He wouldn't have bothered none with me, except that I jumped in and tried to make him stop."

"Hitting your ma, you mean?"

"Yes. I'll be all right, Miss Amy. Truly I will."

"No, Peter, not this time. Your father's done some serious harm to you." Amy ran her fingers over one of Peter's ribs. He flinched and sucked in air again, his lips turning white. "A broken rib can be dangerous. Something has to be done."

"Like what? You gonna go talk to Ma and

make her see the marshal again? So's my pa can come home from jail all in a dither and do worse? Just stay out of it, Miss Amy. You gotta!"

Amy sighed. "Point taken, Peter." She touched a hand to his hair. "Put your shirt back on, hm? I'm going to dismiss class early and take you to my house. The least I can do is wrap those ribs. Then we'll talk. Maybe if we think on it, we can come up with a solution."

When Amy turned, she discovered that Indigo stood in the doorway. Her blue eyes filled with concern, the girl stepped inside. "Is Peter going to be all right, Aunt Amy?"

"I hope so." Placing a hand on the girl's shoulder, Amy said, "Peter doesn't want anyone knowing that he's hurt. I'd appreciate it if you'd keep this secret."

Indigo nodded. "I heard. I won't tell any of the children." She met Amy's gaze and added in a whisper, "I think his pa needs kicking, though."

"Right now I'd like to be the one to do the kicking."

Indigo's delicately shaped mouth drew into a determined line. "Between the two of us, we could do it."

Amy managed a weak smile, remembering a time when she had been as fearless.

"Sometimes you've got more temper than wisdom, my girl. Abe Crenton's a big man."

Indigo patted her leather skirt, where she wore a knife strapped to her thigh. "I could whack him off at the ankles and bring him right down to size."

With a shaky grin, Amy swept past her to dismiss the children. "I'll bear that in mind."

An hour later Amy sat on the edge of her bed, gazing down at a sleeping Peter. With quivering fingertips, she brushed the bright red curls from his forehead, her heart breaking at the thought of his going home again. She considered visiting the marshal, but what could he do, save lock Abe up for several days? In the end the man would return home, furious and dangerous.

Amy dropped her head into her hands, so weary of it all she wanted to weep. Why weren't there better laws to protect little boys like Peter? Women like Alice? The legislation that did exist was rendered impotent by the absolute power men had over the family purse strings of the nation. Even if women filed legal suit for abuse, what did they accomplish? Nine times out of ten, judges delivered light sentences to abusive husbands and fathers. Once the sentences were served, the men gained their release and returned to their homes, undisputed lords of their castles. Didn't the lawmakers realize that those men's families were enslaved by their need for necessities, like shelter and food?

Amy closed her eyes, recalling her many battles with Henry Masters and the degradation she had felt. There had been no way for her to win. He had held all the aces. Slowly but surely she had lost her dignity, and her pride.

She would never forget. She knew that there must be other women and children suffering like treatment. Maybe one day the Peters of the world would grow into men and remember the injustices done to them. Perhaps, through them, the laws could be changed. But for now there was little recourse.

With a sigh Amy pushed up from the bed, took a step, and froze. Swift stood in the bedroom doorway, his shoulder braced against the frame, his gaze riveted to the bandages wrapped so tightly around Peter's chest. A muscle rippled along his jaw. Recovering her composure, Amy closed the distance between them. He eased into the hall so she could follow and close the door.

"How bad is he?"

Still shaken by her thoughts of Henry,

Amy couldn't bring herself to deal with the ugliness immediately. "It's the middle of the day." She glanced at his dusty pant legs. "I thought you were at the mine."

"I was. Indigo paid us a visit."

Amy swept past him and went to the kitchen. Pouring fresh water from the jug, she filled the coffeepot and ladled in several scoops of beans she had ground that morning. "I don't know about you, but I could use a nice hot cup."

Swift leaned a hip against the stove, watching her. "You look like you could use a whiskey or two. I asked you a question, Amy. How badly is Peter hurt?"

"I, um, think he has two broken ribs."

"Jesus!"

Losing the war, Amy felt tears brimming over in her eyes, trailing in hot rivulets down her cheeks. Tears of frustration and anger and pain that ran far deeper than simple empathy for Peter. Swift swore under his breath and crooked a hand around her neck, pulling her against his chest.

"Don't cry, honey. What good will that do?"

Amy pressed her face into the curve of his shoulder, drawing comfort from his smell, a blend of masculine sweat, sun-dried denim, pine, and fresh mountain air. She yearned to wrap her arms around him and never let go, to weep until she had no more tears. "I have to send him back there. Again. It just isn't fair."

Swift bent his head to hers, encircling her waist with his other arm. "I think it's high time somebody had a talk with Abe Crenton. And I've got a sudden urge for a drink."

Amy stiffened. "No! You mustn't interfere, Swift. It'll only make things worse. I learned that the hard way."

Swift ran his hand up her back. She could almost hear the smile in his voice when he spoke. "Amy, love, when you interfered, you did it the proper way. I think he'll understand my language a little better."

"You'll get yourself into trouble. The first thing you know, you'll be in jail."

"For talking?"

"Talking won't change Abe's ways, and you know it."

He pressed his lips to her ear, sending tendrils of sensation threading down her spine. "It's all in what words you say. Trust me, Amy. Someone has to do something. If he isn't stopped, he's gonna go too far one of these times and do hurt that's beyond repair."

Amy made fists in his shirt, knowing that he spoke the truth. "I don't want you getting into trouble."

"I didn't ride two thousand miles looking for it, believe me." He grasped her shoulders and set her away from him. "But sometimes trouble comes. And a man can't turn his back on it. This is one of those times. Do you think I could sleep nights, knowing about this and doing nothing?"

"No," she admitted in a forlorn voice. "Indigo should have known better than to tell you and Hunter. It's like laying tinder and striking a match to it."

"Indigo did exactly right," Swift replied, arching one eyebrow. "She trusts her father and me to have good enough sense not to do anything that can come back on us."

"She's also very young and idealistic," Amy countered. "And she doesn't know you two like I do."

Swift's eyes filled with warmth. "Trust me, Amy. I'm an old hand at trouble, believe me. When Peter wakes up, take him on home. There won't be any more beatings going on there, I guarantee you, not without hell to pay."

Amy touched his shoulder. "Swift . . . you could end up in that cell again. I know how you hate being confined."

"Hate doesn't say it by half." He paused at the doorway of the sitting room. "Which

405

means I'll walk a mile to avoid it. But if it happens, it happens. A few days won't kill me." A grin slanted across his mouth. "Will you bring me an apple pie every evening?"

"Swift, are you positive you won't just make matters worse? If Abe goes home and —" She licked her lips. "It looks as if he used his boots on Peter."

He searched her gaze. "Do you trust me?"

She stared at him, considering the question. "Yes."

"Then don't be afraid to take Peter home."

CHAPTER 18

Swift cut the poker deck and took a drag off his cigarette, smiling at Abe Crenton through a trail of smoke. The saloon owner reclaimed the deck with a skillful sleight of hand and started a new game of seven-card stud, dealing Swift and himself one card, facedown. Swift had sat in on games with some of the best fleecers in Texas. Crenton was a clumsy novice by comparison, good enough to get by in Wolf's Landing, but not nearly smooth enough to escape a trained eye. From what Randall Hamstead said, Abe had a reputation for being a cheat, and Swift was pleased to see him living up to it. To his knowledge, there was no easier way to pick a fight than to call a man on his dealing.

"You threatening me, Lopez?" Crenton asked.

Swift slid his gaze to the surrounding tables. The two strangers, Hank and Steve

Lowdry, recently returned from a buying spree at the general store to rig themselves out for prospecting, sat nearby. He had a feeling the two men were watching him, and that made him uneasy. On second thought, though, maybe two avid listeners would prove helpful later. He forced himself to relax.

"Threatening you? Why would you think that?"

Crenton flipped a second card toward Swift, his blue eyes narrowed. "Why else would you tell me a story like that?"

Swift lifted the corners of his cards. A deuce and a four. He watched as Crenton dealt a second card to himself — from the bottom of the deck. "I enjoy telling stories. Didn't mean for you to take it personal."

Crenton leaned back in his chair. "You tell me a story about a Comanche killin' a wife beater and hangin' his scalp on his gatepost, and you don't expect me to take it personal?"

With a flick of his tongue, Swift moved his cigarette from one corner of his mouth to the other, squinting against the smoke. "You aren't a wife beater, are you?"

"I'm a firm disciplinarian. You got a quarrel with that?"

Remembering Peter's pale little face

against Amy's pillow, Swift tossed a dollar into the pot. Crenton plunked out two, raising him one. "I'm not a man for quarreling, Crenton," Swift replied, meeting the ante with another dollar. "If something's eating me, I usually don't do much talking."

"Ain't no man alive gonna tell me how to tend my family."

Swift smiled. "You do take offense easily, don't you? It was just a story, Crenton. Why, if I had meant it personal, I'd have just said I was going to kick your ass the next time you abused your wife and kids."

Crenton dealt Swift another card, this one face up. A three. Once again the man dealt his own card from the bottom, turning up an ace. Swift gave the table a measuring glance. There were only four more cards coming. He'd have to make his move soon.

Crenton tossed out two more gold pieces and squared his massive shoulders. "If you was to tell me that, my answer would be that the minute you came near me, I'd sic the law on you."

Swift snubbed out his cigarette and shifted on his chair, pushing two dollars forward to meet the bet. From behind him, he heard May Belle's throaty laughter. A jug clinked against glass, followed by the sound of liquor being poured. A nice, peaceful afternoon at the local watering hole, with no one suspecting that all hell was about to break loose. He hated to ruin the mood.

"Well, since we're supposing" — he met Crenton's gaze — "and I do stress that we're just supposing, my reply would be that if I was to come near you, you'd never see me coming and never know what hit you. As for the law? They can't hang a man if they can't prove he's guilty."

"You *are* threatening me," Crenton said with an amazed chuckle. "Seems to me you talk mighty big for a runt-of-the-litter gunslinger who ain't totin' his piece."

"You're a man who puts a lot of stock in size, aren't you? Being built like a bull, I guess you can afford to. Me, I've had to compensate for my lack of bulk, so slinging a gun isn't my only talent." Swift watched Crenton's beefy hands. "Fact is, if I had to choose a weapon, it'd be a knife. My slickest trick is slitting a man's throat before he can blink. You ever seen that done, Crenton? It's a real quiet way to settle differences. You come up from behind. It's all in the timing and wrist movement."

As Crenton started to deal himself another card from the bottom of the deck, Swift whipped his knife from its scabbard, threw it, and pinned the card in question to the table with the blade tip. Crenton froze, his blue gaze riveted to the vibrating knife handle.

"You damn near got my hand, you crazy bastard!"

Swift lunged from his chair and braced his arms on the table. In a booming voice, which he meant to carry, he said, "I'm calling you a card cheat, Crenton."

Crenton drew himself up, the picture of affronted dignity. "You're calling me a what?"

"A cheat! No wonder so many miners lose their paychecks to you in this saloon!"

The Lowdry brothers rose from their chairs, taking their glasses and bottle to another table a safe distance away.

Crenton turned angry red. "Ain't nobody calls me a cheat and gets away with it."

Swift met his gaze. "I don't think I slurred my words."

"You got no call to make such an accusation."

"No call? I saw you dealing from the bottom." With that, Swift overturned Crenton's two cards in the hole, which gave the man three aces showing. Jerking the knife free, he revealed the fourth ace. "Every man in here is my witness. This deck is stacked agains—"

Crenton's fist cut the declaration short, catching Swift along the jaw. Dropping the knife, he reeled from the blow, landing back first on another table, which skidded across the plank floor under his weight. Giving his head a shake, Swift angled an elbow under himself to get up, but before he could, Crenton leaped on him.

"Whoo-ee!" someone yelled.

May Belle cried, "Take it outside, you damn fools!"

The two men rolled onto the floor, their combined weights hitting a chair on the way down. Swift's ribs took the brunt. Holding his middle with one arm, still dazed from the first punch, he staggered to his feet, fighting for breath.

Crenton jumped up. "Wanna call me a cheat again, you no-good son of a bitch! I'll teach you some manners, by Gawd!"

The threat was punctuated by Crenton's boot, which caught Swift square on the chin. With a feeling of detachment, Swift felt himself staggering backward. Then his body hit the wall, making a sound very like a big ball of unbaked bread dough hitting the floor. He blinked, trying to see. In the back of his mind, it occurred to him that letting the other guy take the first punch was a hell of a way to start a fight. And an even worse way to lose one.

After that, he didn't have much time to think. Crenton came at him like a charging bull, head lowered to butt him in the stomach, arms spread, powerful legs thrusting to give his massive weight impetus. Swift blinked again and, at the last second, recovered the presence of mind to shift sideways. Crenton hit the log wall headfirst and crashed to his knees. To Swift's surprise, the saloon owner didn't crumple to the floor unconscious. Instead, he just shook his head and stood back up.

"Well, Lopez. Your mouth got you into this. Now let's see you finish it," someone said with a laugh.

Swift ran his sleeve across his bleeding chin as he gave Crenton a measuring glance. His intention had been to goad the saloon owner into starting a fight so he could teach him a lesson. He hadn't counted on Crenton throwing such a powerful first punch or following through so quickly.

Swift gave his head another shake and leaned forward, arms slightly raised, elbows out. As Crenton came toward him, he circled, playing for time so his head could clear. Swift had done enough scrapping to know that fast footwork and precision with his fists proved good equalizers when he faced a larger man. The problem was, Crenton's first punch had been a solid one, followed by a boot to the jaw. Swift couldn't think clearly, let alone be quick on his feet and precise. If he wasn't careful, he might end up feeling like a mudhole Crenton was stomping dry.

"What'sa matter, Lopez? You yellow?"

The room spun around Swift, then lurched to a stop, making him weave. He blinked and shook his head again. Focusing on Crenton, he tried to imagine being in Peter's or Alice Crenton's shoes, facing this man when he was mean drunk, night after night, with no hope of it ever ending. Those pictures and the knowledge that Amy had trusted him to handle this gave him added incentive. It was high time Crenton got a taste of his own medicine, and he was going to give it to him, or die trying.

"I'm here, Crenton," Swift said in a low voice, beckoning the man forward. "Come and get me."

Crenton grabbed a chair. "I'm comin', you slimy little greaser." He charged, bringing the chair down as he ran.

Swift crouched and sidestepped, sticking out a foot as the saloon owner passed. Crenton tripped and fell, hitting belly first on the chair. Swift didn't give him time to get up. Diving, he grabbed the man by the shoulders, wrenched him backward onto his feet, and then planted his fist in his mouth. Crenton toppled, rolled, and leaped back up. Grabbing another chair, he made a wild throw, which Swift dodged easily. The chair crashed through the saloon window onto the boardwalk. A woman outside screeched and started calling, "Marshal Hilton! Marshal Hilton! A fight! A fight! Come quick!"

His head growing clearer by the second, Swift became aware that the ruckus had drawn a crowd. Years of training enabled him to ignore everything but his opponent. He circled, fingers flexing, body tensed and ready. Crenton grunted and swung, missing his mark. He caught his balance and swung again. Swift shifted and tipped his head, avoiding the blow. Crenton snarled, bent at the waist, and charged again. Swift jumped out of his path, letting the man land on the table where they had been playing poker.

When Crenton stood back up, he held Swift's knife.

Amy, drawn by the commotion, arrived outside the saloon just as Crenton seized the weapon. She elbowed her way through the crowd, rising on tiptoe, trying to see, her heart slamming with fear. Marshal Hilton came up the street at a dead run, one hand clamped over his head to keep his hat on.

"Crenton's got a knife, Marshal!" a man in the crowd yelled.

Amy shoved her way to the front so she could see through the broken window. Swift circled Crenton, leaping back to avoid the slashing knife. Her stomach lurched. When Marshal Hilton made his way to the boardwalk, she ran over to him.

"You have to do something!" she cried. "Crenton's going to kill him!"

Hilton took measure of the situation, one eye narrowed. "Now, Miss Amy! Lopez can handle his own."

"Crenton's got a knife!" As she spoke, Amy threw a frightened glance inside the saloon just in time to see Swift kick the knife from Crenton's grasp.

Hilton folded his arms across his chest and grinned. "Now we're gonna see some fancy footwork."

Amy threw him a horrified glance. "You're not going to just stand here, are you?"

"What do you expect me to do? I learned a long time ago that it's easier to stop a fight once the new wears off." He winced and shook his head, leaning forward to see better through the window. "Abe's been needing a set-down for a long while."

The marshal no sooner spoke than he grabbed Amy and shoved her to one side of the window. The next instant Swift and Crenton came hurtling out, bringing the remaining shards of glass with them. They crashed onto the boardwalk, then rolled into the street. Spectators retreated to a safe distance, forming a half-circle around the combatants, the women screeching.

Crenton jumped up and aimed a lethal kick at Swift's head. Amy gasped and closed her eyes, unable to watch. She heard a fist impact with flesh, a grunt, then a series of quick whops.

"All right, Lopez!" Hilton called. "Now, don't back off!"

Amy opened her eyes to see Swift on top of Crenton, pummeling his face viciously. She wanted to close her eyes again but couldn't. Swift's murderous expression frightened her. He released Crenton and stood up, heaving for breath, staggering slightly before he righted himself.

"Get up," he snarled. "Come on, Crenton! We're just getting started! Or don't you like fighting when you're up against someone close to your own size?"

Crenton rolled onto his stomach and pushed to his knees. Swift circled, waiting until the man gained his feet. The moment the saloon owner did, Swift buried a boot in his belly. Crenton crashed to his knees, moaning and holding his middle.

"That one's for Peter," Swift snarled. "What's the matter? Doesn't it feel good?"

The saloon owner weaved to his feet again and charged, roaring like an enraged beast. Swift sidestepped, turned, and gave Crenton a kick on the rump to help him on his way into a nosedive that buried his bleeding face in the dirt. Amy hugged her waist, feeling sick, wanting it to stop. Since her abduction by the comanchero, violence of any kind nauseated her. As she had discovered the day of the social, even so commonplace a thing as chicken killing made her queasy.

Crenton wasn't ready to admit defeat. He got back up and turned, which proved a mistake. Swift gave him another boot in the belly for his efforts. "That one's for your wife, you miserable bastard!"

Crenton went down, and this time he stayed down, moaning, "I'm finished, I'm finished . . ."

Swift, who looked none too steady on his feet, staggered over to the man, hunkered, and grabbed him by the hair. After giving him a vicious shake, he snarled, "The next time you lay a hand on that boy or anyone else in your family, I'll do worse! Far worse!

Do you understand?" When Crenton didn't reply, Swift gave the man's hair another jerk and nudged him in the ribs with his boot. "Do you understand?"

"Yes! Yes," Crenton moaned. "I won't hit on 'em no more. I swear it!"

"You remember that the next time you feel in the mood to pound on somebody!"

With that, Swift dropped the man's head onto the packed dirt and straightened. Turning back to the boardwalk, he swayed and caught his balance, then strode in a reasonably straight line toward the saloon.

"All right, folks! The show's over," Hilton yelled, stepping out into the street and crossing to Crenton, who still lay crumpled on the ground. "Well, Abe, looks like you met your match this time."

"I want that man arrested," Crenton croaked. "And he's payin' for all damages."

"You want him arrested?" a man from the crowd yelled. "I was in there when it started, Crenton. You cheated at cards, and you threw the first punch. I'd say you're the one to go to jail."

Swift came out of the saloon just then, hat in one hand, sheathing his knife with the other. Hilton turned toward him. "You want to file a complaint, Lopez?"

Swift saw Amy, and his expression hardened. He leveled a cold gaze on Crenton. "What do you say, Crenton? Do you and I have an understanding or not?"

Crenton grimaced, trying to sit up, one hand planted on his ribs. "He threatened me, Marshal! You heard him! Threatened my life just a minute ago!"

Hilton frowned. "I guess with all the noise, Abe, I must've missed that."

"Other people heard! Speak up, somebody!" Crenton threw a wild look at the spectators. No one in the crowd came to Abe's aid, and more than a few looked away with expressions of disgust on their faces. Abe's treatment of his family in the past hadn't earned him much popularity, and even though Alice Crenton no longer dared to make her husband's rages public knowledge, people still remembered the time she'd had Abe tossed in jail. "Somebody had to've heard him!"

Swift swiped at the blood on his chin. "What counts is that you heard me, Crenton. Touch a hair on that boy's head again and we'll see if I was threatening or promising."

Abe glanced at Hilton. "You heard that, didn't you?"

The marshal nodded. "Nothing specific, though." He looked to the crowd. "Any of you hear anything specific?"

None of the bystanders volunteered to speak. Marshal Hilton smiled slightly. "I guess nobody heard anything, Crenton."

Swift came toward Amy, dusting his hat clean on his trousers and reshaping the crumpled crown. As he stepped onto the boardwalk, he clamped it on his head, tipping the brim low over his eyes. She riveted her gaze to his torn knuckles, then to the cut on his chin. "You're bleeding."

"I'm fine."

"Oh, Swift! Your poor hands!"

"I'm fine, I tell you!" He narrowed his gaze. "A lot finer than you're gonna be. What are you doing here?"

"I heard the noise and I —"

He clasped her arm and pulled her none too gently into a walk. Under his breath he said, "Don't you ever come near a fight again. Is that clear?"

"But I —"

He gave her arm a light shake. "No buts. Don't you ever — He could've pulled a gun instead of a knife!"

"Other women were there."

"I don't give a damn about other women! When the dust clears after something like this, I don't ever want to see you standing there again. If I do, I'll kick your little fanny all the way home."

Amy stared at his harsh profile, frightened for an instant by the picture his words conjured. He looked angry enough to kick her now. Taking measure of his broad shoulders and whipcord build, it was a threat she couldn't take lightly. Then the absurdity of it hit her, and she smothered a smile. He had just pummeled a man for being abusive to his wife and children. It didn't seem likely he'd commit the same sin himself.

He threw her a glare. "What's so funny?"

"I —" She shook her head, making a valiant effort to keep a straight face. "Nothing!"

He narrowed his eyes. "I take it you don't think I'd kick your butt?"

Amy fastened her gaze on the planked walkway, amazed to realize that he was exactly right; she didn't believe it for a minute. And knowing he wouldn't felt absolutely wonderful! She lifted her gaze to his. Though she knew the urge coming over her was unforgivably childish and that this was no time to tease, she couldn't resist. "I think you'd have to catch me first."

Before he could react, she bolted away from him, gaining several yards before she whirled and stuck out her tongue at him.

Swift didn't look as if he were particularly amused. She walked backward a moment, poking out her tongue again. He scowled, lengthening his stride, the heels of his boots tapping sharply on the boardwalk. Amy retreated as he advanced, very much aware that seeing him in a temper a month ago would have terrified her.

When he lunged for her, she whirled and ran. Within seconds he caught her around the waist and nearly lifted her off her feet. She laughed and looped her arms around his neck, pleased to see a twinkle had replaced the glitter in his eyes.

"Now what are you going to do, Miss Amy?" he challenged.

"Surrender," she said softly.

His gaze clouded with tenderness. "Promise me you'll never go near a fight again? If anything happened to you . . ."

"I promise."

He bent his head and touched his lips to hers in a fleeting kiss, then seemed to remember where they were, that others might see them. Drawing her into a walk, he angled off the boardwalk into the street. Amy put an arm around his waist and tipped her head back to look at his chin.

"You'd better take care," he warned in a gruff tone. "First thing you know, you'll be fired from your teaching position for cavorting with a gunslinger who brawls in the streets."

At the moment, Amy was too happy to care. "Are you sure you're not badly hurt?"

"Not so bad I can't kick your fanny if it needs it," he replied with a slow grin.

"My fanny is in perfectly good order as it is, thank you."

"Is that so?"

Amy glanced away, embarrassed by what she had said. He chuckled and ran his hand up her side, his fingertips coming dangerously close to her breast. She threw him a look, which he answered with another grin.

"On second thought, maybe I am hurt bad," he tempered, wincing and touching his ribs with exaggerated care, his mouth twitching at the corners in an ill-concealed smile. "You going to tend me until I'm well?"

"Yes." Amy's own smile faded, and she touched a fingertip to his chin. "Until you're well . . . and always."

After cleaning Swift's torn knuckles and the cut on his chin, Amy roused Peter from bed. The child turned ghostly white the moment he stood up. Swift, who had followed Amy into the room, met her gaze over the top of the child's head.

"You know what, partner?" Swift said softly, bending to Peter's eye level. "I got my ribs broke once, and I was so sore I couldn't even breathe, let alone walk."

"I'm fine," Peter said, jutting out his chin.

"You're a tough one, no doubt about that." Swift gave him a slow wink. "But knowing how you're hurting, there's no way I'm taking you home unless I pack you. You'd do the same for me, I'll bet. And never tell anybody I couldn't make it on my own."

Peter placed a shaking hand on his ribs. "If I was big enough, I would."

"Well, it won't be long until you are. I could use a friend I could count on. How about if I help you this time around? Then, when I need a hand, I'll have you to call on."

"Me?"

Swift smiled and very carefully scooped the child into his arms. Amy's throat ached with tears as she watched Peter turn his small face against Swift's shoulder.

"It hurts," Peter whispered.

Swift's mouth hardened. "I know it does, partner. I'll walk real easy, okay?"

"My ma's gonna find out and sass my pa for sure."

Swift raised an eyebrow. "I don't think you need to worry anymore about your pa's temper, Peter. He and I had a long talk, and he agreed to mend his ways."

"He did?"

"Sure did. Miss Amy heard him. Didn't you, Miss Amy?"

"I certainly did."

Peter winced again as Swift turned sideways to get through the doorway. Swift looked as if he were hurting as bad as the child. "I'm being as careful as I can, son."

"I know." Peter bit his lip and sniffed. "Can you make sure Miss Amy don't tell I was a crybaby?"

"She and I already came to an understanding about that when she was doctoring the cut on my chin with alcohol."

"How'd you cut your chin?"

"She told me to sit and I didn't."

Peter managed a wan smile. "Miss Amy didn't do it! And you ain't no crybaby!"

"If something hurts bad enough, anybody's a crybaby."

CHAPTER 19

After delivering Peter to his mother, Swift stretched out on Amy's settee and slept while she baked a deep-dish apple pie, then prepared an evening meal. While she worked she went back over the day, remembering Swift's tenderness with Peter above all else. Her throat constricted with emotion. She loved Swift so much, and he loved her. He had proven it in a hundred different ways. Wasn't it about time she did the same?

She gripped the spoon handle tightly, stirring the vegetables with more force. A funny, fluttery feeling attacked her belly and worked its way up her throat. Knowing what needed to be done and doing it were two different things.

The delicious smells woke Swift, and he came to the kitchen, lightly rubbing his tender ribs, his sleepy eyes warming with appreciation as his gaze settled on the laden table.

"Apple pie, Amy?"

She cast him a nervous smile. "A man doesn't necessarily have to be in jail to get pie. Sometimes he's so wonderful he deserves pie any old time." Running her hands over her apron, she tried to meet his gaze but couldn't quite manage. "I, um, I want tonight to be special."

Swift stepped closer. "Fried chicken?"

"Hunter brought me a hen yesterday."

"Mashed potatoes and gravy? I've died and gone to heaven."

She hoped he didn't notice how her hands were trembling as she set a bowl of vegetables on the table. "I didn't think you believed in heaven."

"Sure I do. Comanche heaven, your heaven, it's probably the same. The gods must keep us Indians and you whites separated so we don't know we're up there together and start another war."

Amy wrinkled her nose. "That won't do. It wouldn't be heaven if I wasn't with you."

He shot her a glance, then slowly grinned. "Why do I have the feeling I've risen in your estimation since that fight?"

"Because you have." She turned back toward the stove and shrugged out of her apron. "Don't misunderstand me. Violence isn't my way. But nothing else worked with

Crenton, and there are no laws to protect his family from him. He'll think twice before he hurts Peter again. And I think —" She broke off and glanced back at him over her shoulder, her eyes stinging with tears. "I thought you were wonderful with Peter. . . ."

Swift crossed the room to her. Taking her by the shoulders, he turned her into his arms and brushed his lips across hers in a light kiss. "I nearly got my butt kicked."

Her eyes widened. "You did?"

"Damned near it." He laughed softly. "If I hadn't been lighter on my feet, he would have had me."

Momentarily forgetting her own dilemma, Amy ran her fingertips along the scar on his cheek, remembering how frightened she had been when Crenton was waving the knife. She could have lost Swift today. "Which only makes you all the more wonderful in my eyes."

His gaze held hers, warm and compelling. "If it has this effect on you, I'll go pick a fight every day."

She gave him a playful shove. "Sit down and eat."

He complied and then took second helpings of everything, including apple pie, complimenting her between bites.

Swift couldn't help but notice that Amy

picked at her food, glancing frequently at the darkness beyond the window, then at the lantern, her mouth curved in a distracted smile.

"Is something wrong?"

She focused. "No . . . nothing."

Swift leaned back in his chair, studying her. "You're nervous about something. Want to talk about it?"

Her mouth tightened. She swallowed, avoiding his gaze. "No. I . . ." Her voice trailed off and her huge blue eyes lifted to his. "Would you excuse me for a moment?"

"Sure."

Swift watched her leave the kitchen, troubled by the expression he had seen in her eyes. She hadn't looked just nervous, but frightened. He thought back over the meal, trying to remember if he had done or said something he shouldn't have. Nothing came to mind.

Pushing to his feet, he began clearing the table. He had just picked up the pie plate when he heard Amy speak his name in a tremulous, uncertain little voice. He turned, pie plate in hand, and froze. She stood just beyond the doorway in the shadows, her hair unbound and flowing around her hips in a shimmering, golden cloud. His gaze dropped, and as it did, so did the pie plate, hitting the floor with a resounding crash, glass and pie filling geysering everywhere.

"Shit!"

The word crackled in the air, so loud it seemed to vibrate the walls. Swift wanted to bite his tongue. Amy jerked and made a startled little sound, crossing her arms over her bare breasts, her small face so pale that Swift feared she might faint. He took a step toward her, his boot crunching on glass, then slipping on a piece of apple. He froze again, staring at her. He knew he shouldn't, but he couldn't help himself. Even splattered with apples, she was the most beautiful thing he'd ever seen. His throat closed off. His temples started to pound. And the wary look on her face made him afraid to move.

"Amy . . ."

She retreated a step. "I shouldn't have — it was a stupid —" She broke off and took another step back. "I have apples all over me."

Swift crunched two more steps through the glass. As he advanced she withdrew, deeper and deeper into the shadows. "Amy, don't —" His foot slipped on an apple and he cursed. "It wasn't stupid." He jumped over the rest of the mess. "Amy, come back here."

Like a wraith, she fled through the shadows toward her bedroom. Swift swore under his breath, took an angry swipe at his pant leg to flick off a slice of apple, then hurried after her. As he entered the hall, the door shut with a *thunk*. He knew it had no lock. Grasping the knob, he turned it slowly. Soft sobs and jerky little whimpers came through the darkness as he opened the door. He wanted to give himself a good kick.

He heard her rattling around. As his eyes grew accustomed to the dark, he saw that she was groping for her clothes, which were slung across the bureau. "Amy," he said softly.

She started and whirled, clutching her pantalets to her breasts. Swift closed the door and leaned against it. She threw a frantic look around her, then riveted her gaze in his direction. He knew she couldn't see him. A tender smile touched his mouth as he imagined her leaving here a few moments ago, trembling with fright, every step an agony, but going to him anyway, wearing nothing but her beautiful hair because she had wanted to please him.

In a husky voice that shook with emotion, he said, "That's the most beautiful gift I've ever — I'm sorry I reacted the way I did." He swallowed. "I, um, the pie — I was so surprised, it just sort of — Did any of the glass cut you?"

"No."

Her voice was barely audible. An ache filled Swift's chest and crawled up his throat. He could see her trembling. "Amy, could we do it one more time, minus the pie and cussing? I've been trying real hard to clean my language up — you know I have — but sometimes words come out before I think."

With a sob she cried, "We can't do it minus the pie. I have apples all over me."

"So? My two favorite things in the whole world are apple pie and you, not necessarily in that order. If I have to go through apples to get to you, I won't complain."

She swiped at her cheek and sniffed. "I — I just want to forget it happened. I'm all sticky." Swift started toward her. "Apples on my legs!" He drew up, smiling through the darkness, watching her. "Apples in my hair!"

He reached out and brushed a tear from her cheek. She jumped and reared back against the dresser.

"Are you trying to startle me out of my wits?"

"I'm sorry. I can see fine, and I forget you can't."

She clutched the underwear to her chest, her eyes luminous as she tried to find him.

"I'm right here, Amy." He cupped her chin in his hand and tipped her face up. "And if you think I can forget you standing there in that doorway, shimmering like gold and moonlight, you're wrong. I'll never forget, not as long as I live. And there's no way I can leave, pretending it didn't happen."

He felt her shiver.

"It's cold in here. Let's go in by the fire."

She shrank back. "No. I'm — The mood isn't — I don't want —"

Swift bent slightly and caught her up in his arms. Where his hands touched, she felt like warm silk. Trembling warm silk. He strode across the room, shifted her in his arms to open the door, kicked it back out of his way, and carried her into the sitting room. When he set her on her feet, she took a step back, still clinging to the pantalets, her hands knotted so tightly her knuckles gleamed white. Swift grasped the muslin.

"Let's get rid of those, shall we?" He gave a little tug. She resisted, throwing a wild glance at the fire. "Amy . . ."

"I've changed my mind," she squeaked. "I was already nervous, and then . . ."

"And then I reacted like an idiot. I'm

sorry, Amy, love. You just took me by surprise. Give me another chance, please?"

He pulled the underwear from her grasp and tossed it aside. When he turned back, his breath caught. Even though she hugged herself, trying to hide behind her crossed arms and splayed fingers, the sight of her, standing naked in firelight, made his senses reel. The pink nipple of one breast peeked at him from between two fingers. Unable to stop himself, he reached out and touched the sensitive tip, in awe because she had found the courage to gift him with her body.

She sucked in breath and repositioned her hands, providing him with a delightful display while she tried to decide what part of her was a priority to keep covered. Regarding her with tender understanding, Swift saw her dilemma. Her breasts were far more ample than her prim dresses hinted; those alone filled her hands. He wished they were filling his. And if she concentrated on just her breasts, that left the rest of her bare.

She finally settled for angling one arm over her chest, palming one plump breast, which left the other peeking out from under her arm. Her other hand flew to the shimmering gold triangle at the apex of her thighs. Given the fact that she had slender hands that did a poor job of covering much, he applauded her choices. "My God, Amy, do you have any idea how beautiful you are?" he asked in a gravelly whisper.

She fastened wide blue eyes on him.

"Your skin is like a moonbeam." He curled a hand over her hip, stepping closer. "And your breasts . . . in all my life, I've never seen — You make me think of those pale pink roses, when the buds first open." He touched her hair with his fingertips, and smoothed it off her shoulder so he could press a kiss there. "You're a sweet dream. I can't believe you're real."

"I'm c-covered with apples."

Swift tilted his head, skimming his lips along the slope of her shoulder to the downy curve of her neck. "When I'm finished, there won't be a trace of apple left on you, I promise."

"S-Swift?"

"Hm?" He captured her earlobe between his teeth, then traced the shape of her ear with his tongue. She shivered and made fists in his shirt, which meant that she'd abandoned the attempt to cover herself. He drew back. "What, Amy?"

She started to hug herself again, but he clamped a hand around her wrists, capturing both before she moved. He stepped back and dropped his gaze. She squeezed her eyes closed, her throat working as she swallowed.

Swift couldn't speak. And even if he had been able to, words couldn't have expressed the emotions that rolled through him. With his free hand he reached to touch her breast, then hesitated, trembling. When his fingertips grazed her shimmering skin, she stiffened and stopped breathing. As he closed his hand on her, he freed her wrists and hugged her close.

"Amy . . ." His voice shook as he breathed her name. "You are so sweet, so incredibly sweet."

"So s-sweet I'm sticky."

"Honey, I don't care if you're sticky." He took a taste of her shoulder. "You're delicious."

"Oh . . . God." She pressed her face against his chest. "I want my clothes. . . . This was a stupid idea. I really sh-shouldn't have — Swift?" She twisted an arm behind her to clamp her hand over his where it had come to rest on her bottom. "What are you — Swift?"

He leaned his head back. "Amy, look at me."

Hesitantly she lifted her face. When she did, he bent his head and pressed his mouth to hers. She made a sound of protest and started to resist, her breath spilling against his lips. He tensed to hold her and drove his tongue into her moist mouth. She froze, then moaned softly, rising on her toes to meet him, her slender arms encircling his neck.

Left to touch her wherever he chose, Swift felt his heart begin to slam. The muscles in his thighs tied into knots. His hands glided over her, trembling, hovering, aching. He settled for returning one palm to her buttock so he could draw her hips closer. The warm flesh of her bottom quivered. He felt her arms spasm around his neck. He pressed his other hand to her slender back, to steady her and hold her, in case she panicked. A little murmur crawled up her throat and into his mouth.

He guessed how frightened she was. His control nearly snapped when she pressed closer and clung to him almost fiercely, seeking comfort from him. The enormity of what he was about to do hit him. Swift squeezed his eyelids closed, shaking as violently as she, so desperately determined to make this beautiful for her that uncertainty held him paralyzed. One wrong move, one thoughtless word. He swallowed, the sound echoing inside his chest, and wrenched his mouth from hers to bury his face in her hair.

"Swift?"

He eased his hand up her back, his fingertips tracing the scars there, his guts twisting because she had trusted him enough to come to him as she had. "It's all right, Amy, love," he whispered, not sure whom he was trying hardest to convince, her or himself. "It's all right."

"You're sh-shaking."

He tightened his hold on her. "I know."

"Why?"

"I'm terrified."

"You're what?"

He gave a jerky laugh. "Scared! I'm so scared I couldn't spit if you yelled fire. If I do this wrong — if I mess it up. I love you so much, Amy. . . ."

To his amazement, he felt her body relax. She leaned her head back, trying to see his face. He straightened and lifted his lashes to meet her gaze. She loosened her arms from his neck to catch his face between her hands. Blue eyes brimming with tears, she rose up to kiss the scar on his cheek, the cut on his chin, then his mouth.

"Oh, Swift . . . don't be afraid," she whispered against his lips, her breath so sweet it intoxicated him. "I wanted to make you happy. . . ."

"Happy? I am happy. I love you so much
—"

"Just tell me that," she pleaded. "The way
you promised to. Tell me you love me, Swift.
Your way, this time, without words. You
can't say I love you wrong, can you?"

He slid his lips to the side of her throat,
loving the feel of her hands on his face. His
mouth encountered a pulse point, and he
pressed his tongue to it. Her heart was pat-
tering so hard and fast that he couldn't keep
up with the beats. He slid his hands to her
waist and drew her slowly toward the floor
until they knelt on the rug.

Pulling away from her, he sat back on his
heels to look at her. She knelt before him,
chin lifted, her gaze clinging to his, her arms
crisscrossed over her body. Very gently he
clasped her wrists and drew her arms to her
sides. A pink flush tinted her white skin.
Swift cupped a breast, lifting it with his
palm. His skin looked as dark as night in
contrast with hers. He bent his head and
touched his tongue to the swollen, rosy peak
of her nipple, smiling slightly when he felt
her pulse throbbing there, too. She was so
scared that she was one big heartbeat, and
he loved her all the more for it.

She gasped at the contact of his tongue,

and her sensitive flesh shrank, its only defense against the rasping caress. Unable to resist, he pulled her into his mouth, catching her around the hips when she jerked to her knees. Her hands flew to his hair. She made tight fists, her breath coming quick and shallow as his tongue dragged across her nipple, teasing the nerve endings there. She whimpered low in her throat when he drew on her, her head falling back when his teeth closed.

Then, as if the starch went out of her, she melted. Supporting her with his arm, he rode her to the floor, switching his attention to the other breast, gratified by the shallow panting sounds she made as he worked her. Amy. His life, his love, a velvet dream in his arms, sweeter than anything he had ever imagined or ever could have conceived possible.

Through the fringe of her eyelashes, Amy saw Swift's black head pressed to her bosom, his dark hands running up her body. Sensation rocked her — so beautiful it took her breath. His shirt rasped against her, warmed by the fire and his skin. She arched toward him, giving herself, all fear leaving her. This was how God had intended it to be. A precious gift. A sacred oneness.

I love you. He said the words in the way

441

he held her, his rock-hard arms so gentle they felt like air around her. *I love you.* His hands told her — not merely touching her, but worshiping her. When he rose above her and jerked off his shirt, golden firelight played on his chest and arms. With a heavy-lidded gaze, Amy looked up at him, finding beauty and sweetness in the sheer maleness of him, the breadth of his rippling shoulders, the tracks of muscles across his belly, the dusting of black hair that ran in a triangle from his chest to his narrow waist. His burnished body gleamed like lacquered wood, rich and hard and sturdy.

When he drew her back into his arms, when her breasts connected with his hot skin, Amy's breath snagged, her senses reeling. Love for him filled her until she ached. She felt no fear. What she did feel was his hand tracing the scars on her back and a tear trailing down the side of her neck.

She clung to him then, filled with a joy that was inexpressible — because Swift Lopez, a hard, embittered man who had never shown weakness, a man who had instilled fear in people clear across Texas, a man who had faced death hundreds, perhaps thousands, of times, held her so tenderly and wept over the pain she had suffered. If he could expose himself so completely to her, she could deny him nothing.

When he moved his hand down her belly, when she felt his fingertips thread through the curls at the apex of her thighs, Amy offered no resistance. Instead she opened for him, trusting him as she had never trusted anyone, surrendering even though she expected pain, reassured because she knew he would hurt her as little as possible. He slid his fingertips lower and Amy whimpered, taken off guard by the electrical sensation that shot through her belly. She had expected him to rise above her, to divest himself of the remainder of his clothing, to take her. What she hadn't counted on was to feel this. Pleasure rolled over her in hot, tingling waves.

Withdrawing slowly, ever so slowly, then thrusting, gently, cautiously, finding a place within her that turned white hot and shivery every time he connected with it. Amy moaned and lifted her hips, unable to draw breath as he increased the pace, thrusting harder and faster until she undulated to meet him, caught up in a sensation that made her mindless. She opened her eyes on a swirling world of firelight and darkness, plummeted through it, that place within her going into spasms that jerked her whole body. She felt as if she might fly apart, but just when she knew she would, Swift's arm drew her close and held her together as wave after quaking wave of indescribable ecstasy rolled over her.

She lay quivering in his arms afterward, chest convulsing for breath, her body filmed with moistness, her heart pounding. He ran gentling hands over her, whispering to her as she returned, measure by measure, to reality. Amy knew that what he had just done to her wasn't all there was to it, that he hadn't found his pleasure yet. Even though she expected it to be painful for her, she fought back her fear because she wanted so badly to please him. But when she started to turn toward him, he slid his hand back to her again, his fingertips stroking lightly over her, not entering her this time. She gasped at the shock of sensation that shot up through her.

"Swift . . ."

"Trust me, Amy," he insisted in a husky voice. "This is how it's supposed to be. Trust me."

Light began to swirl inside her head. Heat built inside her again, white-hot, then more fiery, until her belly knotted around it, twisting and quivering, the tension building until she sobbed and snapped taut, arching toward him, wanting and needing him to press harder. Then rapture, shooting through her, jolt after jolt of it, until she quivered, until she cried out, until she lay spent, too weak to move, to speak.

In a haze, she saw Swift rise over her, gleaming bronze, roped with tendon, becoming aware as her gaze dropped that he had removed the remainder of his clothing. The fear, which she had held so firmly at bay, clutched her with cold fingers, stilling her breath, snapping her taut. Catching her by the hips, he lifted her toward him. She made fists in the rug, tensing, expecting agony.

"Amy, love. Do you trust me?"

Amy clutched the rug more frantically, braced against him. With a choked sob, she nodded.

"Then relax. Show me you trust me, Amy, this one last time." He kneaded her thighs, forcing the stiffness from them, his hands warm and gentle, yet relentless. "Can you do that for me? Let go of the rug."

Memories from long ago, and from only moments ago, spun through her mind. Swift, her dearest friend. He wanted her. And no matter how it might hurt, she wanted to fulfill his needs. She forced her hands to release the braided fibers of the rug, her gaze clinging to his.

"Now take a deep breath," he whispered. "And relax your body. I don't want to hurt you. Relax. There's my girl."

As she exhaled the great draft of air he had told her to inhale, he entered her in one smooth thrust. Amy sucked in breath, her lungs whining at the shock of his invasion. Her temples slammed. She waited, teeth clenched, knowing the pain would come. But it didn't. Then he lowered his body over hers to gather her into his arms. For a moment he didn't move, allowing her to grow accustomed to him.

"Are you all right?"

With a relieved sob, she said, "Yes," scarcely able to believe it. He pressed his face into her hair, his lips near her ear, his breathing fast and shallow.

"Don't be afraid. Trust me, honey. I swear on my life it won't hurt." He began to move within her, striking the rhythm of her nightmares, only now the nightmare had turned to a dream. "I love you, Amy. Hold tight to my neck. Come with me. . . ."

And with that request whispering in her mind, he took her with him to heaven.

CHAPTER 20

Amy drifted back to reality slowly, taking in her surroundings in measures, noticing first the flickering firelight, then the coarseness of the braided rug against her back, the anchor of Swift's body atop hers, the warmth of his breath against her neck, the feel of his hands splayed across her skin. She closed her eyes, savoring the peacefulness and the knowledge that this man who held her so tenderly loved her.

She took a deep breath, absorbing the scents of him, committing them to memory — faint traces of soap, the tang of leather, the smell of tobacco, and the muskiness of his skin. His heart thudded against her breast, a strong, even beat that seemed to throb through her own veins. It felt perfectly right to lie there with him, her limbs drained of strength, her mind drifting. A sense of belonging filled her.

Swift. His name flowed through her like

the chords of a song, sweet and lilting. There was no need for writing on paper, no need for their union to be recognized by law or church. Their vows to one another had been spoken long ago, and as far as she was concerned, a Comanche marriage was enough.

"Are you all right?" he asked huskily.

Amy opened her eyes and ran her fingers lightly over his hair. "I'm —" Tears burned behind her eyelids, and her throat swelled with an ache of gladness. "I'm fine. Better than fine. I feel wonderful."

He touched his lips to her neck, running his tongue across her skin. "You taste wonderful," he murmured. "And you feel even better. I don't want to move."

"Then don't." In truth she didn't want him to, almost feared it, for then she would have no choice but to face reality again. For this little while, she wanted to stay inside the dream Swift had spun around her, to believe in goodness and rightness and love, just for this little while.

"I'll crush you."

He moved slightly, putting an elbow on the rug to lever his chest off her. As his head drew back, Amy looked into his smiling eyes, and her mouth curved in response. After gazing down at her for a long while, he lifted his hand to her face, trailing a fingertip across her cheek. The smell of her clung to him, reminding her of all that had passed between them, and some of his magic slipped away from her.

He drew back a bit more, studying her, his gaze shifting to her uncomfortably warm cheeks. The knowing gleam in his eyes made her feel embarrassed. And instantly conscious of her nakedness. In the wake of that, she felt undignified, remembering how she had writhed and moaned beneath his hands. She could tell by the look in his eyes that he was remembering, too.

The smile in his eyes spread to his mouth. He twisted his shoulders, groping behind him. An instant later, he held up his shirt and spread it over her. Grateful for the shield, Amy hugged the black cloth close, awash in uncertainty. Her first inclination was to scramble for her clothes, but those were in the bedroom and she'd have to walk miles to retrieve them. Not only that, but it felt wrong to scurry away, as if nothing important had occurred. Yet that was what she yearned to do.

"I'm — I'm afraid I'm not very good at this," she whispered.

"If you were, I'd be disappointed. Don't you know that a man likes to think he's the first? That his woman is his and only his?"

Amy's stomach clenched. "Swift, you know that —"

"I'll tell you what I know," he whispered. "You're as sweet and pure and precious as any woman who ever lived. No man's ever kissed you like this." He bent his head to feather a light kiss across her mouth. "Or touched you like I have. Or seen your body like I have. Or made love to you. You're mine and only mine, Amy. That's what I know."

"Oh, Swift . . ." The shirt shifted, and she tugged it back into place.

He laughed softly. "I'd offer to go get your clothes, but I like you this way."

Amy shot a nervous glance toward the dark hallway, which seemed horribly distant. Swift sat up, apparently at ease with his nudity. With a splendid show of rippling muscle, he leaned forward, reaching for his pants. She studied the play of tendon in his back as he moved, fascinated by the way his burnished flesh bulged into steely knots, then relaxed. He rose, affording her a full view of tendon-roped buttocks and corded thighs as he pulled his pants on. The jangle of his belt buckle sounded, the band of leather snapping taut around his lean hips. He retrieved his socks and boots, then sat beside her to put them on.

When finished, he turned his dark head to regard her, his twinkling gaze shifting to the shirt she clutched to her breasts. "Can I talk you out of a smoke?" he asked.

Amy swallowed, horrified at the thought of handing his shirt over, which would leave her naked. He fell back on an elbow and skimmed his hand over the denim, his fingers searching for the pocket that held his tobacco pouch. The pocket in question lay over her right breast, outside in. He dived his hand under the shirt collar, his palm rasping down her chest, then fumbling about as he tried to wrest his tobacco pouch free. The unintentional touches on her breast sent her senses spinning.

Suddenly his hand stilled. His gaze met hers. His white teeth flashed in a rakish grin. Abandoning his quest inside the shirt pocket, he curled his warm fingers around her. "To hell with a smoke," he whispered huskily.

With that, he kissed her. And within seconds Amy found herself losing her grip on the shield of denim, losing her grip on everything. As her senses reeled under his expert coaxing, she dimly recorded the whimpering sounds she was making and realized, vaguely, that Swift had a power over her that she had never allowed anyone else, an enslaving, controlling power that she was helpless to resist, didn't want to resist. She responded to every touch of his hands, every unvoiced command, moaning because surrender would bring ecstasy, ecstasy rapture, and rapture mindlessness. His hands gliding over her body reduced her to a quivering, thoughtless, throbbing puddle of longing, and she eddied dizzily under his light caresses, writhing, arching upward, wanting his fingertips to set her afire as they had earlier.

In a haze of passion, she felt the featherlight gentleness leave him, replaced by a feverish, harsh urgency. The touch of his hands became relentless, his fingers pressing deep into her flesh, staking claim. When he clamped a palm over the now throbbing apex of her thighs, grinding the heel of his hand against her, jolts of sheer sensation ripped through her. His breathing echoed in her head, ragged and quick, the sound of a man burning with need.

When he dragged her hips beneath him, Amy realized he meant to take her quickly. No ecstasy; no mindlessness. For an instant, fear lashed her. He jerked open his belt buckle, unfastened his pants. She felt the steely length of his manhood, thrusting and hot against her thigh, seeking entry. Before she could register that completely, he found her and drove into her, hard. She gasped, her belly convulsing, her insides twisting and clasping. His arms encircled her, snapping taut, almost hurting in their possession of her.

He withdrew and thrust forward, unleashing the power in his body, the impact jarring through her, and him, his invasion deep and fierce. Then, with no preamble, he set a pace, the rhythm furious this time and merciless. She tensed, expecting pain. Instead the rhythm consumed her. She responded instinctively, tucking her legs around his thighs and arching to meet him, increasing the impact, glorying in the slamming bursts of fire that erupted through her, setting her middle aflame, turning it molten.

He was power and might, she the vanquished. Pride and dignity eluded her. She surrendered to the force, rose to absorb it, whimpering as his need became her own, a burning, insatiable need that drove her upward, onward, turning white hot, blinding her. Just as she peaked, Swift froze above her, his face twisting, his shoulders shuddering, his arms in spasms. Then she felt the fire in him erupt into her, a wave of breathtaking heat that rushed and broke, intensifying hers.

With a groan he resumed the pace, slowly at first, his face a sheen of satisfaction, his gaze holding hers as he increased tempo. In the back of her mind, Amy realized he meant to watch her as he thrust her over the edge, but she had come too far to resist, her body more his now than hers. A smile touched his mouth. She saw it, registered it, and then lost contact with reality as his thrusts pushed her past caring.

She heard him whispering to her, urging her on. With a cry she clutched his shoulders, clinging, gasping for breath, her hips arching up to meet him as the climax came. Like Swift, she fell victim to shuddering, convulsive spasms.

When she lay quivering and spent beneath him, he gathered her close, his hot mouth pressing kisses to her breasts, her throat, her face. Exhausted, Amy turned into his embrace, limp and boneless. He held her, stroking a hand from her bottom to her shoulders until sleep stole over her, a deep, mindless, dreamless sleep, her body enveloped by the warmth of him.

Amy woke up to find herself surrounded by darkness. She recognized the softness of her down mattress beneath her. Something warm and damp skimmed her legs. She blinked and stiffened, straining to see.

"Swift?"

He laughed low in his chest. "Who do you think?"

"Wh-what are you doing?" she squeaked, frustrated by the blackness and the familiarity of his hands on her person.

The cloth skimmed up her thigh. "I'm bathing you. I promised, remember? Not a trace of apple when I finished."

She heard a wet plop as he discarded the rag. The covers snapped as he brought them fluttering down over her. His weight sank onto the mattress beside her. The next instant his arm came around her, the sleeve of his shirt abrasive on her waist, his palm leathery on her back.

"I have to leave, golden one. In a couple more hours it'll be dawn, and if anyone sees me sneaking out of here, your reputation will be shot to hell."

Amy could feel his breath on her cheek, the heat of him, but all she could make out of him visually was a blackness before her that was blacker than the night. She made fists in his shirt, suddenly and inexplicably frightened. Once he left, reality might come back between them. She wanted to hold this night close, keep it forever.

"I — I don't want you to go. We're married now, aren't we? Why must you leave?"

His lips grazed hers. "Amy, love, Comanche law doesn't mean squat to the people here. If I stay before we're married their way, they'll look at you as a fallen woman." There was a smile in his voice. "I think we need to find a priest — quick."

"He won't come back here for weeks!"

His tongue touched hers, and he groaned. "Weeks?"

"Weeks," she repeated, hopelessness filling her. "I don't want to wait for weeks. Do you? I want you to stay with me now. A Comanche marriage is good enough. It's everything."

The panic in her voice was unmistakable. Swift drew back to study her shadowed face. "Amy, love, what's wrong?"

"I — I just don't want you to go. I have this horrid feeling that once you do, tonight won't ever have happened."

He ran a hand into her hair. Though he had experienced the same feelings himself, Swift knew by the sound of her voice that he hadn't felt her panic. "Honey, that's crazy."

"I don't care. It's how I feel. If you leave, something might happen. You might never come back."

"I'll be back," he said in a teasing, husky whisper, but as he spoke, the words rang in his head, an echo from the past. Suddenly he understood. Once before they had loved one another — innocently, but just as passionately — and his promises had become dust in a Texas wind. Now, at last, they had reclaimed that feeling of togetherness, and Amy was terrified of it being torn away from her. Swift's heart broke a little as he lay down and drew her close. "Amy, listen to me. Nothing will ever keep us apart again. Nothing. I won't allow it. Besides, I'm just going up the street. It's within hollering distance."

She pressed close, burying her face against his neck. "It seems like a hundred miles."

Swift sighed. "I don't want you to lose your job. I know you need that security, at least for a while."

"I need you more."

"You can have both. We're married now, Amy. You know it; I know it. Nothing and no one can change that." He tucked in his chin to press a kiss atop her head, loving the feel of her silken hair, heavy against his shirt. "And with marriage comes all the things you fear. For the first year or so, while you're walking a circle around me and learning what I'm like when —"

"I don't care about that now." Even as she spoke, Amy knew she was suffering from momentary madness. Later on she would care. There was no getting around that. Henry Masters had left his mark, whether she could admit it right now or not.

Swift closed his eyes, knowing that the scars within her ran too deep to pretend they were healed by one night of lovemaking. He wished that could be, but wishing would never make it so.

"I do care," he whispered, his voice gravelly. He drew her up onto his chest and released his hold on her to catch her face between his hands. "If you lose that job, you'll be dependent on me for everything. Sooner or later that's going to eat at you."

"But —" Amy broke off, despising herself because what he said was true.

He slanted a finger across her mouth. "No buts. You don't have to give up everything to be my wife, Amy. We can go on like we have been until the priest comes. I'll be here every night, for lessons. And maybe I'll stay some nights until right before dawn. Nothing's going to separate us again. I swear it."

Amy let him leave with no further argument. Long after his departure, she lay shivering in her lonely bed, wishing he were there beside her, hating herself because her weakness had held them apart for so long and now it still held them apart.

After school the following day, Amy went by Loretta's for her usual brief visit. To her surprise, both Swift and Hunter were at the house when she walked in. Taken off guard, Amy closed the door, then stood there, uncertain how to greet Swift after their night together.

"Ah, Amy, you're just in time for hot blackberry cobbler!" Loretta exclaimed.

"Th-that sounds wonderful," Amy said weakly, her mind filled with thoughts of apple pie. When she had gotten up this morning, she hadn't found a trace of the mess in her kitchen. Swift had cleaned it up while she slept.

Her gaze collided with his. Memories of their lovemaking spun through her head. She dropped her gaze, groping for her poise, but everything about him reminded her, even his shirt, which only a few short hours ago had lain against her bare breasts.

Swift saw the flush as it started up Amy's neck, and to call it crimson would have been understatement. It flooded her face, inching to her hairline, so obvious that he knew Hunter and Loretta couldn't fail to notice. Tender amusement warmed him, and he bit back a smile. Sweet, precious Amy in her schoolmarm dress, with her glorious hair wound in a prim coronet about her head. To her, their lovemaking last night had been scandalous.

The smile inside him became an ache in his throat as he recalled how tame their joining had actually been. She'd bust her seams when he made real love to her. And if she blushed like this afterward, everyone in town would know what she'd been up to.

Trying to pretend nothing was amiss, Swift rubbed his hands together. "Well, dish that cobbler up, Loretta. I'm so hungry my legs feel hollow."

The attempt at joviality fell flat. Loretta stood frozen, staring at Amy, who was turning a brighter red by the second. Hunter, instead of staring at Amy, had turned his dark blue gaze on Swift, one eyebrow arched in question. When Swift made eye contact with him, Hunter's mouth quirked. He glanced at Amy.

"Amy, love, is something wrong?" Loretta asked.

Amy's eyes seemed to grow larger than the pie plates sitting on the table, startling splashes of blue in contrast with her flushed face. Swift nearly groaned. "N-no, nothing," she squeaked, which was clearly the biggest untruth she had ever uttered. "Wh-why do you ask?"

Loretta threw a glance at Hunter. Amy turned pleading eyes to Swift. To his horror, he felt his neck getting hot, and then the heat spread to his face. Damned if he wasn't blushing. He cleared his throat and raked a hand through his hair, as embarrassed as if he had just been caught tumbling Amy in the hayloft. Hunter, grinning like an ass, turned his attention to the cobbler and picked up the server.

"Well, if nothing's wrong, come on in," he said, darting another knowing look at Swift.

Amy swept off her shawl and hung it on the rack. Approaching the table, she wiped her hands on her skirts, looking so painfully guilty that anyone save a fool could guess why. Loretta's blue eyes slid from her cousin to Swift. And then, as if a contagious disease had infiltrated the household, Loretta's face turned a comely pink. Only Hunter seemed immune. Still grinning, he served four dishes of cobbler, motioning for everyone to take a seat at the table.

All four of them filled their mouths immediately. Swift made an appreciative noise and took a second bite. Loretta, clearly uncomfortable with the lack of pleasantries, glanced up from her plate. "How did those apples I gave you bake up?"

Swift, in the process of swallowing, choked. Everyone, including Amy, turned to watch while he struggled to get his breath. When at last he swallowed and chased the cobbler down with a sip of hot coffee, he managed a shaky, "Excuse me." Amy began blushing all over again. Hunter's grin broadened. Loretta looked totally nonplussed.

Hunter met Swift's gaze. "Are you going to survive that cobbler?"

"It isn't Loretta's cobbler." Swift took another gulp of coffee. "I'm fine. Just went down the wrong pipe, I guess."

Amy bent her head and attacked the berries on her plate as if she had just declared war. Hunter cleared his throat. "Swift and I stopped by to see Peter on the way home, Amy."

She glanced up, her eyes darkening, her high color fading, "Did you? And how is he?"

"Fine. I think Swift's little *talk* with Abe did some good. At least he didn't go home and raise thunder yesterday, like he might have before."

"Is Peter's mother keeping him in bed?"

"And fussing over him like a mother hen," Hunter amplified. Meeting Amy's gaze, he asked, "Why did you never come to me about Peter's problem? As far as I knew, the only time Abe got out of line was back when his wife had him jailed. I had no idea he made a habit of getting drunk and going home mean."

Amy felt her cheeks growing warm again. "I —" Hunter's gaze gave her no quarter. She shrugged. "If I had come to you, you would have confronted Abe, and I was afraid you'd get into trouble."

Hunter's jaw rippled, "It's good Indigo has more faith in my judgment. An ornery man is one thing. Abe Crenton has gone far beyond that. It is not the way of the People to turn away when a man abuses his wife and family. You knew that, Amy."

Amy had witnessed Hunter's mild reproofs hundreds of times when they were directed at his children, but never before had she been a target. For years she had watched him turn those luminous eyes of his on Indigo or Chase, reducing them to heartfelt remorse without even raising his voice. She had often wondered how he managed that. Now she knew. Hunter, in his kind way, struck much deeper than the flesh; the wounded look in his eyes lashed her heart.

"I meant well," she said lamely.

His gaze held hers, and without words he spoke with eloquence.

"If it happens again, I'll come to you," Amy promised.

Hunter's gaze slid to Swift. "If Abe does harm again, take your concerns to your husband. It was his strong arm that defended Alice Crenton and her children yesterday."

Hunter's reference to Swift as her husband meant that he knew what had transpired between her and Swift last night. But before Amy could react to that, Hunter reached out and grasped her hand, in much the same way that Father O'Grady touched her forehead when he gave her absolution. A feeling of peace spread through her, warm and comforting.

For a fleeting instant Amy wished she had grown up with the Comanches, that she had been raised, not by Henry Masters, but by Hunter's father, Many Horses, that she could have basked in love and been reprimanded, not with fist or strap, as had been Henry's way, but with goodness and understanding.

Unlike Amy, Loretta's children didn't know fear; they ran wild and free, holding their heads high with pride. Yet, somehow, despite his gentle ways, Hunter ruled his household, instilling in his children all those virtues he deemed important, loyalty, honesty, pride, and courage. Never did he stress obedience, yet it came, naturally and effortlessly, because Hunter's children loved him far too fiercely to displease him.

Amy's gaze shifted from Hunter to Swift, who seemed absorbed in eating his cobbler, as did Loretta. Their seeming indifference was yet another custom of the People; one's shame was his own, and others did not look upon it. Amy glanced back at Hunter to discover that he had picked up his fork, her transgressions already relegated to yesterday.

As if he sensed the moment of chastisement had passed, Swift glanced up and looked straight into her eyes, his own twinkling. An unbidden smile touched her mouth. Unlike her, Swift had been raised Comanche, and Hunter's ways were his as well. She couldn't help but wonder if he'd be the kind of father Hunter was, unaffected by the noisy chaos in his home, offering direction only when he witnessed a serious transgression, his manner gentle, the reprimand a softly spoken word.

"I wonder where Indigo went after school this time," Loretta remarked. "I expected her home before now."

Hunter lifted his head. "She will come."

"I'll bet she's with that Marshall fellow. He's too old for her, by half. But will she listen to me?"

Amy interrupted to tell them about her confrontation with Indigo the previous afternoon. "I meant to talk with her again later, but the situation with Peter cropped up and I got so caught up in it that I forgot."

Loretta toyed with her fork. "Lands, I wish she'd send that young man packing. Why would a fellow twenty years old be interested in a girl her age? I can't like him."

"She'll send him packing," Hunter replied. "Indigo has eyes that see into tomorrow. She has only to open them."

Swift finished his cobbler and carried his plate to the dish board. Glancing over his shoulder at Amy, he pulled his watch from his pocket. "It's about time for my school lessons. You ready to head over?"

His eyes danced with mischief, and it didn't pass her notice that his gaze swept over her in a meaningful way. Amy rose and carried her plate across the room, careful not to look up at him. After ridding herself of the dish, she turned toward the door. "If I spy Indigo, I'll send her along home, Loretta."

Loretta smiled. "No, don't do that. Like

Hunter says, she has only to open her eyes. I guess I've a bad habit of being overprotective."

Swift took his hat from the rack. After donning it at a jaunty angle, he pulled down Amy's shawl and draped it around her shoulders, grazing her neck and then her breasts with his knuckles as he straightened the woolen folds. Breath snagging, Amy lifted startled blue eyes to his. Before another of her telltale blushes could give him away, Swift, chuckling low in his chest, ushered her out the door, fairly certain Hunter hadn't missed her heightening color and had guessed its cause.

Once on the porch, Amy gathered her shawl close. Swift took her elbow, looking forward to their upcoming *lesson* with lascivious eagerness. He'd be giving her something a little more scandalous to blush about, if he had his way.

"Your cheeks are as red as an overripe apple," he informed her as they went down the porch steps. "We have to walk the length of town. You want everybody we meet to know what we've been up to?"

Her face turned a throbbing scarlet, which set Swift to chuckling again. Placing a hand on her nape, he fingered the silken curls there as he guided her onto the boardwalk.

467

"How long do you plan to blush every time I look at you?"

"It's not my fault I have a fair complexion."

"Why are you so embarrassed?"

Her blue eyes flashed at him. "It isn't funny."

Swift threw back his head and barked with laughter.

"Would you stop! People are staring."

He glanced across the way at Samuel Jones, who was busy sweeping the boardwalk in front of the general store. "Amy, no one's staring. I'll tell you right now, shyness is going to last around me about as long as a candle in a windstorm."

"Is that so?"

"That's a promise. You can wear those prim little collars buttoned up to your chin in public, but not at home."

"Just what shall I wear, then?"

"Your apron, if you're cooking. Otherwise nothing will suit me just fine."

She threw him a thoroughly horrified look.

"My reading and arithmetic lessons fall into the category of otherwise."

She quickened her pace, glancing right and left as if she feared someone might have overheard him. Swift grinned, stepping smartly to keep up with her.

"You are an eager little package, aren't you?"

She nearly tripped over her skirts coming to a halt. Blushing to the roots of her hair, she met his gaze. "You're deliberately tormenting me. Can't you be a gentleman, just once, Swift? It's terribly rude of you to — to talk about it as if you're commenting on the weather!"

As she spun and once again started down the boardwalk at a busy pace, Swift sauntered along behind her, directing his gaze to the tantalizing sway of her hips. Then, as if a lasso had brought her up short, she froze. Swift glanced up to see what was wrong. Steve and Hank Lowdry had just stepped up onto the boardwalk, several feet ahead of her. Amy backed up, her body rigid. Swift quickened his pace to reach her. When he touched her arm, she pressed close to him.

"It's all right, honey."

A shudder coursed through her. "They look like — Who are they?"

Swift looped an arm around her and drew her into a walk, not caring for the moment if the townspeople saw him. "Just a couple of prospectors. Do you want to cross the street?"

"No. I'm not afraid when you're with me."

She pressed closer, belying the words.

Swift gazed ahead at the two men, finding little comfort in the realization that he wasn't the only one who thought they looked like comancheros. Evil. The first instant he had seen them, he had sensed it. And now so did Amy.

To Swift's relief, the two men stepped off the boardwalk onto the street to allow him and Amy to pass. Their spurs chinked in the damp, packed earth. Amy began to shiver. Swift glanced down. Her face, such a brilliant red only moments before, had gone deathly white.

"Wh-why are they here?" She lifted frightened eyes to his. "What could they possibly want in Wolf's Landing?"

"They came for gold."

"Hog spittle!" She threw a look at them over her shoulder. "Men like that don't work for a living."

"I guess they have as much right to dream as anyone."

"Don't you think they look like —" She broke off, as if couldn't bring herself to say the word.

"Like what, Amy?" Swift helped her step off the end of the boardwalk. "Listen to me. They've been here a couple days now. If they were as bad as they look, they'd have already stirred trouble. Hunter visited with them. He said they seemed genuinely interested in finding gold."

As he finished speaking, the hair on Swift's nape prickled. He glanced back to see that the two men had stopped in the street. With their hats pulled low, he couldn't tell if they were looking at him, yet he couldn't discount his wary reaction. He tightened his arm around Amy and picked up their pace.

"If they aren't here for gold," he added, more to himself to her, "then they're taking a long time to make a move."

"A move?" Her face drew tight. "You don't think — Oh, Swift, no. . . . They aren't gunslingers, are they?"

"Not any I recognize." The fear in her expression made him wish he hadn't said anything. He flashed her a slow grin and jostled her with his arm. "Hey, don't look so gloomy. I'm too suspicious by half. It comes with the territory. I came here for a new start, remember? Let's not borrow trouble. The likelihood of anybody following me this far from Texas is mighty slim, don't you think?"

A little color returned to her face. "It is an awfully long way." A smile curved her lips. "Maybe I've just got comancheros on the brain, from keeping company with one."

He narrowed one eye at her. "I am not a

comanchero, never was. If you really thought so, you wouldn't have made lo—"

She pinched his ribs. "Be a gentleman."

"I'm no gentleman, either." He bent his head and nipped her earlobe. "Here in about an hour, I'll have you convinced of that," he whispered huskily.

From the corner of his eye, Swift saw movement at the edge of town. He turned in time to spot Indigo slipping off alone into the woods. Amy followed his gaze. "That girl. I'll give you one guess where she's headed. I wish she wouldn't sneak off alone with him like that."

"Do you think that's where she's going, to meet him? She hunts, you know. And when she isn't hunting, she enjoys walking. She's got a lot of wildness in her."

"A little too much wildness for my peace of mind. She's too sure of herself. She isn't afraid of anything. That could be dangerous around a young man with no scruples."

Swift grinned, remembering the knife Indigo wore strapped to her thigh. "My sympathies are all with Brandon if he steps out of line. That girl's as slick with a knife as any man I've ever seen. And I'll bet she isn't half bad at fistfighting, either. Having Chase to tussle with has given her spunk."

"She's a little slip of a girl, Swift. Brandon's twice her size."

"She could handle three of him and never work up a sweat. Stop worrying. Any fellow who takes that girl on is going to bite off a whole lot more than he expected."

As they walked up the steps of the house, Amy couldn't resist one last look toward the woods where Indigo had disappeared.

CHAPTER 21

Indigo sensed she was in trouble the moment she entered the clearing. Brandon hadn't come alone. Three of his friends were with him, and she didn't like the look in their eyes when they spotted her. She stopped in her tracks.

"Hello, Indigo," Brandon said, stepping toward her. He had removed his tweed jacket and sported a pale blue shirt, the sleeves rolled back to the elbow. She had never seen him so casually attired. As his gaze swept the length of her, he ran a hand over his ribs, much like a man who had just finished a satisfying meal. "I'm glad you decided to come." His mouth tipped in a grin. "So we can make up."

She didn't like the way he said "make up," as if it were a big joke. Though she kept her gaze on Brandon, Indigo saw the others moving toward her. Their half smiles made her blood run cold. She had no idea what they had in mind, but whatever it was boded ill for her.

"Brandon?" she said softly. "Why have you brought your friends with you?"

His blue eyes filled with amusement. "They're here to help me make up with you."

She shifted her gaze to the other young men. Last night, Brandon had tried to put his hand under her blouse, and she had slapped him. They had parted in anger. Today, during noon break at school, he had come to the edge of the playground to ask her to meet him here this afternoon. To make up, he had claimed.

She licked her lips, her mouth dry and tacky. "You need help to apologize?"

"Honey, you're the one who's going to apologize," he said softly. "And you're going to do it on your knees. No Indian slut slaps me and gets away with it."

Indigo finally pried her feet from the dirt. She retreated a step, shocked by the name he had called her. He made her sound like a dirty thing, something so beneath him she wasn't even deserving of his contempt. Hurt cut through her. She had loved him so much. And she had believed all the pretty things he said. Now she realized all of it had been lies.

Falling back on the fierce pride her father had instilled in her, Indigo swallowed the urge to cry and lifted her chin. "I'll go on my knees to no man."

Brandon took another step closer. "Oh, you'll get on your knees. When in the presence of your betters, that's where you belong. You think too highly of yourself, Indigo. God created squaws for one thing, and you're going to learn what it is. You didn't really believe a white man would have any other interest in you, did you?"

One of the other young men laughed, a deep, rumbling sound. She whirled to run and cannoned into a sturdy chest. The impact dazed her. Before she fell, strong arms cinched around her. Dimly she realized there had been someone coming up behind her. There must be five of them. His arms clamped hers to her sides, bruising her, cutting off her breath.

"Who-ee! Isn't she an armful of sweetness?" Lifting her feet off the ground, he swung her around, glancing toward Brandon. "No wonder you've been sniffing her trail. She doesn't even look like a breed. And the way she's put together, who'd guess she's so young?"

"A drop of Indian blood is all it takes," Brandon replied.

"Hey, I'm not complaining. I've always had a secret hankering to have me a white gal with a little fight in her. This is probably as close as I'll ever get."

Blinking to see, Indigo focused on the face of the man who held her, a dark face, one she recognized. Heath Mallory from Jacksonville. She'd seen him attending mass there with his family, a nice, mannerly young man. Only now his face was harsh and menacing, his smile cruel. She tried to shove away from him, but he held her fast. To her horror, she felt him loosen one arm from around her to slide a hand under her leather blouse and chemise. Bile rose in her throat.

"Don't," she cried. "Take your hand off me!"

He groped for her breast. She worked one arm free and elbowed him in the mouth with all her strength. The sickening crunch made blood spurt. His blue eyes grew wild. With a curse he pushed her away, then backhanded her, his knuckles catching her along the cheek. Black spots bounced before her eyes.

Before Indigo could regain her balance, Brandon grabbed her from behind and threw her to the ground. In a flying leap he was upon her, his hands seizing her wrists.

His weight crushed the breath from her. Even if she escaped him, there were five of them, and she knew she didn't stand a chance against them.

Though she tried to fight it off, panic engulfed her. She writhed and screamed, praying someone might, by some miracle, hear her. She kicked and bucked. Despite her struggles, Brandon managed to get a hand under her blouse. She felt his fingers close on her breast. In that horrible, endless moment, she knew they were going to rape her, not because she had done anything to deserve it, but because Comanche blood flowed in her veins. She didn't know exactly what rape entailed, but she had heard enough whispers to guess it would be horrible. The panic within her grew, blinding her, blocking out all rational thought.

Then, almost as if he were beside her, Indigo heard her father's voice. *Never count on strength of arm in a fight, Indigo. Use the skills I've taught you. Stay calm. Take measure of your enemy. Then attack his weak points.* She closed her eyes and forced the panic back, making herself go limp.

Brandon laughed, his fingers pinching hard, punishing her. "Now here's a smart squaw. She knows what she's good for. Don't you, Indigo?"

Slowly Indigo opened her eyes. She met Brandon's gaze, blocking out the touch of his hand. Mistaking her limpness for surrender, he lowered his head and ground his mouth against hers. She suffered the kiss for a moment, waiting, and when he angled his head just right, she sank her teeth into his bottom lip, clenching her jaws together with all her strength.

Brandon snapped taut, unable to pull away without ripping his lip. A low whine erupted from him. She bit down harder. He roared, releasing her wrists to grab her head. The moment he did, Indigo parted her jaws so he could back off, then stiffened her thumbs and jabbed at his eyes. He yelped and reared back, clasping his palms over his face. She slithered out from under him, the taste of his blood in her mouth as she scrambled to her knees.

The other four formed a circle and converged on her. She whipped her knife from under her skirt, aware that Heath Mallory was behind her. "Come on, you *tosi* scum," she hissed, brandishing the gleaming blade. "Which of you wants me first? Let me show you what a squaw is good for."

"Oh, Jesus, my eyes! My eyes!" Brandon knelt nearby, holding his face, rocking wildly.

Indigo knew she hadn't jabbed him hard enough to blind him. Not that her father hadn't taught her how. She quickly took stock of her opponents, struggling against her fear. There had been one constant in all her father's teachings: panic had no place in battle.

Take measure of your enemy. All four of the remaining men outweighed her, and though none had the musculature of her father or Uncle Swift, her only hope of fighting them off was to use her head. She swayed lightly on her feet, side to side, keeping Heath in sight as best she could, the knife poised on her palm.

Heath lunged. Indigo whipped sideways and slashed. The tip of the knife caught his upper arm. He squeaked and leaped back, clasping the wound, blood oozing through his white shirt and between his fingers. "The little bitch cut me!"

"Come closer, *tosi tivo,* and I'll slit your throat," she warned.

One of the others, a lanky redhead, crouched and ran toward her. Indigo scooped dirt and threw it in his eyes, rolling out of his path and leaping to her feet as he dived and hit the ground, his target gone. She whirled, ready for the others. Pride rose in her throat, hot and scalding, making her nape prickle. As she leaned slightly forward at the waist, hands working the air, her feet in constant motion, she wished for a fleeting instant that her father could see her. From the time she was little, he had assured her that size gave a man no edge, and now she was proving it.

Renewed confidence filled her as the remaining three moved in on her, their eyes glittering, their faces shiny with sweat. *Let them come.* Though she was frightened, the knife rested in her hand, as familiar and as easy to wield as part of her body. Though she hated to take a life, she wouldn't hesitate if they leaped on her. Not even her mother's God would condemn her for defending herself.

"Come and get me," she whispered, beckoning a black-haired youth forward. "Come on! Where has your courage gone? Step closer. . . ."

His face drew taut and drained of color. His gaze shifted to the knife. "You haven't got the guts to kill me."

Indigo swallowed. "We will see."

Just as she spoke, something hit her from behind. She glimpsed a blue shirt and realized it was Brandon. She staggered and fell under his weight, nearly losing her grip on the knife. They rolled. He came out on top, pinning her beneath him. Not taking time to think it through, Indigo slashed with the blade, nicking his ear. He roared and jerked to one side. She made a fist in the front of his shirt and shoved the knife against his throat. The instant he felt the cold metal, he froze, his bloodshot eyes widening on hers.

"Don't move," she said. "Don't even breathe, Brandon." She saw the others circling. "Tell them to get back if you value your life."

Brandon's larynx bobbed against the sharp edge of the blade. Blood streamed from his torn bottom lip. "You heard her," he whimpered. "Get back! She really means it!"

"Of course I mean it," she whispered. "I'm a savage, remember? A squaw!"

His body began shaking, a horrible, uncontrollable shaking. Indigo knew the feeling. Only moments ago she had been as terrified. She felt no compassion for him. If he had succeeded in his plan, she would be spread-eagled by now and suffering their abuse.

"Go on!" she yelled at the others. "Get back!"

She didn't want to take her eyes off Brandon, but to be certain his friends were retreating, she knew she must. Tensing, she darted her gaze left, then right. She could see no one, but that didn't mean there wasn't someone standing beyond her line of vision, ready to jump on her. Still, she had no choice but to take a gamble. Lying there, giving them time to think of some way to disarm her, would be a grave mistake.

"All right, Brandon, get up," she instructed. "No sudden moves."

He inched back. She kept the knife pressed to his throat.

"You'll pay for this," he whispered. "I swear to God you'll pay. I'll make you crawl. If it's the last thing I ever do, I'll make you crawl."

Indigo rose to her knees, then to her feet. "I'll never crawl for you or any man, Brandon Marshall. Go back to Boston and your white world if that's what you want from a woman."

"Woman? You? You're a squaw." He touched his torn lip, then his ear, his hand quivering. "You've scarred me for life, you little bitch! You'll pay for this. That's a promise."

Indigo threw a glance at the others, then broke into a run. She was a long way from town, and she knew they would pursue her. Her moccasined feet touched lightly on the ground, the toned muscle in her legs lending her speed as she darted between the trees. Behind her she heard boots pounding the earth. Tears filled her eyes, blinding her. She dashed them away with her leather sleeve. *Indian slut.* The words tore at her.

She had to get away before they caught up with her. She pictured her father's face, her mother's, Chase's. All her life she had been surrounded by love. She had witnessed racial hatred, but only from a distance. Now she'd had a taste of it firsthand. She remembered Brandon's touch. Shame rose in her throat. She was nothing to him! He had never loved her. He'd only wanted to use her.

Their footsteps came closer, closer. Indigo increased her speed, leaping over bushes, running against low-hanging limbs, her lungs whining for breath. Their legs were longer than hers. Her hair fell across her eyes, a blinding veil of brown and gold. Her foot caught on something, and she hurtled to the ground, the impact stunning her. Gasping, clawing her way to her feet, she searched wildly for her knife.

The crashing of their footsteps burst through the trees behind her. Abandoning her search for the weapon, she plunged ahead through the brush, panic making her forget everything her father had taught her. The thrumming of their footsteps came closer and closer, so close she could hear them breathing.

Amy went over the addition on Swift's paper, acutely aware of his shoulder brushing her bodice as she leaned over him to see. Thus far she had managed to keep his mind on academics, but she sensed he had other pursuits planned for when they completed today's lesson. The thought made her nervous, and she found it difficult to concentrate. When he looked at her, she felt shy and awkward. She guessed that he was recalling last night, her nakedness and the shameless way she had responded to him. The lambent gleam in his eyes made her pulse skitter. He wanted her that way again, and he wasn't making any secret of it.

A hot flush crept up her neck. Last night it had taken all her courage to initiate their lovemaking. Now that the worst of her fears had been faced, Swift was playing by an entirely new set of rules. She no longer knew what to expect of him. He clearly didn't feel it was necessary now to restrain himself. And he seemed to find her discomfiture amusing.

It wasn't amusing to Amy. If they were

going to make love later, she didn't want to think about it until it happened. Swift's little hints and knowing grins completely unraveled her.

As if he read her mind, he tipped his dark head back so it rested against her bosom. "I'm tired of adding," he said huskily.

A quivery sensation attacked her belly. She avoided his heated gaze. "We haven't much more to do."

He turned his face toward her, grazing his teeth over the peak of one breast, setting her senses afire even through the layers of cloth. "I want you."

Her legs went weak. He lifted a hand to the buttons of her dress. "Either go into the bedroom with me or find yourself being undressed out here." A button flicked from its hole. "I've waited as long as I'm going to wait." Another button came undone beneath his expert fingers. "I'll make love to you on the table. I swear I will."

"Swift . . . it's broad daylight! The table?" She braced a palm on the surface in question. "That's — you can't be —" Her breath caught. "After supper, maybe we can —"

"After supper, hell. Now, and then again after supper." The teasing tone in his voice was underscored with determination. He straightened so he could run his lips along her exposed collarbone. "God, you're so delicious, I can't get enough of you. Maybe I should make love to you in here." His tongue dipped lower as another button came free. "Taste every sweet inch of you. Have seconds, and then thirds." He slipped an arm around her hips and pulled her toward him, his mouth finding its way to the low neckline of her chemise. "Did you bolt the door?" he asked, his warm breath misting her skin.

Amy couldn't remember if she had bolted the door. With his mouth nibbling her flesh, she couldn't remember much of anything. She ran her hands into his hair, horrified at the image of herself stretched out naked across the table. She wasn't ready for such blatancy. "Swift, I — Please. It's afternoon. Let's wait."

"What difference does the time of day make?"

"I — it's daylight."

"I've waited all my life for you. I'm done with waiting, Amy. We're married, remember. We can make love whenever we like. And right now, I'd like . . ."

"But I — it's — I'm not . . ." His mouth was doing crazy things to her thought processes. She groped for what it was she had meant to say. "I'm not in the mood."

"You let me worry about that," he murmured, still nibbling, still bombarding her with sensations that took her breath away.

He clearly didn't plan to take no for an answer. Amy struggled to speak. "Then let's at least go to the bedroom."

He loosened his hold on her and pushed to his feet. "Lead the way." He caught her wrists. "Don't button the damned dress. It's coming off anyway."

Cheeks flaming, she turned away from him. As she crossed the kitchen, she heard something and hesitated. The sound repeated itself, so faint she almost missed it, a voice that she immediately recognized. "It's Indigo."

He groaned and caught her around the waist to haul her back against him. "She has miserable timing."

With her heart skittering as it was, Amy welcomed the reprieve. "Swift, I have to go see what she wants."

Heaving a sigh, he released her and followed her to the sitting room window. Quickly buttoning her dress, Amy drew the curtains back to peer out. For a moment she couldn't see Indigo. Then she caught a flash of movement at the edge of the woods. Focusing, she saw Brandon Marshall grab Indigo's arm and drag her toward the brush.

The girl knifed upward with her knee, catching him in the groin. Two other youths emerged from the trees. Between the three of them, they overpowered the girl and made fast work of dragging her out of sight.

"Oh, my God!"

Swift tensed beside her. The next instant he swore and ran for the door, Amy following closely on his heels. They burst from the house, then ran down the porch steps and across the yard. Indigo's cries drifted to them from the woods, spurring them forward. Amy's heart began to pound. She lifted her skirts to keep up with Swift as he leveled out into a full run.

When Swift reached the woods, he paused a moment to home in on Indigo's screams, affording Amy a chance to catch up with him. Together they zigzagged between the trees and burst into a small clearing. The sight that greeted them made Amy's legs turn to water. Indigo had been thrown to the ground, and four young men were holding her spread-eagled. Brandon Marshall knelt between her legs and he was wasting no time in jerking up her skirt.

Swift roared with anger and dived into the fray. Taken by surprise, the boys released Indigo and scattered. Swift hit the one closest to him. The next instant the other four converged on him.

Her first thought to get Indigo to safety, Amy darted into the swarm, grabbed the girl's arm, and dragged her away from the men. After helping Indigo to her feet, Amy hurried her to the edge of the clearing. The horrible sound of fists hitting flesh resounded. She whirled, looking for a weapon of some kind so she could go to Swift's aid. She needn't have. Swift had the advantage of surprise, and though the youths were full-grown, they lacked his ruthless precision and deadly speed.

Amy stood frozen. Never had she seen a man fight as Swift did. He tied into the five like a wild man, incapacitating Brandon with a vicious blow to his throat, knocking another down with a well-placed boot directly above his knee and taking out another with his fists. The remaining two fled into the trees.

Still running on rage, Swift collared Brandon Marshall and dragged him across the clearing to Indigo, forcing the younger man to his knees. Amy grabbed a tree limb and brandished it, silent warning to the two young men lying on the ground that she would brain them if they moved.

"Are you all right, Indigo?" Swift asked with deadly calm.

Sobbing and trembling, Indigo nodded, hugging herself as if against the cold.

Swift grabbed a handful of Brandon's hair and jerked his head back. "Beg her forgiveness, you worthless bastard!"

"I won't," Brandon croaked, holding his bruised throat.

Swift cuffed his bloody ear. "Do it, or so help me God, I'll kill you!" There was no mistaking the murderous gleam in Swift's eyes. "I mean it, boy. Don't think I don't."

Swallowing convulsively, Brandon struggled to get the words out. "I'm sorry! I'm sorry. . . ."

"That's not good enough." Swift gave the youth's hair another jerk. "Beg her forgiveness!"

"I beg your forgiveness," Brandon cried. "I beg your forgiveness, Indigo!"

Swift glanced up. "It's up to you, Indigo. Shall I spare his life?"

Indigo's pale countenance tightened. She drew the moment out, studying Brandon's bleeding face as if she had never seen him before.

"For God's sake, you can't let him kill me!" Brandon sobbed. "Indigo, please. . . ."

The girl's mouth twisted with disgust. "Spare him, Uncle Swift. He isn't worth killing."

With that, Indigo spun and left the clearing. Because Amy feared the two boys in the woods might reappear to press a second attack, she was reluctant to follow her niece and leave Swift alone.

He tossed Brandon into the dirt. "Don't ever come to Wolf's Landing again, not if you value your life."

As he turned to leave, Swift's gaze fell to the tree limb Amy held. His dark eyes warmed, and his mouth slanted into a grim smile. Pulling the weapon from her grasp, he took her arm and led her away. When they neared the edge of the clearing, Brandon staggered to his feet. His friends gathered around him.

"They haven't heard the last of this," Brandon cried. "No one humiliates a Marshall and gets away with it! He'd better start wearing his guns if he knows what's good for him."

Swift stiffened but kept walking. Indigo awaited them at the edge of the woods. She flew into Amy's arms.

"It's over, love," Amy whispered, smoothing the girl's tangled hair. "It's over."

"Oh, Aunt Amy! Why did they try to do that to me? Why?"

Amy hugged the girl closer. She had no answers. Indigo was trembling so badly that

Amy feared she might collapse. She glanced at Swift. As if he understood the unspoken message, he scooped Indigo into his arms to carry her home.

"Oh, Uncle Swift!" She wrapped her arms around his neck. "I'm so glad you came! So glad. I dropped my knife. And I couldn't find it. Then they caught up with me."

"You're sure you're all right?" he asked.

"Yes. They didn't — you came before they —" Indigo burst into hysterical tears. "Ma and Aunt Amy tried to tell me, and I wouldn't listen."

Swift struck off at a brisk pace. "Let's get you home to your mother, hm?"

An hour later Indigo was safely tucked into bed in her loft bedroom, sound asleep, her scrapes and bruises tended. Loretta came downstairs to join Hunter, Swift, and Amy before the fire. Amy poured her cousin a mug of hot cocoa. As she handed it to Loretta, she placed a comforting hand on her shoulder.

"Is she okay?"

Pale and shaky, Loretta gave a vague nod, her eyes unfocused. "As okay as a girl can be after something like this." She glanced up and met Amy's gaze. "I guess no one understands better than you how she must be feeling."

Amy's stomach knotted. Memories assailed her. Stepping into that clearing and seeing Indigo being attacked had brought back the past to her. As if Swift sensed how shaken she was, he stepped close and looped an arm around her shoulders. Drawing her to him, he brushed silken lips across her temple.

Grateful for the support, Amy leaned against him, needing the reassurance of his touch. "Oh, Swift, I'm so glad you were at the house. I don't know what I would've done."

His voice taut, he replied, "You looked pretty capable with that tree limb." His eyes twinkled down at her. "I haven't seen you with that look in your eye for years. You'd have done just fine without me."

Amy shivered. "I'm not too sure of that. What if —"

"Let's not think about what ifs. I was there, it's over, and Indigo's all right."

Setting aside her mug, Loretta passed a hand over her eyes. "Physically, anyway. I'm afraid she may never forget. Damn that Brandon Marshall! I'd like to hang him by his toenails and beat him within an inch of his life. I knew this would happen. I just knew it! Why didn't I do something more to stop it?"

Hunter stood in stony silence, gazing down at his wife. After a long while, he hunkered down and drew her into his arms. "Indigo is strong, little one. Her memories of Brandon Marshall will become dust in the wind. You can't spare her everything. And you can't choose her friends. She must learn to judge a man's character herself."

Loretta clung to him. "Oh, Hunter, why did he do such a thing? She's such a sweet girl. A little undisciplined, yes, but she did nothing to deserve this. What's the matter with that young man?"

Hunter closed his eyes. "Here in this town we've built, we forget the rest of the world and all the hatred. Indigo carries my blood. In the eyes of some, that makes her less than human."

Loretta sobbed. "That's so wrong of them, though! I thought by coming here we had escaped the prejudice."

"Here, in this place, we have," he whispered. "It is the world outside Wolf's Landing —" He broke off and ran a hand up her slender back. "Don't cry. Indigo will heal. And she will be more wise now, yes? All will be well. The words of the prophecy promise us that."

Amy recalled a few words of the prophecy

and prayed Hunter was right. A new tomorrow and a new nation where the Comanche and *tosi tivo* will live as one forever. Was such an existence possible? Wolf's Landing was steadily growing, as was Jacksonville. More strangers moved into the area every year, bringing with them their narrow-mindedness and irrational prejudices, not just against Indians, but against every other minority. A person could read one issue of the *Democratic Times* and figure that out. If the poor Chinese dared to so much as get the wrong expression on their faces, they found themselves arrested and heavily fined. Sometimes Amy wondered if Jacksonville's citizens hadn't passed a silent vote to use the Chinese people as a source of city revenue. Could Hunter and his offspring truly live here among the whites in peace? Brandon Marshall wouldn't be the last man to lust after Indigo and consider her fair game because of her Indian blood.

Swift cleared his throat. "I hate to say this, but I'm afraid Brandon may be back looking for trouble. He's a little too arrogant for his own good. I sure wish Marshal Hilton wasn't over in Jacksonville, just in case."

Swift's words intensified Amy's foreboding. She slipped an arm around his waist, no longer frightened just for the Wolfs, but for Swift and for herself. Her premonition of last night, that reality might come between them, came back to haunt her. If Brandon Marshall carried through on his threats, Swift might be forced to strap on his guns. If he did that, the nightmare he had fled in Texas would start all over again here.

She lifted her face to his. "If he challenges you, what will you do?" she asked shakily.

His dark gaze met hers. "I won't pick up my guns again, Amy. You have my word on that. He'll have to shoot an unarmed man. Not even Brandon would be that stupid."

"But —"

"No buts," he said softly. "I came here for a fresh start. I won't let a hothead like Marshall push me around."

The promise in no way lessened Amy's apprehension.

Hunter glanced up. "Indigo is my daughter. If he comes back, he's my problem."

Swift's mouth quirked. "He may not see it that way. I'm the one who made him get on his knees. Let's just hope we've seen the last of him."

Loretta interrupted with a stern, "You're both forgetting Marshal Hilton. He's the law here. I'm sure Brandon won't return before tomorrow when Hilton gets back.

He'll handle any problems, no doubt."

A sound on the loft stairs caught everyone's attention. Amy turned to see Indigo on the bottom step, her face streaked from crying, her arms filled with a bundle of white woman's clothing. Clearly the girl hadn't been sleeping as soundly as they had surmised. She raised her chin and squared her shoulders.

"I've caused no end of trouble, haven't I?" Before anyone could respond, she added, "Well, I won't again. I promise you that." She inclined her head at the bundle in her arms. "I'm burning them. Every last stitch. Don't try to stop me."

Amy's gaze fell to the clothing, dresses, undergarments, and footwear. A swath of delicate pink trailed over Indigo's wrist. Amy recognized the pink gown the girl had worn the night of the social.

Indigo marched across the room toward the back door. As she grabbed the handle, she glanced over her shoulder, her blue eyes swimming with tears. "From this moment on, I am Comanche. I'll never again wear a *tosi* woman's garments. Never!"

Hunter placed a hand on Loretta's shoulder so she couldn't rise from the rocker. Fastening his luminous gaze on his daughter, he said, "A Comanche makes no promises in anger, Indigo, and never is a long time. You cannot deny your mother's blood within you. She is part of your heart."

Tears trailed down Indigo's cheeks, and her mouth began to tremble. Her injured gaze slid to Loretta.

In the same soft voice, Hunter added, "Go do what you must. When you have washed away your anger, we will be here waiting for you with much love in our hearts."

The girl opened the door and slipped out into the dusky twilight. A few minutes later the rosy glow of a bonfire bathed the rear windows of the house. Amy looked out and saw Indigo, back rigid, head held high, tossing one garment after another onto the flames. Dressed in Comanche leathers and knee-high moccasins, with her tawny mane of hair gleaming in the firelight, she looked like a white girl dressed up like an Indian. Amy's heart broke for her. The path Indigo wanted to walk was an impossible one. Any who looked upon her would know she was more white than Comanche.

Amy slipped quietly from the house. As she descended the porch steps and crossed the yard, Indigo turned to regard her. Amy shivered against the cold and held out her hands to the flames, saying nothing. The wind whispered in the naked tree limbs above them, a stark and lonely sound. The smell of winter touched the air, frigid and pure, calling to mind snow-capped peaks in the distance and icicles on the eaves.

"He tried to rape me," Indigo whispered as if she still couldn't quite grasp it. "Him and all his friends. Just because my father is half Comanche."

Amy bit the inside of her cheek, wishing, praying, for the right words to come to her. A string of pitch dripped off a chunk of wood and ignited, snapping and hissing in the flames. Indigo threw the last of her white clothing onto the fire.

She slid a troubled gaze to Amy. "Last summer when Ma and I went to Jacksonville shopping without my father and Chase, we saw a Rogue squaw sitting outside the saloon on the boardwalk. She sat there all afternoon in the hot sun, with nothing to drink and nothing to eat, while her trapper husband drank away his money inside. Ma felt sorry for her and bought her a soda, but she was afraid to accept it."

Amy guessed where Indigo was heading with this and took a deep breath. "Sad things happen, Indigo. This old world of ours can be mighty harsh sometimes."

Indigo shifted her weight, her expression agonized. With the toe of her moccasin, she nudged a half-charred log back onto the fire. "When the squaw's husband came out of the saloon, he was mean drunk. He started hitting her, and everyone on the street just stood there and watched. If she had been a white woman, one of the men would have stopped it, but because she was Rogue, they just —"

Her voice broke, and she swallowed. "I could wind up like that woman, Aunt Amy — if I married a white man. He'd never figure I was as good as him, and he might treat me bad, just like that trapper did his squaw. And white folks wouldn't care. They'd just turn their heads — because I'm a squaw, too."

Amy reached out and clasped one of Indigo's hands. "Not all whites are like Brandon and his friends. Those men in Jacksonville who stood by and watched probably wanted to do something and couldn't find the courage."

Indigo's fingers vised so tightly that Amy's knuckles hurt. "I'm afraid, Aunt Amy."

Amy realized then that Indigo had seen an ugliness today that she hadn't realized existed. "We're all afraid of something, honey. But you can't let fear rule your life." As she spoke, the words rang in her mind, as applicable to her own situation as to the girl's. "When the right man comes along, you'll know, and it won't matter what color skin he has." Or what kind of past.

"Yes! Yes, it will! I'm part Indian. There's no changing that. I'll never trust another white man, *never.* Those five today taught me a lesson I'll never forget. The Indian blood in me makes me next to nothing to them." A tear rolled down her cheek. "The way they think, squaws are only good for one thing."

Amy gathered Indigo into her arms, wishing she could undo what Brandon Marshall had done, knowing she couldn't. Indigo wept against her shoulder, her sobs deep and tearing, her body atremble.

"I loved him," she cried. "I loved him with all my heart. But it wasn't love at all, was it? I just thought it was. He was playing me along the whole time. Lying to me. Pretending he cared. He didn't, not at all. The whole time, he hated me, and I never guessed. Oh, Aunt Amy, I feel so stupid. And so ashamed I want to die."

Amy swayed with her, smoothing her hair, comforting her the only way she knew. She could almost taste the girl's pain. When Indigo quieted at last, Amy sighed and said, "Don't feel ashamed, darling. There are cruel people in this world, and they go through life looking for victims. Pretty, innocent young girls like you make easy targets. Those five young men today — they're the kind you'll see kicking dogs and tormenting children. Your Indian blood was just an excuse they used to vent their meanness."

Indigo stirred and murmured something.

"Just hush, love, and listen to me. You mustn't begin judging all men by the color of their skin." Just as she never should have judged Swift by his comanchero clothing. "If you do, then Brandon has won, don't you see? You'll become as twisted as he is. Be proud of your blood, both the white and the Comanche. If you aren't, then everything your father and mother have stood for, all they've taught you, has gone for naught."

Indigo drew away. Swiping at her cheeks, she gazed thoughtfully into the fire. After a long while she whispered, "I'll try, Aunt Amy."

"That's all anyone can ask of you." Touching a hand to Indigo's hair, Amy managed a smile. "I know you came out here to be alone, so I'm going to go back inside now and leave you to your thoughts. Sometimes we have to work our way through things by ourselves. But while you're doing that, don't forget how much we all love you."

Indigo took a shaky breath. "I'll never forget today, either. It sounds easy, putting it behind me and not letting it change me, but it isn't."

Amy smiled. "Your father says you have eyes that see into tomorrow. It may take time, but you'll recover from this. And you'll be a better person because of it."

Indigo's mouth tightened. "If I have eyes that see into tomorrow, then why was I so blind with Brandon?"

Amy gave her shoulder a pat. "You forgot the most important lesson your parents taught you, that fancy clothes and manners don't make the man. You'll never be fooled by his kind again."

With that, Amy returned to the house, praying with every step that she was right.

CHAPTER 22

En route to the house, it hit Amy with sudden clarity just how close Indigo had come to being raped. Heedful of Swift's warning, she hadn't been allowing herself to think about the what ifs. But now thoughts of what had nearly happened came rushing at her.

Before reaching the porch, Amy began to shake. Insidious at first, the quivering began in her eyelids as she climbed the back steps, then spread downward as she let herself in the kitchen door, quaking along her arms, attacking her hands, then her legs. She had a strange, detached feeling, her thoughts disjointed. She knotted her hands in her skirts to stop their trembling, but the affliction, when conquered there, instantly transmitted itself to her jaws. Her teeth began to chatter.

Amy couldn't imagine what was wrong with her. Everything seemed blurred. As if in a dream, she felt herself moving across the room. She heard Swift's voice, heard herself make some sort of reply. Then, as if awakening from a bout of sleepwalking, she found herself standing over the washbasin on Loretta's dish board, furiously scrubbing her hands with Hunter's knuckle brush. When she realized what she was doing, she couldn't recall how she had gotten to the counter, didn't remember filling the basin. She only knew she had a compulsion to scour herself clean.

The knuckle brush slipped from her frozen fingers and plopped in the sudsy water. Amy stared down at the murky little waves as they rushed outward to the edge of the bowl and slopped over its edge.

She gripped the counter and blinked. Images, painted in blinding color, darted at her from the blackness of her subconscious. Not images of Indigo being attacked, but of herself. For fifteen years she had kept those images at bay, never allowing herself to remember, except in nightmares.

The comancheros had held her captive for nearly two weeks. The memories had lurked inside her head ever since, like a disease. Between sanity and madness, there existed a fragile line. To survive, she had kept her past sequestered in her mind by a thick black curtain. Now the thick black folds were parting, and the pictures were slipping out.

Amy couldn't breathe. She leaned slightly forward, her lungs on fire, belly heaving, her temples throbbing.

"Amy?"

Swift's voice bounced inside her head. Amy-Amy-Amy. She couldn't see him, couldn't see anything except — No! Going rigid, Amy concentrated, driving back the memories. What had happened to Indigo today had nothing to do with her, nothing.

"Amy, are you all right?"

Amy, are you all right-all right-all right-all right? She blinked again. Her lungs rasped and then expanded. Still clutching the dish board, she pried her head around. "Yes, I'm fine."

I'm fine-I'm fine-I'm fine. A hysterical urge to laugh hit her. She gulped it back. Of course she wasn't fine. How could she be fine? She felt water trickling along her arm under her sleeve. Water she didn't remember pouring. She tried to concentrate on the coldness, on the reality of it.

"I thought maybe we'd go to your place for a while," Swift said. "I think Hunter and Loretta could use some time alone."

Alone. Oh, yes, she wanted to be alone.

Just for a few minutes. The memories were gushing out. Like spiders. Crawling all over her. She was going to vomit.

"Honey, are you sure you're all right?"

She brushed at her sleeve. Memories, crawling like spiders. Bile rose up her throat. She rubbed harder. She had to stop. Only a crazy person scrubbed at something that wasn't there.

"I'm fine. Yes, let's go. They need time alone."

Was that her voice? Shaky and high-pitched. Floating, unable to feel her feet, she crossed the room. Fresh air. Breathing . . . that was reality.

On the way out the door, Swift called to Hunter and Loretta. "I'll be coming in late, so don't wait up."

The door thudded closed. Amy hugged her waist and gulped the night air. Swift's announcement that he'd be late made it apparent where he'd be and what he thought he'd be doing. Her belly clenched. She couldn't handle that. Not right now.

She had an urge to flee into the darkness. He took her arm as they descended the steps, the firm grip of his fingers vetoing that idea. She gulped again. The world tipped, a dizzying swirl of moonlight and blackness.

He steered her onto the boardwalk. "Amy, something's bothering you. Can you talk about it?"

Could she talk about it? No. She mustn't even think about it. "It's — h-hard to believe it's already November."

"I take it you don't want to discuss it?"

Discuss it? There weren't words. How could she explain? A black curtain in her mind? He'd think her insane. And she might very well go insane if she didn't regain control. "It's so chilly. Soon it'll be time for Thanksgiving."

He glanced over at her. "There's a full moon. Have you noticed?"

Relieved that he had become sidetracked, Amy glanced up. The moon rested low in the sky, full and milky white, the gnarled limbs of a leafless oak silhouetted against it. She could remember staring up at the moon fifteen years ago, her wrists afire from struggling against the rawhide that bound her to the wagon wheel, her mind filled with dread because morning would eventually come, and with it the men — one after another in an endless visitation.

"Did you know there are three hundred and forty-two slats in this boardwalk?"

She jerked and looked over at him. The boardwalk? Slats? She heard her shoes echoing on the wood and homed in on the sound. "You — you've learned to count that high?"

"Hell, no. Small talk, right? I thought I'd help you out." He tipped his head, regarding her with a slight smile. "Suppose it'll rain tomorrow?"

"There's not a cloud in sight tonight." Amy dropped her chin to stare at her feet. "I — I'm sorry, Swift."

"Never be sorry, Amy. I didn't come into this hoping to change you." His voice grew husky. "Just to love you."

"Some things aren't easy to talk about."

He released her elbow and shoved his hands in his pockets. "I was afraid seeing that today would upset you." Tension threaded his voice. "Just don't shut me out. Or hold me to blame. I can't control what Brandon does."

"It isn't that."

"Isn't it?"

Was that a note of anger she detected? Amy bit her lip. He deserved an explanation. "Seeing that — it brought it all back — the comancheros, the two weeks with them." She doubted Swift had ever run from anything. He would face the memories head-on, then relegate them to yesterday and never again look back. "Indigo came so close. It occurred to me suddenly — how close she had come — and I started remembering."

He kept his hands in his pockets. The breeze picked up, flattening his shirt against his back. He hunched his shoulders. "Can you do your remembering out loud?"

"No."

"You know, Amy, sometimes talking about something helps get it out of your head." She sensed a hesitancy in him before he continued. "There's nothing you need to hide from me. Nothing they did to you could be so bad, nothing you did or felt could be so bad, that I'd ever stop loving you."

"I — I don't want to think about it. I can't."

She expected him to press her. Instead he sighed and said, "Then don't. When the time's right, maybe you'll be able to, hm?"

He drew his hand from his pocket and intertwined his fingers with hers. Before Amy realized what he was about, he had tugged her forward and increased their pace. There was no mistaking what his hurry was or what he had in mind.

Their feet tapped a rhythmic tattoo on the frozen ground. The wind funneled between the store buildings, lifting her skirts, then backlashing to whip them around her legs. She shivered and peered ahead of them into the shadows. What if Brandon Marshall and his friends lurked in the darkness? What if — She cut the thought short. She had to stop thinking negatively.

Swift glanced down at her. "Cold?"

"A little."

"Here in a few minutes, I'll warm you up, Mrs. Lopez."

Even in the moonlight, she could see the twinkle of devilment in his eyes. She glanced away. Could she make love with him tonight, so close on the heels of what had happened to Indigo? And if she couldn't, what then? Would he grow angry? Would he believe she was holding him responsible in some way? It wasn't at all like that, but how could she make him understand?

As they drew near her house, her already accelerated pulse beat became a pounding in her temples. As she walked up the steps and opened the door, what little composure she had left disintegrated. Should she do the ordinary things, light the lamp, lay the fire, dress for bed? What if the memories surrounded her again when he touched her?

When they entered the dark sitting room, he answered one question by tending the lamp himself. Light flared in the globe.

While he adjusted the wick, she stood waiting, mind racing. He straightened and turned toward her, tall and dark, his broad shoulders blocking the lantern's glow. She couldn't read his expression.

"I, um, would you like a cup of coffee?"

"No, thanks."

Though she couldn't see his mouth, she could tell by his voice that he was smiling. He leaned a hip against the table and folded his arms, his body relaxed. She fastened her gaze on his boots. "Shall I lay a fire?"

With a breath of laughter, he said, "We won't need one."

Her throat felt as if it were being squeezed by hard fingers. "I've got leftovers from last night. You didn't eat dinner. Is there anything you'd like?"

"Yes, as a matter of fact, there is something I'd like."

"Some chicken? I have cornbread left over. Mashed potatoes and gravy. It won't take long to heat up."

"No, thanks."

She forced her gaze upward from his boots to the vicinity of his knees. "What would you like, then?"

"You."

The single word hung between them, making her wish she hadn't asked. She licked her lips, then dragged her gaze to his shadowed face. "Well, I guess I'll, um . . ." The words trailed off, the thought lost to her. Pictures of last night flitted through her mind. A shivery sensation pooled at the base of her spine and worked slowly upward, raising goose bumps across her shoulder blades. "Why are you staring at me?"

"I like looking at you. Now it's my turn for a question. Why are you so nervous?"

He shifted and braced his hands on either side of him to push away from the table and pick up the lamp. Holding it high, he ambled toward her, the light playing upon his face as he moved, bathing his features in amber, then shadow. She recalled thinking once that he looked exactly as she imagined the devil, so tall and ebony dark, cloaked all in black. There was something not quite civilized about him, she decided, especially when his eyes got that gleam in them.

"Do you want to go to the bedroom?" he asked.

Amy nodded, hardly able to believe he could be so insensitive. He had to know how unbalanced she felt right now, how fresh everything was in her mind. It wasn't like Swift to disregard her feelings. Her mouth had gone so dry that her tongue cleaved to her teeth. He pressed a large hand to her back and turned her toward the hallway. She moved ahead of him, watching their shadows dance larger than life over the walls. The bedroom doorway yawned like a cavern waiting to swallow her. She stepped into the blackness. He came in behind her, bathing the room with light.

Nothing seemed the same with him there. The space seemed narrower, for one thing. The lace curtains looked too frilly, the bureau cluttered. He made room on the nightstand for the lamp, then sat down on her bed and began unfastening his shirt, his gaze on hers, his mouth tipped in a half smile. He looked out of place sitting there, too dark and rugged to be framed by a backdrop of lace.

She tried to moisten her lips, but her tongue was still parchment dry. His shirt fell open to the waist, revealing a swath of muscled chest and flat belly that gleamed like polished oak in the lamplight. He bent one knee and seized hold of his boot, his gaze still leveled on hers.

"Amy?"

The word was laced with question, and demand. She forced her hands to the collar of her dress and fumbled at the tiny button there. When at last it slipped free, she proceeded to the next, and then the next.

He dropped one boot to the floor, then removed the other one, his attention still riveted on her. Amy wished with all her heart that the lantern would run out of fuel or that he would look away. Neither happened.

"Could you douse the light, please?"

"If I did that, I couldn't see you as well."

That was the general idea. Amy's hands stilled. "I'm not quite ready to undress with the light burning."

He jerked one side of his shirt loose from his belt and ran a hand over his ribs. "You'll never feel ready if you always hide in shadows. I want to see you when I make love to you, Amy. And I want you to see me."

"But —" The word, cut short because she had no idea what she meant to follow it up with, rang in the silence.

"But what?" He jerked the other side of his shirt loose and stood up. "This isn't just shyness, is it?" He moved toward her. "Are you still upset about what happened to Indigo?"

Maybe he would understand, after all. "Yes."

"That's natural." He brushed her hands aside and began unfastening her buttons. "Perfectly natural and understandable."

"It is? Then why can't we —" She clutched

his hands to stop their speedy descent. "By tomorrow night, maybe I'll be feeling better. For tonight, couldn't we —"

"You're going to be feeling better in about two minutes." His fingers evaded hers and continued their downward course until the last button slipped free. He slid back the front plackets of her dress, his warm palms skimming down her arms as he peeled the sleeves toward her wrists. "Trust me, Amy."

A frantic feeling welled within her. "I don't feel comfortable with the light burning."

"You're not supposed to feel comfortable." He dipped his head and feathered a hot kiss across her temple. "You're supposed to feel quivery and weak and breathless."

She felt all those things, and worse. She also felt betrayed because he didn't understand that. Never before had Swift failed to sense what she couldn't put into words.

He tugged on the ribbon that held up her petticoat, then pulled both her dress and the undergarment over her hips, letting them slip to the floor. Next, he advanced on the sash of her pantalets. Amy got the distinct impression that he didn't intend to stop, no matter what she said.

"Swift?"

The pantalets dropped. Her belly knotted and twisted.

"Swift, I —"

He hunkered before her and grasped one of her ankles. After unbuttoning her shoe, he dragged it off, then drew her foot from the leg of her pantalets. She stared down at the back of his dark head while he switched his attention to her other shoe. Within seconds he divested her of the pantalets. Then he slowly lifted his gaze the length of her legs to the black tops of her ribbed hose. Drawing close, he kissed her above the band of cotton on her bare thigh, his lips warm and velvety, his breath moist on her skin. Amy's lungs quit working.

"Swift?" she squeaked. "Please turn out the light."

He rolled one stocking, garter and all, down her thigh, his lips following its descent. "Give me five minutes, Amy, love. If you still feel so tense, I'll turn it out. But first let's try it my way."

He ran a hand behind her leg and bent her knee, tugging the garter and stocking off. She gasped when he nibbled her instep and then her toes. He peeled off the other stocking, then tipped back his head, his hands clasping her thighs, his fingers warm and gentle, yet relentless. His dark eyes met hers, lambent and determined.

"You're not frightened, are you?"

"No, but I —"

"No buts. If you're afraid, just say so." His mouth twisted in a knowing smile. "Shyness doesn't count. Are you frightened?"

"It's just that, after what happened, I don't want to make love. Just thinking about it makes me feel" — she searched for a way to describe it — "shriveled up inside."

He rose and reached for the ribbons of her chemise. "Give me a little more than two minutes on that. Five, maybe? I think I know just the cure. Relax and leave it to me."

"I can't. It's bright as day in here!"

"Close your eyes and you won't notice." The chemise fell open. "Then we'll both be happy."

He bent his head to kiss her bare shoulder as he slipped the chemise down her arms, "Such a beautiful woman and you think I shouldn't look at you?" He ran his lips to her throat, nudging her head back with his jaw. The kisses set her skin afire. "God, Amy, I love you."

"It's freezing in here. I'll take sick."

He chuckled and nipped her below the ear. "You won't either."

"I've got goose bumps. I'll die of croup before the winter's out."

"You won't be cold for long," he promised, and promptly swept her into his arms to carry her to the bed. With a speed that made her dizzy, he dumped her onto the coverlet and straightened to strip off his shirt.

Amy grasped the coverlet to pull it across herself. He clamped a hand over her wrist. "Don't, please."

She abandoned the coverlet and hugged herself instead. By rolling onto her side and drawing up her knees, she managed to hide herself. His eyes warmed on hers. With a flick of his wrist, he unfastened his belt buckle. When he started to peel off his pants, she followed his advice and squeezed her eyes closed. Denim rustled.

"Amy, you saw me last night."

The mattress sank under his weight. His warm hand settled on her hip. The other clasped her knees. He forced her legs to straighten so he could press close to her. The heat of his chest brushed against her arms. His lips grazed her jaw.

"I love you," he whispered. "God, how I love you."

With gentle strength, he forced her arms to her sides and rolled her to her back, pinning her there with his chest. The shock of his hot skin against her breasts made her breath catch. She opened her eyes to find his dark face hovering inches above hers, his brown eyes filled with tenderness.

"Look at me, Amy, love, and say my name," he whispered.

She swallowed. "Swift."

He ran a palm over her waist, up her side, his fingertips grazing the underside of her breast. "Again, Amy, love. No, don't close your eyes. Look at me and say my name."

His hand, warm and sandpapery, closed over her softness. His face drew closer, his eyes still holding hers.

"Swift," she whispered.

He feathered a thumb across the peak of her nipple. She gasped at the electrical sensation that shot through her.

"Again," he commanded.

"S-Swift."

"Swift Lopez." He trailed his lips down her throat. "Say it. And don't ever forget it. Yesterday is over. It's *my* hand on you now."

Tears filled Amy's eyes. She hadn't believed he understood. Now she realized that perhaps he understood too well. Swift Lopez. He touched her with a branding heat, his hands cleansing her in a way that soap and water could never have done.

"They can't hurt you anymore," he whispered raggedly. "Never again. You're mine. Do you understand?"

Amy ran her arms around his neck and clung to him. "Oh, Swift . . . it does hurt. The remembering hurts."

"Tell me." He pressed his lips to her throat.

She began to shake. She clung to him more desperately. "I can't. I'm afraid. I don't let myself remember. Never. Don't you see? I can't. If I do, I'll go mad."

He tightened his arms around her, splaying one hand across her back. Amy felt surrounded by him, by his heat and strength. "Not even when I'm here with you? We'll go mad together. Just one memory, Amy, love. Can't you face just one while I'm holding you? Start at the very beginning. What were you doing when the comancheros came?"

With a choked sob she whispered, "Laundry, Loretta and I were doing laundry. I was stirring the soaked clothes with a paddle, and we didn't hear them coming until it was too late."

The memories hurtled at her. Swift's hand kneaded her back. His arms hardened around her. "It's all right. It's just words, Amy. You can stop whenever you want. Tell me."

"I — I wouldn't go inside when Loretta told me to. Maybe if I had, they wouldn't have taken me. But I —" A shudder shook her. "It was my fault. I didn't mind what she said, and they took me."

"No. That's crazy, Amy. What kind of person would have left Loretta out there all alone?"

"I never minded what anyone said. That time, I paid for it."

"You were too brave for your own good," he amended. "Even if you had gone inside the house, Santos would've gone in after you. What happened next?"

"M-Ma came out with a gun. One of the — comancheros put a knife to my throat. He said he'd kill me if she didn't drop it."

"And so she did?"

"Yes."

"And they took you with them?"

"Y-yes." Amy buried her face against his shoulder.

"And you wished she'd let the man kill you. . . ."

"Why didn't she? It would've been kinder. Oh, God, why didn't she let him kill me!"

He made a fist in her hair. "Because you were meant to be here with me tonight. Because I wouldn't have anyone to love if you had died. No one to love me. Everything has a reason, Amy. All of us have a purpose. Tell me. . . ."

Amy wasn't sure where the words came from. They fell on her ears, shrill and ugly and raw, spewing from her like poison. Once she began talking, she couldn't seem to stop. Swift said nothing. He just held her and stroked her and listened.

Amy knew she was babbling. She talked and talked . . . until she began to feel exhausted, until her body felt leaden and her speech began to slur. Her trembling finally ceased. And then the impossible happened. She ran out of things to say.

Her throat afire from sobbing, she lay quietly beneath him and opened her eyes, incredulous. For fifteen endless years, the black ugliness inside her had seemed bottomless. Now she had poured it all out. All of it, absolutely everything. She felt strangely empty . . . and peaceful.

Swift stirred and pushed up slightly. Combing his fingers through her hair, he trailed whisper-soft kisses across her forehead, then kissed her eyes closed. "Are you all right?" he asked huskily.

"Yes," she whispered, scarcely able to believe it.

"Thank you, Amy, love."

"For what?"

"For trusting me."

She opened her eyes to find that he was smiling.

"I think I know just what to do with those ugly memories of yours," he told her, bending his head to nibble seductively at her shoulder.

"What's that?"

"How about making all new ones?" He trailed his lips to her breast and circled deliciously with his tongue. "Beautiful ones, Amy."

Tears filled her eyes. "I love you, Swift."

He ran his hands over her with a branding heat.

"And I love you. I won't share you with ghosts. I think it's time we bury them, don't you?"

His hands had already begun to work their magic. Amy parted her lips on a sigh. A brilliant kaleidoscope of light swirled inside her head. His fingertips feathered over her like gossamer, making her skin tingle. The lights deepened in hue and spectrum, until she felt as if she were floating within a rainbow.

Swift . . . her love, her salvation, her dream spinner. She melted into him, no longer caring about the lantern burning so brightly beside them, no longer even aware that it existed.

Afterward they slept in each other's arms, drifting together into dreams, contented in the warm cocoon of down. Amy awoke several times to find Swift still curled around her. A smile touched her mouth. Everything really was going to be all right. No Indian wars to keep them apart, no endless waiting for him to return to her. She wasn't even afraid of her nightmares now. When she woke up, Swift would be there and he would set her world back on its axis.

A couple of hours later, he stirred. Amy didn't want him to leave, yet she knew he must. She let her hand trail down his back as he sat up.

"When are you going to make an honest woman of me, Mr. Lopez?" she asked groggily.

"As soon as that damned priest gets back."

Amy grinned. Only Swift would say "damn" and "priest" in the same breath. She wondered what Father O'Grady would think of her Comanche, comanchero, gun-slinging husband and decided the priest, being a man who dealt in souls, would see through Swift's harsh exterior. Swift, a curious blend of killer and saint, outlaw and hero. No one who knew him could doubt that a part of him walked with the angels.

There was a purity within him still untouched by the brutal life he had led, an innocence, for want of a better word. He saw the world differently from most people. To him there was prayer in the fluttering of a leaf, a song of worship in the streaks of a sunset.

"I wish you didn't have to go," she whispered, listening to him dress.

"I'll just be a whistle away."

"Promise?"

She heard him shove on his boots. Then he leaned over her. "Whistle and find out." He kissed her. "Go back to sleep, Amy, love. Then come over for morning coffee at Loretta's. We'll make eyes across the table."

"And you'll come back tomorrow night?"

"Tonight." He nibbled her lips. "It's a little after two. Tomorrow's already here."

Amy's eyes drifted closed. Her last thought was that she had lived fifteen years holding on because tomorrow might bring something absolutely wonderful. And it had.

CHAPTER 23

A piercing scream jerked Swift awake. Groggy and convinced for a moment that he had imagined the shrill cry, he shot up from his pallet by the fireplace. Daylight? It seemed as if he'd just come sneaking in from Amy's and barely got his eyes closed. Another scream came. Amy? Fright filled him. Then he realized the sound came from the wrong end of town. He jerked on his boots and ran to the window to peer out. Up at the Crenton house, he saw Alice down by her front gate. She stood with her shoulders hunched, her hands over her face. The screams undoubtedly had come from her.

Swearing, Swift tore out of the house and down the steps. As he ran, the storefronts blurred in his peripheral vision. Dimly he registered that other people were pouring from their houses behind him, all drawn toward the Crenton place. Something unspeakable had happened. He guessed that by the sound of Alice Crenton's screams. A woman caught up in horror.

When he reached the footpath, he called out, "Mrs. Crenton? What's wrong?"

She whirled and drew her hands from her face. Never had he seen anyone's skin so pale, almost blue-white, like snow in twilight. She stared at him as he ran toward her. Then she began to back away, shaking her head, holding out her hands as if to ward him off.

"Stay away! Oh, merciful God, stay away!"

Swift nearly tripped over his feet coming to a halt. "Mrs. Crenton?"

"What kind of animal are you?"

Swift couldn't imagine what she meant. Then he saw it. A fresh scalp hung on the Crentons' gatepost. The swatch of red hair left him in no doubt that it was Abe Crenton's.

For a moment, Swift couldn't move. All he could do was stare. Blood from the scalp had dripped down the post, staining the weathered-gray wood a reddish black. Slowly and insidiously, the realization came to him that Alice Crenton believed he had killed her husband.

Footfalls echoed behind Swift. A man's voice asked, "Gentle Jesus, man, what have you done?"

Swift heard other people running up. A woman screamed. Another man cried, "I heard you threaten to kill him, but I didn't think you meant it! Oh, Lordy."

Swift pivoted, working his mouth to speak. Randall Hamstead came running up. Swift met his gaze. Randall looked at him for a moment, then paled and glanced away. Off to Swift's left, a woman began to retch. Another began to sob. The Lowdry brothers stood to one side, their attention riveted to the scalp.

Hank Lowdry spat a stream of tobacco juice and wiped his mouth with his grimy leather sleeve. "I'll be damned. A bunch of us heard you threatenin' to scalp him, but none of us thought you'd do it." He started to laugh, then swallowed it back and glanced over at his brother. "He did it! And hung it on the goddamn gatepost! Just like he threatened."

The ground dipped under Swift's feet. Everyone there thought he had done this? It was crazy! Insane! But it also made a terrible sort of sense. Swift Lopez, raised as a Comanche, later a gunslinger and comanchero. A killer. Oh, yes. Who better to blame than him? Especially when the victim had been scalped. Panic banded his chest, making it difficult to breathe. Then the wild urge to laugh came over him.

At last, Swift managed to speak. But when the words finally came, he floundered, uncertain what to say. "I —" He broke off and swallowed. "I didn't do this." He saw Hunter shoving his way through the crowd, and relief flooded through him. "Hunter, tell them! They think *I* did this!"

When Hunter spotted the scalp, he froze. After studying it for an endless moment, he turned his luminous gaze on Swift. There was no mistaking the doubt in his eyes. Swift did laugh then, a shaky, humorless laugh.

"I didn't do this," he repeated, lifting his hands in supplication. "You can't believe I did. Not *you,* Hunter."

"Go get the sheriff!" someone yelled.

"He ain't back yet," another replied.

"Somebody ride to Jacksonville and tell him to get back here straight away! We got us a murder on our hands."

"I'll go," a man yelled. He no sooner spoke than Swift saw him run down the hill.

"We could fetch Mr. Black. He's the coroner. He's authorized to make arrests in case of murder."

"Do it," Joe Shipley barked.

A feeling of unreality washed over Swift.

Good God, they were going to lock him up. He imagined the bars closing in around him, the claustrophobic breathlessness. He considered running, but his feet felt welded to the ground. He looked at the gathering crowd. On every face, he saw accusation and revulsion. This couldn't be happening.

A distant voice yelled, "Here's the body!" Everyone looked toward the Crentons' barn. A man came staggering out. Bracing his hands on his knees, he gagged and took several deep breaths. "His throat's been slit! God have mercy, his throat's been slit!"

Alice Crenton began to keen, a soft, eerie sound that crawled up Swift's spine like icy fingers. He was vaguely aware that Loretta had joined the crowd, Indigo and Chase on either side of her. Her face was deathly white, her large eyes filled with incredulity and horror. She stepped away from the children to stand by Hunter, her gaze riveted to Swift's.

"I didn't do it," Swift repeated.

"If you didn't, who did?" someone asked. "Ain't likely any of us'd scalp the poor bugger."

A general grumble of agreement rose above the crowd. Loretta threw a frightened glance at the scalp. She said nothing, but the sudden doubt that crossed her face spoke volumes. Stung pride burned its way up Swift's throat. He drew back his shoulders and raised his head. He had been guilty of many things in his lifetime, but never lying. If Hunter didn't know that, then there was nothing more that he could say.

Amy was just putting the finishing touches on her hair when a frantic knock drew her to the front door. For an instant she wondered if she had somehow overslept. She glanced at the clock. Right on schedule. She had plenty of time for coffee at Loretta's before work. Puzzled, she drew the portal wide. Indigo stood on the front porch, her face streaked with tears, the bruise on her cheek a livid red, her tawny hair wind-tossed from running.

"Aunt Amy, my father wants you over at our house. Quickly! Something terrible has happened!"

A tingle of alarm slithered up Amy's spine. "What?"

Indigo licked her lips, gulped for air, and then blurted, "Uncle Swift killed Abe Crenton last night! Slit his throat and scalped him!"

Amy's legs nearly buckled. She grabbed for the door to right herself. "What?"

"You heard me! Abe Crenton's dead!

Everyone thinks Uncle Swift did it. Mr. Black put him in jail for murder."

"Oh, my God." Amy hurried out onto the porch. She glanced toward town, then looked over at the schoolhouse. "Indigo, can you run put a note on the schoolhouse door saying that class won't be held today?"

"Yes. Do you have paper for me to write it on?"

Amy was already heading down the steps. "In my bedroom in the top bureau drawer," she called over her shoulder.

Amy broke into a run. Her heels slammed against the earth, the impact jarring through her body. Swift. In jail? For murder? No! It seemed as if the main street of town stretched for miles before her. She lifted her skirts and leaped onto the boardwalk, petticoats flying, pantalets flashing.

Up ahead she saw a large group of men gathered in front of the jailhouse. She cut across the street. As she drew up near them, they closed ranks against her, shoulder to shoulder, barring her path to the jailhouse.

"Ain't nobody goin' in there 'til Marshal Hilton gets back," Mr. Johnson hissed.

Hatred glimmered in the men's eyes. Amy knew a group in this frame of mind could easily become a mob. The small, clapboard jailhouse looked pitifully inadequate. No fortress, certainly. If these men decided to go in after Swift, there was nothing to stop them. The Lowdry brothers stood a little apart from the group, off to her right. Their close proximity made her skin crawl.

She pressed her hands to her waist, horribly aware that approaching the jail had been a mistake. If she said the wrong thing to these men, if she made them any more angry than they already were . . . "I, um —" A tremor ran up the backs of her legs. "I didn't intend to go inside. I just heard the commotion and wondered what was going on."

Hank Lowdry spat tobacco juice. The spray came perilously close to Amy's skirt. "Your friend Mr. Lopez murdered Abe Crenton, that's what. Slit his throat and scalped him!"

Amy flinched at the words. Taking a step back, she said, "Why are you certain Mr. Lopez did it?"

"Don't take a genius to figure it out. We're certain," someone snarled.

Amy sought out the voice. She focused on Joe Shipley, Jeremiah's father. He held a rope coiled in one hand. Holy Mother. Where was Hunter? She darted a glance over her shoulder. Was he aware of how close these men were to lynching his best friend?

"Surely a man's guilt or innocence is something for Marshal Hilton or a jury to decide," she said shakily.

Joe Shipley stepped out from the group. "You think Hilton's God? We pay him wages to keep this goddamn town safe. He's allowed a murderin' savage into our midst. Which just goes to show he ain't no smarter than the next man. Maybe not as smart. The rest of us knew from the first that Lopez meant trouble."

Amy had known Joe Shipley and many of the others for years. Most of them had children who came to her for instruction. She was on friendly terms with their wives. But today they looked like strangers, eyes wild, their faces contorted with rage. If someone didn't calm them down, they were likely to do something terrible.

Lifting her chin, Amy riveted Joe Shipley with her most chilling schoolmarm glare. "Isn't," she corrected softly.

Shipley's eyebrows shot up. "What?"

"*Ain't* is incorrect," she elaborated. "You meant to say *is not,* or, in this case, a contraction thereof, which is *isn't.*"

Shipley's eyes bugged.

Amy stiffened her spine and spent an

agonizing second in heartfelt prayer that Shipley wouldn't decide to throttle her. The veins in his temples were swelling until they looked ready to burst. No wonder Jeremiah was always coming to school quoting his father. The man had a forceful air about him.

Drawing on all her courage, Amy cleared her throat and added, "I'll also remind you to watch your language, Mr. Shipley. You are in the presence of a lady."

A flush crept up Shipley's neck. She continued to stare at him. He shuffled uncomfortably, then cleared his throat.

"I beg your pardon."

Amy gave an almost imperceptible nod. "I realize tempers are running high. But we mustn't forget ourselves in the heat of the moment. School has been canceled for the day, so the children are apt to come by later. It's our responsibility as adults to set an example."

Striving to keep her expression stern, Amy ran her gaze over the other men. Most seemed loath to look her in the eye.

Heartened, she homed in on Michael Bronson. "I'm sure Theodora and little Michael will be out and about today, Mr. Bronson. In fact, you might pass word along to Tess, so she'll know there's no school."

Mike scratched his head and looked sheepish. Relief flooded through Amy. Reminding these men of home and hearth had taken the wind out of their sails, at least momentarily. She doubted it would take much to relight their fuses, though.

"Well." She folded her hands, hoping she looked suitably ladylike and stuffy. "Since Marshal Hilton hasn't returned as yet, I suppose I'll await his arrival over at the Wolfs'." She inclined her head. "Good day to you."

With that, Amy spun and directed her steps across the street. It took all her strength of will not to burst into a run as she climbed the steps to Loretta's house and crossed the porch. Her hand shook as she grasped the knob and opened the front door.

The sight that greeted her when she stepped into the parlor made her stop dead. Rifles lay across the dining table. Hunter stood to one side, checking and loading weapons and issuing orders. Loretta scurried back and forth between the gun cabinet and her husband. Indigo was already back. Both she and Chase were likewise occupied. Amy shut the door and leaned against it.

Hunter glanced up. "Can you remember how to use a rifle?"

"Yes."

Hunter gave a curt nod. "If things get out of hand, we may be the only hope Swift has. Guilty or no, he deserves a fair trial as much as the next man."

"You think he's guilty?"

Grim-lipped, Hunter picked up his Winchester, opened the lever, then threw it closed to bring a cartridge in line with the chamber.

"Answer me! Does Swift admit to it? Surely he said."

Loretta set a handful of cartridges on the table. "Abe's dead, and it looks as if Swift did it. With that crowd milling around over there with a rope at the ready, we haven't had time to get beyond that."

Amy's stomach lurched. "Wh-what does Swift say?"

"That he didn't do it," Loretta said softly. "But the evidence says otherwise."

"But if he says he didn't do it —"

Loretta grabbed a rag and began oiling the barrel of a rifle. She glanced over at her son. "Chase Kelly, go up into the loft and clear the furniture away from the windows, please."

"What for?" Chase asked.

"If there's trouble, we can cover your father better from the second floor. When you have the furniture moved, stay up there and stand watch over the jail. If any of those fools start to go inside, holler down to us."

Chase leaped to do his mother's bidding. Loretta turned toward Indigo. "You can be drawing and locking the shutters at the rear of the house. Bolt the back door as well. If there's trouble, we don't want any back-door callers."

It looked as if the Wolfs were preparing for war. It hit Amy suddenly that Swift's life might not be the only one in peril. "Oh, Hunter, you can't take on the whole town by yourself. This is madness!"

Hunter lifted another rifle, "The madness is out in the street." His gaze caught hers. "Pray Marshal Hilton gets back here in time to calm those fellows down. They aren't thinking straight right now."

"Have they all lost their minds? Swift may not be guilty. How can they contemplate killing a man until they're sure?"

Hunter's mouth thinned. "It looks bad for Swift, Amy. Very bad. Even I —" He broke off and wiped sweat from his forehead with the back of his wrist. "He claims he didn't do it. But if he didn't, who did? It wouldn't look quite so bad for him if he hadn't threatened Abe."

"He didn't say anything specific." Feeling

useless, Amy sorted the .44–40 cartridges from the rest and set them by Hunter's Winchester.

"We're not talking about what Swift said after the fight." Hunter loaded the tube of his seven-shot breech-loading repeater. After inserting the tube into the stock, he raised the Spencer to his shoulder and sighted down its barrel. "He made other threats we weren't aware of." Cheek still aligned with the rifle barrel, he looked up at her. "Inside the saloon before the fight began."

The tormented expression in Hunter's eyes filled Amy with dread. "Wh-what kind of threats?"

Hunter set the loaded rifle aside and pinched the bridge of his nose. Judging by his reluctance to speak, Amy knew she should expect the worst.

"Several people heard Swift tell Abe Crenton a story, about a Comanche who slit a wife beater's throat and hung his scalp on his gatepost, for all to see."

Amy couldn't feel her feet. She laughed, the sound shrill and tremulous. "That's insane! Why would Swift tell him that?"

"To scare him, I imagine."

"But only a fool would tell someone a story like that and then do it!"

"A fool, yes. Or perhaps a man who flew into a rage."

Trapped air shivered up Amy's throat. She gripped a chair back for support. Had Swift gone to the saloon last night after leaving her? Had he become embroiled in a confrontation with Abe Crenton? "I don't think Swift's a fool. And I don't think he's one to act rashly, either. Besides, all he did was tell a story. That's not exactly a threat, is it?"

Hunter ran his hand along the stock of the Spencer. "What is everyone to think, Amy? Swift said the words, and now they have come to be. Who else in this town would slit a man's throat and then scalp him? Me? Scalp taking isn't something a white man would do."

"But Swift says he didn't do it!"

"So he says."

"I have to go talk to him," she whispered.

"Not until Marshal Hilton gets back. Once he gets those men under control, we'll go over and see if we can't get to the bottom of this. Right now, a show of support for Swift could trigger trouble." He motioned for her to take a seat. "All we can do is watch and wait. If they get out of hand . . ." He patted the butt of the Spencer. "I taught you how to shoot this once. Do you remember?"

Amy nodded and sank onto a chair. "You really think I may have to use it, don't you? That they might try to lynch him?"

Loretta laid down the rifle she had been oiling. She took a deep breath and lifted a frightened gaze to Amy's. "That's why we mustn't go over. With Marshal Hilton gone, any kind of confrontation is risky. Tempers are high."

Amy glanced at Hunter. "If — they get out of hand, can we stop them?"

Hunter's face darkened. "We must."

Amy pictured Swift being dragged to a hanging tree. If she had to, could she shoot Joe Shipley or Mike Bronson? Sweat popped out all over her body. She closed her eyes, feeling sick. "You both think he did it, don't you?"

Loretta reached across the table to touch Amy's shoulder. "There's something more Hunter hasn't mentioned. Swift wasn't here last night. I got up a little after one for a drink of water, and he wasn't on his pallet."

Amy sat back in her chair. "You know he was with me."

"But for how long?"

"It was just after two when he left."

Loretta threw a hopeful glance at Hunter. "Judging from the condition of the body, Mr. Black guesses Abe died between midnight and two in the morning, give or take an hour either way. That means Swift might have been with Amy during the time of the murder."

Hunter held up a hand. "You forget the give-or-take of an hour. That's four hours total. Who can say where Swift went after visiting Amy? Unless she can swear Swift was at her house the entire night. . . ."

It wasn't necessary for him to say more. Amy squeezed her eyes closed.

"Marshal Hilton just rode up," Chase yelled from the loft. "And that dad-burned Brandon Marshall and his friends are here, too. Going into the saloon."

Hunter strode to the parlor window and peered out. "What's happening?" Amy asked.

"For now, just a lot of talk. Brandon and his bunch haven't gone down by the jail. Their horses are all in front of the Lucky Nugget. I guess Pete must be tending bar as usual. It's probably a good thing. Maybe they'll get to talking and stay clear of things for a while. If Brandon can stir up tempers, he'll do it, just to get even for what happened yesterday."

"Can you hear anything at all of what the others are saying to Marshal Hilton?" Loretta asked.

Hunter pulled the curtain farther back and motioned them to silence. "They're just telling him what happened." After watching a while longer, he let the curtain fall and turned back to the room. "Well, they didn't try to follow him inside the jail. That's a good sign. Let's give him time to talk with Swift alone. Then we'll go over and see what we can find out."

Loretta puffed air at the tendrils of hair on her forehead. "If anyone can reason with those men, it'll be Marshal Hilton. He's got a way about him."

Amy pressed a hand to her throat, imagining a rope biting into her neck, cutting off her air. She couldn't let that happen to Swift. She just couldn't.

Though the sound was nearly drowned out by a rumble of angry voices outside, Swift heard the door to the jailhouse open and close. Heavy, measured footsteps crossed the planked floor to his cell. He recognized the tread and didn't bother to open his eyes.

"Well, Lopez," Marshal Hilton said in a musing tone. "Looks to me like you're in a hell of a fix. I hate to interrupt your nap, but you've got some questions to answer."

Sweat trickled from behind Swift's ear down his neck. His throat felt parchment dry. "Yeah, it's a hell of a fix all right. Do those fellows out front have a noose ready for me yet?"

Hilton sighed. "Talk never strung anybody up."

Swift could hear a man outside yelling, "Hang the bastard!" It wasn't a very encouraging note.

Hilton heaved another sigh. "Well?"

"Well what?"

"Don't be so goddamn stubborn! From the sound of that bunch out there, this is no time for pride. Did you do it or not?"

"No."

"I reckon that's good enough for me."

That brought Swift's eyes open. He jerked his head around. "You believe me?"

Hilton pursed his lips. "There's some who'd tell me what I wanted to hear, just to get out of here. I know from experience you aren't one of them."

With a thoughtful smile, he braced a shoulder against the bars, reminding Swift of another morning when he'd stood in exactly the same position. This time, though, a word from Amy wouldn't gain Swift his freedom.

Hilton's smile faded, and he frowned. "If you didn't scalp the bastard, who did? Not just anybody knows how to pop a man's scalp off his skull. From what I was told, it was a tidy job."

"I couldn't have done better myself."

"Don't remind me. You really are the most likely fellow to've done it."

"True. You're crazy for believing me. Most wouldn't. Hell, I probably wouldn't."

Hilton chuckled. "That's what I like about you, that straight talk. I was hoping you'd argue and come up with a suspect."

Swift punched the pillow and repositioned it beneath his head. "The truth is, I can't think of anyone else who had words with Abe." Another heavy silence ensued. The voices outside had quieted momentarily. "There's no one I can think of, unless . . ."

"Unless what?"

Swift frowned. "Maybe Alice Crenton —" He groaned and shook his head. "She thinks I did it. So I'm probably barking up the wrong tree. But I was just thinking maybe she'd know something. Something she doesn't even realize is important. Someone Abe crossed, someone he owed money to. There has to be someone who hated him. He did get his throat slit, after all."

"Plenty didn't like him, but I doubt they'd kill him. It can't hurt to talk to Alice, though." He smiled slightly. "Besides, I never mind too much when I've got call to go tapping on her door. She's as sweet as she is pretty and makes the best damned honey bread you ever bit into."

"You've got a soft spot for Alice Crenton?"

Hilton smiled. "If I had thought for a minute that I could've convinced her to divorce Abe, I'd have taken her and all those children away from him quicker than he could blink, and I never would have regretted doing it for a minute. It was the happiest day of my life when you kicked the devil out of him. If it hadn't been for this badge, I'd have tried doing it myself."

The vehemence in Hilton's voice told Swift that the marshal had seriously considered doing just that. He turned to regard the man with new eyes. He wasn't that old, and he still cut a fine figure. Swift supposed the ladies might find him attractive with that strong jaw and those piercing gray-blue eyes. "You must have a high regard for her. Five kids are no small undertaking."

Hilton nodded and rolled his shoulders. "That's another matter, though. Who killed Abe, that's the question."

"A question with no answer." Swift mulled the situation over some more. "I have to tell you, Marshal, even Hunter has his doubts about me this time. If you're looking for votes next election, folks around here aren't going to take kindly to it if you side with me."

Hilton grinned again. "There you go again. Sometimes, Lopez, a man's better off to do some politicking."

"I'm no good at it."

"Yeah, well, I don't suppose I'd be standing here if I thought you were a glib talker." He jabbed a thumb eastward. "I've got a spread five miles from here. When I lost Rose, I took up marshaling because farming was too damned lonely. I can go back to it if I've a mind. Votes don't matter to me."

Swift rose up on an elbow. "I appreciate the loyalty."

Hilton cocked an ear toward the rumble of voices outside. "Loyalty won't save that miserable hide of yours. Answers, that's what we need. Can you swear to your whereabouts last night?"

Swift tensed. "Not for the majority of the night. I was asleep by the hearth, but everyone else was abed. They can't swear I was there."

"You said the majority. You left the house, I take it?"

"From midevening until about two."

Hilton swore. "That's when the coroner thinks the murder happened, between eleven and three, or thereabouts. Where'd you go?"

"Visiting."

"No games, Lopez. Where were you?"

"With a friend."

Hilton gripped the bars and leaned closer. "A woman. This is no time to worry about kissing and telling. Was it Miss Amy? Did you get a powerful itch you needed scratched and go see May Belle? Who were you with?"

Swift said nothing.

"Are you gonna tell me or not?"

"I can't. If those upright citizens out there string me up, her reputation will be all she's got."

"Well, that counts out May Belle. Must've been Miss Amy."

Swift clenched his teeth.

"If she cares about you, she'll come forward on her own accord. Your life is on the line."

"And accounting for my whereabouts until two won't save it."

"There comes a time when honor can be the shovel that digs a man's grave. Her word might make a difference."

Swift jackknifed to a sitting position. "No! Even if she testified I was with her, I could've killed Abe afterward. Hell, I could probably account for my whereabouts until four and it wouldn't do any good. Mr. Black's guesses aren't an exact science. If Abe's body was lying in a drafty place, frigid air could've stiffened him up quicker than normal."

Swift groaned and massaged the back of his neck. "If I'm lucky enough to get a trial, which doesn't sound too likely, that would be brought up in court. You know it, I know it, and" — he jabbed a finger toward the noise — "they know it. If she could swear I was with her until dawn, it might be worth it. But as it is, leave her out of it."

Hilton held up his hands. "All right. It's your neck."

Swift swung his legs over the side of the cot. Bracing his hands on the mattress, he said, "I trust that bit of information is between you and me."

Hilton nodded and scratched his jaw. Swift needed no further assurance, not from Hilton.

"Just for the record," Swift added, "don't be thinking poorly of Miss Amy. We're married, according to my people's laws. We figured that'd do us until the priest got back to Jacksonville."

"I wouldn't think poorly of Miss Amy if she pranced down Main Street in her drawers. She's a fine young woman." He swiped at his nose and sniffed. "I guess I should go see Hunter and let him know what's going on. The last thing I need is him coming over here and having words with anyone standing out there. Once I've warned him off, then I think I'll mosey up to the Crenton place and talk to Alice."

"She's convinced I did it. I'll tell you that right now."

"No need to worry. Just because I'm soft on her doesn't mean she'll do any of my thinking for me. If talking to her doesn't uncover something, then a meeting in the community hall this evening might stir up some useful speculation. There's nothing more enlightening than a bunch of addle-brained people all yakking at once."

Swift met his gaze. "Can I be at that meeting?"

"If you'd like."

"Can you keep those yahoos out there under control?"

"I'll give it my best."

After Marshal Hilton stopped by to speak to Hunter, Amy stood at the parlor window to watch him leave. The men outside gathered around him when he stepped into the street, their voices raised in anger. She tipped her head to catch the words, then wished she hadn't. Hilton, speaking in a low tone, seemed to have some success in calming them down, but Amy had little hope they'd stay that way. Her gaze shifted to the small jailhouse. Swift was locked up in there, charged with murder and, as far as he knew, abandoned by his friends.

Every fiber of her being longed for him, and feared for him. He made the perfect scapegoat. On all counts he was a man the upstanding citizens of Wolf's Landing could condemn, for his Comanche background, the Mexican blood in his veins, and his unsavory past.

Should she go to him? The question echoed in Amy's mind, and she felt guilty even for having to ask it of herself. If their roles had been reversed, Swift would already be at the jail. But he was strong, and God help her, she wasn't. If she was seen anywhere near that jail, she might as well make a public announcement that she was his mistress. She could kiss her job and the respect of all her friends good-bye. If Swift ended up hanging, she'd be left alone, with no job, no home, no security.

She gripped the windowsill until her knuckles hurt. Coward! Did she love the man or not? That was the question. The only question. His guilt or innocence was peripheral. And the answer was yes; she loved him with all her heart. Her place was beside him, the devil take tomorrow.

She turned from the window and faced Hunter. "I'm going over."

Hunter came to the window and peered out. "Those men still look to be in an ugly mood. And you know what Marshal Hilton said. It's not a good idea to go anywhere near there right now."

Amy took a deep, bracing breath. "Yes, well, they're liable to stay in an ugly mood for a spell. My place is with my husband. I'll circle around town and approach the jail from the rear so they won't be likely to see me." She went to the kitchen and confiscated Loretta's milk bucket. "To stand on," she explained as she approached the back door. "So I can talk to him through the window."

Hunter parted the curtain and cast another worried glance at the milling crowd. "I'll come with you."

Amy tightened her grip on the bucket handle. "Can you give us fifteen minutes alone first? There are things —" She waved her hand. "If anyone bothers me, I'll holler."

Hunter's mouth curved in a smile. "Tell him I'll sneak over soon?"

Amy started to nod, then met his gaze. "What I'd really like to be able to tell him is that we all stand behind him." She swallowed a lump of tears, glancing over at Loretta, then back at Hunter. "Maybe he did kill Abe. Maybe, right at first, he panicked and lied. I don't know. But if he says —" Her voice cracked. She transferred the bucket to her other hand. "If, when I talk to him, he still says he didn't do it, then I think we should take his word, no matter how bad it looks."

Hunter's eyes warmed on hers. "I think you're right." He glanced at his wife. Loretta nodded.

Amy hadn't realized she had been holding her breath. She swiped at her cheeks and sniffed. "I, um . . ." She shrugged and turned to go. "Well, I guess I'll head over."

"You tell him I'll bring him hot apple pie and cobbler every day until he's out of there," Loretta called.

Amy couldn't speak around the tears. She merely nodded and let herself out.

The click of the lock resounded inside the room. Hunter scuffed the toe of his moccasin on the braid rug. After a long moment, a broad grin settled on his mouth.

"What on earth is there to smile about?" Loretta asked.

He looked over at her. "I was just thinking how much she's changed since Swift came here. All for the good."

Loretta sighed. "Let's just pray she isn't in for another heartbreak."

CHAPTER 24

Planting one foot on the bucket, Amy grasped the bars of the jailhouse window and hauled herself up. Peering into the gloomy interior, she called, "Swift?"

She heard springs creak. The next instant his dark face appeared. He curled his hands over hers and pressed close. "Amy, what in hell are you doing here?" He glanced right and left. "Someone'll see you. Tongues'll wag for sure."

Amy didn't want to cry, but her wants didn't seem to have much sway at the moment. "You're starting to sound like an old-maid schoolteacher, Mr. Lopez. Let the tongues wag."

His fingers curled more tightly around hers. "You might lose your job."

"I don't care." Amy was surprised to realize she truly meant that. In the end, nothing mattered to her but this man. "Oh, Swift. What're we going to do?"

"Do I have a mouse in my pocket? There's no 'we' to it. I got myself into this mess." He managed to kiss her through the bars. "Amy, as much as I love seeing your sweet face, I don't want you here. You're taking a risk being seen with me."

"Life is a risk."

He drew back. "Things don't look good. I could dance at the business end of a rope before this is over. You can't afford to lose that job. Not now."

There was an echo in every word he said, and Amy didn't like what she heard. Why did it take something as horrible as this to make her see how foolish she had been? Swift was all the security she needed, all that she had ever needed, and she'd been too frightened to realize it. "The devil take the job."

He swore under his breath. "I'll never understand you. Without that job, where in hell will you be if something happens to me? Up the crick, that's where. Get your fanny out of here."

"Shut up, Swift." She leaned her forehead against the bars and smiled at him through tears. "Nothing's going to happen to you. I won't allow it."

His eyes sharpened on hers. "Why don't I like the sound of that? Amy, I want you to stay out of this. If something happens, I want to know you'll be okay. I have to know that. If I go down, I don't want to take you with me."

"I'm going to be fine." For the first time in a very long while, she felt certain of that. "One question. I'm sorry for even asking it, but did you kill him?"

His gaze didn't waver. "No."

That was all Amy needed to hear. She touched her palm to his cheek. "Hunter and Loretta and I — between the three of us, we'll get you out of this. I'll do whatever it takes."

She stepped off the bucket and grabbed it up. Swift tried to catch her arm and missed. "Amy, I don't want you — Amelia Rose Masters, get your fanny back here!"

"Lopez!" she corrected. "And don't you forget it."

With that, she disappeared into the woods.

That evening when Marshal Hilton's meeting at the community hall convened, it didn't take a genius in criminal law to guess how the wind was going to blow. Everyone in town thought Swift was guilty. Joe Shipley didn't have his noose in hand, but Amy guessed it wouldn't take him long to fetch it.

Standing near the coatrack with Hunter and Loretta, Amy tried to monitor the conversations taking place nearby. What she heard made her blood boil. The word *Mexican* surfaced more than once, *gunslinger* was a close runner-up, and *no-good comanchero lowlife* ran a close third. If public opinion was an indicator, Swift didn't have a prayer.

He sat on the fiddler's platform, his wrists bound behind him. When Amy settled her gaze on him, pride filled her. He held his head high and looked his accusers directly in the eye. She could imagine him going to the gallows displaying that same dauntless courage.

She didn't intend to let that happen, of course. Several wild plans came to her. She could go get Swift's guns and somehow untie him. The Spencer repeater still lay on Loretta's table. Amy figured she could bluff her and Swift's way out of here if she had to.

All the ideas were craziness, of course. She couldn't point a lethal weapon at her friends. And running would only condemn Swift to a lifetime of the same. But she had to do something. She couldn't let him die for something he didn't do.

Loretta was called forward for questioning. With obvious reluctance, she gave her testimony. "Yes, Mr. Lopez was gone last night. Around midnight I got up for a drink, and he wasn't asleep by the hearth." When asked if she knew what time Swift had returned to the house, she replied, "I didn't realize last night that it would matter. I went back to bed and didn't get up again until morning." A satisfied buzz went up when Loretta finished speaking. Next came the testimony of several men, the Lowdry brothers included, who had overheard Swift threatening Abe Crenton in the saloon.

Amy could see that the evidence was building against Swift. Not a single person had spoken in his behalf as yet. Then the death blow came. From out of the crowd, Brandon Marshall emerged, tall and faultlessly dressed, his blond hair aglimmer in the lantern light. Turning so everyone could see his mangled face and torn ear, the young man yelled, "I know nothing about Abe Crenton's death, but I can testify to this man's killer instinct. When I heard about this, I knew I had to come and say my piece." With a rigid finger, he directed everyone's attention to his injuries. "He came just that close to killing me. And you know why? For kissing his niece. If it hadn't been for the presence of my friends, he would have killed me. I'll swear to that."

"You're a lying skunk," Indigo cried. Before Hunter could grab the girl's arm, she took several steps toward the fiddler's platform. "You tried to rape me!"

"You're the one who's lying." Brandon waved his friends forward. "I have witnesses. Did I do anything more than kiss that girl?"

Heath Mallory shouldered his way forward. "No, you did not." He shook his fist at Swift. "That man's crazy, I tell you! Crazy mean! He killed Abe Crenton, mark my words. You can see the murder gleaming in his eyes."

It was true; murder *was* gleaming in Swift's eyes. Amy took a step forward, the panic within her building. The buzzing in the crowd had increased to an angry roar. Looking wary, Hilton stepped closer to Swift. "Everyone just keep calm," he warned.

"I'll be calm when that husband killer is six feet under," Mrs. Johnson cried. "No one's safe, I tell you!" She wagged a finger. "I saw you on the boardwalk with my Elmira — don't you think I didn't! Making eyes and sweet-talking her. And her not much more than a baby. I knew then what kind of cloth you were cut from."

"I say we settle this here and now," Joe Shipley roared. "To hell with the folderol of a trial in Jacksonville. One of our own is dead, and this man killed him. We have to take care of our own in this town, or more like him will come. It's best to set an example, right from the first. Murderers hang high in Wolf's Landing. That's our motto."

Things were building to a fever pitch. Amy saw several men pressing closer to the platform. At any second they might surge forward like a wave, overpower Hilton, and drag Swift into the night. And once that happened, there would be no stopping them.

"Wait!" she cried, clawing her way through the crowd to reach the front of the hall. Elbowing Brandon Marshall from the narrow section of unoccupied floor in front of the marshal, she yelled, "You're all wrong! Swift Lopez didn't kill Abe Crenton! He couldn't have! And I can prove it!"

Amy wasn't sure where the words had come from, but once they were out, there was no undoing them. As she turned to regard all the enraged faces gathered around her, she wondered momentarily if she'd lost her mind. But fear for Swift drove her — fear and mindless panic. There would be time enough later to question her actions.

"Swift was with *me* last night," she cried.

"We spent the evening with the Wolfs. Then he took me home, and he" — the lie welled in her throat like acid, then spewed forth — "and he stayed until dawn."

Swift's voice came from behind her. "Amy, don't!"

The expressions on the faces before Amy changed slowly from anger to startled disbelief. A wave of shame broke over her. Fiery heat crept up her neck. She swallowed and continued in a calmer voice. "Swift Lopez *couldn't* have killed Abe Crenton. You've all jumped to the wrong conclusion. He was with me . . . all night long."

Several of the women regarded Amy through narrowed eyes. Harvey Johnson, Elmira's burly father, said, "You must've slept at some point. He could've stepped out, then come back, you none the wiser. Who else would scalp Abe?"

Amy drew herself up, rigid and braced. "I assure you, when Mr. Lopez comes to visit me, the last thing we do is sleep."

Mrs. Johnson gasped and began to fan her hand before her face as if she might faint. Mrs. Shipley squeaked, "That's scandalous!" Several other shocked exclamations were heard, all of which Swift punctuated with velocity and perfect diction by saying,

"Holy shit!" Then, "Amy, have you lost your mind?"

It had taken Amy fifteen years to arrive at this moment, and the way she saw it, she had never been more sane. She was stripped of respect, yes, and most certainly out of a job. And there was no question that she felt humiliated. But none of that mattered. Not when Swift's life hung in the balance.

Amy turned to face Marshal Hilton. The instant she looked into his twinkling gray-blue eyes, she knew that he suspected her of lying. She shot a frightened glance at Swift. Marshal Hilton rolled one shoulder and scratched the back of his neck.

"So Mr. Lopez was" — he cleared his throat — "keeping company with you all last night, was he? And you're willing to swear to that?"

Amy envisioned herself with her hand on the good book. She seldom lied, let alone swore to it. God might strike her dead. Her gaze slid to Swift. For an insane instant, she saw him as he had been that first night they made love, so gentle and patient. Then she remembered how kind he had been to Peter. If the God she so revered didn't want such a man to live, Amy figured it was time she changed religions.

"I will swear to it with my last breath,"

she said softly.

No lightning bolt ripped down from heaven. She took a deep breath and sent up a quick, heartfelt prayer of contrition. Her gaze returned to Swift. Tears shimmered in his eyes. A feeling of certainty swept through Amy. *Let me say I love you my way.* Swift had done just that, in so many different ways. Now it was her turn.

Bolstered by the look in his eyes, Amy turned back to face the crowd. She saw myriad emotions in the gazes she encountered, disgust, hatred, revulsion, scorn. A woman didn't publicly admit to immoral conduct and retain the high regard of sinless folk. For eight years she had cultivated the good opinion of these people. Now she could only wonder why. What they thought wouldn't matter a whit in the long run, anyway.

"I trust that you good gentlemen of Wolf's Landing will find the true killer now?" she said. "Mr. Lopez is innocent."

With that, Amy headed for the door. As if afraid she might somehow contaminate them if her skirts brushed their clothing, the people in the hall stepped aside to make a path for her. Cheeks afire, head held high, Amy walked through their midst. When she reached Loretta and Hunter, she saw that they were both smiling. At least she hadn't lost the high regard of everyone.

The night air embraced Amy when she stepped outside. She gulped it greedily and leaned her back against the building, finding solace in the darkness. She was shaking all over. Closing her eyes, she listened to the voices inside. She could hear Hunter and Loretta talking and guessed they had gone to the fiddler's platform. Soon, Swift would come out. She imagined his arm around her shoulders, the solid wall of his chest warming her. Everything would be all right then. They would shut out the world. Nothing would matter but their being together.

Amy heard a jingling sound near her. She opened her eyes and peered through the darkness, going perfectly still. As always, her night blindness frustrated her. The black figure of a man loomed from the shadows. Almost simultaneously the sharp tip of a knife blade touched her throat. Amy jerked.

"Scream, bitch, and I'll slit your throat just like I did Abe Crenton's."

Terror sluiced down Amy's spine. Instinctively she tried to scream, but all that erupted from her throat was a squeak. The knife pricked her. She felt a bead of blood trail down her neck to pool in the V of her collarbone. The smell of stale sweat filled her nostrils. A leather sleeve grazed her bodice. Then she heard the jangling sound again. Riding spurs. Night blind or no, she knew one of the Lowdry brothers held the knife.

Cruel fingers bit into her arm. The next instant a filthy hand clamped over her mouth. Panic exploded in Amy's mind. She grabbed the man's wrist and sank her teeth into his meaty palm. He swore. Frenzied, Amy tried to twist away. Then, from out of nowhere, something slammed against her head. Bright lights burst before her eyes. She snapped taut, stunned by the blow. Then blackness swooped over her.

Hunter read the note once, then twice. Swift held himself rigid, waiting for his friend to speak. Loretta stood nearby, gripping the back of her rocker. Chase and Indigo, solemn-faced and pale, sat by the hearth. When the silence became unbearable, Loretta cried, "Hunter, for God's sake, what does it say?"

Hunter crumpled the dirt-streaked paper in his fist and raised his gaze to Swift's. "The Lowdry brothers . . ." His throat worked before his next words came forth. "They're not really named Lowdry. They're the Gabriels."

Swift felt as if a gigantic fist had hit him in the guts. Ever since he had walked up on Amy's porch and found the note on her door, he had been praying to her God and all of his that he was alarmed over nothing, that she had left the note for him herself, saying she had gone someplace for a walk because she was upset. All the way back to Hunter's house, he had continued to pray with every running step, his mind racing ahead of him with fear, a part of him knowing that Amy would never venture off alone in the dark.

"Oh, Jesus." Swift bent forward slightly, still feeling as if he'd been hit in the stomach. "Not the Gabriels. Where have they taken her?"

"A mine shack about eight miles up Shallows Creek, the old Geunther place." Hunter took a shaky breath. "They want you to come alone and they stress that you must come wearing your guns."

"No!" Loretta cried. "They're wanting a shoot-out. If you pick up those guns again, Swift, you'll end up in the same mess you faced in Texas. Word will spread. Upstarts will come gunning for you. There has to be another way."

Swift felt sick. "Amy's life is in danger,

Loretta."

A robust knock resounded. Everyone jerked and looked at the door. Loretta finally regained her senses and ran to answer it. Marshal Hilton stepped inside, a broad grin creasing his face.

"Well, if that wasn't a standing performance Miss Amy gave, I never saw one! I don't usually cotton to lying, but this is one time an untruth saved the day." He chuckled and shook his head. "For a minute there, Lopez, I thought that straight talk of yours was going to ruin the whole thing. If you hadn't shut your mouth when you did, I was fixing to shove my hat in it. Those yahoos were an inch away from having a lynching party."

Hilton took several steps into the parlor before he seemed to notice that the others in the adjoining room looked as though death had struck. He came to a stop. "What in hell's wrong? This gives us some time to hunt down the killer. I thought I'd find you celebrating."

Swift finally regained his voice. "Those fellows . . . the Lowdry brothers? Their real name is Gabriel. They came here from Texas, looking for me because I killed their brother. They've taken Amy."

Swift had always known Hilton was quick-minded, but even he was impressed by the speed with which Hilton grasped the situation. "Son of a — They killed Abe and tried to make it look like you did it!" He slapped his jeans. "Dumb ass that I am, I never even thought of them!"

Pain shot behind Swift's eyes. He was the stupid one. The moment Abe Crenton had turned up with his throat slit, he should have been trying to remember who had overheard him threatening Abe. Instead he'd panicked, his one concern being that everyone believed him guilty. He had forgotten all about the Lowdry brothers. In retrospect he felt like a fool. And Amy was paying for it.

"Why in heck did they take Miss Amy?" Hilton wondered aloud.

"To get at me. After her announcement tonight, it was pretty clear that she and I —" Swift threw up his hands. "Hell, I don't know why. Why does their kind do any of the things they do? I guess they hoped that I'd hang. When they saw I wasn't going to, they took her as bait. The bottom line is that I killed their brother Chink. Nobody crosses the Gabriels and gets away with it. What better way to get their revenge than to hurt Amy?"

Hilton's face drew taut. Swift turned his

gaze to the wall hook where his six-shooters hung. He remembered how frightened Amy had been when she saw the two comancheros on the sidewalk. She'd be terrified now. Decision made, he walked to the coatrack and pulled down his gun belt.

"Oh, Swift, no," Loretta cried. "There has to be another way. Amy wouldn't want you to."

Swift strapped on the belt and bent to tie the leather thongs to anchor his holsters to his thighs. "I have no choice." He glanced up. "I guess maybe I never did. Like Amy says, you can't outrun your past. This just proves it."

Hunter stepped to the table and picked up his Spencer. "I will go with you."

Swift doubted the Gabriels had come this far alone. Hunter had no equal as a warrior, but he was no fast gun. "It's me they want. I know you love Amy, but you've got your family to think of."

Hunter gathered extra cartridges and slipped them in his pocket. Shifting his gaze to his wife, he said, "There are some things I must do. My family understands that."

The color drained from Loretta's face. She nodded slowly. Hunter's dark blue eyes filled with a prideful gleam. He smiled and turned back to Swift. "How many do you think there will be?"

"God knows," Swift replied. "The only certainty is that there'll be more than two."

"I'll go saddle up," Hilton inserted.

Hunter held up a hand. "We appreciate the offer, Marshal. But Swift and I will fight this battle the Comanche way. A white man would only confuse matters."

Hilton puffed up his chest. "I'm a damned clean shot, I'll have you know. And you'll be outnumbered. That's not to mention that I'm the law here in Wolf's Landing. Those gents are wanted for murder."

Swift was still staring at Hunter. Memories of times past washed over him, and he felt a flare of hope. If he and Hunter used Comanche warfare strategy, they might be able to pick off the comancheros one at a time without a shoot-out becoming necessary.

"If we work as well together as we once did," Swift told the marshal, "we won't be outnumbered for long." He met Hilton's gaze. "You've proved yourself a loyal friend to me. If you'd like to ride along and stay behind as a backup rifle, I'd be grateful."

Hunter nodded his agreement to that, then spun for the back door. Swift fell in behind him. Hilton glanced at Loretta. "Where in blazes are they going? The horse barn's the other direction."

Loretta pressed a trembling hand to her bodice. "They have to prepare for battle."

A few minutes later, Hunter and Swift reentered the house. Hilton took one look at their faces and barked with laughter. His grin died a quick death when Swift approached him with the paints. Within seconds the marshal's cheeks were streaked, his chin was striped in red, his eye sockets were outlined with graphite, and his teeth were blackened.

"Will he do?" Swift asked Hunter.

Hunter, busily checking his arrows and war ax, looked up. "His forehead and hands need something."

Swift smeared the places in question. Hilton cocked an eyebrow. "Is this Comanche medicine?"

"You could say that," Swift replied. "It'll keep you from glowing in the dark and getting your butt shot off."

Hilton shrugged and bent his head so Swift could get his brow. "That's good enough medicine for me."

"It always was for us, too," Hunter shot back. He sheathed his ax and went to hug his family goodbye. When he drew Loretta into his arms, he said, "Pray on your beads, little one." He turned toward Chase and chucked him under the chin. "You pray, too, eh? Say many hell Marys so I come home safely."

"Hail," Loretta corrected.

Hunter bent to kiss his daughter, then scrubbed to remove the paint he left on her cheek. Swift, anxious to be gone, waited by the front door. Loretta followed the men out when they exited the house. Standing on the porch, she waved them off.

As Swift started into the barn, she called, "Don't use those guns unless you have to. Your future may ride on it."

As far as Swift could see, he wouldn't have a future to worry about if something happened to Amy.

The first thing Amy became aware of was pain slicing through the back of her head. She frowned and tried to rub the spot, only to find her wrists were bound behind her back. She surfaced to consciousness by measures, first becoming aware that she was lying facedown on a cold wooden floor. Dust and grit filmed her tongue. She no sooner registered that than she heard boots scuffling and spurs jangling. From the corner of her eye, she saw a man sitting down beside her on a wooden crate. She slitted her eyes and turned her head toward him.

A Mexican spur gleamed back at her in the feeble firelight. Her gaze inched up his leather pant leg, taking in the silver conchae along the side seam, coming to rest on the deadly looking six-shooter at his hip. She glanced up at his swarthy face, shadowed by a sweat-rimmed hat. Steve Lowdry.

Memory came rushing back to her — standing outside the community hall, a man looming out of the darkness to grab her arm, a knife pricking her throat. She had struggled, and something had hit her on the head. After that, blackness.

She shot a quick glance around the dimly lit room, taking in the cobwebs and filth. A deserted mine shack? In the shadows across the room, she saw two other men, one standing at a window, another sitting on the floor with his back to the wall. Silver conchae glinted in the firelight. The stench of their unwashed bodies surrounded her. Comancheros.

Such an icy terror clutched Amy that for a moment she felt like a corpse in the first stages of rigor mortis. Her heart stopped. Her lungs quit working. A bone-deep cold seeped through her body.

When at last her heart started up again, it did so with a painful lurch against her rib cage. A breath shivered down her throat and stopped midway, leaving her starved for oxygen and working her lips like a beached fish. A heavy, urgent ache centered low in her belly.

"Well, now. Lookee here who's awake."

Lowdry lifted his boot and toed Amy on the hip, rolling her onto her back. Her arms felt as if they might break, twisted as they were under her weight. She closed her eyes. Not seeing was to retain her sanity. If she looked into Steve Lowdry's face, she might lose her grip.

She heard a rustle of movement. A heavy hand settled on her midriff.

"Say, there, you playin' possum, honey? That's a good name for her, ain't it, Poke?" The hand grabbed her hair. "Curls like honey. What else you got like honey, honey?"

One of the men from across the room laughed. "Lopez won't get here for a spell. Wha'd'ya say we do a little samplin' and find out?"

Lowdry chuckled. "Wha'd'ya say to that, pretty thing?"

A third voice, gruff and gravelly, said, "You know what they say about gals named Honey, don't ya?" He guffawed. "They're easy to spread."

The hand released Amy's hair. The next instant hard fingers gripped her ankle and began dragging her across the room. The planked floor barked her twisted arms, slivering through the sleeves of her dress. She clenched her teeth. Heat from the fire washed over her body. Behind her eyelids she could see golden light. Lowdry released her ankle and let it fall to the floor.

Amy kept her teeth clenched and her eyes closed. She knew what was coming. Fear fragmented her thoughts. Her nostrils narrowed, making it difficult to breathe, but she knew if she opened her mouth, she'd start screaming. And once she started, she might never stop.

Steve Lowdry grasped the front of her bodice. His stench made her want to gag. "What you got under there, honey?"

The cloth of her dress stretched taut against her back. Amy knew it would rip at any second. She gulped down a whimper. His voice oozed over her like slime. She could hear the saliva in his mouth working, the short, excited pace of his breathing. What did she have under there? It was a question calculated to terrify her. And it was working. She imagined those hands on her body.

A hundred unvoiced pleas crowded into her throat. But before she could utter them, pictures from the past splashed across her mind with blinding clarity. She saw herself as a child, struggling helplessly, sobbing and begging for mercy. Above the echo of that little girl's voice, she heard male laughter. Her terror and frantic pleas had gained her nothing then and would gain her nothing now. Men like these enjoyed hearing a woman scream. They raped and brutalized not for sexual gratification, but for the sheer violence of it.

A sudden calm came over Amy. She was no longer a terrified little girl. And she'd be damned if she'd give these animals the satisfaction they sought. She was no stranger to pain, after all. She knew from experience that no matter how badly something hurt, the agony eventually passed. She couldn't prevent these men from violating her body, but she could retain her dignity, regardless of what they did to her.

Let me say it my way, just once. The words slipped into her mind from nowhere, the sound of Swift's voice, husky soft and silken, echoing and reechoing. She imagined his dark face, the way his eyes clouded with tenderness when he looked at her, the way his hands whispered over her, making her feel cherished. These men couldn't steal that from her.

Her bodice ripped. Amy felt cool air sifting through her chemise. Fingers dug in around her breast, inflicting pain. She tensed, knowing that this was only the beginning.

Let me say it my way. The calm remained with her. Swift had given her so many things — love and laughter and hope — but the greatest gift of all had been a renewed sense of self. *Courage is taking three steps when it terrifies you.* Tears gathered behind her eyelids. No matter what these men did to her tonight, she would survive it. And when morning came, she would turn her face toward the horizon and never look back.

The hand tightened cruelly. "Hey, sweet thing? You dead or somethin'? I like my women with a little life in them."

Amy remained limp and concentrated on separating her mind from reality. She remembered the day she and Swift had chased the chickens until the feathers flew. Once again she floated in his arms to the strains of a waltz, in moonlight touched with magic. With the memories came the certainty that tomorrow would indeed come. Tonight was only an instant out of a lifetime.

The door to the shack crashed open, the sudden sound reeling Amy back to the present. Startled, she opened her eyes to see Hank Lowdry bursting inside. He slammed the door closed behind him and glared down at the man hunkered next to her.

"Damn it to hell, Billy Bo! What do you think yer doin'?"

"Just havin' a little fun. Doggone it, Sly. You near gave me heart failure."

"Good. You can fun around later. Lopez ain't comin' to have tea."

Swift was coming? Amy dragged her gaze to the man who had been tormenting her, a man whom she had known as Steve Lowdry. Billy Bo? The name was so ludicrous she nearly laughed, albeit hysterically. He jerked her torn bodice back into place and rose. Amy's skin crawled where he had touched her.

"I can fun around and be ready," he complained. "Since when do you git so nervous over taking on one man? There's five of us."

Five? Amy slid her gaze around the shadowy room. Including the newly arrived Sly, alias Hank Lowdry, she counted four men, which meant another must be outside. Doing what? Waiting to ambush Swift? Oh, God, Swift was coming here. These horrible men must be using her as bait. Swift wouldn't realize how many guns he was up against. He was walking right into a trap.

Sly moved to a window and rubbed angrily at a square of grimy glass so he could see out. "Lopez slapped leather against twenty of Chink's best men. Are you forgettin' that? And he plugged Chink in the bargain. Get your mind out of your britches and stick to business."

Billy Bo gave Amy a lingering look. Then, reaching under his hat to scratch, he ambled across the room, his spur rowels dragging on the planks. "What'd'ya want me ta do?"

"Keep watch, you dumb ass. Before you get it shot off." Sly drew his six-shooter and checked for cartridges. Then he pressed close to the window again. "Douse that damned fire, Poke! Who in hell built it, anyway?"

"I did," the third man snarled back. "It's colder'n a witch's tit in here."

Amy heard spurs chinking toward the hearth. Water splashed and hissed. Smoke roiled over her. She turned her face into her shoulder, glad for the darkness. Five men? And Swift was expecting only two. She had to do something. The question was, what?

Swift drew Diablo to a halt in the dark shadows beneath a tree. The smell of smoke drifted to him. Hunter was somewhere off to his left. Hilton was on a stand about a hundred yards behind him. Light from the full moon bathed the clearing ahead. Perfect. He and Hunter would be able see one another well enough to communicate by sign language as they advanced on the mine shack.

Forcing thoughts of Amy out of his mind, Swift closed his eyes, trying to absorb the smells and sounds around him, to become a part of them. The words he had said to Hunter that first night in Wolf's Landing came back to haunt him. *That place within me that was once Comanche is dead.* If that was true, then Amy was as good as dead.

Swift opened his eyes and stared up through the gnarled tree branches at the moon. Mother Moon. His heart twisted. It had been so long since he had begun denying his Indian heritage. Could he still taste a man's sweat on the air at a hundred yards? Could he still distinguish the sounds of an animal from those of a man, those of friend from foe? Could he still move through the darkness like a shadow? Warble like a night bird? Hoot like an owl? Cry like a coyote? Would he remember the signals he had been trained to use in battle?

Fear crawled up Swift's spine. A picture of Amy flashed in his head. And now the Gabriel brothers had her in that mine shack.

Her worst dread, and it had come to pass. He had to get her out of there.

An owl hooted. The hair on Swift's nape prickled. Without moving his body, he slid his gaze across the clearing. He saw Hunter crouched behind a bush. His hands flashed. Swift deciphered the signal and stiffened. *There's a man ahead of you.*

Swift lay forward along Diablo's neck and cupped his hand over the horse's muzzle. The animal grew motionless. A smile touched Swift's mouth. Some things were never forgotten. He slid off the horse like a wraith and flattened himself to the ground. Tipping his head back, he worked his throat. "Hoo-hoo! Hoo-hoo!" Rolling onto his side, he signaled back to Hunter. *I will take him.* Hunter nodded and melted into the black shadows.

"Goddamn it! Rodriguez should be here by now!" Sly turned from the window. The bright moonlight enabled Amy to see him as he pulled his timepiece from his pocket. He tipped it toward the light. "We were supposed to change the watch ten minutes ago. Something's happened."

"He's probably sittin' out there asleep!" Billy Bo grumbled from somewhere near Amy's head.

Sly jabbed a thumb at the door. "Poke, go see what the hell's keepin' him. One of you report back to me within five minutes. Fernandez," he snarled at the third man. "I want you on the roof. Move it!"

"Why can't Billy Bo or Fernandez go check on Rodriguez?" Poke argued. "If something's happened, why's it gotta be my neck on the line?"

"Because I said!"

The man named Fernandez leaped to do Sly's bidding and quietly exited the shack. From the shadows Amy heard Poke shoving up from the floor, still muttering under his breath. "I'll tell ya why it's me and Fernandez that's gotta go. It's 'cause we don't hearken to the last name Gabriel, that's why."

"Quit yer goddamn bellyaching!" Sly shot back. He glanced up at the roof, cocking an ear at the thumping sound of footsteps above them. "He sounds like a herd of horses up there. Don't he know to be quiet?"

Poke stepped into a shaft of moonlight and clamped his hat on his head. Amy was glad that his snoring had stopped. It seemed to her that she'd been lying in the same position for hours, listening to him sputter and smack his lips.

Hours. Had it been that long? Or had only minutes passed? Amy had no idea. She only knew that she couldn't work the ropes on her wrists loose, that there was nothing, absolutely nothing, she would be able to do if Swift needed help. He would come for her. Of that, she had no doubt. And he might die for his efforts.

Poke pulled his gun and made sure it was loaded. With a last curse to show his displeasure, he opened the door and stepped outside. Shortly after the portal closed behind him, the hoot of an owl drifted through the night.

Amy registered the sound and nearly discarded it. Then she froze and stared through the darkness at Sly's dark silhouette against the window. He was hunched over, doing something with his hands. A moment later a lucifer flared, spraying sparks. The light of the flame bathed his craggy face as he dipped his head to light his cigarette. Amy swallowed and glanced beyond him at the window. If he had heard the owl, he didn't realize the significance of it. At least he hadn't yet. But he might at any moment, if she didn't distract him.

She swallowed again. Until now she had been as unobtrusive as possible, terrified to call attention to herself. But if Swift was out there, she couldn't just lie here doing nothing.

"Why —" Her voice cracked. She licked her lips. What if the sound she had heard was just an owl? What if Swift was still back in Wolf's Landing? What if — She shoved the thoughts away and focused on the opposite. What if Swift was out there? Sly Gabriel might spy him creeping toward the mine shack and kill him. "Wh-why are you doing this?"

"Doin' what?" Sly turned his head from the window to peer at her. "Havin' a smoke?"

"N-no. Wh-why did you kill Abe Crenton?"

"We didn't like his looks."

He turned back to the window. Amy's pulse quickened. "No, seriously. I'd really like to know. What purpose did killing him serve?"

"None. That's why we ended up having to take you."

He obviously wasn't going to talk, not unless she spurred him into it. Amy stared at his hulking shape. "Ah, so your plan fell apart?"

He turned to look at her again. "Only because you're a lyin' bitch. Lopez wasn't with you all night last night."

"How can you know where he was?"

"We were watchin' him, that's how." He leaned his hips against the windowsill, completely turning his back on the window. "He left your place about two. We waited until after he left to kill Crenton."

"So he wouldn't have an alibi for the time of death." Amy felt some genuine curiosity stirring. "You wanted him to hang, that's clear. But why? If you wanted him dead so badly, surely you could have thought of a dozen more expedient ways to accomplish it."

He laughed softly. "Exped— what?"

"Expedient . . . faster ways."

He shrugged. "Fast ain't always healthy."

"I'm afraid you've lost me again."

"We saw a way to kill him legal. Bein's we're strangers to these parts, it was a darned sight safer than doin' it ourselves. Especially since Lopez went righteous on us and quit wearin' his guns."

"I'd think being strangers would have served you well. No one knew who you really were. As for him not wearing his guns, I'd think that would make it easier, not more difficult."

A breath of laughter escaped him, the inference being that she was incredibly stupid. "Sure, if we wanted to gun down an unarmed man and have every lawman in the place after us. There ain't many roads outa here. If the law took after us —" He took a drag off his cigarette and flicked ashes, which flared orange en route to the floor. "Well, you get the idea. I'd hang just as dead whether they knew my real name or not. We don't know these mountains good enough to strike off through uncharted territory to avoid the roads."

It was beginning to make sense to Amy. She slid a glance toward the window. "So you decided to kill Crenton, make it look as if Swift did it, and let him hang for it."

"Lopez threatened to slit the man's throat in front of a dozen witnesses. It was too good to pass up. All we had to do was carry through on his threat. Me and Billy Bo have taken our share of scalps, so we do a clean job. A few years back, the army paid good for Injun hair."

Amy's stomach knotted. Injun hair. Human life meant nothing to him. Her throat felt dry. She swallowed the nausea down. "One more question, just to satisfy my curiosity. Why do you want Mr. Lopez dead?"

"He gunned down my brother Chink."

"Why?"

"Over a woman." He laughed again. "A

589

yellow-hair, like you. The man's got a thing for blondes, don't he?"

For just an instant, a pang of jealousy cut through Amy. Then she swept it aside. She could never doubt Swift's love for her. If he had killed Chink Gabriel over a woman, he must have had reasons other than the obvious.

"I'd say your brother must have liked blondes, too," she came back softly.

"It didn't matter to him what color their hair was," Sly snarled. "He was just havin' some fun. And Lopez killed him over it."

The hatred in Sly Gabriel's voice chilled Amy. She wondered if his brother Chink's idea of having fun with a woman had been anything like Billy Bo's.

Chapter 25

It seemed to Amy that several more hours had dragged by since Sly Gabriel had ended their conversation and returned his attention to the window. She knew that much time couldn't have elapsed. Sly had instructed Poke to report back to him within five minutes, and Poke still hadn't returned. If even one hour had gone by, Sly would be getting antsy by now, wondering what was amiss.

As if he read her thoughts, Sly pulled his watch from his pocket and checked the time. He swore and turned back to the window. "That goddamn Lopez is out there, Billy Bo," he hissed to his brother. "I think he's tryin' to pick us off one by one."

"How in hell you know that?" Amy heard Billy Bo shuffling from the shadows. "I ain't seen nothin'."

Sly drew his gun and rechecked the ammunition, which told Amy how nervous he was. He had already checked the weapon once. "Rodriguez never came in to change the watch. Now Poke hasn't come back." His voice trembled slightly. "The son of a bitch is out there. I feel it in my guts."

Billy Bo pressed closer to the window and peered out. "What we gonna do?"

"Well, we ain't gonna sit in here and wait to get our throats slit, I can tell ya that. Grab the woman!"

Billy Bo turned toward Amy. "What're we gonna do with her?"

"We'll use her to force him into the open," Sly replied. "Lopez'll show himself if we start carvin' on her a little."

An icy cold pooled in Amy's belly. Billy Bo approached and grabbed her bound wrists to jerk her to her feet. Her arms twisted upward behind her back. Pain knifed through her shoulders. She gasped and staggered against him. Heaving up on her wrists again, he sent her reeling toward the door. Amy clenched her teeth to keep from screaming.

Sly threw the door wide. Billy Bo steered Amy out into the yard. Releasing his hold on her wrists, he snaked an arm around her waist, jerking her back against him.

Using Amy and his brother as a shield, Sly Gabriel came up from behind. "Lopez!

Hey, Lopez, we know y're out there!" Sly roared. "Take a nice long look at yer lady, amigo. Here in a minute, she won't have a nose." He pressed in closer to Billy Bo. "If that don't bring you out, next he'll slice off her ears."

As if to demonstrate his willingness to start cutting, Billy Bo pulled his knife and pressed the sharp side of the blade against Amy's upper lip. She swallowed down a whimper. A single sound from her might make Swift do something rash.

"I'm gonna count to ten, Lopez," Sly called. "If you aren't in plain sight by the time I finish, we start carvin'."

Fernandez whispered down from the roof. "Want me to take him out, boss?"

"You think y're up there for a nap?" Sly retorted in a low voice.

Amy scanned the clearing. Moonlight bathed the immediate area in front of the shack, but when she tried to see farther into the shadows, her night blindness hindered her. Was Swift out there? Did he realize Fernandez was lying on the roof, ready to pick him off? Oh, God. She rolled her eyes downward to stare at the knife under her nose. If she screamed a warning, Billy Bo would probably flinch and cut her.

A horrible quivering seized her. She

imagined Swift stepping out into the moon-light . . . imagined him getting shot. A scar on her face was nothing if it meant he might live. She braced herself, inhaled slowly, and then screamed, "There's a man on the roof!"

Billy Bo did flinch. Luckily, when he jerked, the knife dropped a fraction, rather than slicing upward.

"Goddamn it, Billy Bo, shut her up," Sly cried.

Billy Bo swore and clamped his hand over her mouth, grinding the knife handle against her lips. Amy's legs nearly folded. She closed her eyes on a wave of relief, praying Swift had heard her.

As if in answer to her prayer, a wonder-fully familiar, silken voice came from out of the darkness. "Let her go, Gabriel. It's me you want, not the woman. I'm wearing my guns. You'll get your gunfight, so you can call it self-defense. So do the decent thing and get her out of there."

Amy stared into the darkness beyond the clearing, her heart slamming. Swift. She wanted to run to him. Every muscle in her body strained against Billy Bo's hold.

"Show yerself," Sly ordered.

"Not until you get the woman out of harm's way."

"So you can pick us off? How dumb do ya think we are, Lopez? Show yerself right now, or she dies."

A shadow moved. Amy tried to twist her mouth free of Billy Bo's hand. He clamped down all the harder. She knew Swift's chances would be decreased if she remained in his line of fire. He'd have to pick and choose his targets, which would slow him down. Even if he shot Sly and Fernandez, he wouldn't risk aiming at Billy Bo for fear of hitting her. Billy Bo would undoubtedly take advantage and reward Swift with a bullet.

The knife blade pressed against her cheek. She knew Billy Bo would slit her throat with little provocation. Her life or Swift's? Without him she wouldn't have much of a life, anyway. She shifted her weight to one foot. Then, before Billy Bo could guess her intent, she knifed up with her knee and dug the heel of her shoe into his shin, shoving downward with all her might.

Taken by surprise, he jerked back a little and howled with pain. The instant he moved, Amy took advantage of the marginal space between their bodies and made a wild grab. She found her mark and clenched her hands into fists. Billy Bo shrieked. Amy fully expected him to kill her. She was taken totally by surprise when he let go of her completely and grappled for her hands, trying to free himself.

Total confusion erupted. Sly cursed. Billy Bo made a gargling sound and cried, "She's got me by my bullets! Get her off me! She's got me by my bullets!"

The hiss of an arrow penetrated the darkness. Almost simultaneously, Fernandez grunted and came sliding down the roof to fall in a lifeless heap behind them. The impact of his body startled Sly. In all the confusion, it took Amy a moment to realize that Billy Bo had released her.

"Amy, drop to the ground!" Swift yelled.

Swift's words penetrated Amy's terror. She released her screeching victim and threw herself headlong into the dirt. Gasping to recapture the air she had knocked out of herself, she looked up to see Swift step into the moonlight. Dressed all in black, with the guns gleaming like silver death on his hips, he looked like Lucifer himself. His six-shooter flashed. Orange fire spurted into the night. An explosion of noise rent the air above her. Bodies thudded onto the ground. Then silence fell, an eerie, unnatural silence.

His hand still poised to fan the hammer spur of his weapon, Swift took three running steps, ducked into a crouch, and spun to check the clearing around them. Amy had never seen anyone move with such speed or precision. Seemingly satisfied that no one lurked in the surrounding brush, he closed the remaining distance between them.

"Amy, are there any others?"

Dazed by how quickly everything had happened, she gulped, still trying to get her breath. "No, I don't think so. F-five, there were five."

Swift holstered his gun and knelt on one knee to untie her hands and gather her into his arms. He was shaking violently. "Are you all right? Did they hurt you? Amy, are you all right?"

Never had anyone felt so good. Amy wrapped her arms around his neck and clung to him. "I'm fine. Are you? Oh, Swift, I was so afraid they'd kill you!"

He tightened his hold on her and buried his face in the curve of her neck. For several moments they clung to one another. Then Hunter and Marshal Hilton emerged from the darkness.

"She okay?" Hilton barked.

"Yes, I think so." Swift glanced up at Hunter. "You took out Fernandez?"

Hunter smiled. "He was hard to miss lying up there on the roof. Are you sure Amy's all right?"

A quivery breath rushed up from Swift's chest. Though still shaking, he gave a low laugh. "She's fine. Finer than fine. She's glorious."

Hilton walked around them to survey the dead men. He turned back to look at Swift, scratching his head. "I've never seen shootin' like that in my whole life, Lopez. You're something to envy when you're handling those guns."

Swift tensed. Amy felt the change and pulled back to look up at him. A bleak expression hooded his face. He glanced toward the Gabriel brothers and swallowed. "Believe me, Marshal, being fast with a gun is nothing to envy. Every quick draw for a thousand miles will be paying me calls when the word gets out."

Amy's feeling of deliverance shattered. Swift had come two thousand miles to escape his reputation as a gunslinger. Tonight his past had caught up with him. His plan of making a home in Wolf's Landing and living peaceably there might now be an impossible dream.

Amy threw a frightened glance at the bodies behind her. The comancheros had exacted their revenge after all.

"Don't," Swift whispered. He cupped his

palm to her cheek and forced her head back around. "Don't look, Amy, love. You've seen enough ugliness to last you a lifetime."

Amy nodded and pressed her forehead to his shoulder.

"I think I'd better get you home," he added.

Amy offered no resistance when he rose and scooped her into his arms. She drew little comfort from his closeness and warmth. One thought monopolized her mind. Swift was going to be forced to leave Wolf's Landing, and she had a dreadful premonition that he didn't intend to take her with him.

Hunter and Marshal Hilton parted company with Swift and Amy when they reached Wolf's Landing. Hunter and Hilton went on into town to recruit volunteers so they might return to the mine shack for the five outlaws' bodies. Swift made his excuses, saying that he wanted to remain with Amy to "get her settled in."

Ignoring her protests, Swift carried Amy from his horse to the house, ensconcing her on the sofa while he lit the lantern and built fires in the fireplace and stove. When he finished with that, he put on a pot of coffee. While that was heating, he returned to the sofa and checked her over for injuries. His concern in no way bolstered Amy's mood. She knew Swift too well to ignore the look in his eyes. He was searching for a way to tell her he had to leave.

In all fairness, she could see why he felt she should stay behind. He'd be living on the trail, constantly looking over his shoulder. That was no life for a married man. As much as she hated to admit it, her recent behavior indicated that the security of home and hearth were everything to her. Who could blame him for thinking she would be happier left behind in Wolf's Landing? Even if the townspeople never forgave her, she would have the security of Hunter and Loretta here.

The problem was, she wouldn't be happier. She wouldn't be happy, period. Tonight's lessons had been harsh, but Amy had learned them well. Swift was her cornerstone. Without him, all the security and material wealth in the world would mean nothing.

While he went to pour each of them a mug of coffee, Amy disregarded his adamant orders that she remain on the sofa and went to her bedroom. Moments later he came searching for her.

"What are you doing?" he asked.

She turned from her bureau, a pair of pantalets in hand. "Packing. I shouldn't take more than two changes of clothing, should I? I've never lived on the trail before."

His gaze dropped to the undergarment in her hand. His larynx bobbed, and he glanced away. She was relieved that he didn't pretend not to know what she was talking about. "Amy, you don't have any idea what you're getting into. The gossip you stirred up tonight will surely die down. Here in Wolf's Landing, you'll have —" He broke off and waved a hand at the house. "With me, you'll never know from one day to the next where your next meal is coming from. Or if you'll even live to have another meal."

The picture his words conjured filled Amy with a moment's dread. Then her resolve swept it away. "Swift, understand something. One day with you is worth a lifetime without you."

His gaze flew to hers. She saw hope flicker in the depths of his eyes. "Honey, I know you love me. I can't ask you to run with me, though. There's a limit to what you can do to prove your feelings. What if you get pregnant? Or sick?"

"We'll lay over someplace." She pursed her lips. "There's nothing to say we can't change your name from Lopez to something else, nothing to say we can't eventually start over in a new place. I've always had a hankering to see California. The mining's good there. Or maybe we could try Nevada."

"You truly want to go with me? I thought — After everything you've said, I didn't think you'd —"

Amy's heart broke a little. Had her love up to now been so shallow? "You thought wrong, Swift. I'm going with you. Just try to leave me behind. We're married, remember? Where you go, I go. That's the way it's supposed to be. What's mine is yours, what's yours is mine. You know how it goes. That means your troubles are mine, too."

"But everything you valued — the safety here, having your own house. You'll have none of that. If the thought of being totally dependent upon me here in Wolf's Landing bothered you, how're you going to feel a thousand miles from here, with no one but me to turn to?" He studied her for a long moment. "Think long and hard on that. If you go with me, I can't guarantee I'll be noble enough to bring you home if you decide to change your mind. I'd rather cut the ties now than go through the heartbreak of that."

Tucking her pantalets under one arm, Amy whispered, "My home is where you are."

Tears filled his eyes. She slowly crossed the room to him. "Please don't leave me, Swift," she said softly.

He groaned and grabbed her into his arms, hugging her so tightly she could scarcely breathe. The pantalets slipped to the floor. "Leave you? Amy, love, I thought that was what you'd want. Leave you? It'd be more like cutting out my heart."

"Not to mention breaking mine," she cried in a shaky voice. "Since I just got it back, I'd like to keep it in one piece for a while."

She felt his lips curve in a smile and knew her meaning wasn't lost on him. Comanche heart had nothing to do with fearlessness and everything to do with a person's sense of self. The gifts Swift had given her could never be stolen from her unless she allowed it.

She rose up on her tiptoes. "I love you, Swift."

"And I —" A sharp knock on the door interrupted him. He arched an eyebrow. "What now?"

Amy smiled. "Things can't go downhill. It can only be good news."

He relaxed slightly and drew away. "Not the way my luck runs."

Together they went to answer the door and found Marshal Hilton standing on the porch. Nudging his hat back, the marshal flashed a slow grin. "I just thought I'd drop by and tell you the news."

Swift pulled the door wider. "Come in out of the cold."

"No, that's okay. I can't stay but a second. I'm kind of anxious to go up to the Crenton place and check on Alice and the kids." He grinned again. "It's a nasty job, but someone's got to do it."

Amy entwined her fingers with Swift's. "You mentioned news, Marshal?"

Marshal Hilton scratched his chin and frowned. "Well, the damnedest thing happened tonight. You remember those two Lowdry brothers? The rough-looking pair you were worried about a few days back?"

Swift wondered if the marshal had suffered a memory lapse. He tightened his grip on Amy's hand. "Of course, I remember them. What —"

"Well," the marshal went on, interrupting him, "it seems they were part of a small gang. Five of them in all. Real rough characters. They're the ones who killed Abe Crenton. God only knows why, but you can't always figure fellows like that. Abe must have got on their bad side somehow."

He paused and slid twinkling eyes to Amy. "I guess they got to fighting among themselves tonight. That's how it looked, anyway. Had a big shoot-out up at the Geunther place. Not a one of them lived to tell about it. I've gotten a group of men together to go up and get the bodies. Hunter rode up ahead of them to —"

He scratched his head again. "He said something about an arrow he had to dispose of. Anyway, he's going to organize everything. Which leaves me with the rest of the evening off to check on Alice and the kids."

It took Amy only a minute to grasp the marshal's meaning. A surge of happiness shot through her. She glanced up at Swift's puzzled face and pressed closer to his side. "Thank you, Marshal Hilton," she said softly. "That's a fine thing for you to do. We'll be forever grateful."

The marshal nodded and winked. As he turned to leave, he called, "I told you, Lopez. If you planned to put your back to the wall in my town, you had a friend." Lifting his hand in farewell, he quickened his stride. "Welcome to Wolf's Landing. I wish you and your lady happy."

Swift narrowed his eyes, watching Hilton's

silhouette merge with the darkness. "Is he serious? He's going to cover it up?"

Amy nodded. "It certainly sounds that way."

"Do you realize what that means?" He let out a joyful whoop and swirled her around the room. "I'm free! We don't have to leave Wolf's Landing! No one's going to know about the gunfight!" He lifted her off her feet and did another spin. "It's a miracle."

Amy let her head fall back so she could look up at his wonderfully dear face. In that instant it seemed to her that her life flashed before her eyes, a long and trying journey that had led her inexorably to this moment. *Keep your eyes always on the horizon, golden one. What lies behind you is for yesterday.* She smiled, keeping her gaze on his beloved face. Was the horizon a distant line of purple over snowcapped mountain peaks? Amy didn't believe so.

Swift tightened his arm around her waist and swept her in another circle around the room. A waltz step. Still looking up at him, she floated to the imaginary music that seemed to thrum inside her. Swift Lopez, her horizon and all her tomorrows. At long last, what lay behind her had become a yesterday she could no longer see.

The employees of Thorndike Press hope you have enjoyed this Large Print book. All our Thorndike, Wheeler, and Kennebec Large Print titles are designed for easy reading, and all our books are made to last. Other Thorndike Press Large Print books are available at your library, through selected bookstores, or directly from us.

For information about titles, please call:
 (800) 223-1244

or visit our Web site at:
 http://gale.cengage.com/thorndike

To share your comments, please write:
 Publisher
 Thorndike Press
 295 Kennedy Memorial Drive
 Waterville, ME 04901